Bound in Stone: Volume One

First novel in
The Soulstone Chronicles

By
K. M. Frontain

CreateSpace version ISBN 978-1-927397-11-4

~~~

Original cover art by Dallas Williams
www.dallasillustration.com

Cover design and layout by K. M. Frontain

~~~

To Paul Squassoni, whose kindness, encouragement and patronage made the cover art for this print edition possible. Thank you from this grateful word wright.

~~~

And once again,
To my husband, JC, for his faith.
And for my son, Alex, for his ears.

Author's Foreword

The Soulstone Chronicles began as a set of questions inspired by a game, Dungeons and Dragons. Something we Dungeon Masters noticed— something I myself was guilty of when I first played the game—we discovered it was a habit of new players to want perfect characters. Perfect charisma, perfect agility, perfect speed, strength, wisdom, intelligence. You get the idea.

Strict dungeon masters allowed one roll of the dice to determine the strength of each attribute of a player character. As you can imagine, a bad roll could be a really upsetting occurrence for a novice.

Oh, no! My thief has five speed!

And suddenly the planned character cannot be a thief. Suddenly one isn't sure if one likes Dungeons and Dragons. Maybe playing it isn't all that fun.

Most Dungeon Masters, at least most of the ones I've met, have allowed three dice rolls per attribute, and the player could pick the best of the three or had to use an average. For newcomers, this salvaged many player characters and made the game worth playing. But we Dungeon Masters always smiled our wry smiles.

Yeah, who wants to play a flawed character? Really?

Experienced players sometimes do. It's a challenge. But new players to the game usually don't want a flawed character. Yet they should have fun; and so, the best of three rolls.

But still, I thought, way back when, what happens if someone really is perfect, has perfect speed, perfect strength, agility? What if they are perfectly beautiful and have absolutely spectacular charisma? Off the chart charisma? So much charisma they might wish maybe they hadn't any at all?

Could such a state be a curse to a super being?

And that was the beginning of my epic. Let's make a god, I thought, and play with a few questions. Let's see how he really likes being gorgeous, irresistible, indestructible. What happens if he's truly immortal or as close to it as possible? Does power really corrupt, especially if one has plenty of time to think how best to use that power? Is heaven real? Could there be a true hell? Is the soul real? If it is, is it a form of power too? Does it take precedence over matter, the rules of matter? What happens if a soul doesn't pop in for an occasional revisit to the place of creation?

What if you discover that *everything* really is your fault?

Now mush in a bit of science and ecology while world building, dump my character into a position where he has all that power, but then give him no control of it. Make him absolutely ignorant of his true potential. Let's see what happens.

And there you have my Kehfrey, the mortal avatar we meet at age seven, child prodigy in a world that would better match ours in the seventeenth century, a god who doesn't remember he is one. I had a lot of fun messing him up. I shoved him into an untenable situation and let the story unfold. I hope you enjoy his journey as much as I did.

All the best,
K.M. Frontain

Chapter One

The knife was butcher sharp and, in the boy's hands, too large. A killer's knife. A bloodletter. His father's weapon, but not a favourite. A bit too heavy in the tang for a perfect cast; good only for rough work in close quarters. The boy turned it slowly, playing with the light that shone on the metal, casting the rays this way and that about the confines of his most recent home. In his view, the blade was pretty and worth more attention than the ugly squalor his father had plopped the family into this time, but his mother, when she looked up from her meal, saw disobedience and potential disaster.

"Kehfrey!" She lurched up and knocked the side of his head. He dropped the knife, stunned by the blow. "How many times have I told you not to touch your father's weapons?"

"I was being careful!"

He didn't dare retrieve the weapon from the floor, and she made the laborious effort to fetch it herself. Upon rising, she tossed the blade onto the table and placed a supporting hand to her back.

"Careful? There's no such thing as careful when it comes to boys. I hope this isn't another one."

He looked at her big belly and a glint of calculation brightened the hazel of his eyes. "I hope you give me a sister, Mum. Perce has a sister. She gets pies from the bakery all the time and she never pays for them. All she has to do is smile at the baker's boy."

"Is that so?" She squinted suspiciously. "Pies? You think a sister is good only for winning pies for a pest of an older brother?" His expression tightened with dismay, but then he smiled up at her, his best smile, the winning one. She smiled back. "You were always the sweetest of them, Kehfrey," she said and then pasted an unforgiving frown where the approval had been. "And the most mischievous! I swear you have elf in you."

"I do not! I swear you never went near them!"

She couldn't help laughing at the inanity of the retort, but paused to think what it might mean, that her littlest boy would defend his honour so quickly. The suspicion returned, this time bearing the stench of her life's beginnings, the decaying corpse of which still plagued her soul. "Who told you such a thing?"

A tardy spurt of wisdom kept his mouth shut, but she was on to him.

"It was Wilf, wasn't it? He's been teasing you over that red hair again."

Kehfrey nodded, glowering. She sighed with impatience, angry with the boy, disappointed with her eldest son for teasing him, weary of the little digs to her remaining pride.

"Wilf is only jealous he didn't get red hair," she said for the umpteenth time. "He thinks the marks would go for him if he had it."

"He gets enough marks with his blond hair." The boy scuffed the packed dirt with his heel and raised dust that didn't satisfy his ire. The fine, dry motes only made him sneeze.

"Yes, he does," Canella agreed. "But that's beside the point. Your father has the same hair, Kehfrey. You know you're his boy. I never went near elves. You have my word on it."

He glowered at the dirt. "Easy enough to swear you haven't been near elves. There are never any about in any case."

She considered smacking him again, but discovered herself too hot and weary to bother. She sat on the single chair in that shabby room of earthen floor and mud packed walls, a place too poor for proper mortar, a place she doubted she would dwell a week within. But there it was, not so much home but the safest place of the moment.

The chair creaked as she leant closer to the table. Using the confiscated knife, she cut a chunk from a loaf of dry bread sitting on the bare planks and dunked it in her beer.

"Your father is thinking you'll do nicely with him tonight," she said around a mouthful. Manners. She'd had them once, but they weren't much use to her now. Not often. Blunt scorn better suited the men with which her husband consorted. Blunt scorn was what most of them deserved.

"Really?" Kehfrey said, jumping up from the squalid floor. "He's taking me?"

"Mmm," she mumbled. "He says you're quicker than Gamis."

"I *am* quicker! I've been practicing!" He hopped a triumphal dance on the pocked floor.

"That's not why he's taking you, though." She glanced absently out the window at a passing walker. A man, he sweated profusely and mopped his brow as he went by. She thought he lived down the street a ways, the house with the vines climbing to the roof. Fellow was likely well-to-do. He might make a good hit before they left this place or perhaps after.

Kehfrey's bottom waggling ceased. He straightened and peered over at her, his face blank with bewilderment. At the same moment, he scratched a fleabite that had begun to itch. Turning from the window, his mother saw him raising welts on the pale skin of his scrawny belly. Her lips thinned with distaste, but she didn't comment. Hard enough to get the money for the proper herbs and expensive dips; she wouldn't waste them on a boy who loved to dive in trash. Looking down, she adjusted her bodice, pulling the cinch looser beneath her breasts to accommodate her expanded belly.

"He says he needs you because you're smaller," she said eventually. She wiped her moist forehead with her grubby apron and hoped her skin wasn't as red as the man who had walked by.

"Smaller!" Kehfrey cried. "I won't be later. I'll be bigger than Wilf."

2

"I don't think so, baby boy," said Wilf, just then stepping through the open door.

The eldest son and their mother's favourite, Wilf was boss when father was gone. He was also the bane of Kehfrey's life. Too late to avoid it, Kehfrey caught a rough shove that sent his little body flying across the room. He smacked against the wall and stood there rubbing his bruised shoulder as the dust settled. Wilf continued to the table. Their mother ignored the violence and smiled a welcome at the young man.

"What have you brought?"

"Food, of course."

He set the sack he carried on the table and stood back proudly. He wore his new suit, a hunter green outfit of perfect cut and fit, a pristine white linen shirt beneath vest and jacket. Because of his industry, he required such expenses on occasion; his marks would pass him over if he didn't look outstanding. His mother, however, wasn't a mark and not interested in admiring him. Hot, sweaty, covered in filthy clothes, Canella just wanted the comfort of a good meal and hopefully bath money. One of the luxuries for which she and her older boys shared a love was a nice relaxing soak, but her sons often had them for free bathing in their lovers' tubs. Thinking this, she was no longer as pleased with the offering of food and drink.

"Where's the money?" she said, brows lowering.

Wilf cast her a wry glower, but dug into his tunic all the same and handed over a pouch that jingled nicely. She dumped six silver pieces onto the table and cried out in delight at the sight of a single gold coin. She looked at Wilf with an approving smile. He pulled off his wide hat and gave her a jaunty bow. His hair flew back as he rose, a dramatic wave of flaxen, the colour a gift she had passed to him.

"Oh, you're good!" she said. "Which one gave the bonus?"

"Mistress Nas."

"My, my! Why the bonus? What did you do to deserve it?"

"Mum! Not in front of Kehfrey. And not in front of you either."

Kehfrey loosed a contemptuous snort. "I bet he buggered her but good!" He ran out the door with Wilf roaring after him.

"Wilf!" Canella barked. "Leave off! Pop needs him tonight. I can't have him all banged up and useless."

Wilf stalled at the entrance and glared out at his little brother, who once again danced his wild victory march, bottom waving insultingly. Wilf grimaced and stalked back in. "He's a waste of time. Why haven't you sent him out with Vik to help troll for clients? He should be working. He's seven. He's been seven for months. I was working at seven."

"Hi, now!" she protested. "He's smaller than you were, and *you* weren't working the flesh trade at that age. And you know Vik's tastes. I won't have our Kehfrey exposed to that. You take him out if you're so damned concerned. He's certain to attract a mommy type. Vik did for you."

3

"I don't *do* mommy types any more. Gods, Mum! I'm seventeen years old." He stomped over to the table and took three of the silver coins back. "I need new stockings," he said.

"You just bought clothing last week." She looked at his suit pointedly. "You spent enough on that set. What do you need with more?"

He decided a change of subject was in order. "Why are you letting Pop take Kehfrey if you're so concerned for his welfare?" He opened the sack he'd brought, exposing a round of yellow cheese and a bottle of wine. Canella smiled with delight and leant toward the food. Wilf pocketed the three coins.

"The gang needs a small one tonight," she said and handed Wilf the bottle for uncorking. He set to with his dagger and had the cork out shortly. She shot back a swig, lowered the bottle and smiled in appreciation. "Very good year."

"From Mistress Nas's private stock. Cheese from her pantry, too."

"So you paid for none of it." She held her hand out, indicating she wanted the coins back. He glowered and dug into his pocket, but only gave her one. This, of course, prompted a reproving scowl. He riposted with his best winning smile. Smirking, she dropped her hand and let him keep his gains, knowing he likely had more than just two coins hiding away somewhere on his person.

"You're a good son," she said.

The compliment provoked a flush of discomfort. "Don't start that, Mum."

He knew exactly what she was about, digging the guilt out of him with maternal approval. She indicated their shared comprehension with a widening smirk.

"I swear Kehfrey takes after you more than Pop," he grumbled and stomped over to the open window to stare out at his diminutive brother. Kehfrey was off in the shadow of the rickety buildings to the other side of the street and speaking with his new friend Perce, gesticulating wildly, obviously in the middle of another of his outrageous tales. "I don't know why I should feel guilty. I do my share," Wilf said.

"You shouldn't," Canella replied. "You *are* a good son, and I think you should keep your share."

"You're such a bother, Mum. None of us would still be here except for you," he said with a mix of affection and sour irritation. "You're the glue of the family. For love of you, we do our share and give our gains."

He turned. She didn't like his expression. She must look so very tired, not the least beautiful, not even pretty. Just enormously pregnant. A bloated face above shabby clothing, bloated limbs beneath. Her hair was still a lovely blond, the same as his, but her locks were lank and pasted to her skull. Remembering this, she put her bonnet back on to hide her oily head. One could hardly tell her for a noble-born woman. She seemed like any other worn-out pauper.

Wilf must have been thinking likewise. He retrieved another silver and set it on the table.

"Well, now," she said self-consciously. "Everyone needs a safe place to sortie from. That's what family is, however much of a bother." She slipped the coin into her bodice with the first. The gold she would present to her husband Kehfen, but the silvers were hers.

"That's my grandfather talking in you," Wilf said. "The old bastard." He squatted by the table to look her in the eyes. "Honestly I don't think you should let Pop take Kehfrey. You know his line of work is more dangerous than Vik's and mine. If they are caught ...."

"There's nothing I can do about it." Resignation made her gaze veer away. "Kehfen's connections wouldn't take it well if we didn't make ourselves useful from time to time."

"We've done our share! We get the targets, don't we?"

She looked up again, irritated by his forcing the issue. "Yes, but Pop put up with a lot of grief from the Syndicate over both you and Vik before whoring became a part of the family business. If not, you'd likely have been forced to pickpocket and been hung long before now. Kehfen stood up for you. He saved you from the burglary trade. You're just lucky you and Vik were so cussed inept, or you would have been called to do the night jobs."

"Must be the flaxen hair, Mum. Your side of the family and all. Good for nothing but charming everyone." He plucked the bottle from her hand and drank to the birth gifts she had bestowed upon him.

She laughed, knowing the snide comment for truth, but deep within she hurt. She was too accustomed to crude, to laugh so easily. She wished he wouldn't dig at her for her blunder. She hadn't meant to make him a bastard, and Kehfen had fixed it by marrying her, hadn't he? Didn't she deserve credit for marrying? Shouldn't Wilf blame the man who had sired him and left her a soiled thing for her father to toss onto the family stoop, to be brushed away like the spare crumbs of a beggar's leavings?

Wilf gave her a gift of compassion. His next words roughly mimicked her thoughts. "Kehfen's been a good father to us overall," he said and drank some more wine. He handed the bottle back. Glancing around, he scowled at the lack of seating. "When are we going to get more chairs?"

"Not much point if we have to take off again suddenly."

"Kehfrey won't like that much," Wilf said, lifting to a stand. His legs were getting all kinked, crouching like that. He hated crouching, or any other cramped position for that matter.

Outside, his little brother moved from a similar position, but he shot up like a jack-in-the-box, both arms flailing and startling his young companion. That brat was so damned random. "He's got that boy Perce all agog with his wild stories," Wilf continued.

Canella sighed. "Kehfrey will get on fine. All he needs are his wild stories. He doesn't have to pack any of them."

"Well, there's a perfect statement, if any." He squinted thoughtfully. "Is he good enough?"

"Better than Gamis."

"Really?"

"Why shouldn't he be? He does take after his father the most."

"Yes, I suppose." Wilf shifted, a small motion that hinted nervousness. "Which place are they hitting? Are they using one I cased?"

"I'm not certain. It may be. You usually spot the good ones."

"I don't know, Mum. I've been getting a bad feeling lately. I think we should move again."

She looked at him sharply. "Why do you say that?"

"There's a fellow hanging about with Mistress Nas's lot. He's pleasant enough, some Lord Velmis or something. He's a foreigner from Omera."

"And what has this to do with us moving so soon?"

"The last target I named to Pop was his. He said he was renting the place. He invited me in too quickly, I think. I had a weird feeling about it. Thought he was looking for someone like Vik at the time. Now I'm not so sure." His gaze veered to the side, but he couldn't avoid her stare for more than a second. Concern outweighed guilt, and he confronted his mother fully again. "Will you tell Pop?"

She nodded. "Go look out the window."

"I wasn't followed."

"If you think we should move, then you may have reason to feel it. Don't ignore the wisdom of your gut, boy. Go and look. Now!"

Just then, Kehfrey re-entered muttering curses beneath his breath. His skullcap was off and twisted in his grimy hands, his ginger hair askew and dusty as if he'd spun on his head, which he might have done. He glared at Wilf. "You were followed! There's a man standing over by the corner, watching this door. Now we're going to have to move again. I'm not going to get any pie."

Wilf blanched. He and his mother didn't think to doubt the boy. As much as Wilf liked to rile the minuscule fellow, and Canella to be disgusted with him, Kehfrey was usually never wrong when he got an impression. He was a perfectly odd child, but wholly suited to living by his wits, as a child of thieves must.

Wilf grabbed the coins on the table, tossed them into his pouch and shoved the leather packet back into his tunic. Kehfrey popped his dirty cap back on his head, seized the cheese and bread, and stuffed them into the sack. His mother kept the wine bottle. Prodded by Canella's elbow, the knife toppled onto the packed dirt and, in their haste, none of them noticed the loss.

Wilf helped his mother up while hissing at Kehfrey for details. "Quick, boy! Tell me what he looked like?" He ushered their mother into the back room, and they stepped across a number of sloppily strewn sleeping palettes toward a corner of the wall.

6

"Not much point," Kehfrey said. "He had a big beard, all black and curly. Looked fake to me."

"Is that how you spotted him?" Canella asked.

"No! He was staring at the door an awful lot." They reached the back wall of the lodging. "Me first!" he said. "I can check for spies." He pulled a pair of boards aside and scurried through the opening. He was gone for less than a minute and came back with a bright smile of reassurance marred by a gap from a missing tooth. "All clear."

Canella handed the open bottle to him, and Wilf proceeded to help shove her very pregnant body through the hole. She had a time of it, swearing she would drop the baby from her womb there and then. They eventually issued into the narrow alley, little more than a place to dump refuse even the poor ignored. They stood outside the hole and listened. The overhanging roofs almost connected above the lane, darkening it so much it seemed in permanent twilight. The heat wave had intensified the stink of sewage, and the shelter of the alley had made of the odour a noxious vapour. Canella ended the stillness putting her soiled apron over her nose in an attempt to keep from gagging.

Kehfrey stepped a few paces off and whispered at a curious large rat that had poked its head out of the rubbish. It took fright and scampered off. Canella frowned over her apron, thinking she'd heard him tell the greasy thing to make itself scarce. She'd have thought a stone would do better for the task. Rats were known to take a chunk out of young flesh now and again. She considered berating Kehfrey for his lack of wisdom, but he'd been in this alley often, never returning with anything but innocuous bits of garbage and fleabites, and there was nowhere a person could run from fleabites.

"You really will need to buy new stockings," she said to Wilf, looking down at the scum on their clothes.

Wilf scowled and kicked a pile of rubbish further into the muck. This lifted the stench to appalling proportions, and she finally did gag, but he didn't notice her distress as he surveyed his attire. "And breeches and shoes," he added caustically.

"Don't do that," Kehfrey said. "She'll barf the baby out."

Wilf at last noticed his mother's misery and took her arm. He led her through the dimness toward the cluttered end of the lane. Here fresher air filtered through the fetid atmosphere. It was almost worse to have the better air. The stench of human waste in the alley seemed that much more putrid after each purer gust from the street, where city ordinances prevented the worst sort of pollution.

To the side and unseen by the boy's family, the heavyset rat poked its nose out of the rubbish and eyed Kehfrey expectantly. The boy flicked his fingers negatively, which sent it off again.

Canella issued a muffled order through her handkerchief. "Kehfrey, go back and leave a warning for your Pop." The boy seemed to have no use for his nose and no fear of losing it to a rat bite. Let him risk the horrid trip back. The watcher wouldn't bother with a small boy.

Kehfrey turned about, but stalled and offered his own suggestion. "Do you want me to distract the spy?"

"No!"

"But I can lead him away long enough for Wilf to get his spare breeches and stockings."

"No!" Wilf said. He didn't want his old breeches and stockings. "I can get new ones. I can't get a new brother. Now go!"

"Yes, you can. Mum might have one now. You don't like me anyway."

"Shut your gob, Kehfrey," Canella said. "We want to keep you. None of your wild ideas, now. And Wilf does too like you."

"Does not!"

They were coming to the end of the alley and were forced to stop bickering. Wilf jerked his head at the boy, blue eyes warning him to get on with his duty or else. Sulkily, Kehfrey handed over the wine, bread and cheese and made his way back to their recent home. He crawled through the hole, followed by the rat. It bit his worn-out heel for attention. He hissed at the pest that the cheese had gone with his mum and that it had best be off looking for her crumbs under the table. As the rat went to the indicated area, Kehfrey fetched a piece of charcoal from the cold brazier and went out to visit Perce again. He sauntered into the open with the utmost equanimity, but remained at his side of the street.

"Why'd you leave without finishing the story?" Perce demanded with a hurt voice. He'd been waiting in the centre of the lane. The moment he realized the other boy wasn't going to cross to his side, he ran to meet him.

Kehfrey eyed him wisely. He and Perce were the same age, but they were widely separated in experience. Perce was larger and his clothing less worn. They had not been handed down through a multitude of previous owners. He was the image of a well-kept innocent who had never starved a day of his life. Kehfrey had just made Perce promise him a pie for the rest of the story, but now he'd have to go without to keep the watcher from being the wiser.

Feigning to mess about as any child, he told the remaining half of the narrative while drawing on the wall of his building. He created a sloppy picture of the constricted street, including a rather ugly dark-bearded man. In the corner where he scribbled a mess of trash, the warning sign was clear for any who knew to see it.

Five times he surreptitiously ordered the rat back into the house and out of view. A rat that big often ended up as some beggar's roast. He'd warned the damned thing, but it was a stubborn cuss. Thought of nothing but food. The first time they had met, it had been in the middle of the night, the rat on the verge of biting off one of his brother Gamis's toes. Aside from thinking this funny, Kehfrey had been amazed at the size of the pest, for which reason he had warned it off from eating people parts. A rat that big needed to be preserved to see how much bigger it could get. He was peeved he'd have to abandon his project before ascertaining if the rodent could grow any fatter without letting it resort to human appendages again.

"That's an awful picture," Perce said after Kehfrey had finished.

Kehfrey knew it. He'd been drawing his worst. The boy followed him to the other side of the door, where he offered the charcoal. "You draw on this side. I'll come back later to see if it's better."

"Where are you going?" Perce asked.

"Mum wants me to massage her feet. She's going to have my sister, you know."

"She's as big as a cow."

"I know," said Kehfrey, laughing. "I'm going to have a giant sister."

He smacked his naive friend on the shoulder and headed back in. He grabbed his father's knife from under the table, having at last noticed it, and found the worn out sheath for it lying beneath the cold brazier. He tucked the knife into its home and hid the weapon beneath his tunic at his back. In the back room, he found the rat scuffling about inside his grubby blankets. He shook his head at it.

"Don't be stupid. I didn't hide food in there." He poked it with a toe and had to shake it off when it grappled with him for fun. Eventually he managed to toss it back onto the mat. "I'm leaving now. You keep away from people, you hear? The desperate ones eat rats as easily as desperate rats eat people."

It ignored him, once more rummaging inside the blanket. The boy shook his head again. Fat rat! Thought of nothing but eating, just like his brother Gamis.

"Bye, Gamis," he said. Smirking, he met Wilf and his mother in the alley shortly after.

"What was with the huge drawing?" Wilf said. He'd been spying as best he could from the distance. A mountain of ant-infested rubbish closed off the end of the alley. He had been bitten on his legs when the insects had crawled up his stockings.

"I couldn't just draw the warning sign," Kehfrey said.

"I hope you didn't leave one of your cussed works of art. Everyone will be staring at it then."

"Trust me. I was brilliant. It's crud." Kehfrey laughed and said, "Perce is drawing another one on the other side of the door right now."

"Is the spy in the same place?" Canella asked, to which Kehfrey nodded. "How are we going to get out of this alley without him seeing?"

"I told you I should distract him," Kehfrey huffed. His brother and mother looked at each other worriedly. "You know I'm right. The longer you stand around here, the more likely a friend of his will show up to cover this alley. If I distract him, that'll give you time to get out without getting torn apart by ants. You can climb that end over there. It's has something in it the ants don't like."

"What exactly?" Wilf said.

"A body. These ants like regular rubbish."

"Oh, gods!" his mother whispered, at last noticing the horde of flies lifting off that side of the alley entrance.

"Don't worry, it's completely covered. I buried him again after I looked. He's so rotten even the rats won't eat him now."

Canella almost turned green.

"All right! Go!" Wilf relented.

Grinning, Kehfrey darted back down the disgusting alley and arrived at his friend's side in seconds. "You win!" he told Perce.

Perce left off drawing and glared at him. "I'm not done!"

"Let's go get the pie now," Kehfrey said impatiently.

"I have to wait for my sister to come home from the dressmaker's," Perce hedged.

"Oh, come on! You already have a pie. I saw her come in with it this morning. You know she's not likely to get a second today."

"But my mother—"

"Tell her I stole it," Kehfrey suggested. "Come on! You promised!"

"I can't tell her that! I wouldn't do that to a friend!" Perce looked at Kehfrey as if he'd just grown two heads. Both heads would have had the same challenging grin had this been the case.

"Go on, now. I give you permission. You aren't afraid to snatch a pie, are you? I'll share it with you."

A crafty gleam entered Perce's brown eyes. Ah, ha! Kehfrey knew instantly this sort of theft had occurred before in Perce's household. In silent accord, they hurried across the street to Perce's building, where Perce told Kehfrey to wait at the bottom while he rushed up the rickety flight to the second floor. He returned quickly with the goods.

"Mum was sleeping," he said with a triumphant grin. He dunked his fingers in the pie and gobbled a mouthful.

"Here now!" Kehfrey protested. He grabbed the tin and made off with it. Perce shouted and chased after him. Despite his smaller stature, Kehfrey was quicker. He dodged nimbly away and headed for his target.

"Good-bye, pie," Kehfrey said sorrowfully to it.

Just before he reached the bearded man, he pretended to trip. The pie flew into the air and struck the target dead on the chest. Kehfrey rolled to his feet. Because the man looked uncertain as to whether he should be angry or amused, Kehfrey determined he needed help deciding.

"What did you do that for?" he shouted. "You ruined my pie, you big uglier-than-a-cow's-butt fart from a goosed pig!"

The spy lunged at him. Kehfrey darted away. Perce screamed and ran home. While Perce called desperately for his mother, Kehfrey dashed up the street away from his family. He had his escape route planned. He was on it before his pursuer managed to get within three arm lengths of him. Seizing the vines on a trellis, he scrambled up the wall of a building. Of course the owner of the building came out to bellow at him.

"Get off my vine, you elf-begotten brat!" This man wiped his sweaty face with a dirty rag as he stepped into view.

"Little bastard threw a pie at me!" the pursuer said.

"Threw a pie at you? I wouldn't waste a pie on you! Pig fart!" Kehfrey clawed the last of the distance up the vine, turned on the roof and glared jubilantly down. This particular edifice belonged to a single well-to-do family. It had no outer stairs on the front leading to an upper flat, therefore no way up to the eaves but the vine. "You owe me a pie!" he hollered down, quite safe from reprisal.

"Come down here!" the pursuer shouted back.

"Not on my vine!" the vine owner said. "You get off my roof, boy!"

"What do you want? For me to fly?" Kehfrey scrambled further back from the edge.

"You'll fly to a hell when I get my hands on you!" the bearded man shouted.

"Is that ugly beard real? I just have to know. You look like you pasted on something from between a woman's legs. I should know. I've seen what they have up there. All you have to do is stand under a stairwell. You must know, too, because what you have on your face is a perfect match."

The pursuer grabbed the vines with the obvious intent of climbing up them. The vine owner protested, but when this amounted to nothing, he grabbed the climber by the legs and shouted for his neighbours to get the constabulary.

"I *am* the constabulary!" the bearded man hollered. He dropped down from the vines and stared up at Kehfrey, a sudden narrowing of suspicion to the lids of his eyes. The sweaty proprietor stepped back to gaze at the officer nervously.

"Come down here, boy," the constable said. "I'll go easy on you."

Kehfrey lifted a disbelieving brow. He decided it was time to leave. If his brother hadn't spirited his mother away by now, then he had been born into a family of complete idiots.

"Taste the pie and tell me how it was first," he said. The constable scowled. The pie had fallen to the street long ago. Only a stain on the constable's tunic remained to remind Kehfrey of the missed opportunity and, off in the distance, a fat rat gobbling the flung treat in plain view of everyone. Damned stupid rat.

"Come down here and taste it yourself," the constable said.

Grinning, Kehfrey just backed away. Loose slate skittered down the slope onto the heads below. The constable cursed some interesting insults, all of which Kehfrey committed to memory as he scuttled up the incline. Shortly he'd gone over the apex onto the other side. By then the constable had left off cursing, and Kehfrey caught a clear view of him heading for the alley.

Kehfrey rose and balanced on the point of the roof. The vine owner shouted he'd break his fool neck. Kehfrey ignored him because he'd most certainly break his fool neck getting caught and hung. He ran down the roof, likely convincing the owner he truly was mad, and took a running leap onto the building at the opposite side of the alley. He was quicker going up this incline, using his momentum to reach the peak. He gripped it firmly, hauled himself over and hung down the other side by his fingertips.

Presently he heard the constable wading through the rubbish, mouthing curses still, some of which were directed at his own person. Kehfrey listened intently. After a moment, the constable called out to him. "Hey, boy! Come out! I have all day to catch you! You aren't getting away from me!"

There ensued a loud racket, the sound of refuse being tossed about and rats squeaking in protest. Kehfrey waited a few minutes more, long enough to hear the constable berate himself for getting distracted by a brat boy, whom he described with a number of commonplace invectives. No longer interested, Kehfrey crept down the roof toward the street on the further side.

The awning waited just below, open as usual, one floor lower down, large and green and very inviting. He had already attracted attention from passers-by on the street. He hung off the gutter to an outcry of concern and dropped down onto canvas. The awning dipped perilously, threatening to collapse. The proprietor shouted from beneath. Kehfrey rolled down the canvas and hung by his hands off the edge.

"Hi there, Master Cobbler," he greeted brightly. "Wilf will be coming by to order new shoes from you. Mind you don't make him the too fancy ones that Vik likes."

The cobbler, standing between two displays of his finest work, blinked in surprise. Recognising the offender, he scowled thunderously. "Get off my awning, brat!"

Grinning, Kehfrey thumped to the ground. His skullcap was half off, his red hair awry, his face grubby with dirt and charcoal and his faded clothing further torn from the climb up the vine. He looked every inch the irrepressible hellion. He took off, running into the crowd and out of view. The cobbler shouted something after him, but since it wasn't a very interesting criticism, Kehfrey ignored him and continued on.

From behind the cobbler, a tiny woman wearing a violet hooded cape stepped out to get a clearer view of the fleeing boy. The cobbler remembered his customer and gave a polite bow. He wiped the sweat from his forehead with his apron as he straightened. He'd chafed his skin from having done this all day long. The weather had been hot for days and endless days. Amazingly his customer wore a silk cape without exhibiting the least perspiration. Odd little creature. Must have lived to the south for some time. Had blood made of water perhaps.

"Sorry, milady," he apologized. "That Kehfrey is a mischievous runt. Pay him no mind. Pay him no mind. No harm done."

"Indeed?" said the small women, and she had the barest trace of a foreign accent that made his spine tingle with appreciation. Such a hot little voice. Warm like stones in the sun. If she were any lovelier, he thought he might melt. "Is it a habit of his to jump onto your awning?" she went on.

The cobbler shook his head firmly. "No, lady, not at all. But one can never tell with the boy. One can never tell. Seems to clamber about everywhere. Consorts with any sort of odd creature. Seen him up on the roofs one evening, with rats the size of dogs."

He picked up the shoe he'd dropped when Kehfrey had surprised them and dusted it off. He hoped the brat hadn't lost him a customer. He'd tell the Syndicate what for the next time they came to collect his dues, he would.

"How much did you say?" the woman asked.

The cobbler looked down into bright green eyes and felt himself melting after all. She was a looker, she was.

"Twenty silvers," he said. She took out a purse from beneath the violet cape and handed him three gold pieces. He blinked at the coins in surprise. "I'll have to get change for this."

She stopped him with a slight touch to the arm. "There will be a man coming this way soon," she said. "Don't mention that you know the boy, and I'll come back with another gold piece." She turned to leave.

"The shoes, milady!" the cobbler reminded, obfuscated by her strange interest in the brat.

"When I come back," she said, tucking a lock of very curly dark hair beneath her hood. "*If* you don't say you know the boy. And I'll *know* if you do say." She walked into the crowd, which parted for her at once. She was small, but she carried herself like a highborn woman, and that commanded more respect than size.

Just minutes after, a man did arrive in the street asking about the boy. Bystanders pointed him toward the cobbler's shop. "Here, you!" he called.

The cobbler set down the pretty shoes he'd been pondering and faced the visitor. He was a mess, the searcher, his stockings covered in grime. "Yes?" the cobbler answered, his wide eyes blinking in apparent surprise.

"Did a boy come down onto your awning just now?" the man demanded. He tugged at his beard, which came off in sweaty chunks.

The cobbler eyed this development with interest. "You'll be much better off without it. It's quiet hideous. I'm sure it's too hot as well."

"The boy!" the man snapped.

"Wasn't just now. Been gone minutes. You've missed him."

"Do you know anything about the brat?"

"Not a thing. Just that he almost broke my awning. Could have strapped him one myself if I'd caught him. Have some fine belts for the job. Would you care to see one? I worked them myself."

The man turned away in disgust, pulling the last of the false beard off his face as he did, and at last the shoemaker recognised the officer.

"Oh! That's you High Commissioner," he said. "Back on the beat again? Keeping your fingers in the pie?"

The officer whipped about, his expression harsh. "What would you know about pie?" he snapped.

The cobbler's eyes widened. "Why nothing! It's only an expression. I meant only that it's odd of you to be chasing after scamps when you have others to do the nasty work for you."

"You shut your mouth," the city officer snarled. "Shut your mouth, or I'll shut it for you."

The cobbler blanched. The High Commissioner sneered and presented his back. Scratching at the exposed skin of his cheek, he stomped away, the crowd of bystanders looking on in deferential fascination. It was as the cobbler said, very odd for the official to bother himself with a nuisance gamin. He disappeared around a corner, at which point the cobbler sighed his relief, put the shoes down and took a seat on his stool.

"Yes, that Kehfrey. He's a rare one," he muttered. Perhaps this time Wilf would want shoes as fancy as Vik's. The cobbler shook his head. He doubted it. Vik was a phenomenon of his own make, just like little Kehfrey. Well. Not exactly alike, it should be hoped. "Wouldn't have tattled in any case," he grumbled. "Get a right good bit of business my way because of that family. Every fancy boy wants my shoes, and fancy boys always get their lovers to pay for the best."

A gold piece was a gold piece, whoever gave it, perverts included.

He hoped the lady came back as promised. She was a rare looker, she was.

***

Kehfrey decided a stop at Vik's likeliest location was in order. The place wasn't very far off, and if his mother and Wilf hadn't already visited, he would save them the trouble.

He was in luck and found Vik lounging on the steps of the fountain, one of a number of young men surrounding the celebrated artist, Astabe. The fountain was territory, Astabe's territory, and he made regular use of it, especially on days such as this, when the wind was so frail that it wouldn't pass over the door stoops or the window ledges, and the sun wanted to bake everyone indoors. The boughs of a large beech shaded the fountain. The granite steps stayed cool for hours, up until the shelter receded and the sun fired the stones to scorching hot. Then the water running out of the fish heads did little good unless you sat in the fountain, but that was against city law; a day in the pillory if you were caught and without the benefit of any shade at all.

Kehfrey jogged up to within ten yards of the fountain and hopped the rest of the way like a silly child with nothing better to do. Everyone ignored him except Vik, who cast furtive motions with one hand indicating he should go away. Now! But Kehfrey continued bouncing until he'd come up close enough to see what the artist worked on in the muted light. The moment he made out the subject, he stopped still and stared in shock. A slender male figure lay exposed on the canvas, one arm over the eyes as if the subject slept. The face hid in shadow, leaving the body as the focus of the piece. Kehfrey gaped at the painting. Presently he couldn't contain himself any longer.

"That's the smallest whanger in existence! Even mine is bigger! Which of you modelled it?"

The artist, who'd been dabbing at his rendering of the nude as if he were teasing the flesh of his two-dimensional creation, jerked and left a wide mark with his brush. He cursed and rushed to wipe the error away. Kehfrey laughed uproariously and tagged the mockery with a cruelty.

"Leave it. It's an improvement."

"Who is this devil child?" Astabe roared.

Vik had by now risen with the intention of chasing his brother down the street. "I'll get rid of the brat," he said and stomped down the steps toward the unwelcome caller. A cape of blue silk trimmed with black ermine swirled with his motion. He wore a hat of matching colour on his head. Beneath the cape, he had dressed in the most vivid hues of yellow and gold imaginable. Somehow, despite the awful brightness, the ensemble worked. He looked stunning, at least so his friends told him. Kehfrey just thought he looked stunning, plain and simply stunning, and showed his opinion by covering his eyes in a pretence of going blind.

"My eyes! My eyes!"

Vik grabbed his ear and hauled him down the street.

"My ear!" the boy changed his cry.

"Box him one!" Astabe shouted after them.

Vik ignored his current lover and continued stomping away. "What's happened?" he demanded between a series of loud semi-false profanities.

"Change of residence. Watch out not to be followed," Kehfrey hissed. "And how can you wear that cape in this heat? Or that gods awful suit! Looks good on you, by the way. Heavens know why. The colours all clash."

"Fashion sometimes dictates suffering," Vik replied equably. "And now that I know your tastes are going to lead toward drab and boring, I feel very sorry for you."

He released his brother's ear and gave him a mock shove with his ornate shoe. Kehfrey made the required sprawl to the earth and lost his skullcap. He rolled over and performed his best poor-little-boy impression, but his unappreciative brother already stalked toward his client, his last act of disdain an arrogant flourish, flaxen hair tossed over the shoulder.

Well, at least the hair matched the suit. Kehfrey's false hurt changed to a scowl. "Just tell me who modelled for the portrait! I didn't see a face!"

Vik stomped back. "He can't just paint a big whanger. It would offend his patron."

To this, his little brother grimaced in disbelief. "What for?"

"Because," Vik replied impatiently.

"So the great artist has to paint one that looks like it was poked into a bowl of ice?"

"That's about it," Vik agreed.

Kehfrey considered this as his brother returned to Astabe. Shaking his head in mystification, Kehfrey picked himself off the dirt and turned, at which time he found himself face to face with a well-dressed girl in a violet cape and matching dress. He squinted up at her and revised his estimation. Not a girl, just an unusually small woman. Very pretty, though. Her crinoline didn't give the skirt nearly the girth he usually saw on upper-class women, but the quality of the clothes was the highest. Her perfume filled his nostrils, smelling of flowers, hundreds of them. The scent was enough to bury him.

"Your brother is very attractive," the woman said softly.

"I was thinking the same thing about you," he answered. Smiling, she lowered her hood, and he changed his mind. She was more than pretty. She was exceptional. She had very clean skin, curly dark hair and wondrously green eyes. There was a serious gleam to them, however.

"Tell your father to take another target tonight," she said.

His gaze narrowed. "What are you talking about?"

"I'm a seeress," she told him. "Take another target."

Terror bumps rose all over his body. Despite a warning tightness in his guts, he remained frozen before her. "And if not?" he said.

"You will pay for your family's corruption," she answered.

He blinked. "What's this corruption bit?"

She smirked slightly. "Corruption is what your family works at." Seeing that he didn't understand or didn't want to, she was more explicit. "Thieving and whoring," she said.

He scowled. Thinking it unwise to speak with her further, he made to dart away.

"I'll trade you," she offered.

He stalled in his tracks. Bartering was one of his favourite pastimes when he got a chance at it, which was seldom since he usually only had bits of garbage to deal with. His hazel eyes narrowed with distrust, but his unremitting curiosity fixed him in place. "For what?" he inquired.

"Your knife for this." She held out her hand. On the palm rested a small stone. Grey and smooth, only a strange symbol painted on the surface distinguished it from any other stone.

"How did you know about my knife?" he said, backing away.

"I told you. I'm a seeress." She remained motionless with her hand out. "This stone will save you. I can see your father going to the target even if you tell him. His partners won't listen."

"Then I'll keep the knife. It's worth more than a stone, even to the metal collector. It's worth enough to feed us a week."

"The knife won't save you, not even to feed you."

"And what's the cussed rock supposed to do?"

"You're going to be caught, Kehfrey," she said, ignoring his question. "You're going to be caught. You will die."

If he hadn't already been nervous beforehand, this pronouncement might have given him a chill despite the blasting heat of the sun. Her words frightened, but he determined to hear whatever she had to tell him. Outrageous as her prediction seemed, he believed her. "Don't leave me in the dark, woman!" he barked with his child-high voice. "Tell me what to do with the cussed rock!"

She smiled again. This time the gesture was wide with delight. "You're just the wildest brash boy. Why should I bother?"

"I don't care why! Keep bothering!" He danced nervously on his feet. "You've bothered this much, haven't you?" Settling down, he pulled the knife out from the back of his tunic and presented it to her. She accepted it and placed the rock on his palm. "What's the sign mean?" he said. "What must I do exactly?"

She bent and whispered in his ear, pushing his hair aside with a light touch of her fingers. He shivered listening to the answer, and his face had a shocked pallor when she straightened. The spine-freezing chill had arrived after all. There was something. Not in the answer. No. It was something later, something bad, and it had nothing to do with him. It had to do with her.

"Is it catchy?" he said.

She frowned in mystification. "Is what catchy?"

"Seeing." By the gods, but she looked good even wearing a scowl.

"Odd child. No. You're born with it or not."

"Oh." But she'd touched him and he'd known. He wanted her to touch him again.

He wasn't to get his wish.

"You have to hold the stone. No matter what, don't let go."

She walked away, violet skirts swishing against parched dirt. Kehfrey stared after her, feeling as if the light of the day had abandoned him. The blasting heat on his skin said otherwise, but he was so damned frozen inside what did sunlight matter?

"Kehfrey?"

The boy turned to see his brother at his back, following the seeress's departure with a suspicious gleam to the blue of his eyes.

"Who was that woman?" Vik said. He stepped another pace forward and craned to see. The diminutive woman had just disappeared into the crowd.

"Just a fortune teller," Kehfrey said dismissively.

"Why did you give her a knife?"

"Payment. Go back to your lover. He's got to realize we know each other by now."

"I told him I thought you were rather sweet looking. He's wondering if he should paint you into his Hell's Gate."

Kehfrey found that mildly interesting. "As what exactly? A soul going to a hell?"

"A devil," Vik said, a bright note of amusement in his voice.

Kehfrey canted to see beyond his brother. Vik's lover glared at him. Kehfrey blinked, taken aback. Astabe's glare seemed sort of hungry and smouldering.

"Vik?"

"What?"

"What's that hungry look mean?"

His brother's head turned with an audible snap, and his flaxen hair whipped about beneath his hat. "Son of a bitch! Forget sitting for him! Go find Mum!"

"No problem," Kehfrey said and fled down the dusty street. That hungry look was worse than knowing you were about to die.

***

He found his mother sitting alone at the meeting place. The exposed areas of the old city cemetery were nearly empty because of the high temperature. Those who had chosen the site for relief from the heat wave were hidden within the shade of the trees. Canella had selected an expansive willow close to a decrepit mausoleum. She was alone. No doubt the bloody handkerchief she held in her lap had won her the shelter. Pretending to hack consumption on all and sundry could clear a space of competitive citizens in short order. Kehfrey thumped up, disturbing a lot of dust on the path, and she sneezed violently, furthering her image of sickness.

"Aiie! I almost lost hold of my bladder, you brat! Settle down!" She glared, but he merely smirked and squatted down at a safe distance. Mum was feeling cranky.

"Missed your afternoon nap," he remarked.

"Where were you? I missed my nap worrying over you. And where's your cap?"

"I went to see Vik. Lost my cap getting here."

"I should have guessed. You'll have to steal another. You warned Vik, then?"

He nodded. "Where's Wilf?"

"Gone to fetch Pop," she answered.

"I'm hungry," he said.

She proffered the sack of cheese and the half-filled bottle of wine. He pulled a long draught and forced himself to swallow. He didn't like the sour taste of wine, but he was thirsty enough to drink anything.

"Gaah! It's awful!" He handed the bottle back

She laughed, and of a sudden their relation was more easily discernable to those looking on. Mother and son had the same smile. "You'll change your mind when you get older," she said.

By his expression, he didn't believe her. She watched him pull a chunk of cheese from the wedge and ignore the dry bread. He had a wiggly tooth up in front, not quite ready to go. She knew he didn't want it to go. He already had a gap left by another missing tooth. As it was, when he smiled, no matter how sweet he intended the expression, a hint of devil's mischief arrived with the gesture. Ah, but he was his father's child. Kehfen smiled that way, but little Kehfrey managed to imitate his father with the lips she had given him.

"Where did you find Vik?" she asked.

"With the *Great* Astabe," he said, his tone sour. "He wanted me for his Hell's Gate."

"Really?" She thought this interesting. Perhaps the artist would be willing to pay to have her Kehfrey sit for him.

"Vik decided it wasn't a good idea," he informed her, perfectly alert to her pecuniary musings. Her blue eyes had taken on a calculating sharpness.

"Why not?" she said. Her gaze narrowed with suspicion. "Vik wouldn't pass up an opportunity. You're making a tale again."

"Swear it, Mum. Vik sent me off. Astabe had a funny look on his face."

"A funny look? What sort of funny look?"

"You know. Pop's sort of funny look when you think I'm sleeping."

"Kehfrey!" she barked. The rebuke broke off and her eyes widened in alarm. "You stay away from that Astabe!"

He nodded resolutely and carefully bit into the cheese.

"And stop being awake when Pop is looking funny."

He laughed and then suffered for his amusement. He choked on the cheese, coughed and spluttered yellow bits everywhere. His mother shoved the wine at him. He swallowed, but his throat refused to clear and he swallowed more until it did. He'd drunk a sixth of the bottle by then. When she received the bottle back, she looked at the volume wisely.

"You're going to be drunk," she told him.

He shrugged, thinking he might as well get drunk before he died. He mightn't have a chance later. All the same, he tried not to choke again as he finished his meal. Choking to death wasn't his idea of a glorious demise. If he were going to expire, he'd do it in a spectacular way. Yes, he would.

His eldest brother arrived with his father and Gamis not long afterward. By then, Kehfrey entertained his mother with a fantastical tale, one that included a giant of monumental proportions who vaguely resembled a certain renowned artist. Kehfrey was in the process of killing the great entity when his father's hand clapped onto his small shoulder and thrilled him better than his finest nightmare. Screeching, he whirled and sent a fist flying toward his father's groin, but Kehfen was ready for the attack and caught his wrist. Everyone burst out laughing, but for the startled waif.

"Careful, boy," Kehfen warned. He looked over at his wife, and there was the devil's mischief hinting through the beard. "Don't hurt the only valuables Kortin lets me keep."

Kehfrey recovered from the surprise and wriggled out of his father's grasp. Kehfen let him go, smiling still as his youngest danced away off balance. The child toppled onto the dry earth and sent up a cloud of dust. He coughed and lay there with a muzzy expression. Kehfen laughed and went to sit with his wife.

"What's with him?" Gamis said. The second youngest, Gamis was the only one to have been born with sandy brown hair. He had also inherited hazel irises from his father, a trait he shared with Kehfrey. Gamis was ten.

"He's drunk," his mother said.

"Is he, now?" Kehfen muttered. He scratched at his beard. White hairs peppered the chin area. "Well, just so long as he's not by nightfall."

Canella looked at him in surprise. "You aren't still doing the hit?"

"Might do." He swept his hat off and leant back against the willow tree, to then pull his greying ginger hair off his sweating forehead. The air felt good on his scalp. He regretted the dark clothing he must habitually wear. Poor Gamis looked little better off. Perspiration stained the front and back of his brown tunic.

"Hiswil sent one of the gang to check the place out early," Kehfen continued. "If it looks like a set-up, we'll abandon." He gazed at his youngest son thoughtfully. It appeared Kehfrey had fallen asleep on the dirt, one hand thrust inside his breech's pocket. "Go get your brother out of the sun," he ordered Wilf.

The eldest boy fetched the little fellow up and laid him beside his mother. "Is he really better than Gamis?" Wilf asked. Gamis flushed with anger and that was answer enough.

"He's better," Kehfen confirmed.

"But you've only taken him to the trainers a few times. How can he be better already?"

"The gods only know. Maldin says he's never seen the like."

"What do you mean exactly?" Wilf settled down next to the sleeping child.

"He's faster with every lock he's been given to pick. He's faster than Maldin! He's even picked a few Maldin has trouble with."

"He's good at pick-pocketing, too," Gamis put in quickly, coming to crouch in the shade to the other side of Wilf. "He should be sent out to do that."

"Shut your mouth, Gamis." Quieting his voice, Kehfen continued the rebuke in a low hiss. "None of my boys does the picking trade. I never let you take the risk. Why should I make Kehfrey?"

"You only said that to get Kehfrey out of your way," Wilf taunted. "You're jealous." Gamis turned away with a sullen scowl. Wilf eyed him and then focused his attention on his stepfather. "What about the other skills?"

"He's fine by them. He has an instinct for just about every trick we've shown him. If he didn't look like me, I'd swear he was a devil's changeling."

Wilf scrutinized the man pensively. Because of the beard, he really wasn't certain what Kehfen looked like, but the nose was fine and hooked, the forehead smooth despite his age, the lips well shaped. He wasn't a tall man, and Kehfrey showed every sign he would end up just as slight as his father. Wilf smirked. "I called him an elf the other day."

"And he's upset over it still," Canella snapped. "You shouldn't tease him so."

"Oh, come on, Mum. He can take it. You heard the insult he sent my way."

"And what was that?" Kehfen asked.

Canella smirked this time. "Wilf had a fine bonus today," she said casually.

Wilf flushed.

"Really?" Kehfen responded. He eyed Wilf meaningfully. Wilf handed him a single silver coin. His mother said nothing, but grinned wider. "Where's the rest?" Kehfen asked.

"I need new breeches and stockings, for gods' sakes!" Wilf pointed at the fouled ones he now wore. "Washing won't get this out."

Kehfen let the matter drop. "What was the insult, then?"

"He said I buggered Mistress Nas but good," Wilf replied, grinning now.

Kehfen laughed. "Did you?"

"Not last night."

The three older family members chortled, but Gamis wrinkled his nose in distaste. "I don't know how you can do that stuff. She's an ugly old slut."

"She's an ugly old *rich* slut," Wilf amended. "And she feels just fine if you pretend otherwise." Gamis only glowered disbelievingly. Wilf decided he needed further riling. "You must be more into Vik's tastes," he said.

Gamis dove on him. They rolled away, lifting a swarm of dry motes into the air. Seven years the senior and with the advantage of size, Wilf shortly had Gamis pinned down. While Gamis shouted at the elder boy to get off, Kehfen complacently opened the sack and pulled out the remaining cheese.

"That Wilf takes after you," Canella said, feeling rather sleepy.

Kehfen laughed. "How's that possible?"

"You raised him!" she said, now feeling petulant.

He only laughed again. "He takes after his grandfather. Do you think that old bastard will ever acknowledge him?"

She shook her head. "I don't know. He's lost every son he's had, true born or bastard. If he were really going to forgive me, you'd think he would have made a motion to do so by now."

"Everything will go to his brother's get, then," Kehfen said. Noting her downcast face, he opted for reassurance. "He knows where to get a message to us."

She nodded. "Let's not worry about it. It isn't likely."

That old sadness settled in her mind, she ordered Wilf to release his brother. Beforehand tickling a furious but laughing Gamis under the arm, Wilf straightened and retreated. Gamis leapt to his feet and thumped away to a distant tree, to share the shade with a few other overheated denizens of Wistal, all of whom looked disinclined to be talkative, which was fine by him.

Kehfrey woke with a start, rolled and jumped to his feet. He wobbled uncertainly.

"Sit yourself down, boy," Kehfen said.

The boy thudded back onto his bottom. His head continued weaving. "The world is moving too quickly," he said, for which his parents laughed at him. He blinked at them owlishly. "It *is* going too quickly! Faster than the fastest, fastest, fastest bird! Only it's not a bird. It's round like a peach, but without the crevice. Something is keeping us on the world, but I didn't see what." This only had them laughing harder. Kehfrey grimaced. "It's spinning around like a fat, round top and we should all be flung off!" he screeched.

Wilf stepped up, grinning widely. "Give him the rest of the wine, Pop. That'll shut him up."

"No, I don't think so. Take him to the well and dunk some water over his head. I think he may be too hot."

"I am not!" Kehfrey protested, but Wilf grabbed him all the same. Slung over his brother's shoulder, he went shrieking out of the cemetery and toward the well further down the street.

Kehfen frowned as the two boys departed. "He still has his hand in his pocket," he said. Wasn't that odd? What did the boy have in there?

The arrival of his first natural son distracted him from this silent worry. Vik sauntered over and stood before them, refusing to sit or squat. He wouldn't soil his beautiful clothing for that. Kehfen scowled and declined to look at him. Vik, on his part, declined to look hurt, although he was.

"I came to see what the whole thing is about," he said.

His mother smiled, but sadness over Kehfen's obvious rejection weakened the gesture. Vik was fifteen years old. He was probably their most handsome child, but also their most disappointing. He was well aware of it, but stood straight and proud nonetheless.

"Wilf thinks the target tonight may be a set up. Someone followed him home from Mistress Nas's villa," she said. This information produced a concerned frown on Vik's handsome face.

"Anything odd in your group?" Kehfen said, looking at him at last.

Vik shook his head. "I haven't been invited anywhere new lately. There's been no real change in my group. They're a silly lot for the most part. All they ever talk about is art, clothing and who's had who. I don't think they have me linked to Wilf."

"If you don't like them, why do you consort with them?" Kehfen said.

His son would not respond. Vik spurned the irresolvable argument with a quiet retreat, his countenance inexpressive. It was the perfect criticism, aimed at a father possessed of an outsized measure of blunt fire and a meagre share of cool comportment.

"Kehfen!" Canella rebuked him.

Her husband averted his face, but the glimpse of disgust she caught told her once again he wasn't prepared to listen. Thinking it best not to call Vik back, she watched him depart, a cheerless expression on her face. Vik seldom visited. He kept his gains to himself and rented his own place to sleep. When he did visit, he showed up during his father's absences with the expressed purpose of detailing a possible target, but she knew he came to share a rare moment with his favourite brother. If not for Kehfrey, Canella suspected he would have stopped calling altogether.

Wilf returned with a soaking wet Kehfrey to divert her from her upset. She looked at the dripping boy and smiled. Aside from being somewhat cleaner, his hair was further askew and he was patently furious, lips compressed and eyes bright with discontent. Sweet and sour like a pickle.

"My little pickle!" she said. "What are you so angry about now?"

"Tell him to give it back!" he shouted.

Kehfen frowned at the two. "Give what back?"

"My stone!" Kehfrey shouted more loudly. He charged Wilf and pummelled him with his fists. Wilf plucked him off his feet and held his kicking and squirming body at a distance. Water droplets sprayed off the infuriated child.

"Wilf! Give him back his stone!" Canella barked. Wilf dropped the boy, who fell on his bottom and cried out in pain.

"Careful with him," Kehfen said. "I need him walking tonight."

Wilf scowled and dug into his tunic. His eyes widened in dismay, but the startled expression quickly transformed into a glare bent upon Kehfrey. "Give it back!" he shouted.

"Give what back?" Kehfen said, his voice rising as well.

"My pouch! He took it!"

"Serves you right for taking my stone!" the little boy retorted.

Wilf made to lunge at him, but Kehfen issued a sharp reprimand. Looking at his stepfather's irritated countenance, it was evident only a trade would suffice. Wilf thrust his hand in his tunic and located the stone. He threw it at Kehfrey's feet. Kehfrey withdrew the pouch from beneath his ratty garment and tossed it up. Wilf looked inside at once, for which Kehfrey glowered at him.

"I didn't have time to get anything out of it, idiot."

He snatched his stone up and scrabbled over to his mother before Wilf had time to react. Wilf concluded he'd best leave the troublesome brat alone and headed over to Gamis's tree, where he sat down without a word. Gamis shifted away from him, but seeing that his half brother was intent on glaring at Kehfrey, he decided he could suffer Wilf's presence after all and settled down again.

Kehfen looked at Kehfrey suspiciously. "What's with the stone?" he asked.

"Just a lucky charm," the boy said.

Kehfen stared at him. "What sort of stone is a lucky charm? It looked like a plain rock to me."

"I took it from the palm of the most beautiful woman in the world," the boy said proudly. "It's going to save my life."

His father and mother exchanged knowing glances, believing another wild story imminent. "And why did this beautiful woman give it to you?" Kehfen said.

"Because I'm irresistible of course. Why else would she?"

"Why else? No other reason comes to my mind," Kehfen admitted dryly. "Yours?" he said to his wife. She smiled and shook her head. "And how will the stone save your life?" he asked the child.

"It's going to keep me from dying when I get shot by a crossbow bolt tonight," he told them, astonishing both into perfect, horrified silence. "She's a seer," he spoke into the profound hush. "She says your gang will go ahead with the theft despite the warning, and I'm going to pay for my family's corruption."

"Did anyone see this woman with you?" Canella demanded. "Anyone real? That we know?"

"Vik did. Can I have some more wine?"

"No!" they both barked.

Kehfen stood and took off after Vik.

"Kehfrey," Canella said, her tone urgent. "Think carefully. Could the woman have followed you from home? Could she have been with the bearded man?"

He shook his head. "She wasn't."

"How can you be certain?"

"I just am," he said flatly, looking into her eyes without wavering.

She regarded him with some awe. Her littlest boy had the bearing of someone far beyond his years. Somehow his hazel eyes just seemed too wise. "Kehfrey," she began again. "She could have been playing a trick on you."

"If so, it won't matter much after tonight, then," he retorted smartly. He jumped to his feet and raced out of the cemetery. She called to him, but he refused to return, instead climbed up onto the distant well and commenced to hop one-footed around the edge, careless of toppling within. She looked across the sunlit dirt at Wilf, but the older boy had fallen asleep next to a drowsy Gamis. Despite the heat of the day, Canella had a chill inside her guts. She wished Kehfen would come back quickly.

***

Kehfen didn't manage to catch up to Vik until the fountain. He discovered his son standing alone before the low wall of the pool, looking down at the water with a melancholic air. The shade had retreated from the granite and exposed it to the harsh sun, forcing the artist and his group of young men to abandon the idyllic setting. Astabe's territory had become a repudiated, lonely place.

"Vik," Kehfen called.

Vik turned in surprise. "What are you doing here?"

Kehfen slowed to a walk and stopped beside him. "Did Kehfrey talk to some strange woman today?"

A brief hint of disappointment flickered in Vik's eyes. He had hoped his father had followed to make peace with him. He veiled the regret and responded flatly to the question. "I saw him with a woman, yes."

"What did she look like?"

Vik regarded his father narrowly. "Small, beautiful. Very green eyes."

"Did she give Kehfrey anything?"

He nodded. "I saw them make an exchange."

"Of what?"

"He gave her a knife. I didn't see what Kehfrey got. It was very small." In response to this, his father hissed a diatribe against the unknown woman, to which Vik listened in growing alarm. "What's this all about?" he asked.

"She gave Kehfrey a stone. He thinks he's going to be shot with a quarrel tonight. Gods busted boy! Wasted metal for a stone. I'll black his ass for him."

Vik blanched. "Don't be so hard. He said she was a fortune teller."

"What sort of fortune teller singles out Kehfrey of all people and convinces him to give away a valuable bit of metal? He's never been that stupid," his father said caustically. "I've got to go back and look at this stone."

He hastened back the way he'd come. Vik stared after him, wondering if he should follow. He decided against it, averting his head to peer down at the shimmering water. He hoped Kehfrey was all right. Of all his siblings, Kehfrey was the only one who didn't seem to mind a roach for a brother. Perhaps he was still too young to understand, but Vik hoped he was wiser than the rest, if there was any such thing as wisdom concerning someone of his type.

He grimaced and in an almost dismissive manner walked away from the water. He knew where Astabe would have gone in the heat of the late afternoon. Vik decided he would visit the family meeting place tomorrow. By then, one of his kin would have marked the location of their new abode in the code of the Syndicate.

***

"Let me see the gods busted stone!" Kehfen snarled.

"No!" Daring to perch on a high, thin branch in a tree, Kehfrey glared down with a pugnacious expression that spoke ill of his father's blunt method. "If you take it from me, I may as well go jump in the well and drown. I may as well dive on my head here and now."

"I'll give it back," Kehfen pretended to bargain.

"Liar!" Kehfrey said immediately.

"You little brat! How dare you call me a liar!"

"I call it as I see it."

His father flushed. A few bystanders tittered at his back, and he turned to glare with an expression as contentious as his son's. He delivered the look with far more menace, and the witnesses hurried away, but only to watch at a safer distance.

"You swear it to me; then I'll come down," Kehfrey offered.

His brother Gamis snorted in amusement. "He'll still black your ass after," he called up. Kehfen sent Gamis a stony look. Gamis decided he had best shut up and sidled away to a safer distance as well.

"Fine. I'll swear," said Kehfen. "Come down."

"Swear first," Kehfrey countered. Kehfen scowled, his lips compressing into a thin line.

"Oh, just swear!" Canella said. "You know he can tell if you lie."

"He's unnatural!" Kehfen hissed.

"He's yours!" she hissed back. "You made him. It must come from you."

He glowered at her, but without much force. Kehfen seldom put the full weight of his condemnation on Canella. He hated it when she cried. And she always did.

"Hurry up," Kehfrey shouted down. "I've got to pass water. You don't want me to do it up here, do you?"

Kehfen bestowed upon his youngest the fullness of his withering regard, but Kehfrey hung on and refused to wither. Kehfen found his flat stare unnerving, as usual simultaneously perturbed and proud that his smallest child bore up under his censure better than the rest of the family put together. Kehfen had no idea how he'd be able to manage the boy later. Damned urchin was only seven. What would he be like at fourteen?

"The child just isn't natural," he said again.

His wife but shoved him indelicately toward the tree. Relenting, he lifted both hands and performed the necessary guild signs close to his chest. The boy promptly slipped down until he hung from the branch he'd been seated upon. Swinging, he dropped down to the next one, then the next. His mother shut her eyes and refused to look. Presently, she heard a thump nearby.

"Is he down?" she asked.

"Yes," Kehfrey answered. "You can look now. I didn't break anything."

She opened her eyes in time to see Kehfen snatch the boy off his feet and shake him furiously.

"You awful brat!" was the least nasty epithet he hurled at his son.

"Kehfen!" Canella protested. "Just look at the stone first!" She was impatient to see it herself. Punishing Kehfrey could wait. It wasn't as if the boy would run. He never ran. Often as not, he'd talk his way out of getting flogged. Well, except with Wilf. He and Wilf had their contentions, sibling rivalry gone all out of proportion, what with Wilf being so much older. Canella would have thought the boy would be more resentful of Gamis, but Kehfrey seldom bothered with Gamis except to bedevil him, and he bedevilled everyone; only he really meant if with Wilf for some inexplicable reason of his own.

Responding to Canella's prompt, Kehfen dropped the child and shoved a palm out. The boy placed the stone in his father's hand without hesitation, and Kehfen examined it suspiciously. After a moment, he frowned down at his son. "You traded a knife for this. It has a stupid, meaningless mark on it."

"I know that," Kehfrey huffed mutinously.

Canella snatched the stone from her husband and looked it over. Sighing in frustration, she handed it back to the child.

"I can't believe it. My wise child taken in by a pretty face." She turned with a flounce of her ratty skirts. "Well, at least we know his weakness while he's young." She stomped over to the willow tree, scattering pigeons from her path.

Kehfrey flushed bright red as Wilf and Gamis laughed at him, but the knowing smirk on his father's face fuelled a keen bitterness that tightened the child's fingers around the stone until his knuckles turned white.

"You were taken, boy. She had the better deal with the knife. The metal collector will give her ten silvers for it, if she doesn't keep it for herself. Even off balance, it still had more value as a knife than as recycled metal." Kehfen turned his back on the boy. "Keep your fool stone. It'll remind you of how you were duped today."

His brothers' guffaws grew louder. Mouthing curses, Kehfrey pocketed the stone and stomped off to a distant, almost barren tree that showed signs it did duty as a pissing post. He relieved himself upon it. To the side, the bystanders were moving off now that the entertainment had finished. Kehfrey snorted to himself.

"I'm going to live." He settled his breeches around his waist and stuck his hand back into his pocket. He withdrew the stone to inspect the symbol inscribed upon it. "Healing," he whispered. All he had to do was hold on tight. "I can do that."

He dropped the stone back into his pocket and, looking about, located a group of children near his age playing hoops in the street. The sun crept toward its resting place, giving the streets more shade and permitting the local inhabitants to venture out from their daytime hideaways. Kehfrey wandered over to the children. If they let him, he would amaze them with some of his tricks. He bet the fat nurse on the stoop had some treats. She was the one he really had to impress.

"Hi, there!" He jogged closer, his hurt forgotten. Shortly he had his marks agog over his manipulation of the hoops.

From the distance, his parents observed silently. Despite having made themselves feel better putting Kehfrey down, they were both apprehensive. While they watched him clowning for treats, a messenger arrived from the Syndicate. Kehfen lifted up and approached the man. Listening to the message, his face tightened into an emotionless mask. Canella knew instantly the hit was still on for the night.

Chapter Two

Kehfen escorted his family to a safe house that evening, an old tenement building whose topmost half served as a whorehouse. Up top wasn't much better than below. It catered to a poor district frequented by unrefined customers. The best payers at the establishment were in fact the thieves who held truck in the bottommost portion, a dilapidated common area wherein fallen plaster exposed weathered and mouldy wood. The walls, repaired or not, had gone brown from the years of unwashed filth. The ceiling had water stains and cracks, and knife marks ticked all surfaces. Coarse, hard-spirited men had flaunted their deadlier arts in the house for decades.

In a dim corner of this neglected but heavily populated tenement, Canella settled onto a dirty pallet and fell into a fretful doze. Kehfen ordered Wilf to keep her company, knowing unreliable Gamis would be off the second his back was turned, eager to play a game of Acquisition with the older boys and young men scattered about the building. Wilf wouldn't abandon his mother in this place. Safe houses were safe enough for the men of the Syndicate, but not much so for the women. Most of those were upstairs and less well off than slaves.

"Tell her not to have the baby now," Kehfen half joked to the young man.

Wilf smirked, but his regard was serious above the grin. They were in mutual accord concerning Canella's safety. Kehfen gripped Wilf's shoulder in farewell, rose and headed for the stairs to the cellar. He descended, but paused with his head just above the trap and peered about for the boy he must present to his team. It wasn't difficult to spot his smallest child, to whom he had passed on a disgraceful bush of ginger hair and the palest skin outside of albino that dared boast no freckles. Kehfrey had pestered some fool into a toss with darts, betting his silly stone for a silver and, quite unsurprisingly to his father, he'd just pierced three times the chalk target drawn on the unfinished wood of the tenement wall. Kehfrey's astounded mark, who'd expected worse from the miniscule runt, hesitated to make good on the wager.

"Are you a devil child? Are you an elf? Are you really a midget passing yourself off as a boy?"

"I'm seven years old and completely human. Don't be a poor loser. Pay up!"

Kehfrey ended the demand with a grimy palm held upward. To a chorus of laughter and jeers, the irritated mark dropped the silver onto his waiting hand. Grinning, the boy strode away toward his father's visible head, never having lost track of Kehfen's movements despite slipping off to make the small profit.

"Hi, Pop! You look dee-cap-ee-tate-ed," he said, practicing a word he'd recently acquired. Two days earlier he'd never heard of a better one for chopping off heads, but then a freakish accident involving dropped cargo had taken the head off a dockworker. Everyone had been talking about the gory mess. Kehfrey had spent the night sleepless, mulling over the possible sensations that came with decapitation. The next morning he'd been too sick to eat breakfast. Today he effected his resolution never to consider how decapitation felt again.

A few guffaws met the boy's smart-mouthed observation. "Hells' balls! Is that one of your brats, Kehfen?" the loser said. "I should have guessed, what with the innocent face and devil's hair. He up and scammed me out of a silver. He's got your perfect aim, gods blast you both."

More laughter littered the air following this sarcasm. For answer, Kehfen merely smirked and ducked beneath the floor, and Kehfrey stomped down the steps after him. "Stop thumping, Kehfrey," he said, keeping his voice low. He wouldn't ruin his reputation of cocky sureness berating the boy publicly. "Bloody castrated bulls' butts, you make me wonder. You didn't do that at practice two days ago."

"I'm not practicing now."

"Stop it anyway. It's giving me a headache."

Kehfrey thought it wasn't his thumping giving his father a headache, but the worry over what might happen tonight, but he was wise enough not to say so. He trailed his father the rest of the way down in silence.

At the end of a short passage, his father knocked on a heavy wooden door. This opened into a large, musty chamber that held in its centre a weathered table with a single chair. In the midst of the dank squalor, a golden candelabrum stood slightly off centre on the table. Only two lit candles were in the holders, though the fancy piece had places for three more. Kehfen's team leader sat on the single chair with two men flanking him. One other, a very tall man, lurked in the shadows at the rear of the room. A fourth, an older fellow, shut the door and rounded the table to stand near the leader.

"Kehfen," Hiswil welcomed flatly. He remained seated. He was a stocky man with a bald head. He compensated for this shortcoming with a prominent moustache. It curved away from his lips, crossed his cheeks, and met his sideburns at the further sides. Only a tiny slit of a beard decorated his chin, which was just as well. His lower lip could bear no further adornment, being somewhat too generous. The outsized moustache balanced the disproportions south and north.

Hiswil awarded the little boy following Kehfen a misgiving regard. Kehfrey's diminutive stature made him seem younger than he actually was. "You're sure he's ready for this?"

"He'll do, but if you have someone else in mind, say so," Kehfen said.

Hiswil squinted shrewdly. "Your Gamis won't fit down the chimneys anymore. Nor will most of the others. Those who can are too clumsy for the job, being too young for it. Your Kehfrey is the best we have for this."

30

"Then why did you ask?" Kehfen said sourly.

"Just to see how you'd take it," Kehfrey piped up from behind.

Hiswil bent a menacing gaze on the boy. "Is he going to tweet like that on the job?"

Kehfrey chose to answer despite the warning tone. "I'm not an idiot. I know when to shut up."

"Is that so?" Hiswil sat forward in his chair as if he might lunge over the table.

"Shut up, Kehfrey," Kehfen ordered his son.

"Right," Kehfrey grumbled, just loud enough to be heard. "Can't say nothing 'cause I'm not tall enough to smack any of you back."

One of Hiswil's men snorted in outrage. "You *ought* to smack him one, Kehfen. He's got too much mouth."

"Shut up, Lerny."

Lerny, the scruffy old fellow who'd closed the door, had a scraggly grey beard and a face of crags and peaks. He glowered at Kehfen but shut up nevertheless. Kehfen was the shortest man in the room except for Hiswil, but no one who wanted his skin intact challenged him. Kehfen had a gift for murder as well as thievery, and if he'd been more disposed to the former, he'd have been working the extortion racket of the syndicate. Sometimes the bosses of the other rings visited theirs to solicit favours, Kehfen's services in particular. It seemed he had a knack for getting certain jobs done quietly and in a less messy manner than most. Knowing this, Lerny was reluctant to rile the man.

"He's got no manners," Hiswil said, who was as deft at cutting into bodies as Kehfen, but disinclined to the strenuous activity. "That's what comes of not disciplining your boys. We should put this one in pick-pocketing after tonight. He should earn his keep."

"Not my boy," Kehfen replied stiffly. Hiswil rose to his feet, but Kehfen refused to back down. "My family has done its share. We've provided more useful targets than everyone else combined. Are you saying Kortin doesn't think so?"

Hiswil sat again. "Except tonight may not be so useful," he sneered. "Isn't that right, Kehfen?"

"If you think that, why are we still doing the job?" the child said.

Hiswil bolted to an angry stand. "I thought we decided that boy was to keep his mouth shut!"

The child's father was inclined to press for answers, however. "Answer the question, Hiswil," Kehfen said. "Why did Kortin order the go ahead if you think it's not a good idea?"

Hiswil lifted his glare to him. "Kortin says something is going down. We have to see if this target is a part of it."

"What does Kortin think is going down?"

"He's not certain. Your boy Wilf isn't the only caser who's been followed home recently, and there have been three exchangers arrested in the past week, all of them who'd never a suspicion on them before. We may have to go out of the city to fence the goods if this keeps up."

Kehfen's expression became grimmer. "I don't want my Kehfrey involved."

"Your Kehfrey is the only one small enough to get down the cussed chimney. We have no choice. You damned well know the doors and windows will have wards up on this one. The mark is rich enough to afford the service."

"But what did the scout see today? If the target is compromised, why go?"

"I saw nothing," the man at the back said, stepping forward from out of the shadows. He was tall and very dark skinned. His hair hung down from his head in thick locks. His entire outfit—tunic, pants and boots—was jet black, and he had a horde of knives sheathed in various locations on his person. A curved sword in a lacquered sheath hung at his hip. The pommel bore a golden tassel. Kehfrey thought he looked fantastical, so dark as to have been made of the earth itself.

As if sensing his regard, the extraordinary man slowly glanced down, brown irises a pair of sharp stones in fields of bright sclera. As indolently, he averted his gaze, but Kehfrey had the oddest sense more interest lay behind that stolid expression than the dark man would have liked exposed.

"The servants wandered the mansion and the grounds just as could be expected," the foreigner continued. He had a thick accent, but the words were clear enough. "There was only one thing that bothered me about them."

"And what was that, Olomo?" Kehfen said.

"There were no women," Olomo answered. "That's just not natural."

Kehfen agreed, albeit silently. He fixed his regard on Hiswil. "What haven't you told me yet? Don't shove shit back up my ass, Hiswil. I know Kortin told you more about this than you've said."

"Bugger off, Kehfen," Hiswil growled.

Kehfen headed for the door, dragging Kehfrey back with him.

"Get back here!"

"Go to a hell! I'm seeing Kortin myself." Kehfen heard the chair topple.

"Rook may have hit the wrong manor a few months back," came a belated response.

Kortin's son! Kehfen halted and closed his eyes in disgust as Hiswil continued speaking.

"He did a house his father told him to ignore. We've had odd things happening since."

Kehfen turned and lifted a brow in question.

Hiswil paused a second to right his chair. He sat on it and sighed. "Bloody buggering idiot. If Rook takes over the Syndicate, I'm off to Lordun."

"Not likely," Olomo said. "Kortin will do him first."

"He wouldn't kill his own son!" Lerny cried in shock.

Olomo eyed him flatly. "He would have someone else do him."

"He's right," Hiswil agreed. "Kortin has other children. Rook may have bungled his last. Kortin's pissed. He told me Rook left a sign linking the robbery to him."

"What the hells sort of sign could he possibly have left?" Kehfen asked.

"He visited his father prior to the hit. They argued. Apparently Rook took off with a bottle from the personal stock and left it inside the house later."

"Gods in a hell!" Kehfen muttered. "The idiot!" This meant Kortin's identity, with which only a few trusted men were familiar, had been compromised. Kortin had a vineyard just outside the city, a lovely piece of land. His dim-witted son may have taken that haven from him. "Do you think he did it on purpose?"

"Kortin asked me the same thing when I saw him," Hiswil confessed. "This gets worse." A small movement distracted him, and he looked down at Kehfrey, who stood behind his father scratching an itch and listening carefully. Hiswil had almost forgotten the boy. "You understand this, boy? None of what we say here gets blabbed about to anyone."

"I told you I wasn't an idiot."

Hiswil leant back in his chair and deliberated the boy. "He takes after you," he said presently, looking at the child's father. Kehfen rolled his eyes in exasperation, admitting it wordlessly. Hiswil nodded and continued the report. "Since the hit, there have been strange things happening at the villa. Servants have disappeared and returned, remembering nothing about where they've been. There's no sign of injury on any of them."

"They were abducted," Kehfen said with certainty.

"Probably, but since they know little of Kortin's life before his entry into the legitimate world, they weren't of much use to whoever took them. The thing is, they all have nightmares now. They wake up screaming their heads off, but whenever they're asked what they dreamed of, they don't remember. On top of that, Kortin's been getting notes from someone, notes that show up inside the villa without a messenger delivering them, demanding that he return what was stolen."

"And has he?"

"A coach was hired to deliver a package not long after the notes started coming. According to Kortin, the driver didn't rifle the contents. The notes are still coming."

"That means Rook kept something back," Kehfrey just had to put in. Hiswil, rather than shouting at him, nodded in concurrence.

"He's a smart boy," Lerny muttered, but everyone ignored the old man. Their attention stayed on Hiswil, who continued speaking.

"Rook has disappeared. Kortin doesn't think it's the hidden enemy who's responsible. The notes are still coming. Rook may have taken off with whatever he stole."

"And what has this to do with the man following Wilf and the hit tonight?" Kehfen said. "Does this mean the constabulary have become involved?"

"Yes. Whoever Rook pissed off, he's higher up the city ladder than we supposed. This may be an attempt to catch one of us for questioning."

"Who is this person?"

"We don't know yet. Since this happened, Kortin's been having trouble coordinating with the other bosses. We do know this man operates from out of the house Rook hit. There are highborn visitors going in and out of it, but there's never a party going on. They arrive serious and they leave serious."

"Why the hells are we going to tonight's target if we already know all this?" Kehfen said angrily. "The target is a trap!"

"Because Kortin needs to know just how much they know! Your boy has to get us in, and we have to get someone out. This time, *we* take someone."

Kehfen stiffened in outrage. "I'm a thief, not a kidnapper!"

"Well, tonight you're a kidnapper!"

"We shouldn't be going to this house," Kehfrey interjected.

Hiswil glared down at him. "What?" he said warningly.

"We should be going back to the house Rook hit. That's where you find the answers. This other house is a waste of time. You're just taking us to visit a yard where the dogs are all hungry."

"He's got a point," Olomo remarked, looking piercingly at the child a second time.

Hiswil regarded the boy unblinkingly, smoothing his moustache in a manner suggesting he considered the idea. "I do believe the child may be as smart as Lerny thinks," he said, proving at least he had listened to the old man. He looked at Kehfen. "The only problem is, it's the same house."

"What? The same house! My son was invited into the same house? How the hells did this unknown enemy link Wilf to Kortin? What the hells is going on?"

"Since your Wilf reported this house, Kortin is wondering if the enemy is hoping to catch a rival outfit and get some answers from it."

"Only problem is, we're the only outfit," Lerny cackled.

"Wilf is well known among the gentry," Hiswil pointed out. "There are some who know who his mother is, some who know who her husband is, and there are those who know you for a thief and murderer and who wouldn't be averse to divulging that information for a few silvers."

"Bloody hells," Kehfen said. "This enemy thinks I'm a ringleader."

For the first time since they arrived, Hiswil smiled. It was an amused, but dark grin. "You've got to admit it. Wilf has been invited into many houses that have been hit by our portion of the Syndicate. You make a very likely ringleader."

"As if!" Kehfen scoffed. "I'm not the one with the booty to pay for a house and vineyard."

"Quit your whining, Kehfen. You had your chance at more booty and wasted it pissing Kortin off one time too many."

"Eh?" Kehfrey whispered. "You been pissing off the boss, Pop? How come?"

"Quiet, Kehfrey!"

But the little boy's voice had carried in the dim confines. "He been saying no too much," Lerny answered, his ugly leer mocking the child. "No, you can't has my fine-mannered wife to lure marks into alleys. No, you can't has my boy Wilf for thug work. No, you can't has pretty Vik as a lure or for working the picking trade. And no, you can't has sweet-faced little Kehfrey working pick pocket neither. But maybe he'll sell you to the whore ring, seeing as how you can't keep your mouth shut. Maybe it wants filling with something."

"Piss off, Lerny!" Kehfrey said. "Come here; I'll fill your mouth with one of my feet. Or is that your ass I'm looking at? Don't bother turning around to show me. I doubt I'll be able to tell your ass from your face. Likely they both stink equally."

"He's got a real mouth on him!"

"Shut up, Lerny!" Kehfen spat. "You say one wrong word about anyone in my family again, I'll gut you."

"I was just teasing, Kehfen," Lerny protested.

"Shut! Up!"

Lerny shut up and backed a few paces.

"Why didn't he mention Gamis?" Kehfrey wondered.

"Will you just shut up, boy!" Kehfen huffed in exasperation.

"Gamis isn't pretty enough for the other trades and he does fine at quiet work on night jobs," Hiswil answered. He gave Kehfen a derisive grin. "But if what Master Locksmith Maldin says is true, this brat of yours will do us even better at night jobs. If he can keep his mouth shut."

"He can keep his mouth shut," Kehfen said grimly, and Kehfrey proved him right by lowering his eyes in apology and shutting up at last. Kehfen redirected the conversation back to Kortin's predicament. "What about the other Syndicate leaders? What's been happening on their end?"

"There have been some attempts to get the whores to talk. Nothing serious. The begging and pick-pocketing ring has had a few unfortunates roughed up. That's all."

"Right," Kehfen muttered, heaving a deep breath after. "Doesn't the protection racket owe us one? Their people are more into this line of thing."

"We're on our own on this. Kortin has called in all his favours with the extortion and protection gang. They're searching for Rook. We do this hit, Kehfen. You have no choice but to agree. Your family isn't safe so long as this situation remains unresolved. The constabulary aren't cooperating. The Big Boss says his hands are tied. It's up to us."

The Big Boss, he ran the entire Syndicate, and if his hands were tied, then every criminal ring was in trouble. Peering down at Kehfrey's ginger head worriedly, Kehfen nodded in defeat. "Fine. When do we leave?"

"We have a few hours. Get the boy to rest."

Kehfen gave a small weary shake of his head and pulled his son from the dank room. Before they left, Kehfrey looked back to find Olomo gazing at him intently. Kehfrey averted his face and followed his father up the stairs, saying nothing until the door shut with a thud behind them, but after he could not contain his curiosity. "What's with the tall dark man? Where'd he come from?"

"Some southern land across the western mountains. He came to us two years ago, barely talking our language."

"Why'd he come?" On the few occasions his father had brought him for training, he'd never seen the outlandish fellow.

"He says he's on a quest," Kehfen said at the top of the stairwell, turning to look down at his youngest.

Kehfrey was agog over this revelation, his mouth open in wonder. He looked so young and appealing, but Kehfen knew better than to think him innocent. The child was a canny monster at times. A week ago after listening to the idle gossip of his elder brothers, he'd absconded with his mother's second pair of underthings and sold them for three times they were worth to a pervert with a fetish for unwashed intimate apparel. He'd crossed the vast city and been missing into the night.

That had been the first time Kehfen had ever whipped his littlest boy with a belt, but damn, he was proud of his guile, though he couldn't say aught of it for fear his wife would wallop him one as well. She had liked thinking of her Kehfrey as a little angel; only he wasn't the least bit like one under the winning smile. Besides, Kehfen didn't want yet another of his sons working the whoring ring of the syndicate, even as a pimp who sold odoriferous undergarments. There was such a thing as pride, even in a man such as him.

"What's the quest about?" Kehfrey said, ever eager to hear a new and fantastic story.

Kehfen disappointed him. "No idea. Wouldn't tell us. I first saw him in a tavern on the waterfront. He took a liking to me and started following me around. That's how he got into the Syndicate."

"What does he like you for?" Kehfrey said, wishing there was more to know.

Kehfen scowled down at him. "Can't someone like me?"

Kehfrey considered this with mock seriousness. "I suppose," he said after a moment.

His father gave him a playful cuff to the head, only fluffing his messy hair more. "Go lie down with your Mum."

Grinning, Kehfrey trotted off to his dormant mother and settled on the pallet next to her. Wilf, who'd been sitting quietly nearby, watched him. He knew what to expect. With infuriating quickness, Kehfrey dropped to sleep in seconds. Wilf shook his head wryly.

"How does he do that?" He'd never learned the way of it. He just couldn't seem to stop thinking.

Kehfen squatted next to him. Keeping his voice low and placing a hand over his mouth to prevent the lip readers from eavesdropping, he conveyed to Wilf the gist of the conference below. If Wilf had thought to sleep that night, the possibility rapidly vanished. He'd be thinking furiously from that point on.

***

The manor was several miles outside of the city proper. Kehfrey sat behind his father as they rode down the dark path. Warm air drew sweat from their skin despite that the sun had fallen hours ago. Lerny kept swearing over the humidity, inevitably causing Hiswil to shush him with a curse, but the threatening tone never dissuaded the old fellow for long. With the stubbornness of a man who'd long ago lost track of at least a half portion of reality, he spoke up again.

"Bloody gonna rain soon," he muttered. "Gonna get stuck in a thunner storm, we are."

Kehfrey peered up through blackened boughs at the patchy moonlit sky. There were clouds up there, but they weren't thunderheads, not yet. The heat and humidity would scorch the land for another day at least. He decided Lerny only wished for a thunderstorm. The past few days had been insufferably hot and muggy.

He stretched out from behind his father and looked forward. Trees bordered the path, making their journey seem to be one through an unending tunnel with a broken ceiling. Since they'd turned off from the main road, they had kept the horses at a walk. They followed Olomo, who led his mount by the reins. Olomo didn't seem to mind the darkness. He strode along as if he were in the full light of the sun. Kehfrey could barely see the tall man, let alone the ground beneath the hooves of his father's mount, but Olomo never once stumbled or faltered, walking with preternatural skill in the gloom.

Dark night, dark path, dark man. The three seemed a perfect trinity.

The horses eventually clomped to a halt on the further side of the manor grounds, just at the edge of a small glimmering lake, the surface of which was as smooth as glass. In the distance, the peaked roof of the target loomed behind some shadowy trees. The rest of the manor remained hidden from view.

"Off you get, boy," Hiswil ordered.

Kehfrey turned his head and found the stocky man waiting to assist him from the horse. He put his arms out and settled them on Hiswil's broad shoulders. Hiswil pulled him from the saddle. Kehfrey clutched at the man's heavyset body, tightening his grip as if he were frightened. Hiswil hastily settled him on the grass and moved away.

To his son's back, Kehfen dismounted and handed the reins to Lerny. "Try not to talk them deaf," he teased the old man.

"Very funny," Lerny grumbled. "Them likes me, unlike some folks."

Kehfen chuckled and moved off with the boy trotting after him. The gang followed Olomo around the pond, hugging the tree line, their steps placed with discretion on soft grasses that gave no alert to their passage. They continued in this manner just to the rear of the building, where they paused, well hidden beneath branches, and scrutinized the windows.

Kehfrey panned his gaze over of the structure. A long building of two wings and a somewhat taller centre hall, the manor had been constructed of cut blocks. He couldn't discern the colour, but he suspected it was the habitual grey granite transported down from the lowland quarries broaching the borders of mountainous Stohar. Damned, but he'd love to visit Stohar. It was supposed to be full of ogres.

The gang of thieves had navigated the grounds at the back of the manor and come out near the kitchen. A good smell scented the air, a rich bread odour that made Kehfrey hungry. Though the pleasant scent filled the muggy atmosphere, no light issued from where the kitchen should have been, a set of windows and a door near a vegetable garden hedged by multiple stacks of chopped wood.

The servants' floor, the attic from which numerous dark chimneys sprouted, was dim as well. Faint light brushed the glass panes of three rooms on the second level, where the owner of the manor would somewhere have his chamber. A brightly illuminated window glared at the dark from one end, but only the dance of flames in a fireplace lit another window on the closer wing. A suspicious darkness obscured the entirety of the first floor, except for one casement with flickering light playing on the panes. Directly below the other with a fire in the hearth, this one also had a lit fire.

"Odd time for a fire," one of the men remarked.

"It'll have to be the other side," Hiswil said, and they all looked at the further end of the rectangular structure. No sign of smoke rose from the grouped chimneys at that end, but it also had the brightly lit room on the second floor. For a brief second, a figure showed in the window and receded again, the first signs of life they had distinguished.

Oddly, this reassured the boy, though he knew it made that end of the house more problematic. He'd have to be quieter than a rat on the way down the chimney past that chamber. "What if they'd all been smoking?" he whispered.

"Then we would have needed to use the heat and smoke potion," Hiswil said. "Damned expensive job if we had. Why the hells is a fire lit now? It's too cussed hot."

"I don't like it," Mur said. He was an unremarkable fellow who tended to speak little, but expected to be heard when he did. "It's like they want us to use the cold chimney."

"I think we should back out," Kehfen added. "We're sending my Kehfrey into a trap."

Hiswil considered the option, mulling over Kortin's very likely anger if they fled before making the attempt. "You all want to explain to Kortin why we didn't even try a look inside?" he demanded. The men were silent, but he heard Kehfen's breath hiss out in a near mute noise of frustration. Hiswil understood the man's fear, but Kehfen knew what was at stake and what the punishment would be if they failed this task. The boy had to go in.

"All right," Kehfen breathed angrily. "But we use the potion, gods bust it. If they know we use chimneys, then they want us to come down the unlit ones. If not, they think the light of the fire will keep us away from this part of the house."

Hiswil cursed, but knew Kehfen was right. "Fine. Let's go."

Olomo led them through the ornamental garden to the corner of the manor, using everything for cover—rose bushes, statues, clumps of flowering plants. They reached the end of the house, where they stared at the target window for a few moments longer before scuttling in closer, just to the side of the outer chimney.

Shoved to the wall, Kehfrey noticed signs that vines had recently garnished the granite. Dark marks remained where creepers had once grasped the stone face. The evicted ivy had pulled away mementos of home and left chipped areas in some places. It seemed the master of the house had decided to rid his walls of a convenient ladder after Rook's little visit.

Hiswil was the best tosser. He stepped away from the wall, shrugged a rope off his shoulder and settled it to the ground. The end had a grappling hook attached to it. Hiswil slung a short length of the rope out from his fingers, whirled the hook in the air three times and tossed it up with a tiny snort of effort. Kehfrey watched it fly out of sight. It didn't come back down.

"Nice toss," he whispered.

He thought he saw Hiswil grin in the darkness while tugging on the line. When the man moved back, Kehfrey's father stepped up to the rope. Hiswil passed something to him, but Kehfrey didn't see what. His father pocketed it too quickly. Kehfen checked that the rope would hold his weight and, with more coiled rope upon his back, scurried up the building. He performed this task in the same manner he might have done something ordinary, effortlessly and without thought, but not a single heavy thud sounded against the wall.

Within a minute, his shadowy figure signalled from the roof. A second rope came down. Hiswil stepped away expectantly. The grappling hook fell with a dull thud nearby. Hiswil gathered it up and commenced to wind the cord.

"Up you go, boy."

Without hesitation, Kehfrey placed his small hands on the second rope and climbed. He hauled himself up without worrying about the height he attained. Heights didn't bother him the least. At the top, his father pulled him onto the roof.

"Creep up behind here," Kehfen whispered, indicating a place where a set of chimneys formed a safe niche for the boy to rest within.

Kehfrey stood on the indicated tiles and peeked down into the larger flue. He assumed the smaller one led down into an upper bedchamber. Looking at it, he was glad to be going down the other. He didn't like this part of the job at all. While training in pipes, he had found the enclosed spaces disturbing, but at least the large chimney was bigger than the smallest pipe he'd practiced within.

"You take the smaller one," his father said.

Kehfrey suffered a small prickle of anxiety. "Why that one?"

"Because the lower floor is a trap. They'll be down there for certain, fire or no. Hiswil can damned well climb for a change."

"Fine by me," he said, reasoning that this just meant the journey down would be shorter, if tighter.

"Just keep your head and you'll be fine," Kehfen said softly. "Listen before you go into the open. If you see no one in the room, open the window." He took another rope off his shoulder and fashioned a halter for Kehfrey's small frame. "Look for the ward sign first, mind!" he added.

"I'm not—"

"An idiot," his father ended. He gave Kehfrey a quick peck on the cheek. "Remember; keep your head. I'm here to haul you up if you need it. Three sharp tugs. Don't panic when you reach the damper."

"I remember. Stop fussing."

The boy waved smoke from his face and endeavoured not to cough while his father wound the other end of the line around the chimney. Once done, Kehfen fished inside his pocket, pulled out a vial and unstoppered it.

"Drink. And don't choke on it no matter what," he instructed.

"Is it bad?" Kehfrey said, taking the vial gingerly.

"It's disgusting. But if you don't swallow it all, the smoke will asphyxiate you and the fire will burn you next. Usually we get the boys to practice downing disgusting brews beforehand, but we hadn't the time with you. Not much call for the potion in the summer months."

Kehfrey grimaced. "What was that word? Ass-fix-ee what?"

"Asphyxiate. Drink, you bothersome brat. Grit your teeth no matter what."

The boy pinched his nose and swallowed in one gulp. Despite his resolve, he almost vomited the noxious fluid back up. His father clamped a hand over his mouth and chin. Another hand shoved down on his head and locked his jaw shut. Thinking his father seemed very accustomed to the potion's effect on younger thieves, Kehfrey gritted his teeth with a will. It wasn't so bad. He'd smelled and tasted worse in the back alleys, worming his way into messes of which he didn't dare tell his mother.

When it looked as if he would keep the concoction down, his father released his mouth and eyed him worriedly. "Well?" he demanded.

"Dee-licious!"

Kehfen grinned. "Right. Absolutely best-tasting potion you'll ever have." He lifted Kehfrey and set him on the lip of the smaller chimney. "Down you go." Kehfrey slipped inside the hole and hung by his fingers alone when his over-anxious father decided last minute advice was necessary.

"Remember! Three tugs if you need help. Use the flare at the window when you're down," Kehfen whispered in a rush.

"I got it! Just let me work, gods bust it! What do you take me for? Some sort of half-baked baby that's about to ooze out of this cruddy hole?"

He thought he saw his father grin, but it might have been a grimace. Of a sudden, he noticed the smoke no longer interfered with his breathing. He could smell it, but it didn't make him cough. Shrugging off his wonder over this mysterious effect, and ignoring the fear shivering in his guts where bread smells had earlier provoked the hollowness of hunger, he braced his feet and shoulders against the sides of the chimney and crept down the dark cavity.

He spent the initial few minutes working his way downward in the pitch-blackness until he met the first obstruction. He was expecting it. He'd descended to the damper. This portion of the chimney had been designed to create the proper draft: a simple mechanical flap with a lever outside to adjust it. Just beneath, firelight flickered. Oddly he felt no heat whatsoever. He was in fact feeling the coolest he'd been in days. As well, the fear in his guts had decided to settle. All in all, he was pretty damned comfortable for a boy on his first job, down in one of the narrower chimneys of a brooding manor scoured of its festive ivy.

Distractedly he wondered who the figure in the other window on the opposite side had been. Possibly it had been this mysterious owner, but the shape had seemed small for a man, almost childlike. Mayhap the fellow had children?

He listened intently before he forced the metal damper. Hearing nothing, he pressed the flap open with a foot. It creaked ominously and he paused to listen again. After a minute of perfect silence, he shoved at the metal further. The flap opened fully, dividing the flue in half. He sent his father two warning tugs. Then, careful not to make any noise, he worked himself around the narrowing.

The chimney immediately widened. He'd arrived at the smoke dome and could no longer use both sides of the structure to press against. His father supported his entire weight now, but that was no matter. He was too little to count for much, just a tad over three stones, hardly a bother for his father's solid musculature. With nary a jerk, Kehfen lowered him down until he had found a small ledge at the lower throat of the dome. Kehfrey perched on this small shelf, propped by one hand on the damper. The rope looped down past his shoulder and he gave his father a second set of warning tugs. His father pulled the slack until the line tautened.

Peering down at the fire, Kehfrey noted glowing coals with only one log freshly placed on the andiron. Flames leapt around the wood, but he felt no heat. He waited and listened for noises in the chamber. A minute of caution followed. He tugged the rope once and his father lowered him down the remaining distance.

Heading straight for the burning log, he shoved hastily against the slanting wall. He thumped down at the back of the hearth and stared out at the darkened room like an imp glaring from a hellhole, the pupils of his eyes having caught the light of the fire and turned him into a soot-covered demon child. A crackle and snap from the fresh log caught his attention. He began to recoil, but froze with his arm above the flames. The fire licked at his clothing and fingers, but his shabby garments did not burn, nor did his skin singe. He blinked at his sleeve. For a second, he'd seen a glow that wasn't fire, a glow that lit upon his arm, green and extraordinary, but he'd blinked and the aura had vanished. The arm was once again an ordinary arm, but for the fact it should be roasting in the heat.

"Hells pop my eyes," he murmured. He dismissed the conundrum and looked out at the room again.

Having been in near darkness up until then, the room seemed bright to him. It was a bedchamber, from the looks of it unused. Dust covers made a mystery of many of the furnishings. For another long minute, he eyed the sheets suspiciously. His father tugged on the rope, signalling for attention. Kehfrey gave him one tug in answer. Everything was fine. He was inside.

He crept into the room, straightened and stared at the open door. The hallway beyond was dark. One hand in his breeches pocket, he approached the doorway. He paused just before it, listening again. He heard nothing and crept further forward to peek out. A single wall-mounted candelabrum lit one end, and this barely cast any light. He spotted no one in the corridor.

He was about to retreat when he paused to stare at the candelabrum again. It didn't hold candles. There were blown-glass glow sticks in the sconces. Damn. The target had to be rich as all the heavens to afford such things. Kehfrey had only seen glow sticks through storefront windows in the past and only in the shady times of the day, when the light of the sun wouldn't destroy the biotic liquid in the interior of the glass tubes. But there were never any in the windows after dark when the shops had closed. The storekeepers always locked them up for the night to deter thieves hoping for an easy pinch.

Kehfrey stared at the wondrous objects for another pent second and then pulled back into the room. He withdrew behind the door, where he dipped into his other pocket and pulled out a small bottle of oil with a glass pipette inside. Stoppering one end with his finger, he lifted the filled pipette and dropped the oil on every hinge he could reach. He wasn't tall enough for the last one and played with the idea of dragging a chair over, but decided against it. The chairs looked heavy beneath the cloths and would certainly scrape on the floor were he to move any. He would just have to shut the door and hope it didn't squeak. He tucked the bottle away and shoved the wood with prudent slowness.

He was lucky. The hinges were already well oiled, and the door closed softly. He discovered no key in the lock, so dug into his pocket again, this time for a wooden wedge that he lodged under the door. This measure wasn't meant to keep anyone out for a protracted length of time, only long enough for him to get back up the chimney.

He at last went to the window. It was built of multiple panes, so well crafted that the firelight reflected perfect compound images of everything in the room, including him. He'd never seen such flawless glass before, only poorly blown, opaque and warped panes that made everything beyond cloudy. And he'd thought the owners of these wonders wealthy. The man who owned this place was richer by far. Perfect glass panes and glow sticks. Rich man. Very rich man. Must eat pie every day, for breakfast, lunch and supper. And for snacks too.

Kehfrey stepped onto the ledge to look the casement over and quickly found the signs of warding placed by a priest. The marks decorated the wood near the latches, one on each side of the mullion that divided the window in twain. He stared suspiciously at the glyphs. They didn't look right to him. They seemed different than the holy marks he'd been shown whilst in training.

After a moment, he shrugged, thinking the symbols must change depending on who made them. He rubbed the chalk off with his finger and afterward worked at the latches. Both were stiff, but he managed to move one. He opened that side of the window and stepped down off the casement. He took a flare from his pocket, swiped the magic end across the ledge and watched it glow a faint green. Did it have inside it the same stuff as the glow sticks? He wasn't certain. The colour wasn't quite the same and also not as bright, and it came in a tube of dried intestine. Use once and toss; that's what his father had said.

He waved the flare before the window and thought he heard in response a muffled curse from below. He grinned. Hiswil didn't like climbing.

His task accomplished, he tugged once on the rope, waited a few seconds and tugged once again. An answering set of jerks vibrated down the line not long after and then the rope went limp. Kehfrey returned to the chimney, tossed the fading flare on the hearth, and commenced to wind the rope into a coil. Interestingly, the hemp didn't burn as he pulled it though the fire, and he figured it must share his magical protection so long as it touched his body.

His father arrived first, using the rope already attached to the roof. Kehfen peered in cautiously and crept over the sill. He undid Kehfrey's halter and set the coiled rope to the side of the window.

"Why didn't the rope burn? Or my clothes?" Kehfrey whispered.

"It's how the magic works."

"Tells me shit, that does."

"How should I cruddy know?"

"There was a glow."

"Shut your gob, Kehfrey," his father hissed. "Now's not the time."

Lips sealed in a thin line, Kehfrey looked away. There'd been a glow. Likely it had been on the rope as well, but it was too late to check. His father mightn't know, but it seemed to Kehfrey the magic had spilled from his pores and set a glow on everything he'd contacted.

Mur poked his head above the sill not long after and glowered at them both. "Why the damned upper floor?" he demanded.

"The lower floor is suspiciously dark," Kehfen said, to which Mur nodded in concession. Kehfen helped him into the room. Olomo, then Hiswil followed his ascent, leaving one man below to see after the prisoner they planned to lower down. Hiswil didn't bother asking about the upper floor. He seemed to have already guessed why Kehfen had sent his son into it.

"I want Kehfrey out of the house now," Kehfen said.

Kehfrey scowled, little liking the idea of deserting his father, but he saw Hiswil's answering nod and resigned himself to the short exile. In any case, hiding in the bushes beat getting skewered by a crossbow bolt, didn't it?

The father jerked his head peremptorily, and the boy climbed out the window. Kehfrey crept down the wall, pausing once to the side of a window on the lower floor. He listened with his ear pressed to the stone but heard nothing. As his father had stated, it was suspiciously dark inside the room. Cautious not to reveal his silhouette to anyone who might be inside, he continued downward. He settled on the grass, immediately putting his hand into his pocket for reassurance. The stone was still there, cool and comforting. He turned, looking for the fourth adult of their team. He blinked at the darkness. A massive surge of alarm filled his guts. He saw no sign of the rear man.

He didn't wait an instant. He snatched the rope and climbed. He arrived at the upper window within seconds. "Hi, there!" he hissed.

The three men whirled toward him. Olomo stood at the fore, in front of the opened doorway. Kehfen rushed back to his son.

"What are you about?" he whispered. "Get back down!"

"Man below is gone!"

Kehfen hauled him in. Looking down after, he discovered the fourth member of their team had indeed vanished. He pulled back in and looked at Hiswil in shock. "Ofmen is missing!"

Hiswil waved him forward. "We find a room on the opposite side and get out now!"

With a quick glance to either end of the hall, Olomo rushed out and ducked into a room on the other side. Hiswil dashed after him. Kehfen looked carefully at both ends of the passage and then pushed Kehfrey toward the opposite room and hurried after his son. Mur, cursing beneath his breath, delayed not at all and crossed on his heels. He'd had the foresight to fetch up Kehfrey's discarded wooden wedge. He shut the door and shoved the wedge beneath.

"We're bloody buggered," he said. He dug into his pocket and worked the lock with a pick, for once trying to do the opposite of his standard practice. He was locking it. He succeeded and crept backward toward them.

Olomo had already opened the window. Hiswil set his grappling hook against the sill and tossed the rope down.

"It's on the front side, but we have no choice," he whispered. With his chunky body pasted to the wall, he risked a cautious look out. The expansive driveway lay below, curving toward the entrance from the main gate, which was far to the fore of the mansion and nearly hidden by trees and shrubbery. The yard, fortunately, was not lit. Even so, Hiswil snarled a nasty expletive as he set himself over the sill and started down.

"You go next," Olomo said to Kehfen. "I will watch the boy."

Kehfen looked at him nervously and then nodded. He didn't want Kehfrey going down to another surprise. He peeked out. Hiswil had almost reached the ground. Kehfen heaved himself over the edge and began the descent.

Mur shifted apprehensively behind Olomo, glancing at the door with baleful eyes. He thought he had heard something. He stepped back, inadvertently shoving the dark man.

The door burst inward. A strange flash of power sundered the panels and nearly blinded them. Wood fell from frame and hinges, and black-garbed men rushed into the room, a reek of sulphur arriving with them. A snapping noise sounded. Mur cried out. Seeming to have appeared there magically, a quarrel transfixed his throat. He gurgled and slumped to his knees, choking to death. Olomo threw a dagger at the attacker. It struck in the chest, and the victim slumped to the side. A second dagger toppled an enemy revealed behind.

"Out, Kehfrey!" Olomo ordered.

The little boy had apparently frozen in shock. Olomo threw a third dagger and put out an arm to shove the child toward the window, but Kehfrey thudded against the windowsill and slid down it. Only then did Olomo perceive the deathly stillness of the boy. A trail of blood traced the downward path of his body. A red blemish spread upon his chest. The eyes stared sightlessly.

Hesitating no longer, Olomo dove out the window, grabbing the rope as he passed. He slammed against the outer wall. The impact forced a grunt from him, but he made no sound of pain sliding down, though he burned raw his hands from the rapid descent.

"Where's Kehfrey?" Kehfen said when Olomo slid within earshot.

"Dead!" Olomo barked, thumping down beside him.

The boy's father stared at him, white-faced, and then grabbed the rope, clearly intending to climb back up it. Olomo whacked him on the head with the haft of a dagger, heaved the limp body up and raced off into the shadows. He found Hiswil at the large pond and shoved Kehfen's unconscious body at him.

"Take him home. His boy is dead. Mur is dead."

"He's your friend!" Hiswil said. "You take him!"

"I go back," Olomo said resolutely.

"What? What the hells for?"

"The men who attacked are my kind."

"What?" Lerny said. "Dark-skinned men?"

"No. Assassins. Whoever the enemy is, he has bought men of my trade for this task. I must go to them."

"And again, what the hells for?" Hiswil demanded.

"They are what my quest is about. I will find Ishpaäf now. The small, flame-haired thief has led the way as foretold."

"Ishpif? Ishpof? What's that?" Lerny said. "Here now, Hiswil! Let the great giant man go! I'm out of here! Poor Kehfen. His poor little boy. Help me get the man on a horse." He went to the insentient thief and with Hiswil's help placed Kehfen athwart a mount.

Hiswil cursed upon looking back. Olomo had disappeared. "Bloody buggering hells. We're in for shit."

"He won't talk," Lerny said. He clucked at the horse to set it in motion. "He's never talked before."

Hiswil emitted a noncommittal grunt. He tied the reins of the remaining horses pommel to pommel and took up the lead. It was still too dark to ride. Distressed over the deaths of Mur and the boy, he glared fearfully at the darkened patches beneath the trees.

Were they in there? Were the assassins nearby, looking for them? He'd been given no time to ask, but he didn't want to stick around and wait for an answer. Clicking at the lead horse, he led the string away.

***

Inside the chamber, someone entered with a glow stick and went about uncovering the ones waiting in sconces, pulling off dark felt to let the radiance of the biotic jelly illuminate the room. The space brightened, revealing the dead thief and the little boy. The child sat lifelessly beneath a corner of the sill, one hand in a pocket. His eyes were shut as if he slept, but the dark stain on his chest and the one on the wall told another story. The projectile that had killed him rested half buried in the wood higher up the windowsill.

"Quarrel went right through him," the light bearer said. "Boy was too small."

A second man entered and grunted in agreement. He bent over the child. "We're not going to please him. He wanted more than one of them alive. Even this child might have had his uses."

"Children know nothing. The man we took may be enough," said the first speaker, who had been the merciless shooter responsible for the child's death. He thought he had been compassionate. What the master did to men, the assassin would not see done to a child, even one who was a burglar's get. The killing the master did was honourless and vile.

"Did you see the daggers in our brothers?" he said, distracting from the child's seemingly pointless assassination.

The other straightened and nodded. "They had one of our kind with them. The marks on the hafts are strange."

"Not so strange," a heavily accented voice spoke from the window.

Both men turned with crossbows ready. The dark man who had thwarted them minutes earlier stared inward from just below the sill.

"I seek Ishpaäf," he said, his eyes burning with eagerness. The two assassins straightened and lowered their weapons.

"You killed three of our brothers," the first defender said angrily.

"Had I a choice?" Olomo demanded.

The man glowered, but shook his head. "Get in," he said.

Olomo climbed through the window and looked at him expectantly. "I am Olomo, First Line of Pek Tom. You see the mark of my faction on my daggers. You will take me to your group master," he said.

"You're Ysepian."

"Yes."

"I am group master," the first defender replied. "I am Simre, First Line of Pek Tol."

"I would see the vessel," Olomo said. "Do you have it?"

Simre made a curt motion of his head that could have been affirmative or negative. "You will wait. This business must be seen to. You will answer questions."

"I will not," responded the Ysepian. "I do not spy."

"You will be paid."

"I am paid for assassinations! Do not insult me again!"

As Olomo had expected, this refusal only prompted the men of the Tol faction to nod approvingly. Any other answer would have been the death of him. He peered at his counterparts from Pek Tol intently. They were both white-skinned, just as the rest of the people of this particular northern land tended to be, but their speech was that of the land of Amek, a land of deserts and plains and of a darker-skinned breed of men. There was a tale to be told here, and Olomo wanted to hear it, but it wasn't to be now.

"You must leave the house," Simre said. "The one who hired us will not understand. We will meet with you later. Go to the south of the manor. There is a gardener's hut there."

Olomo nodded and began to move, but Simre's cohort stalled him. "What led you to us?" he demanded.

Olomo turned his head and answered. "The small flame-haired thief." He indicated the child. "Our holy leader prophesied him. He was to lead the way to Ishpaäf."

"And now he is dead. You will not reach Ishpaäf. Your prophet has misled you," said the second assassin. Olomo swivelled to face him, dark skin reddening over cheeks and forehead, but Simre rebuked the underling before violence ensued.

"Go out!"

The subordinate bowed with an unrepentant expression and left the room. He met more of his brethren in the hall and bent his head to whisper to them.

"Do you not have the Vessel?" Olomo said, turning his gaze from the dismissed assassin. "Why did you not tell me at once?"

"I will explain later," Simre offered tensely.

"No! I must return to the other flame-haired thief. He must have been the correct one all along."

"Even with this other thief, Ishpaäf is unattainable," Simre said. "I have seen the Vessel. It is near, but it is protected from us."

"Then take me to it."

"That is not possible. I have said that I will explain later. You must go now."

Olomo was prepared to continue arguing, but at that moment Kehfrey inhaled sharply, startling everyone. Olomo looked down in surprise and realized the boy had moved since he'd abandoned him for dead. His eyes were shut, where before they had been open and unseeing, and his hand had come out of his pocket. The fingers were empty.

"The boy lives!" Olomo pulled the bloody tunic up from the small chest. Shoving his fingers in the tear made by the bolt, he ripped the worn fabric asunder and used a ragged end to swipe away blood. He touched the small body and found no wound, just a white mark where the quarrel must have punctured the flesh. "The boy lives!" he repeated in wonder, watching the little chest rise and fall steadily. "The prophecy is true. This *is* the flame-haired thief who will lead me to Ishpaäf."

Simre stepped up, his expression urgent. "Quickly! Get the boy out of here and to the gardener's house. If the one who hired us finds him, we will lose our opportunity." Olomo nodded agreement, and together they belted the boy to his back with a sash. "Go to the back window," Simre instructed.

Waved on by the other assassins, Olomo dashed across the hall and over to the room he'd entered earlier. There he used the rope Kehfen had left behind and then raced under the trees, heading for the southern

48

grounds of the manor. He located the gardener's house and approached it cautiously. Outside the door, he hesitated. Bound by their code to do so, the members of the other faction must lead him to the Vessel, but he wasn't certain of them yet.

After a moment's thought, he left the door and headed toward a drooping bush. Crouched beneath, he detached the boy from his back and settled down next to the child. He set one hand on a dagger and the other on the child's chest to feel the swelling and emptying of Kehfrey's lungs. The child remained unconscious, and Olomo thought it best not to awaken him. Whatever miraculous healing he had undergone, he had lost a copious volume of blood. The boy had to rest and regain his strength.

The dawn hinted its arrival with a rose blush to the east.

"I am the mantis," Olomo whispered. He stilled himself and thought nothing. He was the mantis, waiting to strike.

Beneath his hand, the boy was a leaf, alert and waiting to blow off with the first available wind.

***

"He's not going to be happy," Simre's second uttered.

The last of his words echoed back to them from the end of the cellar. Simre stared flatly at the man without answering. The second didn't seem to care that he was not acknowledged. He gazed at the single living captive and did not look up as the silence lengthened.

They were in the wine cellar, a low and dim hall of dark shadows that had a fetid stench lurking beneath the scent of soured wine. Most of the barrels standing on the packed earth were old and empty. The master produced no wine and only purchased it already bottled. A few smaller kegs of new beer were scattered closer to the stairs.

The captured thief lay on the cold floor in the centremost aisle, naked, gagged, and tied with his arms and legs spread. The lines of rope drifted off into the shadows, fixed to barely visible barrels heavy with stale water. The dead thief had been laid out to the side of the living one. The assassins had dropped the body carelessly, and its staring eyes pointed in the direction of the frightened cohort. The prisoner kept his head turned away. Occasionally he groaned futile pleas for mercy despite his gagged mouth, but the assassins ignored his whimpers. He had soiled himself and the reek of his waste added to the foulness that already lurked in the dark.

A green ball of energy hovered at the base of a chain hanging from a hook. Its glow filtered down through the shadow and turned the pale skin of captive and capturers a ghastly cadaverous colour. Beyond the aberrant illumination, in the dark that it failed to brighten, shuffling noises sounded, occasionally a grunt, once a recognisable word.

"*Hungry!*"

Simre kept his back to the creators of the noise. He was afraid of them, but beneath the light lay safety. He would not show fear before his companion. His second, a true fanatic of Pek, perhaps truer than him, never showed fear. This was possibly the reason he had never become first. A man with no fear was not always wise.

The master at last arrived. Simre sensed his impending entrance before his physical manifestation. The shadows deepened in the cellar, turning from natural to ominous. The master always led with this horrific darkness. Even in broad daylight, the shadows grew thicker wherever he went.

The door above opened, and he descended the stairs, his steps even, unhurried. He walked the aisle toward them and stopped at their sides. Simre didn't look at him.

"One dead thief. One living." The soft words punctured the quiet. The portentous shadows swallowed any echo they might have made. "How many escaped?"

"At least three," Simre reported. He turned to watch the man, repressing a deep and righteous anger.

"Did they manage to take anything?" the master said.

"No. They were alerted to our presence early. They had no time to steal. They fled."

"What alerted them?"

"One of them noticed this one missing." He pointed at the living thief. "They fled out the other side of the building."

"How is that possible? You told me the entire bottom floor was prepared."

"They gained entrance on the second floor through a lit fireplace," Simre answered flatly.

The master, who had been staring at the living thief all this time, looked at Simre. "Not as well prepared as you thought, were you, assassin?" he derided.

Simre said nothing in response. The master turned away, to once more stare down at the captive. The thief whimpered, now shivering uncontrollably on the floor. In the weird light, the eyes that looked down on him seemed colder and deader than poor Mur's.

"Remove his gag," the master ordered.

Simre bent and pulled the gag from out of the thief's mouth. The prisoner coughed. He tongue worked, but no sound came out. When at last he spoke, his voice was raspy and almost unintelligible. Even so, they recognized the plea.

"Mercy!"

The master smiled, but compassion did not brighten the gesture. He stepped to the side of the dead thief, crouched and placed a hand on the still chest. "What's your name?" he asked the living captive.

"Ofmen."

"Ofmen," the master repeated.

He smiled again, looked down at the corpse and spoke. The words were distinguishable, common Winfellan, but the manner in which they were spoken resembled that of prayer. He crouched over dead Mur like a priest healing the wounded, but as they watched, darkness swelled around the hand pressed upon the thief's unbreathing chest. It oozed like a slug over his torso and abruptly sank inward.

At the top of the stairs leading down to the cellar, several assassins stood outside the closed door, tense with expectancy. A few minutes had passed since the master had descended. Presently they heard what they had anticipated. A scream filtered through the thick wood. Then another. And another.

***

It was noon and Olomo yet sat next to Kehfrey, his hand on the boy's chest, feeling the steady movement of his breathing. Though the sun had crested the trees of the manor grounds long ago, the child had not awakened. The fiery orb once again scorched the air with intense summer rays, but a hot, humid breeze gusted swollen clouds overhead. Today it would rain.

A small noise sundered the quiet behind and to the side, but Olomo remained immobile beneath the canopy of foliage. A cat chasing a mouse darted past the bush. It caught the rodent and crouched. The feline glared about suspiciously. Then, with mouse in teeth, it dashed away.

Into the small clearing, Simre walked. "Come out," he said. He looked toward the cottage only briefly. His gaze darted from bush to bush.

"I arrive," Olomo warned. He edged out from beneath the drooping branches and into the open, but remained close beside the shrub. He glowered at his counterpart from Pek Tol. "You were long in coming."

"There was a matter to see to," Simre said, moving up to him. "It went on longer than I had expected. The child?"

"Is well. He sleeps. You have much to tell me, Simre, First Line of Pek Tol. Why do northern white men speak the language of Amek? Why are they assassins? Where is the Vessel?"

"We were purchased as children by the Pek Tol faction," Simre answered. "Our House resides in a province of Amek. This is why we speak the language. Our holy leader foresaw that the Vessel would come to the land of Winfel. This is why the faction purchased white-skinned children. We were sent to find the Vessel and bring it back to Pek Tol."

"And you found it?"

Simre nodded. "The Vessel is in the hands of the sorcerer who owns this place, but he has placed wards of power over it. We have made a bargain with him: our services for the Vessel."

"You bartered like merchants over Ishpaäf!" Olomo's lips curled down with derision.

Simre scowled. "There was no choice. You will see for yourself shortly."

"Will I?"

"You will be introduced as who you are, Olomo, First Line of Pek Tom, seeking Ishpaäf just as we are," Simre informed him.

"And the boy?"

"Introduce him as your servant if you like, but do not draw attention to him. The sorcerer enjoys the company of boys, albeit older ones usually."

Olomo glowered and spat, uttering an insulting word after. Simre did not respond to his revulsion. The Amek had relaxed views on sexuality. Ysepians were more unforgiving. Olomo remembered this and decided to drop the topic. He bent to look beneath the bush and blinked in surprise.

The boy had disappeared. Olomo hissed in alarm.

"What is it?" Simre said.

"The child is gone," he whispered. Motionless but for his eyes, he peered under the bush. Presently he spotted the child hiding further off beneath a smaller shrub. The sun had filtered through the leaves and betrayed him. The white skin of his chest hinted between the foliage. "He is in the further bush, the small one with white flowers."

"The azalea?"

"Yes," Olomo confirmed.

"He was very quiet. Like a master."

"Yes. It only makes sense. He is meant to lead us to Ishpaäf."

"I won't lead you anywhere!" Kehfrey shouted from beneath his spoiled sanctuary. "I'm going back to my Pop!"

Olomo gaped at him in surprise. They had been conversing in Amek, yet the child had spoken in his native language as if he'd understood.

Kehfrey darted out from his cover. Simre, who had been ready for the move, arrested his flight, racing around the bush and snatching the child into the air.

"Let go!" Kehfrey shrieked. He kicked backward, but the assassin merely held him at arm length, large hands beneath small armpits. Kehfrey settled for spitting. He turned his head as far as he could and aimed well. Simre blinked beneath the spittle and glowered.

"The child is spirited," he said wryly. "Who taught him Amek?"

"I don't know," Olomo answered, rounding the bush. "His family speaks only Winfellan. Who taught you, child?"

"Let me go!" the child answered in his native language.

"Who taught you Amek?" Olomo insisted.

"I don't know what you're talking about! Let me go!"

Olomo frowned in puzzlement and issued a warning, still using the Amek tongue. "Desist shouting. Your life is at risk."

"It already got risked! Butt for brains here shot me! I want to go home! Go play with your damned friend by yourself!" Kehfrey tried to kick again, but only ended up swinging his legs uselessly. He grabbed Simre's hands and scratched them. Simre loosed a small pained sound, but refused to drop him.

"Stop that!" Olomo barked, this time in Ysepian. "Stop or I will punish you!"

Kehfrey glared at him, but stilled his wild manoeuvring. "I want to go home," he repeated.

"You understand me?" Olomo said, again in his native tongue.

"Yes," the boy said sullenly.

"Do you know what language I speak?"

"The same one as mine! What do I care? You have an awful accent in any case."

Olomo peered at him narrowly and glanced at Simre. The Amek assassin's gaze was riveted to the boy. An awed expression had settled over his features. Presently Olomo spoke to Kehfrey again, this time in Winfellan.

"Do I sound different speaking now?"

"You sound worse," the boy said spitefully. "Let me down!"

"And how do I sound now?" Olomo asked in Amek.

Kehfrey looked at him distraughtly, frowning and with tears leaking from the corners of his eyes. "What are you on about? What's this got to do with letting me go?"

"You aren't going anywhere," Olomo said. "You are remaining with us. If you wish your family to live, you *must* remain with us."

Kehfrey eyed him and then wiped the liquid from his cheeks with a grimy shirtsleeve. When he looked at Olomo again, his distress had receded and been replaced with a determined countenance. "What exactly are you?" he asked.

"We are assassins," Simre answered.

The boy looked back at his captor with a mix of wry humour and curiosity. He hung limply in the man's arms, no longer struggling, but he still had the obstinacy to utter a snide response. "I already know that about you."

Simre gave no apology for the murder. "Will you run if I let you down?" he said.

"No," Kehfrey answered.

"Swear it using your guild signs," Olomo ordered. The boy scowled and his lips pressed tight together.

"Boy," Simre said, "the Ysepian is correct. The only chance your family has to survive is if you cooperate with us. Swear your oath."

"Tell me what this is about first. I won't swear an oath blind."

Simre glowered, but respect tempered his irritation. "He is wilful, but he is oddly wise for his age. This gift for languages ...."

"What are you talking about?" Kehfrey said. "What gift with languages?"

"He will lead us to Ishpaäf," Olomo repeated with fervour.

"You've both cracked your noggins, haven't you?" said Kehfrey.

"Set the child down. I will tell him why I came to Winfel," Olomo continued.

"He will run," Simre said.

"He has short legs, you cussed great idiot! You will outrun him!" Kehfrey interjected. "Let me down! My underarms are getting sore. And so is this hole you made in my chest. All this stretching can't be good for it."

Simre dropped him. The boy landed on his feet and straightened. He peered at the tall men warily, noting that Olomo towered over the other as they both towered over him. He wondered if the man was some sort of giant.

A breeze gusted through the garden. His torn tunic gaped open and revealed the whiteness of his skin where the sun hadn't touched it. The Ysepian squatted and put his hand on the boy's chest. Most of the blood had welled out of the back of the wound, leaving Kehfrey's front relatively clean. Kehfrey eyed Olomo suspiciously and then looked down at the dark hand. The index finger pointed. Following the indication, he noticed the spot where the bolt had punctured his chest.

"What happened to the quarrel?" he wondered.

"It went through you," Olomo said. His hand dropped. "How did you survive?"

"I picked up a spelled stone the day before the hit," came the simple, if unexpected answer. "Traded a knife for it. Well, then? What's this Ishpish thing?"

Olomo smiled unpleasantly with a show of teeth and threat in the eyes. "Ishpaäf! Say it correctly and don't pretend you cannot."

"Ishpaäf," Kehfrey muttered mulishly, his pronunciation perfect. He glared at Olomo expectantly.

"Ishpaäf is a state of being," the Ysepian told him. "It is perfection. Pure serenity. It is a higher state of existence in which the powers of the spirit expand to their fullest extent. Do you understand?"

Kehfrey nodded. "What's it to do with this vessel you were talking about?"

"How long have you been awake?" Olomo said, his anger heightening and making his voice louder.

"About an hour," the boy lied.

"And you never moved. You never opened your eyes."

"Well, your hand was too big for my father's and you smell different. And you were so hellish still! How was I to know if you were friendly? I decided to wait and see."

For hours and hours and hours. And he'd been itchy. His fleabites had second fleabites; he was certain.

The Ysepian glowered. "Such patience in action, yet such an impatient mouth. You will learn to restrain your words."

"Get on with this Ishpaäf thing! What does this vessel have to do with me?"

"*The Vessel* contains the ashes of Amut. It is he who first attained Ishpaäf, who taught it to the rest of his holy order, but few of his followers were able to achieve the perfect state. Amut pitied his fellow men and ordered the Vessel readied. He set himself afire and before he died shouted that the pure who seek Ishpaäf would learn the secret of attaining it by looking upon his ashes."

"He set himself on fire?" Kehfrey cried. "He set himself on fire! How can anyone learn Ishpaäf from an idiot who set himself on fire?"

Olomo smacked him across the mouth. Kehfrey's little face whipped back toward him, a defiant glare fixed over the pallid features. Olomo stood and towered over the boy again. "You will learn to restrain your words!" he directed. "You are destined to lead us to Ishpaäf. How this can be so is a mystery, but you *will* learn respect."

"Your friend already said the Vessel is here. You don't need me to lead you anywhere," Kehfrey said. Not very wise of him, but he wasn't inclined toward cowardice, even if pretending meant keeping a semblance of his face intact.

"The Vessel is warded from us," Simre reminded. "No one can reach it. If Olomo's holy man is correct, you will be the one to regain the Vessel for us."

"And how does that help my family?"

"We will not kill them," Simre said plainly.

"What if this sorcerer tells you to? You said you were working for him."

"I see no need to tell him about your family. Our agreement was to help him in order to obtain the vessel. If hurting your family endangers reaching Ishpaäf, we cannot obey his edicts. Besides, we don't trust him."

The child considered this, his expression flat and enigmatic. Olomo crossed his arms and looked down at him expectantly. Presently the boy spoke. "Fine, I'll help you, but you have to swear not to kill my family," he said.

Neither man took offence over the stipulation. They made the appropriate gestures and so swore.

"Now you," Olomo said. Kehfrey performed the ritual motions and the pact was created. Satisfied, Olomo nodded at Simre. "He will not run now."

Simre inclined his head in acceptance. "Give me your shirt," he directed the child. "I will dunk it in the watering barrel. We can't have you arriving bloodied."

Kehfrey pulled his worn tunic off. Simre walked to the gardener's cottage and dunked the bloodied garment in a large barrel of rainwater standing by the door. He wrung it out and handed it back to the child, who plastered it back on, thankful for the wet because it cooled him somewhat. The new day had already grown swelteringly hot.

As the boy shrugged on the tunic, Olomo noted the remaining bloodstains only added to the general dirt of the old garment. He wasn't pleased to have the boy improperly dressed just before meeting this mysterious sorcerer, but there was no time to find something else to wear. He settled for tying the loose ends together, such that the garment didn't gape so much. Kehfrey suffered his touch, but backed two steps the moment Olomo straightened.

"We will go to the manor now," Simre said and walked away. "Perhaps the boy should stay outside, guarded by one of mine."

But Olomo wouldn't have the blessed child from his side. He wasn't a fool. He had shared no oaths with the members of Pek Tol. Though tradition dictated that the Vessel should visit all factions, nothing bound his rivals to let him walk the journey with them or to walk the journey at all. If Simre's ambition were too great, a rival might lose his opportunity and his life. Olomo felt his best option was to keep the child close to hand.

"The child remains with me, who was prophesied to learn from him," he said with a forbidding tone and followed after his counterpart.

To this thinly veiled warning, Simre shrugged and kept on. Olomo did not turn back to be certain of Kehfrey, but this was hardly necessary. The boy created a small din to the rear. Grumbling beneath his breath, he stomped petulantly after the men.

"Be quiet!" Olomo commanded without turning.

"I am quiet," the child protested.

"Not when you mumble. Not when you stomp your feet. Be quiet now," he said resolutely. "You are sworn to help us. Do as we do."

The stomping and mumbling ceased, and the three continued on without speaking, only now their passage through the gardens sounded like two. After a minute, his certainty finally put in doubt, Olomo turned to see if the boy was still there. Kehfrey looked away from the myriad flowers at which he'd been gazing and halted to glare at his keeper. Rather than being angered by the boy's obvious disrespect, Olomo merely looked pleased. He turned and followed Simre to the manor.

Kehfrey stalked on again, once more looking at the flowers. They had altered from dark spiky clumps over short-cut lawn, as they had been in darkness, to spread-wide wonders of colour and scent. Wouldn't his mum love those, he thought, and planned stealing a few for her. He considered selling a few bouquets in the flower market later when he got the chance, the moment he could get these Ishpishers off his back. If he were very careful, he might manage to snatch an old rag somewhere, perhaps from the kitchen, and turn it into a wetted sack. He'd pick that entire bed bare. He doubted the sorcerer would fuss over one fancy bed of flowers out of what seemed hundreds. Would he?

But what had Rook taken to make him fuss this much?

Chapter Three

Vik stood in the centre of the barren room, his face white and his expression bleak. His father's features mirrored his countenance, only Kehfen's had also gone blotchy from weeping. Vik looked toward his brothers, hoping not to see the horrible truth confirmed there. Gamis refused to look back at him. Crouched against a wall, he was on the verge of crying. His endeavour to refrain was almost as harsh a sight as if he already wept. Wilf didn't try to stop, just shed tears silently as he stared at Vik from where he sat on the floor.

"How could you let this happen?" Vik demanded. "Why did you go ahead with the hit if you knew it was a trap?"

"Kortin's son Rook did a hit on the house without approval," Kehfen explained succinctly and unemotionally. "He stole something the owner wants back badly. Rook took off with whatever it was, and Kortin can't find him. Weird things have been happening at Kortin's villa since. Demands to return the item keep appearing in the house. Servants disappear and return without any memory of where they've been. Kortin ordered the hit to go ahead because he wanted a hostage to question."

"Why didn't the protection racket do the job?"

"Kortin ran out of favours. They're looking for Rook instead."

Vik stared at him numbly. The news of Kehfrey's death still hadn't sunk in completely. He resisted the truth of it even now. "How's Mum?" he asked.

"She's sleeping. The midwife said to let her unless the baby awakens. She said the delivery was normal."

Vik's expression altered from bleak to scathing. "Normal! You call being shocked into labour because of Kehfrey's death normal?"

Kehfen looked at him without responding. He blamed himself for his little boy's death. Vik only expressed what he himself thought.

When Vik understood his father would not reply to the accusation, he questioned him again. "Where was this hit?"

This elicited a reaction, a wary one. "Wilf, shut your mouth," Kehfen warned the elder brother, and then faced his firstborn cagily. "What do you want to know for? I know you loved Kehfrey more than anyone, but do you really think I'm going to let you run off and get yourself killed trying to get revenge?"

Vik took a step toward him. His face remained impassive, but his eyes glimmered with unshed tears and his fingers closed into fists. "I'll use the people I know to find out more about the house that was hit."

"What could you hope to do with your lot that the Syndicate couldn't?"

"*My lot* have avenues of inquiry the Syndicate does not!" Vik spat, his countenance now grim and condemning. For once in his life, he didn't care what his father thought of his choice in company. Kehfen's choice in company had led to the death of his little brother.

"What do you hope to gain from that?" his father asked.

"The truth! The truth about who lives in this house. The truth about what it is this enemy thinks is missing. Your damned Syndicate didn't help you there. It only got Kehfrey killed."

Wilf had come to a stand while listening to the altercation. Now he stepped forward and confronted Vik. "And then what?" he said.

"Then I tell you what I learned and we decide from there," Vik promised.

Kehfen eyed him warily. Presently, he nodded. "All right. But you do nothing without my word!"

Vik agreed with a small motion of assent, his eyes not quite meeting his father's.

"Make the oath!" Kehfen demanded.

The boy hesitated. Kehfen crossed his arms, a mounting repudiation in the gesture. Vik, scowling the entire time, made the oath, after which Kehfen went limp with gloomy resignation.

"All right. It's outside the city. There's a manor on Portway. Old Prince Gormil built it for one of his high-class whores and used it for entertaining his less savoury friends. Some unknown party purchased it recently. Is that enough for you?"

Vik nodded and walked toward the decrepit door that led out of the bleak room in which his father had chosen to house the remaining members of their family. The wood had wormholes in it. So did the dirty planks of the floor, which creaked ominously with his every step. His hand was on the rusted latch when Kehfen delayed him.

"You have a sister," he said softly.

Vik pivoted a quarter turn, looking back with a blank expression. "Red hair?"

"No, flaxen again."

"Oh. That's nice," he answered flatly. He opened the door and departed without another word. On the outside, the door had been painted a bright red, this so customers knew which whore's chamber to visit. His mother had given birth to his first sister in a house of prostitution. At least she'd had one of the better rooms.

In the corner, after Vik had gone, Gamis at last wept.

***

"Who is this?"

Simre stepped a pace forward and made the introduction. "Olomo, First Line of Pek Tom."

The master's lids narrowed a fraction. "Why are you here?" he said.

Olomo answered, his tone stiff, his words precise. "I was sent here by our Holy Leader. He foresaw that the Vessel would be in the city of Wistal in Winfel."

"Indeed." The master was evidently not the least happy with the explanation. His upper lip thinned. His dark eyes fixed on Simre. "Your holy men are irritatingly accurate."

Simre bowed shortly in proud acknowledgement.

They were in a lush hall of dark wood and gold gilt. The master stood on the lowest step of the main stairs, one hand on the burnished rail. Olomo shot a quick glance at the hand. It was relaxed. He examined the master again. No sign of tension betrayed the owner of the limb, who was a man of average height, at least for these northern climes.

Olomo thought him nondescript, without a feature to set him off from anyone. His hair was brown. His eyes were brown, his face regular, neither handsome nor ugly. He was plain and forgettable, even his choice of clothing unremarkable, the colours bland, the cut of the cloth simple. Outwardly the master appeared ordinary, very ordinary, perhaps too much so, given that he was a practitioner of dark arts.

"And this boy?" the sorcerer said. "Why does a warrior from Ysep have a miniscule, dirty boy of pale complexion in his shadow?"

Olomo didn't look down to see what the boy was about. Kehfrey had been warned to remain quiet and respectful. He had better do so. "The boy is my apprentice," Olomo said dismissively. He endeavoured to get the man's attention off the child. "How do you know I am from Ysep?"

"Your accent is dreadfully Ysepian," the sorcerer observed.

Olomo thought he heard the faintest of snorts from the boy. The master, in the meantime, had not finished speaking.

"You roll Ruls too much and place excessive accent on syllables containing a letter Lys."

Olomo decided it best not to respond to the criticism. Unfortunately his attempt to distract hadn't worked.

"Why did you choose this boy for apprenticeship?" the sorcerer said, and his gaze came to rest on the child once again.

"He shows natural skill for our ways."

This statement did not put the sorcerer off, but focused his interest further. The disapproving tension of his lips relaxed and became the faintest of upward curls. "He's a born killer?"

"We are *all* born killers," Olomo parried with quiet fanaticism.

The master smiled outright. Suddenly he didn't look ordinary at all. He was striking, yet all the more sinister and cold. "Has Simre told you of our agreement?" he inquired, the smile fading.

"He has."

"And you? What will you do?"

"I will honour the agreement."

The master considered this. When he spoke again, he watched the Ysepian with a careful, measuring air. "What will you do when I give Simre the Vessel? Will you fight him for it?"

"That is not necessary."

"And why not? How can you attain Ishpaäf if the Vessel is in the hands of another faction of Pek?"

"The Vessel will begin the Divine Journey," Simre said. "All factions will be visited. It is preordained."

"How convenient." The master stepped down onto the floor and approached the Ysepian. "I suppose you want to see it."

"Yes," Olomo said. The master stood before him, more than half a foot shorter and unafraid. Outwardly impassive, Olomo tensed. He felt threatened, yet the sorcerer did nothing but gaze at him. However unpretentious the man appeared on first inspection, an indelible sense of menace emanated from him and could not be discounted as false.

The sorcerer looked at Olomo for several seconds, a little test that Olomo determined to pass. He seemed to win concession. The master's gaze shot away, down at the boy unfortunately, and then up again, a shrewd gleam displaying briefly in the eyes. "Come, then," he said and headed back up the stairs.

Olomo looked askance at Simre, who nodded a reassurance. Olomo stepped after the sinister northerner, followed by Kehfrey and Simre. The master led them up the polished stairs and along a hall lined with expensive side tables and chairs. Nearly at the end, he stopped at a door and peered at it without touching. Olomo regarded him suspiciously.

"Why do you not open the door?"

"It is warded," the sorcerer responded.

"Even from you?" Olomo said, scepticism plain in his voice.

"The best wards guard against everything. They make no distinctions. Now be quiet."

Kehfrey dared a step to the side of the Ysepian for a better view. A glow shone on the wood, a strange black glow. The blackness spread away from the handle as if it were some sort of living jelly, faint but noxious. The master moved closer and pushed the latch down. A blast of heat blew into the hall from out of the revealed room.

"Be careful not to touch the door as you enter," the master warned and passed within the chamber without looking at them.

Olomo approached the entrance and stared distrustfully at the open door. The structure didn't seem unusual to him in any way. Warily he walked through. Nothing untoward occurred. He looked behind at Kehfrey, to discover the boy squinting at the wood with obvious interest. "Get in!" he ordered.

"The glow went back over the handle," Kehfrey whispered to him.

"What?" he hissed. He heard a movement behind. He turned to find a woman staring past him at the boy. She was small and lovely, but visibly distressed. Her eyes had white circles about them and sweat soaked her violet gown. Olomo looked at her face again. Mistrust mounted at the sight of unusually vivid irises.

She waved the boy forward insistently. Olomo missed Kehfrey's response, eyes widening in recognition and surprise. Unaccountably, within the manor of his enemy, Kehfrey had rediscovered the seeress, but she was not impeccably presented as before. The woman's hair was lank with moisture, her forehead beaded with sweat, her pretty dress drenched down the neck and beneath both breasts. She was pale, her breathing uneven, and she stood as if she might fall any second.

"You should not stay there," she said to the child, her voice hoarse, and he realized she'd had no water for hours. "The ward has a tendency to leap out at the unwary."

"Why were you locked in the room?" he cried. "Are you a prisoner?" She'd been the figure in the window last night! It had been her! Here! Suffering this horrid heat!

"She is my slave," the master said from somewhere beyond Olomo. "She is being punished for a misdeed."

Kehfrey stepped into the furnace-like heat, moving to the side of Olomo far enough to see the sinister man. The master stood near the fireplace, peering down at it. Kehfrey glanced around quickly. The chamber was well appointed, clean and obviously in use, no sign of dust covers anywhere. The single armchair was rich, upholstered in lush velvet cloth, and had the company of a table and a large writing desk whose shelves were covered with odd artefacts rather than writing material. A heavy chest with a damaged lock, sitting alongside a small bookshelf partially filled with largish books, rounded out the furnishings. The window of the room had been flung wide to let in the breeze, but this was too faint and too warm to amend the sweltering heat.

"How is it that your apprentice sees the aura of the ward, Olomo, First Line of Pek Tom?" the sorcerer said softly.

Kehfrey's attention snapped back toward him. Upon ending his inspection of the chamber, the boy had been staring at the woman again, who had been staring back with an uneasy expression. At this point, Olomo stepped in front and blocked Kehfrey's view of their disturbing host, who still gazed at the fireplace with a dispassionate expression on his cold face. Kehfrey's skin crawled despite that the Ysepian shielded him. He felt as if the master's attention lay entirely on him. The terrible heat within the room worsened his discomfort. Why was a fire permitted during a heat wave?

Facing the master, Olomo fought to contain his annoyance. He was irritated over the child's unnecessary interest in the woman and also displeased the sorcerer had heard Kehfrey's unwise whisper. "The boy is unusually gifted," he was forced to admit.

The assassin's attempt to shelter the child at last prompted the master to react. He rounded Olomo to face off with Kehfrey. "What is your name, boy?" he asked.

Olomo made a sign with his hand, a movement both hasty and curt. As a result, Kehfrey stared at the master without answering. The black aura he'd seen on the wood of the door shadowed the sorcerer as well, but it wavered over him, darker in some places, sometimes completely vanishing only to return again.

The silence lengthened, and Olomo did not correct Kehfrey's insolence, which sharpened the boy's inclination toward reticence. The woman walked over to stand beside her master. Glancing at her face, Kehfrey discerned a careful neutrality that alarmed him. Her eyes had grown piercingly green in her pale face. He had the distinct impression she would have overtly constrained him from giving a response if she dared.

"What's she your slave for? I heard you like boys," he said, wisdom swamped by indignation on her behalf.

And now the Ysepian saw fit to correct him. Olomo turned and slapped him hard. Kehfrey thudded to the floor. He picked himself up quickly.

"What did you do that for? It was only a question!"

"It was forward! It is not your place to ask," Olomo barked. "You will wait outside the room. I will deal with you later."

"A moment," the master said. "I want the boy to stay."

"His punishment is of no concern to you," Olomo said.

"His punishment doesn't interest me," the man riposted. "You will permit him to stay. *He* interests me."

Olomo scowled. "I do not see what interest you might have in a disobedient apprentice."

"You said yourself that he is gifted. I would know more. Obviously he has more gifts than your kind has a use for."

"He has more mouth than the followers of Pek have a use for," Olomo uttered scathingly.

The sorcerer smiled, the curl derisive. "Then you would not be averse to selling him to me?"

Olomo was momentarily silent, but disapproval was evident in the disgusted look he bent upon the shorter man. "This boy is not for sale," he said presently.

"I don't want him for that." The master's gaze shot toward Simre, who looked down, a red flush creeping up his neck.

"He is still not for sale," Olomo maintained.

The master looked away from the Amek assassin. A hint of resentment clouded his eyes, but it faded, and the sorcerer's expression became enigmatic once more. "You would keep an unsuitable, ill-mannered apprentice?"

"His ill manners can be beaten out of him."

"Not bloody likely!" Kehfrey said. "You smack me again and you can kiss your own ass before I lead you to—mmm!"

The master's gaze fixed on Simre again. The Amek assassin had walked up behind the child and covered his mouth with a hand. "What are you doing, Simre? What was the boy about to give away?"

"They think he will lead them to Ishpaäf," the woman said flatly.

Olomo's disconcerted expression transformed into a snarl of outrage. He directed his anger at the child, thinking the boy had somehow managed to betray them and reveal his destiny to the tiny woman. He had, but not in any manner Olomo suspected. The woman's master smiled.

"My slave is sighted," he informed the assassin. "A very gifted seeress. So? This boy was foretold by one of your holy men, I take it?"

Once again Olomo was forced to admit something he would have preferred to remain unspoken. "He was foretold by my holy leader."

"But he's Winfellan. He must have led you to this house. How?" The sorcerer glared at Simre. "Take your hand off the boy's mouth, Simre."

Simre hesitated and, caught in his grip, Kehfrey watched the shadowy aura darken over the master. Simre seemed to perceive the darkness as well and released him. The menace dissipated, leaving the room inexplicably cooler than before.

"Who are you, boy?" the sorcerer demanded.

"I'm a thief," Kehfrey told him. "You bloody got my Pop in trouble!"

"So. You are one of the ones who took my property."

"My Pop had nothing to do with that hit. Rook did that. He kept whatever he took. You should have asked the Syndicate to help you instead of worrying the bosses."

"Syndicate?"

"Damned right! What sort of idiot tries to take over the city without bringing the local underworld into it?"

While the sorcerer coolly mulled over this impertinent response, Olomo couldn't believe he was listening to it. "You promised to help us!" he blurted.

"I *am* helping you," Kehfrey said. "If we get this fellow on the Syndicate's side, we get this business done with quicker, and I don't have to worry over my family. Then you can have your stupid Ishpishy." During this small speech, the boy hadn't taken his eyes off their sinister host, but at the end of his explanation, he glanced at the woman to discover her skin even paler and her eyes wide with fear.

For him? How odd.

"What would you know of my purpose here?" the sorcerer said. His tone was ice. The response he gained was modulated to melt it.

"That's gods cussed obvious. You're cruddy evil! Look at you. You're black all over, when that shadowy shit doesn't disappear for a moment, I mean. Of course you're here to take over the city."

The sorcerer stared down at the preposterous child in astonishment. "And how does that follow?"

"Because it's the same in every story you hear. The sorcerer is always trying to take over."

The woman burst out laughing, but it was a panicky sound. "The boy is mad," she said.

"Is that what you see?"

She shook her head quickly. "An opinion, Master," she whispered fearfully.

Kehfrey blinked as a drop of sweat fell into his eye. He rubbed at it anxiously and then grabbed an end of his torn tunic with one hand and wiped his forehead. Already the cloth had dried.

The master seemed to notice the child's ripped apparel for the first time. "Why is your tunic torn?"

"Fell out of the house," he lied flatly. "Why do you have a fire going in the summer? It's too damned hot in here."

"Go and see," the man suggested.

Kehfrey eyed him, gauging his safety, but presently decided he was already in up to his head and might as well sink it the rest of the way down. Exhibiting more bravery than he should perhaps have done, he stomped past his disquieting host and over to the fire, where he halted to stare in awe. "Why isn't it burning? That fire's just not natural, is it? It's going in circles! Like little marching men!"

"What do you see in there?" Olomo demanded.

"A nice little box. And the marching fire men."

"The Vessel!" The Ysepian darted past the master and toward the hearth. With an eagerness that bordered panic, he crouched down and looked within. The Vessel was indeed there. It floated in midair, a plain but well-crafted box with only one gilded symbol on the lid. A fire burned around the artefact though fed by nothing, and it scorched the box not at all. As the child had described, the flames danced about the wood, a parade of tiny waving dervishes that marched relentlessly. Disregarding the aberrant combustion, Olomo lifted a hand toward his goal.

"Don't touch it!" the woman cried. "The flames will leap out at you. Nothing natural will put out the fire."

The assassin withdrew his hand. He looked at the poker that stood in a stand of utensils. If he were quick, he could shove the precious relic out.

"I wouldn't bother, if I were you," the sorcerer said. "The fire is spelled to follow the Vessel."

"He does not lie," Simre confirmed. "Before, he had the Vessel in a room below where we could all look upon it. I made an attempt. My clothing caught fire." He pulled up his shirt and revealed a huge patch of injured skin. "He took pity on me."

"But I may not again," the sorcerer uttered and the hint of resentment had returned to his dark eyes.

"How did the Vessel come to you?" Olomo demanded, rising to glare at the sorcerer from a more impressive height. "How did you get our most holiest of relics?"

"I acquired it when I acquired my slave." The master stepped toward them, his gaze fixed on the boy, who rose and looked at him

64

dispassionately, but such a wealth of raw spirit and cunning intelligence lay behind those hazel eyes, the child could not hide his worth. The sorcerer intended to obtain him and pondered his best course to go about winning this little game while he made the child's skin prickle with misgiving.

The woman had remained motionless. Olomo's ire focused on her. "Her? She is but a young woman. The Vessel was stolen over five hundred years ago."

"She is a half elf. She's older than all of us combined."

"You!" Olomo cried. "You are the elf! You are the accursed thief!"

She refused to respond, but Kehfrey's pretence of calm punctured. He gaped at her. She was an elf? She didn't have red hair.

At the same moment, the sorcerer's narrow regard fixed on the child's ginger hair, which was so bright not even the grime of Wistal could hide the fire of its hue. Lice crawled in that twisted mess, and the child stank like a cesspit. Most city spawn did, but hopefully the urchin would clean up nicely.

"Tell me why you took it?" Olomo demanded of the seeress.

"Because I could!" she snapped. "Because none of you could have reached Ishpaäf. I knew Amut. He was my mentor. He never taught you what you've become."

"And you bring the Vessel to a sorcerer instead!"

"That wasn't my intention. I was betrayed." She scowled and averted her face, then stalked away to the other side of the room, refusing to speak further.

Olomo turned on Simre. "Why didn't you kill her? She is the elf of legend."

"Because I told him not to," the sorcerer said. "And you will not as well." Olomo looked at the master, whose attention yet rested on the child. "I want this boy," the master added.

"He is not for sale," Olomo reiterated.

"I will give you the Vessel now."

Olomo stared at him, stunned.

"We take the bargain!" Simre cried.

Kehfrey whitened. This was a very bad turn of events. Staring at his enemy, he felt as if the sorcerer's dark eyes ate his disquiet, consumed it like the most scrumptious of meals. The sensation made his flesh prickle, and a desire to cringe away, as if avoiding the cut of a knife, manifested as an almost unbearable rigidity in his spine. The master's heavy attention lacerated to the bone. It was a presentiment he could have done without, but it stayed with him for decades, long after he and the sorcerer parted company. Just now however, he felt sick and light-headed and also peculiarly clammy and cold.

"No!" said Olomo, and the boy's dizziness momentarily brightened with hope.

"Olomo!" Simre snapped. "Think! The boy *has* led us to Ishpaäf. We will have the Vessel through him. His part is done."

Olomo gaped at his counterpart, his flesh almost grey beneath his dark exterior. "Yes," he whispered. "It is so."

"Then it is a bargain?" the sorcerer said.

"Yes," he agreed.

Kehfrey looked at the assassin numbly, but then his young features turned down in a fierce scowl as outrage eclipsed the sickness of his body. "Bloody buggering shit from a black bat!" he cried and kicked his betrayer hard in the shin. Olomo yelped and hopped away. Kehfrey judiciously ducked behind the sorcerer. If the man intended to be his master, he might as well make use of him. "Go take your stupid box, ugly diseased bull's butt end!"

The sorcerer laughed. It wasn't a pleasant sound. He lifted an arm toward the hearth and spoke terrible words. Kehfrey cried out and slapped his hands over his ears, but the words echoed on in his head. They pounded! They pounded horribly! The vertigo returned and he slumped to the carpet, insentient.

Within the hearth, the unnatural fire died and the sanctified box dropped onto the old ashes lying on the bricks. Olomo stared at the container in awe, but the more alert Simre rushed past him, grabbed the box and straightened, his eyes wild with triumph.

"We have the Vessel!" he whispered. He turned to Olomo. "Come!" he cried and rushed out the door without a backward glance at those remaining within.

Slowly, as if he were drugged, Olomo stepped toward the entrance. The master watched him depart, saying not a word. Simre's voice echoed back into the room, shouting commands in Amek. Answering cries of joy reverberated faintly from below. Olomo disappeared around the bend of the entrance, and the sorcerer at last looked down at his prize. The woman already knelt at the child's side.

"Why did he pass out?" he demanded.

"Loss of blood, I think. And the heat."

He crouched and brushed the boy's sundered tunic aside. "This is what you wasted a spelled stone on?" He placed a finger on the white mark over Kehfrey's heart. She did not answer. "You think I cannot perceive my own work?"

Again she did not respond. He struck her and she fell backwards to the floor. She did not rise after. Her face remained averted, her posture subdued.

"You lied to me. You could have avoided this sweltering room, slave. You could have told me about this child instead of saying you'd lost the stone. What did you see for this boy?"

"His death. A quarrel straight through the heart."

"And you gave him the stone meant for Minister Lolte. Why did you not say?"

"I didn't see any of this other stuff," she protested. "I didn't see the dark assassin. I didn't see the boy's relation to them."

"But you saw that he was one of the thieves to come to my house!" he roared. "You said nothing of that!" Standing, he withdrew a chain out from beneath his tunic and placed his fingers on a specific flat medallion hanging thereon. "I command you to tell me what you've seen for this boy."

"I see a brightness around him! A brightness that swells and swells beyond comprehension! I don't understand it! I can't—! He's important! He's so important that I am but a speck crawling on his surface, unable to see the extent of his skin!"

"What do you mean?" he shouted. "This says nothing to me! What do you mean by it?"

"I don't know! He's—! Oh! It hurts! It hurts!"

"What else? Tell me his immediate future, you sorry bitch!"

"I see the dark assassin returning!" she cried, the words bursting from her without volition. "I see him begging to have the boy back!"

"Why?"

"Because they will not achieve Ishpaäf!"

"And the boy will?"

"Yes!"

"When will Olomo come back?"

"In two years! When the Vessel has travelled to every faction! They will send Olomo back for the child!"

"And what will happen if we tell him this now?"

She cringed on the floor and sobbed as if in pain. "It fades! It fades!"

"Answer me!"

"He will stay," she cried. "Not Simre. He will not believe. Olomo will kill him and stay with the boy. He will teach him the ways."

"He will make an assassin of him?"

"Yes."

"Get up," the sorcerer commanded. "Go to Olomo and tell him now."

She pulled at the nearby armchair until she stood on unsteady legs, then stumbled out of the door into the hall. A few seconds after she had vanished from view, he heard a thud. He listened, but no further noises ensued. He stalked toward the entrance and looked out. The woman had collapsed. He uttered a mild curse as he walked over to her. Carefully he raised the power, the milder and more generous sort, and sent healing into her. She awakened with a cry of alarm. The sorcerer lifted his hand from her chest and straightened.

"Hurry up!" he snarled, turned his back on her and strode away. With a satisfied smile, he listened to her run down the stairs.

Back in the room, he walked to the armchair and sat. He studied the unconscious boy and played with the idea of awakening him. He decided he would not. The child was wilful and disrespectful. The woman would have to be handy in the future to remove the boy if necessary, whenever the child angered him. This extraordinary city urchin would be useful, but not if physical punishment broke his will.

The sorcerer smiled witheringly. "But you will be broken, yet not so that you would notice," he said to the insensate body. "What I can't decide is whether you'd make a better assassin or apprentice. You will have to show me, won't you?"

A shout lifted into the air from outside. He went to the window. Down in the driveway, the woman ran toward Olomo, who lagged behind the Amek assassins. Simre called to the Ysepian to ignore her, but Olomo halted and turned. A hand rose to finger the haft of one of his knives.

The sorcerer's eyes narrowed. His began a spell, but his lips ceased moving almost at once. Motionless, the assassin listened to the woman's pleading. A minute passed and he took heed without question. His eyes seemed to grow larger in his dark face. Eventually he glanced up at the sorcerer's window. Their eyes met. The assassin turned and marched away. The woman stared after him, forlorn on the limestone gravel. Slowly she pivoted, looked at her master and nodded achievement of his command. Satisfied, the sorcerer moved away. Half turned, he halted

The boy had escaped. In a rush, he strode from the room, only to pull up in surprise. The child crouched to the side of the door with his hands over his ears. He looked up as his master entered the hall.

"Oh!" the child cried. "Are you done, then?"

"Done what?"

"Are you done speaking those horrible words?"

The sorcerer peered down at him narrowly. "Exactly how do the words bother you?"

"They ring inside my head. They just go on and on."

The sorcerer frowned pensively. "I will have to think about you. You are a strange child." And apparently destined to be some sort of incomprehensible brightness. That woman was a useless nit.

"What about my family, then?" the boy asked. "Can I go back and tell them you will wait for them to get Rook?"

"Not until I learn more about this Syndicate of yours."

"But you must have learned everything from the man you took last night. Or did the assassins kill him?"

"I killed him. After he talked," he said coldly.

"Oh," the child uttered. Aside from a slight nervous shift in his posture, the boy showed no sign of fear.

"Are you wondering if I will kill you?" the sorcerer said.

"It crossed my mind."

"Yet you risked being outspoken. Why?"

The child heaved a great sigh. "Because even if I helped the assassins, my family would be in danger from you later, wouldn't they?"

"You think rather far ahead for a child."

"My Pop says I'm unnatural as children go."

"Does he? Does he also say why?"

The child shrugged in mystification. "No. Hasn't a clue."

"Nor have I. As I have said, I will have to think on you. Tell me your name."

The boy hesitated, but then answered, his voice almost a whisper. "Kehfrey," he said nervously. The sorcerer smiled. The dark aura surrounding him deepened. The boy frowned at the manifestation.

"Why do you look at me like that?" the sorcerer said, his smile dropping away.

"I see stuff around you, black stuff. I must be sick."

"You've lost blood, but you're not sick," the master said. "What you see is real, but only those with the gift can see it."

"Oh," the boy murmured. "So why did that black stuff around you get darker?"

His new master hesitated over the answer. "A name grants power to the receiver," the man said, deciding to give the truth. He wondered what the boy would do with it.

"Oh," said the child, taking his enslavement rather calmly. "Why is that?"

"Can you read?"

"No. Well, except for our guild signs."

"Would you like to learn?"

"Is that how I'm supposed to get the answer to my question?" Kehfrey asked, somewhat irritated, but also intrigued with the idea of literacy. He'd always wondered what it would be like to be able to read.

The sorcerer smiled and walked away without answering. He was an interesting child. Very interesting.

"What about my family, then?" the boy called.

"Go to the kitchen and eat," the sorcerer directed without turning. "I have a visitor to prepare for. I will discuss this later."

"Aren't you worried I'll just run off?"

"No," came the answer, drifting back softly. "You have given me your name. Now you are mine to call."

Kehfrey gaped after him apprehensively. The sorcerer let himself into another chamber and shut the door behind. Presently the child lifted himself and walked toward the stairs. He met the woman just as her foot settled on the top step.

"Hi, now," he greeted. "I still have the stone. Is the magic all used up?"

"Yes," she said. Her hair was still lank around her head and she looked weary to the point of falling apart. The deep circles around her eyes seemed deeper and beneath her nose a smear of blood had been wiped halfway across her cheek.

"Why did he punish you?" he asked.

"It's of no consequence. What are you doing?"

"Going to the kitchen to eat." A perplexed frown darkened his expression. "What happened after I hit the floor?"

"Olomo left with Simre. He'll be back."

"He will? Why?"

"Because I told him he can't achieve Ishpaäf without you," she said. The boy opened his mouth to ask yet another question. "Enough about it!" she snapped.

He stepped back from her, and she continued in a gentler tone, disliking the guilty expression on his face. She suspected the child well understood he was the cause of her master's recent abuse.

"I will take you to the kitchen, if you like," she offered. He nodded circumspectly and followed her down the stairs.

"Why did you want to save me?" he asked at the bottom.

"Because I saw you die."

"That's no reason. You must see lots of people die. Why bother with me?" She didn't answer, but continued onward. He pouted at her back. "Does he have your name?"

She froze and then whirled toward him. "Did he ask you yours again?"

"Yes."

"And did you tell him?"

"Yes. Just my given name."

"Was he holding his chains?"

"No."

She frowned in a surprised manner, then knelt in front of him. "Don't tell him again. Not all of it. He will be prepared next time."

"He said I was his to call," the child told her.

"You are, but not completely. He wasn't ready to trap you fully. And he only had your given name. The surrender wasn't absolute."

The child nodded in understanding. "But does he have yours? Is that why you're a slave?"

"Yes," she admitted. "But he only had it once and through trickery. He had help from someone who betrayed me."

"If you're a slave, does that mean he can force you to do anything?"

"Yes," she said, and then amended the answer. "Almost."

"Even give your name again?"

"No. That he cannot do."

"Why is that?"

She smiled suddenly. "You're a pest. I should have let you die."

He smiled back, all devilish and impenitent. The red hair standing on end gave credence to the illusion. "But I'm just too irresistible, right?"

"Right," she agreed. "Perfectly irresistible." She lifted herself and continued away. Kehfrey scampered after her. She heard an intake of breath preparatory to another round of questions and cut him off. "No more questions. You eat. You take a bath."

"A bath! What for?"

"You smell, O irresistible one," she intoned.

"I do not!"

"Yes, you do. You're just used to it."

"How old are you?" he said, changing the subject.

70

"No more questions," she insisted.

"Why don't you have red hair? Don't elves have red hair? Is it because you're a half elf?"

"Oh! What a child!"

"Why did that Amut fellow burn himself? Couldn't he find an easier way for everyone to reach Ishpishy?"

She sighed and shoved a door open.

"Will you tell me your name?" he continued relentlessly. "I can't do anything with it."

"You could give it to him," she snapped, turning on him.

"I swear never to do so," he said, gazing at her earnestly. "I swear on my soul."

She frowned down at him. "Be careful what you swear on."

"But this is important. I want you to trust me."

She laughed in surprise. "Why?"

"Because I like you."

She smiled. He presented his affection as if declaring a rare gift. "You are a very odd child."

"Is that why you saved me? Do you like odd people?"

"And you are annoyingly persistent." She marched into a side hall. "The kitchen is this way."

"My name is Kehfrey. See? I trust you."

She shook her head in disgust. "You be quiet!"

"Why were you in the shoemaker's stall yesterday?"

"Oh, gods! I was buying shoes!"

"So you saw me by chance."

She stopped and turned on him again. "Did you see me in the stall?" She had thought the portly shoemaker had hidden her with his bulk.

"No," the boy admitted.

"Then how did you know I was there?"

"You stink," he said and laughed at her shocked expression.

"I do not!" she protested.

"Yes, you do. I smelled you in the stall. It was the same smell at the fountain later."

She scowled at him. "What smell?"

"Flowers. I think."

"That's not stink! That's perfume!"

"Not if it knocks you out, it isn't."

"Oh!" she hissed. She whirled and stomped to the kitchen, murmuring imprecations with every step. Oddly the boy discontinued to pester her with questions.

Kehfrey didn't want to ask more questions. He was listening raptly to her curses. They were very, very imaginative. And naughty. He was delighted and therefore disinclined to interrupt.

***

"Why do you want to know about *that* house?" Someren said. "Nobody wants to know about *that* house."

"*You* know about that house."

"I do not!"

"Yes, you do," Vik insisted, "or you wouldn't be adamant that nobody wants to know about that house. What is there about *that* house nobody wants to know about?"

Exasperated, Someren rolled eyes beneath heavily painted lids, but moved closer to Vik after and simpered like a girl. Vik was not impressed. He preferred men to act like men. If he'd wanted a girl, he would have gone out and acquired one. He pretended he was impressed all the same and wrapped an arm around Someren's cinched waist. He thrust his groin up against the puffed skirt girding the other's legs. Someren smiled in anticipation.

"Tell me what you know," Vik whispered in Someren's ear.

"I'll tell you after," Someren whispered back.

Vik bit a lobe lightly, tasting the powder that lightened skin. He set a hand on the whitened cheek and shoved a thumb between lips painted rosy red. The greasy residue smelled of raspberries, but he knew it tasted of wax and oil. Disgusting, but not so bad as the powder. Someren whimpered against him.

"Tell me now, or there will be no after, or next, or again," Vik threatened. His mark pulled away, withdrawing so abruptly Vik's thumb smeared red paint across the cheek. The effect made Someren clownish instead of feminized.

"You are cruel!" Someren shouted. "Don't think I don't know what you're doing! You're just going to use me and leave!" Catching sight of the damage to his cosmetics, he gasped in outrage and flounced to his dressing table. He sat, fluttering his rose skirts like the daintiest of females, though he loomed toward six feet—a gaunt, well-cinched six feet.

His visitor was not so easily dissuaded from his purpose. Vik rounded in front and straddled his body. Someren turned his head and sulked. "You are cruel," he repeated.

"I know," Vik said unapologetically. "Now tell me what you know." He pulled the man's head back by the hair, twisting his fingers in the locks, destroying hours of careful work on the intricate coiffure. With the other hand, he smeared the lip paint across Someren's face, his movements insulting, challenging and ever so erotically right for his victim.

Someren gasped, his features washing with a strange mix of pleasure and pain. "You promise not to leave right after?" he whispered.

"I promise."

Someren smiled, a ghastly mess of paint and lust. "I want you to hurt me," he said.

"I know." Vik's blue eyes stared a cold pledge. "Now talk."

***

"What's his name?"

"Whose name?"

"The sorcerer's?"

"Marun," she told him.

"Is it his real one?"

"I don't think so."

"What's yours?"

She sighed tiredly. "When will you cease to question?"

"When I run out of questions." He heard her moving beyond the screen. "Where are you going?"

"Nowhere! I'm just lying down!"

"Oh." He splashed the water in the copper tub, hitting a bubble and creating two smaller ones. Bubbles. They were simply wonderful. He'd never seen such pretty things before. Well, except for the woman, whose name he still didn't know. "So make up a name," he called to her. "I can't call you nothing."

She was silent a moment, and then her voice drifted over to him, sounding tired and distant. "Call me Nicky, then. Now wash! And shut up!"

Satisfied, he pulled the cloth out from beneath the water, found the soap and scrubbed his neck. She'd told him he had a ring around it blacker than a slave's collar. She'd also said he was sprouting plants in his well-fertilized ears and guessed that he could likely grow mushrooms in his nether regions. There were also enough lice on his head to dissatisfy an entire army, and fleas in plenty to feast upon and kill a better-bred boy in one night. This last hadn't impressed Kehfrey much, but he had washed his nether regions and his hair. He hadn't found any mushrooms, but there were a lot of drowned lice in the water.

A small noise from beyond the flowery screen alerted him to a shifting motion on the bed. A few minutes later, he heard snoring. He grinned, thinking she wasn't going to like it when he told her about that. Should get a few good curses out of her.

Eventually, his skin wrinkled like a pink prune, he ventured out of the clouded water. He pulled a towel around himself and peeked around the screen. His saviour of yesterday still snored, lying across the bed without any covers. She had taken her violet overdress off, the crinoline too, and wore only a white slip. Though she had shoved the window wide to let in the breeze, the wind was still hot and humid, hardly refreshing at all, and she looked even now as if she suffered from the elevated temperature. He wished he could do something to help her, shut off the sun for a few hours or something, but he was only a naked boy in a sorcerer's lush guest bedroom with a tub of submerged fleas and lice behind him. He fit in this place about as well as a cow in clogs.

He walked around the screen and searched for his clothing, but they were nowhere to be found. Had she meant it when she'd called them hell spawn and said they should be burned before they spread disease? He looked in the hearth. It was filled with wood, but not lit. He didn't see his clothes in there. He scowled worriedly. What was he to do now? He had no clothes!

Lightning flashed in the distance. A warning toll of thunder followed the burst. At the window, he gazed at dark clouds creeping northward across the sky, a sheet of slanting grey travelling beneath them. The downpour seemed bent on remaining remote, which was a pity since he'd like to be cooler. But there was hope yet. The flowers in the bed he planned to pillage had partially closed, and above, the leaves of the trees had turned up in preparation for the downfall. Funny how he'd managed to become a part of the property, a tuber in the flowerbed.

He looked over at Nicky. She was a flower. Of a certainty, she was. Her bosoms were nice under that gauzy slip, shapely and not too big. He'd managed to see bigger ones on occasion. The larger types tended toward sagging, but they had an interesting if funny way of flopping about.

Well, as much as he liked looking at this luscious bloom that was actually an ancient woman with perfect tits for her size, he had clothing to find. Pulling the towel tighter, he walked to the door, opened it and peeked out warily. He thought he heard someone on the stairs, but the sound receded. Standing there uncertainly, he considered filching some clothing off of one of the kitchen boys. They must have quarters upstairs in the attic.

He poked his head further out and looked toward the end of the hall. Yes, there was a door at the end. He pondered the deed, but decided against it. He didn't want to be caught thieving naked. That was just too embarrassing.

Across the hall and a short way down, a door suddenly opened. Catching sight of the child, the master of the house paused with his hand on the latch. Kehfrey stared back, frozen, wishing most frantically that he'd found clothing before encountering the sorcerer a second time. In his short life, he couldn't remember being naked. Ever. Well, he knew he'd been born thus, but that didn't count.

The master shut the door and walked toward the child. He looked past the boy and discovered the woman sleeping on the guest bed. She was snoring heavily, a fact he seemed to find amusing. A small derisive upturn of his mouth occurred, and the child thought it must be his idea of a smile.

"What are you both doing in there?" the master said.

"She made me wash," the towelled boy explained, whispering for her benefit. "She said I was growing plants in my ears." The sorcerer perused him, gaze glancing off hair, shoulders, chest, feet and making Kehfrey feel jittery, but he didn't give in to the urge to shuffle about, merely stood with apparent calm and waited for his master to speak again.

"Why are you standing in the corridor undressed?" Marun asked.

"She did something with my clothes. I can't find them. She said they stunk."

"They did stink," the sorcerer observed flatly. "Go back in the room."

"What about my clothes, then?"

"She'll see to it later. Go!" he said irritably.

Eyeing the cloud of dark thickening around him, Kehfrey decided to obey, but he listened at the door to the sorcerer's receding steps. When the sound of his movement had sufficiently softened, the child opened the door a crack and peeked out. He caught sight of Marun's back just as he walked out of view down the stairs. In the clear, Kehfrey reconsidered ransacking the rooms for clothes. He heard a noise behind him, looked and found the woman turning in her sleep. Now that was a nicely shaped rump, wasn't it? She was small, but built for admiring. But this didn't get him clothing.

Sighing heavily, he shut the door and walked over to the bed. She had thrown herself down near the pillows. The entire foot of the bed was free. He crept up and lay down on the soft mattress. With another dissatisfied sigh, he shut his eyes and tried to sleep.

Ah, hells! The flower snored like a pig.

***

A pace behind the nobleman Someren had introduced him to, Vik walked into the hall of the enemy and peered about. At first glance the hall seemed innocuous, just another rich man's entryway with a rich man's gilded décor. The foyer was immense, carved doors lining either side, more hinting beyond the lower expanse of the broad staircase that led up to the second floor. At the top, the balustrade spread to either side like wings, revealing more shut doors until the walls of the upper hall commenced and blocked the view. Fine furnishings of intricately crafted wood and sumptuous upholstery lived up there and also down in the foyer, the chairs and tables of new fashion and showing very little wear.

Polished wood gleamed like glass where shadows did not protect the veneer, and whorls of pith were vivid in the sunlight that blasted through the higher windows to the fore of the house. The gilding on the moulding showed the only sign of wear, but this was not a bad effect. Vik saw nothing untoward, nothing he could pin as ominous or incriminating. Everything was rich, beautiful and mundane. And yet here his youngest brother had died.

Despite the terrible heat, Vik wore his best clothes, a suit of deepest blue trimmed with black. The outfit was subtler than his other suits, but he looked his best in it. He'd been hoping to make an impression on Lord Rhet and he had. He'd fascinated the nobleman enough that Rhet had consented to keep him near during this small visit to the countryside. The lord seemed to regret his decision now. He shifted nervously, fidgeting with a brass button on his sleeve.

In comparison to Rhet, Vik seemed dull. The nobleman sported an outfit of garish orange and red. His eyelids were painted to fit, a burnt orange shade. Rhet directed this colourful gaze toward the stairs, hinting far less joviality than he had displayed during the coach ride. A servant had disappeared up the flight not long ago. This man came down now, and Rhet put his hands behind his back to hide his nerves.

"The Master will be down shortly," the servant informed them. "If you would wait in the library, milord?" He bowed and indicated a door to the right.

Lord Rhet turned to his latest find and smiled winsomely at him. "You had better go out to the coach, my pet. This won't take long."

He looked Vik up and down with frank appreciation. Vik disregarded the vulgar appraisal. He considered pleading with Rhet to let him stand in the hall and wait, but decided against it. He'd only just met the nobleman and didn't want him suspicious. There was also that promise he'd given his father, but which he'd broken by entering the manor. Best to just leave. Smiling politely, he bowed to the exact degree due a lord from a cultured commoner.

As he rose, he heard a noise at the top of the stairs. A man descended. He was a nondescript fellow wearing clothes of good cut but of exceedingly boring colour. His regard, however, wasn't the least bland. Dark eyes shot blatant ill will. To hide his discomfort, Vik bowed and walked out the door a servant held open for him.

"Lord Rhet," Marun greeted as the door shut. "Who was that?"

"No one of consequence," Rhet hastened to say. "I didn't want to let him get away, you understand? I just found him. He's a beauty, isn't he?"

"Yes, a beauty. Come in to the library." The sorcerer preceded the nobleman out of the hall.

Rhet did not comment on the insult. He followed like a dutiful servant, shutting the door upon entering the library. The master of the manor walked to the window and looked out at the driveway. The beautiful youth paced back and forth before the coach, glaring angrily toward the manor entrance. Marun's eyes narrowed.

"What happened with Minister Lolte?" he asked. He heard Rhet behind, the noise of his feet shifting uncertainly on a squeaky board.

"Oh! Lord Hosten visited him. Uncle's in a bad way, though. Barely made it through the interview."

"I have another stone ready for him. You will take this one personally."

"Yes, of course," Rhet agreed equably, although his host's words had not been a request.

"And the interview went how?"

On the gravel, Rhet's find had spotted the sorcerer looking out at him. The youth stared back and then presented his back and stalked away. He rounded the coach, stepped off into the garden and out of view. Marun turned and looked at Rhet without interest. The nobleman had been speaking, but he hadn't paid attention.

"So it all went pretty much as we expected," Rhet ended. He fluttered at his sweating face with a handkerchief.

"Good," Marun answered. He withdrew a small stone from his pocket and handed it to Rhet. "For Lolte."

"I will take it to him personally," the lord assured, clutching the stone tightly.

"Of course you will," he said calmly, ignoring Rhet's obvious anxiety. "Tell me where you found the beauty."

Rhet hesitated. "The beauty?" he asked faintly.

"Your find? The boy?" Sevet reminded, staring the nobleman down.

"Oh, him! Someren introduced us just an hour ago." Rhet tittered. "Pretty thing, isn't he?"

Marun had been to Someren's establishment just last night, but the pimp hadn't mentioned acquiring a new boy of the quality currently walking the manor gardens. Why had the pimp gone to Rhet with the boy and not him? "Someren? Isn't it a little early for you to be visiting his establishment?"

Rhet simpered and waved the question off as if it had been a jest rather than a criticism. "Oh, yes, but he came to me today."

"Someren came to see you? Why?"

"Oh, he came to ask a favour. Nothing serious. The constabulary are roughing up his boys a bit, threatening to shut him down. But they're always doing that. Nothing to worry over."

"And Someren went to you of course."

"Well, naturally. I am Lolte's nephew. Minister of Justice and all!" Rhet laughed nervously. Marun smiled. Rhet smiled back, but it was a weak gesture marred by a nervous tic.

"And your beauty came with him?" the sorcerer said. "Was he the bribe?"

"No, actually," the nobleman denied and coughed into his hand. His throat was dry, but he didn't dare ask for a drink. His host didn't offer him one. "The boy is an acquaintance of his."

The sorcerer's brow furrowed. "An acquaintance? Not a new acquisition?"

"No, he's on his own," Rhet assured him. "Although Someren looked as if he'd like him to be one of his boys."

"He works independently?"

"I believe so. He has other connections. I don't know who exactly. As I've said, I only met him an hour ago. I believe he mentioned posing for Astabe. I think I know which one."

"The angel forcing the devils back through the gates of hell," Marun said.

"Yes! That's it! Have you seen his work in progress?"

"Yes," he admitted. "But I don't recall seeing the boy there at the time."

"Oh, Someren says Vik comes and goes at will. He's very independent."

"Vik," Marun whispered. He turned away from the anxious, sweating lord and walked back to the window. The boy had returned from the garden and currently talked to the coachman with his head canted to view the driver. The posture revealed a firm line of chin and a smooth column of neck. Granted his pale colouration might account for a lack of facial hair, but his height suggested he approached sixteen. Perhaps he shaved already. Only touching him would determine such.

"When you leave, Rhet," Marun spoke coldly, "you will leave without the boy."

Rhet gasped from the rear. "But—!"

"It is time to leave, Lord Rhet," he said without turning.

Rhet left. Marun smiled evilly.

***

Vik turned expectantly when he heard the door of the manor open. Lord Rhet rushed out, skittering down the flight of steps as fast as his skinny legs could carry him without seeming to run, the sight of which alarmed Vik. "Lord Rhet?" he cried. "Whatever is the matter?"

"Nothing! Nothing!" Rhet barked. His abrupt manner did not reassure, nor did his ensuing actions. He hauled the door of the coach open and launched inward. Not only did Vik gape, but also Rhet's footman, to see the pampered lord lunge into his vehicle without the customary assistance.

Pulling his nerves together, Vik placed a foot onto the step and commenced to climb in, but the nobleman leaned forward and shoved him away. Vik gawped in blank amazement as the man hauled the door shut with a bang.

"Sorry!" Rhet said. He thumped the roof of the coach. "Get moving!"

"But—!" Vik protested. "But you brought me here! There's a storm coming!"

"Sorry! I can't take you back! He wants you!"

The coachman cast the boy a sympathetic glance and snapped his whip in the air over the backs of his team. The horses snorted and thrust forward. The footman grabbed the rear of the vehicle, and Vik gaped after it in horror. He stood there and felt his stomach fall into a chasm as his ride disappeared around the bend of the drive.

"Gods bust it!" he cried, mimicking little Kehfrey's favourite curse. He clenched his teeth so tightly his jaw ached. His oath to his father was truly forsworn. He hadn't the excuse of Rhet dragging him along for the ride, not when the scrawny nit of a man had virtually dumped him in the enemy's lap. He had only meant to scout the place out and cozen the rest of the secrets from that skinny-legged, over-perfumed roach afterward.

A gust whipped his hair into his eyes and he pulled the strands away angrily. "Gods bust it," he repeated, whispering this time.

His situation was worse than that of breaking an oath. His family had no idea where he'd gone. Not a good thing. He considered marching back to the city on foot, a walk of an hour at least. He'd get caught in the storm for certain, but it would be safer all around, except for the possibility of getting pneumonia. Yet he might be able to avoid that nasty consequence if he cadged a lift on the way. He took a determined step forward.

"Where are you going?" someone demanded from behind.

He whirled. The enemy stood on the lowest step of the manor. There was no malevolence in that dark regard now, just cool watchfulness.

"I was about to start walking home," Vik said.

"Didn't Rhet tell you that you were invited to stay?" the other replied calmly.

"He mentioned something of the sort."

"And you refuse my hospitality?"

Vik considered him, musing upon his best response to this. "I normally don't take invitations from men of whom I haven't any prior knowledge," he said presently, opting for polite caution.

"Wise of you, I'm sure," the man said. He stepped down onto the gravel and toward him. "Anything could happen to a boy alone with a stranger. Just about anything."

Vik backed a pace. Why had he thought the man nondescript before? There was nothing nondescript about him. He was cold and menacing. Terribly menacing. Vik considered running. It sounded like a very good idea to him. He retreated another pace.

"Are you going to run?" the man said, approaching closer.

Anger heated Vik's otherwise frightened thoughts. "Are you suggesting that would be wise as well?"

The man halted and smiled. The gesture did nothing to soften the menace exuding from him, but it also altered him from plain to arresting. "Why run?" he said. "Isn't this what you do for a living?"

"*I* choose to whom I render my services," Vik said frigidly. "I choose! And I don't choose some menacing stranger who frightens highborn lords out of his door. Who the hells *are* you?"

"Your next lover, of course," the other said with certainty. He moved forward again.

Staring in amazement, Vik forgot about running. Hands rose, clasped his head and drew him closer. The enemy's lips were warm on his flesh, but with their touch, the chill in Vik's centre seemed to become a solid mass of foreboding. He snatched at the unwelcome hands, but his suitor clutched at his wrists and held him fast, the lips now twisting into a mocking sneer.

"Is that the type you are? The kind who like to protest? Who like rough treatment?"

"No! I don't enjoy pain!" Vik performed a quick manoeuvre Wilf had taught him and freed his arms. He backed off several feet, rubbing his wrenched wrists while the man regarded him darkly. "Is that the type *you* are? Someone who likes to give pain?" Vik demanded in turn. "You should visit Someren's establishment. I gave him a fine black eye earlier."

"Did you?" came an interested reply.

"We are perhaps mismatched," he suggested.

"I think not," the other denied. "I don't like overly perfumed men who pretend to be women."

The youth's expression acquired a confused cast. Marun remained where he was, watching closely. The boy's cheeks had flushed from the confrontation and the heat. The high wind whipped his straw hair about, blinding him regularly, occasionally veiling a fine straight nose beneath pale blue eyes. The brows above arched with more elegance than could be found on most peers of the realm, and to the south, the cleft in the chin was at once delicate and manly. His bottom lip was a perfect expanse of subtle pink, the top a set of thin, but sweet curves that gave a hint of arrogance to the expression. Pleasantly, there were no signs of cosmetics on the boy's skin to mar this perfection. He was faultless, the perfect angel. Astabe could be lauded for his choice.

"What is your name?" Marun asked.

Vik eyed him uneasily, thinking again he should just run.

"What are you worried about?" the enemy posed. "I am a poor host for not making introductions, and therefore hardly worthy as your suitor. Tell me your name, at least, before you show me your fine backside running from my view."

"Your sarcasm is hardly soothing my apprehension," Vik replied witheringly.

"Then I'll curb my poor temper. I apologise. Most abjectly. Please tell me your name."

Looking at him uncertainly, Vik opened his mouth to answer, but an unexpected interruption ensued and also a discovery most unnerving and unanticipated.

"Shut your mouth!" a familiar voice shouted from the direction of the manor.

Vik looked up in surprise. His eyes bugged. "Kehfrey?"

Was he dreaming? Was that his dead brother's ghost standing in the doorway wearing a towel?

A towel?

"Kehfrey?" he cried again.

"Don't give him your name, fool! He's a sorcerer! He uses names to make slaves of people!" the false ghost hollered.

"Kehfrey!" Vik shouted a third time and rushed past the stunned sorcerer. He darted up the steps toward his brother. "You're alive!"

"Of course I'm alive. The bloody stone worked."

Vik ignored this strange answer and hauled Kehfrey up, towel and all. "We're getting out of here!" He turned with his brother in his arms, only to find the sorcerer standing below and looking at them coldly.

"So. Someren's little visit to Rhet was no coincidence," he said icily.

"No, it wasn't." Vik set Kehfrey down and slapped his right forearm. A dagger appeared in his hand.

Marun eyed the weapon without a sign of worry. "That's what I felt attached to your wrist earlier. Interesting contraption."

"And effective," Vik said frostily. "Back off."

"Of what interest is this boy to you?" the enemy demanded without moving.

"He's my brother," he said tightly.

"Your brother?" Marun looked at Kehfrey, weighing what he saw all over again. "It would appear that your family worries over you as much as you them," he remarked presently and stepped upward, all trace of displeasure vanished from his features. Even so, Vik crouched, ready to gut him. "That won't hurt me," Marun said and walked by the two without looking at them. "Come back inside, Kehfrey."

As Vik straightened in confusion, Kehfrey stomped back in the house, slapping his bare feet grumpily on the marble floor. "What do you mean it won't hurt you?" he said.

"Kehfrey!" Vik cried. He rushed into the manor and snatched the boy's arm, at once commencing to haul him away.

"Leave off, Vik!"

"No! You're coming home!"

"He is home!" the sorcerer barked, turning in the middle of the hall.

Vik paused to gape at him. "What the hells are you on about?"

"The boy is mine now," he said flatly.

"What? He's what?" Vik stepped forward, the dagger rising. He ignored the strange icy cold that flooded the hall. "You fucking baby fondler!"

Kehfrey tried to correct his brother. "Vik, don't! He's not into that."

Vik shoved him backward once again. "Kehfrey, get out of this house!"

"He's not into that! He said so! It's true!"

Marun's gaze darted down to the boy and conveyed a brief flash of puzzlement. Contempt quickly replaced it when his regard reverted to Kehfrey's brother. "I don't bugger children. I have other uses for the boy."

"Such as what?" Vik challenged.

"He might make a fine apprentice," the sorcerer informed the youth.

The statement stunned both brothers. While they were mentally preoccupied with this pronouncement, Marun took the opportunity to inspect each bewildered face. Kehfrey's bath had cleaned him up nicely as he'd hoped. Perhaps better than he'd hoped. The urchin was actually a beautiful child, bearing a definite resemblance to the elder brother. He could see it now that he'd been alerted, but the younger didn't have the cleft in the chin, and his nose was delicately hooked rather than straight. But the lips, the lips were the same combination of sweetness and arrogance.

"Are all the members of your family this beautiful?" curiosity prompted Marun to ask.

Kehfrey snorted and stomped back to Vik's side. "Except for Gamis," he said ungenerously. "He's an ugly butthead."

"Kehfrey!" Vik pulled the boy behind him, his eyes never leaving the enemy, to whom he said, "We're going home. I don't care what use you think you have for him."

"Leave off, Vik," Kehfrey said impatiently. "I made a deal with him to keep the rest of you safe."

Vik straightened and gaped as the child thrust forward again. "What? What deal?"

"I believe he wishes to negotiate an alliance with the Syndicate for me," Marun said with a wry voice.

"Shit! You told him about the Syndicate?" Vik cried, aghast over his brother's imprudence.

"No. He didn't," Marun denied. "The thief my assassins caught last night told me. Would you like to see what's left of him?"

The siblings eyed him warily. "*Would* we like to see it?" Kehfrey asked in turn.

Marun smiled coldly. "Probably not. But a look might be useful. The Syndicate might find your reports educational during the negotiations."

Kehfrey lifted the towel higher around his chest. "Fine. Lead on," he said, accepting the challenge.

Marun smiled again, a sort of amused and sardonic uplift of one corner of his mouth. He turned away.

"No!" Vik rejected.

"Oh, come on!" Kehfrey called. He flounced off after the sorcerer, pulling his long towel up heroically when it slipped again. Lips pressed thinly in trepidation and disapproval, Vik shoved his dagger into its hidden sheath and stalked after his intrepid but very foolish brother, thinking he was as foolish for following. But with the Syndicate's existence tossed out into the open, he felt he had no choice but to stay and brazen out the dangerous game into which Kehfrey had fallen.

The sorcerer led them toward the kitchen. As he opened the door, a silence descended on the space, a domain of metal pots and implements that hung practically everywhere against a backdrop of wood washed to dullness. The master ignored the cook and his helpers. Following in on Kehfrey's footsteps, Vik noticed there wasn't a woman amongst the staff, who were of various ages to be certain, but none female. Marun walked out of the kitchen through another door on the further side. The next corridor boasted a series of windows that afforded a view of the kitchen garden. Within this bright passage, Marun approached yet another door. This one was fashioned from heavy oak and had a bar athwart it.

"You have a prison in the manor?" Kehfrey said.

"This is the wine cellar," Marun told him.

"What's it doing with a bar on the outside?"

"You will see," the sorcerer answered ominously.

He lifted the bar off the hooks and let it drop. It swung down and thudded to the side of the door. The loud knell sounded like a knocker meant to alert the occupants within. What occupants there might be in that cellar, the brothers had no idea. Only grim imaginings came to mind.

The sorcerer pushed the latch and opened the door, afterward descending into the darkness without hesitation. Kehfrey paused and then scurried after him. Swearing beneath his breath, Vik followed, grabbing the boy by the shoulder to slow his progress to a more cautious one.

"It's nice and cool down here," Kehfrey remarked. "Where have you gone?"

His master's voice wandered the darkness to them, a muffled sound in the fetid gloom. "Here," he said.

Both brothers hesitated at the bottom, neither of them liking the smell or the obscurity. "Well, that's useful. Where's here?" the younger said.

A green flame erupted in the darkness. Kehfrey blinked in astonishment. Marun stood in the centre of a wide aisle created of old barrels, a witch flame in the palm of his right hand. "Come forward," he said.

"He's going to kill us!" Vik hissed. His words carried despite the softness with which they were uttered.

"I will not," the sorcerer denied and strode back toward them. Vik pulled Kehfrey behind him. The enemy's lips curled scornfully. The man halted before Vik and held the uncanny flame higher.

The light transformed the youth's flaxen hair into a green horror and cast a glow over his skin that made him ghastly to look upon. He seemed a pale-eyed corpse within the radiance. But oddly the witch light had turned Kehfrey's ginger hair a luscious brown and his fair skin had become as verdant as leaves. He gave the illusion of a glowing wood sprite come down into the dark with them. It was as if the illumination collected over him, as if he attracted it. Odd.

"As I stated already, I have uses for the boy," Marun said, dragging his eyes away from the child. "And as for you ...." He grabbed Vik by the back of the neck and pulled him forward to bestow upon him a rough and demanding kiss. Vik gasped against his lips, but shortly managed to shove him away.

"Get off my brother's face!" little Kehfrey shouted, an outraged defender oblivious of his minuscule size. "You don't just grab him!"

"Don't I?" Marun replied, his mouth forming another of his small, sinister smiles.

"No!" the boy affirmed.

"What do I do, then?"

"Uh ...!" Kehfrey fumbled, surprised an adult should pose such a direct question about an undisclosed activity.

"Oh, leave off!" Vik protested. "He's only a little boy!"

"He's unusually precocious, wouldn't you say?" Marun observed.

Vik glowered, unable to refute this, uncertain he should. Kehfrey's precocity might be all that saved them from this disaster.

Seeing that his challenge wasn't to be met, Marun turned his back on them and walked down the aisle a second time. "Come now!" he said.

Kehfrey looked at his brother, shrugged away his unease and walked forward resolutely. Not so easily brave, Vik hissed between his teeth and followed. The sorcerer had stopped where he'd been standing previously. The brothers approached warily. Neither of them saw a dead thief anywhere, at least not in the weird light glowing above the sorcerer's palm.

"So. This is educational," Kehfrey said.

The master looked down at him witheringly. "Have patience, brat. He's in the dark for a reason."

"What reason?"

"The dead don't enjoy the light."

Kehfrey and Vik gaped at him; then they heard the shuffling. Marun smiled at their shocked faces. Vik was first to turn his head and see them. He choked on his own spit trying to scream. The moment Kehfrey became aware of the others, he lost his towel, his fingers having gone useless with fear. And suddenly the green luminosity scattered from him. He stood naked and white in the gloom, his skin seeming as dead as the two thieves shuffling toward them. Marun stared at the child in fascination, but the boy only had eyes for the approaching horrors.

Mur's ghoul was in better shape. Ofmen's was accountable for the shuffling noise. His corpse hauled itself toward them, both legs missing up to the knees. The hands held the remains of severed limbs. The joints scraped across the floor, only a few strips of flesh yet hanging off the bone. Kehfrey stared at bloody mouths and realized where the flesh of the thief's legs had gone.

"I've seen enough now!" he blurted. It seemed to him he heard a distant thud. He hoped it wasn't the door shutting them in.

"Are you sure?" Marun said.

"Yes!" he squeaked.

"Best pick up your towel, then," his master suggested.

"They might get me if I look down!"

"I don't think so. See? They're holding still now."

Kehfrey grasped that the horrors were indeed motionless. They had stopped between two stands of barrels at least seven feet away. "Why did they stop?" he said breathily.

"I willed them to," the master informed him.

84

"Right." Carefully he knelt and groped for his towel without looking. It was at this moment he realized Vik was missing from his side. "Vik!" he cried. Then he noticed his brother sprawled to the side. "Vik?"

"He fainted," Marun told him.

Kehfrey looked up. The sorcerer's face betrayed a glint of cold humour. "You think that's funny?" the boy said petulantly.

"Yes. You didn't faint, and you're only a little boy."

"Of course I didn't faint!"

"Why not?"

Kehfrey looked up blankly. "I don't know," he admitted. He pulled his towel around his waist and shivered in the cold air. "Can we go now?"

"Hold out your hand," his master commanded.

"Why?"

"Do it!" Marun snapped.

The shadows in the room swelled around them, and Kehfrey heard the ghouls groan in a fashion suggestive of pleasure. He held out his hand quickly. Marun lowered his right hand and deposited the witch light onto the child's unsteady palm.

"Keep it as high as you can," he said.

Kehfrey lifted his arm obediently. The sorcerer stared at him as if he were perplexed. "Should I hold it higher?" the boy said.

His master didn't answer. Upon accepting the flame, Kehfrey had turned into a woodland sprite again. Marun could fathom no reason for this effect. He bent and lifted Vik. He carried the youth toward the stairs.

Kehfrey rushed after him, glancing back to be certain the ghouls didn't follow. He was almost on Marun's heels as the man ascended the steps. When they walked out of the open entrance, Kehfrey realized it hadn't been the door he had heard thud while they were in the wine cellar. It had been Vik falling to the earth.

Marun directed Kehfrey to shut the thick door and bar it again, but after shutting the door only, the boy stood indecisively with the witch light still in his palm, uncertain what to do with it. The bar was too heavy for him to lift with only one hand.

"Put the light out," the sorcerer snapped.

Kehfrey looked up questioningly, but Marun did not speak further, merely watched narrowly without offering a suggestion how to go about dousing the unnatural fire. Slowly Kehfrey closed his fingers around the green flame. He shivered and then bared his palm again. There was nothing in it. Quickly he pulled the bar up and onto the holders, losing his towel in the process. He snatched the cloth up, but the master had already turned away and was marching out the further door, turning sideways so that Vik's head wasn't knocked.

"Where are we going now?" Kehfrey asked, catching up in the kitchen. They both ignored the silent, fearful servants.

"*You* are going back to your room," the sorcerer said coldly.

"What about my brother?"

"You will not concern yourself about him."

"That's not likely, is it? He's my brother. Are you going to hurt him?"

"No."

"But you hurt Ofmen. You like hurting people."

Marun halted and glared down at him. "I like hurting my enemies. Are you and your brother my enemies?"

Kehfrey stalled before him and shook his head firmly. Still scowling, Marun turned away once more. Kehfrey pursued him up the main stairs, but he stopped before his door and watched from there as Marun continue on to his own. Just before he reached it, Kehfrey shouted at him.

"You didn't ask! You can't just grab a fellow without asking!"

Marun looked at him angrily. "Yes, I can!" he snarled.

With a word of power, he sent his door flying open. Kehfrey shrieked in pain and clutched his ears. His towel fell to the ground once again. Marun shook his head in mystification over the boy's reaction, a mystification clouded yet by anger, and strode into his room with Vik, kicking the door shut with a bang after. Kehfrey stared at the closed door, grimacing with pain and worry.

His door opened and revealed the woman, still in her slip, her eyes puffy from sleep but wide with anxiety. "What are you doing out here?" she cried. "Was that Marun? Did you make him angry?"

"Yes!" He grabbed his towel and pulled it up over his groin. "He's in there buggering my brother!" he shouted and stomped into the room.

The woman stared after him in shock and then confusion. "What? What are you saying?"

But Kehfrey threw himself on the bed and sobbed into the cover without answering. Shaking her head in bewilderment, Nicky shut the door and went to comfort him.

Chapter Four

He floated. He was high enough above them still, out of reach of blood-reddened mouths and flesh-fouled teeth. He was desperate to remain out of reach, but he was sinking. Inevitability dragged him downward. Floating ... floating was impossible.

He choked again on the scream that just wouldn't come out, and it was as if his own helplessness dropped him further down. He willed himself back up, but the impossibility of floating was a heavy anchor. Everything moved slowly, everything that was him, his body, his mind. Only they moved quickly, with their bleached arms reaching, their soiled mouths grinning, their dead eyes insisting he must die. They had the power, and he had nothing but his weakness and his terror, plummeting him into their grasps. And then he had pain.

He was caught! He smothered! Intrusion!

"No!"

Jerking awake, he gasped for breath. He lay on his stomach, his face half turned toward a pillow. Someone was over him, sheathed deep inside. That same someone reached beneath and grabbed flesh made tumescent by terror. The pain turned into coarse pleasure.

"Gods!" he uttered hoarsely. He knew who it was. He knew and he burst with racking shudders.

"You're too quick," his rapist said and punished him with a brutal shove inward.

Teeth locked together, Vik worked his arms beneath and pushed his chest and head up enough to let his body respire freely, but he kept his face down, refusing to look back. Let the bastard finish. Let him finish and then he would leave.

But the master finished and refused to part from him. His larger frame remained overtop, trapping Vik to a submissive posture. "Tell me something, *Vik*," Marun whispered in his ear. "Tell me why the constables sent to follow your brother Wilf knew nothing about you?"

Vik declined to answer. Lips touched his shoulder. The gesture was gentle, but he shivered with fear.

"I have what is supposed to be a complete report on my desk, direct from the Minister of Justice's office," his captor said.

There came the sound of metal tinkling, and the lips crossed over Vik's shoulder to his other side. The cool touch of fine chains trailed along his back, and his skin prickled with apprehension. Power, he felt such power in the light stroke, the weight of it heavier than the chains themselves.

"I know who your mother is," the violator went on, "Canella, disowned daughter of Baron Harte, now married to a known thief, a man named

Kehfen who has defeated all pursuits, avoided innumerable traps and murdered a number of ambitious professional man hunters, one of whom was found buried under a pile of rubbish just yesterday. I know who Canella's children are. Her first child is Wilf, likely the bastard son of the late Lord Ghemet. She has another boy named Gamis and the last child is Kehfrey. She is currently with child again. Where, Vik, are you in all that?"

"Second son," Vik answered, seeing no use in further silence. The sorcerer already knew too much, enough to hunt his family down and murder them all. "Get off me!"

"Second son," Marun repeated. "Why did Lolte's spies get the information wrong?"

"I don't live with my family. Not since I was thirteen."

"Why aren't you living with your family?"

"Get off me!" Vik shouted. He jerked upward. The sorcerer pressed him back down. The man's body felt hot, but the chains and the power were a cold burn on his back.

"Where did you live instead when you left your family at thirteen?"

"With a friend."

"A friend? Do you still live with him?"

"No!"

"Why not?"

"It's not your business. Get off!"

"Was he your lover? Did he dump you?"

"No! I dumped him."

"Why?"

"He lied! Alright? He said he loved me, but then he expected things as if he had a right to them."

"Things?"

"Things I didn't want to do," Vik admitted. "Not with him. Not yet."

"This friend? How old was he?"

"Sixteen."

"And he let you go that easily? He didn't try to stop you?"

Vik clawed the sheets with his hands. Would this man never shut up and let him off the bed? "Yes, he tried to stop me," he said.

"And what did you do? What happened? How did a stripling stop a boy three years older than him?"

"I hit him," Vik said. "I hit him until he gave up."

"You beat a boy older than you? Was he smaller?"

"No. I'm stronger than I look ... at least when my temper is up."

"Is it so?" Vik's captor breathed. After a short pause, the sorcerer asked another question, and Vik shut his eyes in frustration. "How old are you now?"

"Fifteen."

"So young?"

It was a whisper. Another kiss on the back of his neck made Vik shiver again.

88

"Are you afraid?"

"Yes," he admitted.

"And after you left this importunate first lover, where did you go then?"

Vik attempted a detailed answer, hoping the questions would end after. "To someone I met when I helped Wilf trawl for clients, an old man who could only watch and wish. I spent two years in his service, pretending to be a servant in training as a gentleman's gentleman. But when he died, I was dismissed at once."

"I see. And your actual services were?"

"Damn it. He watched! He just watched!"

"While you did what?"

"While I did myself! Will you just get off me!"

"Which of your parent's doesn't approve of you, Vik?" his captor goaded. "Or is it both?"

"My father! Get off!" Vik howled.

The sorcerer lifted away. Vik rolled off the mattress and came up ready to fight, but Marun just lay upon the bed and considered him. Vik refused to look at any part of him but his face. His defiance merely caused his foe to smile, a cold and sardonic gesture. The sorcerer's next question threw Vik's mutinous expression off.

"Why didn't Minister Lolte tell me about the Syndicate?"

Vik straightened and gaped at him. "What? Minister Lolte ...?"

"Yes, Minister Lolte." Marun's gaze cast downward, a slow perusal. He was slender, this Vik, a willowy creature, already tall at fifteen, no doubt destined to be taller. Odd how he was brother to the diminutive mystery, the rapscallion boy who no doubt scurried through the manor at this moment, causing yet more trouble. This Vik showed every sign of becoming more exquisite as he matured. He had an air to him that seemed beyond human, beyond mortality. Marun wanted to crush that impression of divinity beneath him again. Soon. Very soon.

"How should I bloody know why Lolte said nothing about the Syndicate?" the youth replied.

The sorcerer regarded him, his expression inscrutable; then he crept off the bed and walked away. At his washstand, he poured water into a bowl, and Vik stared at his back, his mind blanked by what he perceived. Some time in the past, the master of the manor had been whipped until his back had become a network of crossing lines. Callus upon callus, white-ridged flesh snarled with lines of near red; what could he feel there? What could he possibly feel?

"Perhaps your father knows?" Marun suggested as he began to wash.

"My father isn't in charge of the thieving ring." Vik pulled his eyes off the mutilated flesh, away from portentous gold hinting at the neck. He scanned the room hurriedly. Opulently decorated in red and gold, it was just another uninteresting rich man's room.

"Who is?" Marun said.

"Bugger off! I'm not giving away my father's business."

Marun looked back and eyed him flatly. "You're very loyal to a father who doesn't approve of you." He averted his face and continued washing.

Vik spied his suit strewn upon the floor at the foot of the bed. He darted over and snatched the clothing up.

"I'll just take them off you again," his captor said calmly without looking at him. He set aside the cloth he'd been using and faced Vik. "Put the clothes down."

Vik ignored him. He'd been seeking for his weapon, but couldn't see it anywhere. The sorcerer walked toward him. Vik backed off and glanced toward the door.

"I put a spell on it," the sorcerer told him. "You can't open it."

Vik looked at the man wrathfully. "Where's my brother?"

"Back in his room. Safe. Are you avoiding your own dilemma?"

By now Vik had retreated until he was against a desk. He edged sideways. Marun halted and watched him quietly. Vik froze, his clothes in his hands like a shield. Quite useless, he knew.

"And what now?" the master said.

"I don't seem to have the next move," he retorted.

Marun smiled faintly. "Are you going to beg me to free you?"

"Would you?"

"No."

"Then shut up about it!"

Marun smiled outright. Once more the gesture took the plain austerity from his face. He was striking, but his smile was yet filled with sinister overtones that boasted no affability. "You have some of your brother's character, I see."

Vik merely regarded him, his quiet as much an accusation as any verbal protest he might have mustered. Marun stepped forward again until he had the boy pressed against the desk. He pulled the garments from limp hands. He dropped them. He tugged Vik forward by the hips and covered lips with his own.

To crush. To crush this beautiful, beautiful angel in his arms. Such perfect ecstasy.

***

"Your brother is here?" she repeated.

"I just said that!"

"The one I saw at the fountain yesterday?"

"Yes!"

"Why?"

He sighed impatiently. She'd spent the last quarter hour trying to stop him from crying and get him to talk, but now that he was talking, she couldn't seem to understand a word he said. He rubbed at his reddened eyes and sniffed.

"Please, don't cry again," she pleaded.

"I'm not going to cry again! Unless you keep misunderstanding everything I say!"

"Oh, please. I'm just surprised your family actually dared to get you."

"Not my family! Vik!"

"All right. Vik," she repeated. "But now he's in Marun's room?"

"Yes," he said glumly. "And Marun didn't ask."

She stared at him before responding. "Marun forgot how to ask long ago," she said at last. The little boy looked at her sadly and then averted his face. "How did you find out Vik was here?"

"I couldn't sleep because of you snoring and went downstairs."

"I was snoring?"

"Like a cussed pig."

She glowered. "I was tired. I only snore when I'm very tired."

"Then you were tired like three cussed pigs. No! Four!"

"I'll give you pigs!" She pounced on him. He shrieked and rolled away. He lost his towel and shrieked again. Nicky snatched it before he did.

"Let go!" He grabbed it and pulled.

"Make me!" she challenged, grinning like a wild woman and hauling back. Kehfrey gave a giant tug. She let go suddenly and he tumbled off the bed.

"Ow!"

"You win!"

Unamused, Kehfrey pulled the towel over his middle. "What about my clothes, then?"

"I sent them away," she reported unsympathetically.

"Well, I don't want to wear a towel all day!"

"Then take it off."

Kehfrey snapped his mouth shut and glowered at her. Smiling, she relented.

"I ordered one of the men to fetch you new clothes. They may have them already."

"No one said a thing in the kitchen," he cried, getting up hastily.

"In the kitchen? You were in the kitchen again?"

"Marun led us through."

"Marun? Us?"

"On the way to the cellar," he added.

"You went to the cellar with Marun?" she said flatly, her expression very blank.

"To see the dead men," the little boy continued.

It took her a moment to work a query around this fact. "Why did Marun take you both to see the dead men exactly?"

"To give us a lesson so that we could convince the Syndicate to cooperate with him," he said impatiently.

She stared at him, her eyes growing wider. "You will be betrayed," she uttered.

Kehfrey blinked, opened his mouth, shut it again. She didn't look right. Her eyes had gone ... muzzy.

"You will be betrayed by your father's people," she amended.

"Why?" the child demanded.

"To draw Marun into a trap," she whispered.

"And will that help any of us? Letting him get drawn into a trap?"

Her eyes squinted and her head bowed. She pressed her fingers to her temples, crushing dark hair that fell over her face. "No. It won't help," she said hoarsely. "He will come prepared." Her back curled until her forehead touched the mattress. "Your family will still suffer."

"Stop looking!" he cried. "You're making yourself sick!"

She raised her face. Her nose bled. "You hear the lies in their mouths," she whispered.

"I said stop looking!" He pounced on the bed and shook her.

She rolled onto her back. "I need a drink," she croaked, staring blankly at the ceiling.

He slid off the bed and rushed to the washstand. He found a cup on it, but when he looked in the pitcher, he discovered it empty. The only water in the room was bath water, dirty bath water.

"Well, I can't give her that." Hearing her move, he turned. She had sat up. Now she moved off the bed unsteadily. "Don't get up!" he cried. "You aren't well!"

He rushed back and hovered in front of her, uncertain what to do. She stared down at him almost vacantly, her nose bloodied, the stain smeared across her cheek where she'd rubbed it. Her face was white and her eyes overly bright.

"It's all right," she said dully. "I'm too hot. I think I'll just get in the tub."

She stripped the slip down to her waist before reaching the screen. She passed from view. He blinked after her, indecisive, watching the shadow of her figure as she let the slip fall the rest of the way down and onto the floor. Her silhouette stepped into the tub and sank down until the head rested against the curved back.

"I'm going to find you some drinking water," he called.

She didn't answer. He hesitated and then rushed forward to be certain she hadn't expired in his dirty bath water. Gazing down at her, it was evident that she was still breathing. Her breasts bobbed in a very interesting manner.

"Nicky?"

"Yes?" she whispered.

"Are you all right?"

"Yes," she said, so faintly he barely heard. He swallowed nervously and backed off.

"I wonder where the bubbles went?" Perhaps his dirt, or whatever drowning fleas were left swimming in the soup, had popped them all. "Oh, get off bubbles!" he whispered. "It's not bubbles she's wanting."

His determination growing, he went to the door and peeked out. No one was in the hall. He hauled his towel up, stepped out and shut the door behind.

"Here I go to the kitchen again." He awarded a perfectly livid glance to the master's bedchamber door. "If Vik comes out with any sign of hurt, I'll give you what for!"

The innocent door wisely refused to respond, and Kehfrey stomped toward the stairs.

"They cruddy better have my new clothes. I'm sick of this towel. If I drop it one more time, I'm tossing it out a window and walking butt naked the rest of the day. See if I don't!"

As he walked down the stairs, he heard a deep rumbling noise. He paused and looked out the tall windows decorating the hall. Rain had begun to pelt the glass. The storm had finally arrived.

***

"Gods damn it! We have to go!" Wilf said.

His stepfather paced away from him, thinking with his head down. They were alone in the bare room. Gamis had asked permission to see his friends below in the common area. Kehfen had let him go. The boy would only have made noise and awakened his mother and infant sister had he stayed.

"Not you," he said at last. "I go. Alone!"

"What! I'm going, too!"

"No!" he said, looking up. "You stay here with your mother. If I disappear too, you and Gamis will be all she has left."

"Shit!" Wilf jerked back a step, too angered to remain in place. Kehfen had used the one argument he couldn't fight.

"There's no certainty Vik went there," the thief said, endeavouring to calm the young man. "He promised."

"I told you! I went to his favourite haunts. One of his friends said they saw him in Lord Rhet's coach. Vik told them he was going for a ride outside the city."

"I know that. But we can't be certain Rhet went to the manor."

Wilf made an impatient smashing motion with his arm. "You think Vik went for a God's cussed ride for nothing? He's there!"

"He gave oath!"

"He broke it!"

Kehfen hissed in frustration. Of all the things that had gone between him and his firstborn natural son, a foresworn oath had never been one. "You stay here," he repeated. "Take care of your mother."

"You can't go alone!" Wilf insisted.

"I'll go to Kortin's villa and see about help," he offered.

"You think Hiswil will go with you?"

Kehfen shrugged his shoulders uncertainly. Wilf opened his mouth to argue further. Both started when someone banged on the door. They turned. Dust filtered down from the frame. They stared at the falling motes, silent and suspicious.

"It is I! Olomo!" the knocker announced.

Kehfen snatched his knife from his waist, and Wilf matched the motion. Hiswil had related Olomo's strange departure at the manor. Kehfen no longer trusted the foreigner. Olomo's actions of the night before were suspect. Kehfrey had died in the man's care.

There was a momentary quiet beyond the door, and then Olomo continued speaking, his voice urgent, so urgent his accent made his speech almost unintelligible. "You must come with me to the manor! Kehfrey is alive!"

Kehfen slowly straightened and his mouth opened in hopeful surprise. He stepped forward.

Wilf pulled him back. "It's a trick!" he hissed "Hiswil said he admitted to being an assassin. Olomo told him there were more in that house."

"Kehfen!" Olomo called. "I killed the leader of the Pek Tol faction. I have the Vessel. We must return for Kehfrey. The boy is alive and well."

Kehfen pulled his arm out of Wilf's grasp and stepped toward the door. "What are you going on about?" he called. He left the door shut.

"Kehfrey is alive," Olomo repeated. "He is in the manor."

"You said he died," Wilf accused. "You're a traitor!"

"Yes, he died," Olomo answered, "but he lives again."

"How can that be?" Kehfen demanded. He stared at the door intently.

"I do not know exactly," Olomo responded. "I only know the quarrel went straight through him. He was dead, but when I returned, he began to breathe again. He said he had a stone."

"That stone!" Wilf whispered.

"A quarrel!" Kehfen uttered in awe.

"What about it?" Wilf said. "We can't trust what he says."

"Kehfrey said a crossbow bolt would kill him. He said the stone would save his life. He had his hand in his pocket constantly."

Hastily Kehfen moved forward and unlocked the door. Wilf readied for an attack. The swinging door revealed Olomo, but he leaned against the hall on the further side, in no condition to assail anyone. A large red stain had spread down his left side. Blood seeped from a wound beneath his heart and dripped onto the floor. With his right arm he cradled a wooden box against his side. Kehfen stared at him in shock.

"You're bloody dying!" he said.

"I will not die. The knife but scraped across my ribs. It bleeds too much, however. I need to stop it."

Kehfen darted forward and dragged him into the bare room. He pushed the taller man down until he sat on the floor. "Get me something to bind it with," he said to Wilf.

94

"We have nothing but the mattress Mum sleeps on. The baby has nothing but a shawl."

"Then give me your tunic," Kehfen said.

"I'll give you my undershirt," Wilf offered.

"Hells, no. You've sweated in that all yesterday and today. I can smell you from here. The tunic is cleaner."

Angrily Wilf hauled his tunic off and handed it to Kehfen, to then watch resentfully as his stepfather ripped the fine green fabric into bandages.

"How did you do this?" Kehfen asked as he began to wind the dressing around the Ysepian's chest.

"I fought Simre for the Vessel," Olomo answered bleakly, indicating the wooden box at his side. "I killed his followers. I have sinned."

"Sinned!" Wilf sneered. "You abandoned Pop for that damned box!"

Olomo looked up sorrowfully. "I have sinned. I left the one foretold to lead us to Ishpaäf in the hands of a sorcerer."

Kehfen froze. "Sorcerer?"

"Yes," Olomo said tiredly. "He who owns the house is a powerful sorcerer."

"Kehfrey is with a sorcerer?" Kehfen demanded.

"Yes," Olomo affirmed.

"You left my son with a sorcerer!" he shouted. In the further room, Canella's voice lifted querulously.

"Hsst!" Wilf warned needlessly.

"Go calm her down," Kehfen said. "Tell her Kehfrey's alive and I'm going to fetch him."

"What? We can't do that yet. Olomo could be lying to us."

"I do not lie," Olomo said with some of his former pride. "I have spoken the truth. An assassin has no need for lies when he is not on mission. Kehfrey lives."

"And is in a sorcerer's house!" Wilf hissed back. His mother called again. "If you leave with him, what's to say that you won't just disappear and never come back?" he said to Kehfen.

"Your father will come back," Olomo assured him. "After he sees to his son's apprenticeship."

"What?" Kehfen cried.

"We have no time for this argument. You must come with me now. The boy must be taught the ways. We must see the sorcerer. We must secure his cooperation."

"How the gods cussed hells will we do that? He's after Kortin!"

"Kehfrey has suggested the sorcerer make a pact with the Syndicate. I believe the sorcerer is willing to listen."

"Shit!" Wilf swore. Again his mother called. An infant's wail joined her cry.

"She has given birth," Olomo said.

"A girl." Kehfen knotted the bandage and stood, offering Olomo a hand up. The assassin accepted it and lifted himself with a stifled grunt of pain. "Go in to your Mum," Kehfen snapped at Wilf.

Wilf scowled. "Go in yourself. Tell her what you're about to do."

"No, gods bust it! She'll keep me hours explaining. You go."

Wilf eyed him angrily. After a brief clash of wills, he grabbed Kehfen and hugged him hard. He let go and stomped to the door of the inner chamber. "Be careful," he said over his shoulder.

"I will be," Kehfen replied. Outside, thunder peeled. "Crud! Of all the times for it to start raining. Come on," he snapped at Olomo. "Before she yells at me to get in there."

Olomo followed him out the door, the Vessel clutched tightly beneath his right arm.

***

Marun's servants sat in the kitchen like soldiers besieged. The kitchen staff, the household staff, they were all to be found in that one room. Despite the heat, they gathered near the cooking area like beleaguered men near a fire in the dark, loath to abandon the comfort of flames. Flames could ward off ghouls.

Kehfrey stood in the corner of the kitchen, his clean hair glinting the same colour as the copper pots hanging off the hooks overhead. Where the light hit the crinkles, it gleamed perhaps redder than copper, but the effect was ephemeral, shifting with the motions of his body.

He held the new suit of clothes one of the staff had handed him, wondering if he should dress here or dress upstairs. Apprehending that going back up would require coming back down again to fetch water, he determined to damn any modesty he had left and dress in the kitchen.

"Why are you all here?" he said to the men huddled there. "When do you ever get any work done? Some of you lot aren't kitchen help."

"We work when he's elsewhere," a young man in dark grey livery told him.

"If we can help it," another added.

"And if you can't?" Kehfrey looked past the cook. Was that pie on the counter over there?

"Then we move very quietly," said an older man who wore the same livery as the other household staff, but who also bore a fancy cravat with gold thread along the edges. Kehfrey took him for the boss of this terrorized gang. "Why does he have you?" this man said.

"Have me? He doesn't have me."

"He has you," the man insisted. "He has all of us."

"Does he? Are you all slaves?" Their flat stares were answer enough. "Right," Kehfrey said. He glanced sideways. The cook had moved out of the way. That was definitely pie, several of them. What would it take to get his hands on one?

He let his towel drop and started with the new black breeches, ignoring the staring men. He put a foot in one leg. Lightning clapped close by outside. Startled, he looked out the kitchen window and discovered a pair of familiar eyes staring in at him in shock. Kehfrey yelped in surprise, lost his balance and tumbled forward. His baby tooth snapped loose as he hit the floor.

"Aiie! Crud!"

He swallowed blood. His tooth lay on the stone floor. A gust of wind swirled around him. Looking up, he saw the boss rushing out the door. Two others followed quickly. Hurriedly, Kehfrey snatched his tooth up and pulled his breeches on. He was about to rush out, half naked, when the men came back, hauling a twisting and cursing Gamis between them.

"Get off him! He's just my brother!"

"Another one?" said the older man, dripping water from his face. The last of them shut the door on the torrential rain.

"Yes, another one. Put him down, then," Kehfrey snapped.

"The Master must be informed," the older servant said flatly.

"So I'll tell him. Here now, Gamis. Get your butt on that seat."

He crossed over to his brother and pulled him away from the semi-stupefied servants. Gamis, on his part, had been hanging quiescent between them the moment Kehfrey had spoken. He was dripping copiously. Kehfrey directed his bewildered brother over to an empty chair and shoved him down. Then he rushed back for his abandoned towel and threw it over Gamis's shoulders.

"There you go. Just sit there and drip dry." He darted toward the pies and hustled back with one. "Save me half."

"Here, now!" the cook said.

"Hear what? The Master? I'll see to it!" Kehfrey darted toward the inner door. "Wait a minute!" he said, pulling up sharply. He ran to the counter, grabbed a fork and tossed it at Gamis, who caught it and continued to gape at him. The cook gaped at Gamis and then at Kehfrey. Eyeing him wisely, Kehfrey decided the man wasn't going to protest further. "Where's the water for drinking?" he asked the rotund fellow.

"In the barrel," came the answer.

Kehfrey found the indicated vessel near the door. A row of clean pitchers stood on a shelf above it. He grabbed one and filled it and then rushed out the door. He came back seconds later, almost bumping into a pursuer. It was the older servant who had insisted they were all slaves.

"What are you doing?" this man demanded.

"Getting water for Nicky." Kehfrey darted around him. "Mind you save that half for me!" he shouted at befuddled Gamis and circuited the servant nimbly.

"Gods bust it!" he heard his brother exclaim. "Isn't he dead?"

Kehfrey grinned, ran out the corridor into the entry hall and headed up the stairs. "Not for a long time," he whispered to himself. "Tried it and didn't care for it."

"Wait, you!" shouted the servant.

Kehfrey heard a gasp of horror. He turned at the top of the stairs to find the man standing fearfully in the centre of the hall, both hands clapped over his mouth. "I said I'd tell him! Go back and hide!"

The door down the hall opened. Marun stalked out of his room and glared at Kehfrey. "What did you do now?" he demanded. He glanced over the balustrade and saw his butler, white faced and anxious in the foyer. The sorcerer's gaze returned to Kehfrey. The boy had to be the one at fault. The butler never dared to displease. Ever.

Kehfrey looked his master up and down. "You're naked," he said needlessly.

"And you're not. Where did you get those breeches?"

"Staff fetched a suit for me."

"Why aren't you wearing the rest of it?"

"Gamis distracted me. But don't worry! I have him busy eating pie."

Marun blinked at him. From inside the room, Vik shouted. "Kehfrey! Get Gamis and run!"

The sorcerer shut the door on him. "Is your entire family going to drop in to see you one by one?" Marun said, his expression cynical.

"Have you hurt Vik?" Kehfrey demanded.

"No. Unless you count his pride. Go and tell your other brother he's invited to stay for supper." He opened the door. Vik, with only breeches on, attempted to dart out. Marun caught him and shoved him back in. "And if any other members of your family show up, be certain to have the staff set places for them," he directed as he pressed Vik inward.

"Where'd you get all those scars, then?" Kehfrey hollered as the door thudded to. He waited for an answer, but the door stayed shut. His door, however, opened. Nicky poked her head out, dripping wet and with soapy water running down from her hair.

"Kehfrey! What are you doing now?" she whispered. She shut one eye as the soap threatened it. She had apparently recovered enough to begin washing her hair.

"I was getting you drinking water," he whispered back.

He rushed forward and handed the pitcher to her. She wore only a towel. It gaped as she snatched the pitcher, which was too heavy for one hand. Caught between losing the towel and dumping the pitcher, she opted for losing the towel. Kehfrey's face lengthened as if it would follow the towel down. She couldn't help grinning at his shocked expression, but then the grin faded.

"What happened to your face?" she said.

"Uh ... fell on the floor," he reported. Wasn't that interesting? Everything about her seemed very well placed, even when it wasn't bobbing in water. And that was such an interesting cleft between her legs. What an oddly pretty junction. Better than most he managed a peek at.

"And the tooth?" she whispered. "Where is it?"

"In my pocket," he said, his eyes still on the junction.

"Quick! Swallow it!" she ordered him.

"What? Why?"

"Do you want *him* to get it?"

Kehfrey blinked. Comprehension dawned and he thrust his hand in his new breeches to pull the tooth out and toss it into his mouth. She handed the pitcher back to him and picked up her towel. When she'd risen, the boy had already swallowed the tooth and spilled a large quantity of water onto his chest. She wiped the spill from him with the towel, exhibiting no apparent concern over her nakedness. He gaped at her. After a moment, his brows furrowed pensively.

"What?" she said.

"Mum wouldn't be caught without clothes."

"Your mother is probably less than a tenth my age," she pointed out. "You live as long as I do, and some things just don't bother you anymore."

"Why not?"

"Because they just don't seem important. In some places, they aren't."

He looked at the parts that everyone else hid. "They look important to me," he said. She laughed, grabbed the pitcher from him and shut the door on his astonished face. "Hi, now!" he objected.

She opened the door a crack. She was still smiling. "What?"

"What's to stop him from getting my tooth when it comes out the other end?"

She laughed again. "Not even *he* will look there," she said. The door snicked shut.

Frowning, Kehfrey wandered back to the stairs and walked down them slowly. "What would he do with it, I wonder?" Three more steps down, he suddenly remembered the pie. "Gamis!" he hissed.

He had better have saved him that half!

***

"Pop said you were dead," Gamis told him.

"I was dead." He shoved another mouthful of pie into his face. Oh, it was so good!

"You were not! Or you'd still be dead," his brother retorted. Kehfrey glowered at him, dripping a gob of berry from one side of his mouth. "You eat like a pig," Gamis added.

Kehfrey ignored the insult. He wasn't going to waste a taste of pie on that feeble slight. He took his time and chewed the pie thoroughly. The drip was duly shoved in the moment he had room for it.

"Where'd you get that mark on your chest?" Gamis asked. His little brother sat across the kitchen table in only his breeches, having decided to forgo dressing until he'd finished the pie. Kehfrey hadn't trusted Gamis not to eat the rest of it while he was occupied.

"Told you. I was dead," he said.

"What the hells do you mean?" Gamis shouted.

"Here, now!" the butler hissed. "Be quiet! If he comes down, I'll tan you both!"

"Why are you here?" Kehfrey demanded of Gamis. "Why are you here alone?"

"Pop made Wilf and Vik promise not to do anything stupid or dangerous. So there was only me left to check the place out for your body."

"You came to get my body?"

"I wanted to bury it."

"Very nice of you," Kehfrey said sarcastically.

Gamis scowled. "Well, fine! I won't bother seeing you properly buried a second time." Kehfrey grinned at that. Gamis grinned back. "Give me another piece," he cajoled.

"You had your half! You had half of mine!"

"Vik disappeared," Gamis informed him then.

"Vik is here," Kehfrey informed him in turn.

Gamis's mouth dropped open. "What? He broke a sworn oath!"

"I don't think so," Kehfrey defended. "He wouldn't." Would he? Ah, damn! He'd gone and gotten Vik in trouble. And buggered. "Ah, fuck!"

"Watch your language, boy," the butler said.

Kehfrey ignored him and so did Gamis, who continued speaking. "Then what's he doing here? Pop told him not to do anything without his leave."

"We can ask him when he comes down," Kehfrey mumbled around a mouthful. If Vik ever did come down. Damned sorcerer. Shoving Vik back into the room like that. Where'd the cold-hearted brute get all those scars on his back? Those had been interesting. A veritable maze.

"Come down from where?" Gamis asked.

"The master's bedroom," the butler said with a nasty tone. Kehfrey turned his head and glared at the man, who eyed him repressively. The butler had yet to forgive the boy for provoking him to shout in the main hall.

"The master's bedroom?" Gamis repeated. "Bloody hells!"

"You're invited to supper," Kehfrey said.

"Bloody buggered-to-death misbegotten he-goats!"

Kehfrey snickered and almost choked on crust. The cook shoved a mug of beer at him. He took it gratefully and downed a fair quantity.

"Careful, boy! That's a strong stout."

"It's stout, all right. Gaah! It's cussed warm."

"It's stout. It's supposed to be warm."

"Not this warm!"

"No ice this time of year," the cook said regretfully. "Have to order it weeks ahead and it don't last long. Very expensive."

"Why don't you keep the stout in the cellar?" he said. "It's cool enough."

"Only keep the new beer down there until it's settled enough for drinking."

100

"Why not bring up the settled beer?"

The cook looked at him pointedly.

"Right," he said after a moment. "Forgot."

"Forgot what?" Gamis wanted to know.

"The master's got ghouls in the wine cellar," Kehfrey said. He looked at the last of his pie regretfully and shoved it into his mouth. It was so good!

Gamis stared at him in disbelief. "There's no such thing. That's just another of your stories."

"It's no story," said the butler. "There are ghouls in the cellar."

"Who gets the wine out? Or the beer that's ready?" Kehfrey asked, disregarding Gamis's awed expression.

"The master," one of the younger men said. "The last one of us he sent down, he sent to punish him."

"You mean he's had other ghouls down there before the two I saw today?"

The servant nodded gravely.

"They're still down there," the cook whispered fearfully.

"Did he make it back up?" Gamis asked. "The servant, I mean."

"No," the butler said. "He's one of *them* now."

Gamis gaped at him. His blank gaze settled on his little brother, and he wondered if Kehfrey was a ghoul. He insisted he'd been dead, didn't he?

"Can I have more pie?" Kehfrey piped up in the silence.

"No," the sorcerer answered from the hall door.

Gamis yelped in fright. Kehfrey turned, wiping his mouth hastily with the back of his hand.

"You were supposed to have dressed," Marun said to the child. The master was quite properly clothed in a suit of dull maroon. Only the white undershirt beneath his tunic provided any brightness to his outfit.

"I didn't want to get pie on my new suit," Kehfrey explained. The master's expression frosted over. "I'm coming," the boy said flatly and left the bench to seek his clothes, which the butler had wisely placed on a clean counter. Kehfrey hauled on his undershirt and tunic, and afterward sat to pull on the stockings that had been provided. He buttoned them under the cuffs of his breeches. The butler handed him a pair of shoes. They were a fine set, fashioned of black leather and sporting brass buckles. Kehfrey slipped them on and stood. They felt good on his feet.

"How did you know what size I needed?" His old shoes had been too large, handed down from Gamis. There had been holes in the soles.

"Never mind that," his master said. "Come." He left the kitchen. Obediently Kehfrey followed after him.

"Kehfrey!" Gamis hissed, standing at the corridor door where he peeked out anxiously.

"Just wait there!" Kehfrey hissed back.

Marun turned his head and looked coldly at Gamis. The boy gasped and pulled his head back behind the door. The sorcerer gave a slight disapproving shake of his head. "He doesn't have the same courage as you, but he is not quite the ugly butthead you said he was."

"When I said that, I was being kind. And I just told him there were ghouls in your basement. What do you expect him to do? Ask to see your nasty pets?"

"I expect you to behave more respectfully!" Marun snapped, looking down at the child warningly. His eyes narrowed. The gamin's upper lip was swollen. "What happened to your lip?"

"Fell on it and lost my tooth," Kehfrey said, grimacing so that his master could see the double gap formed by the two missing teeth in his upper jaw. His little tongue poked out momentarily.

Marun wasn't certain if it was a taunt or not and let the incident go. "Where is the tooth?" he asked, his eyes intent on the child's mouth. This boy .... He had that otherworldly air to him as well. He shared an exquisite structural beauty with his brother Vik. The features of his face were refined and almost vulnerable in their childish sensuality.

"Swallowed it," the boy announced. "Might come out the other end tomorrow."

But certainly his vulgar character did not match his features. Marun gazed down at him flatly and then turned about. Behind, Kehfrey grinned wickedly, not a speck of vulnerability left unspoiled on his young face.

The master continued on until they were in the main hall. From there he led the boy into the library. Inside he pulled a sheet of parchment from a desk drawer, sat down and wrote several symbols on the sheet. Kehfrey, who had looked around at the many shelves with interest up until then, watched him curiously.

"These are letters," Marun said. He listed their names and sounds. "I want you to memorize them."

"I got it," the boy said.

Marun eyed him suspiciously. "Are you saying you understand my orders or that you have already memorized the letters?"

"Already memorized them of course."

Without a word, Marun pulled another parchment from the drawer. He placed it on the desk, stood and offered Kehfrey the seat. Kehfrey sat. Marun took the previous paper away. "Fine," he said. "Write the symbol for Sen."

Without hesitation, Kehfrey reproduced what he'd seen Marun inscribe. The sorcerer stared at the letter a second. It was a perfectly formed Sen, without a wobble to it. Anyone looking at it would not have thought a child had written it, especially an illiterate one.

"Pi!" he snapped.

Kehfrey wrote Pi. Once again the penmanship was flawless. Marun listed the remaining seven letters he'd chosen for the day. The boy scratched them down perfectly with the exception of blotting ink on the last. This occurred after the child discovered he was running out of ink and dipped the nib into the well for more. He didn't wipe the excess off and blotched the symbol.

"Sorry, never used a quill before," he said apologetically.

"Never?"

"Just chalk and charcoal," he explained, his pale features solemn. He repeated the letter, etching it without error.

Marun eyed him thoughtfully. "Write the word rain," he commanded.

Hazel eyes huge and wary in his young face, Kehfrey turned his head down. Frowning, he put the letters together. He wrote the word with only one error. Marun took the quill from him and wrote the word correctly.

"Oh," the boy uttered.

"I find it hard to believe no one taught you to read or write," Marun snapped.

"No one did," he said, looking at his master earnestly.

"Then how do you know how to spell rain?"

"I didn't. I got it wrong. You never showed me that other letter."

"Yet you did spell most of it."

"Isn't that what the letters are for?" The boy's red brows almost met over his nose. "I thought you were testing me."

"I *was* testing you."

Kehfrey blinked at him cagily. The sorcerer stared back suspiciously. A loud knock sounded from the front door. Distracted, they looked through the open library entrance. The butler appeared in the hall, paused when he saw his master, swallowed nervously and rushed on. Marun heard the outer door open and then the announcement of the visitors, which on this occasion was an unusual and startled yelp.

"Hells!" he hissed. He stalked forward, a spell forming on his lips. He ceased the casting the moment he discovered who stood in the hall. "Olomo," he greeted.

"I have returned for the boy," the Ysepian assassin proclaimed.

Marun looked from him to the slight man at his side. Once again family had arrived for Kehfrey. This short man had to be the child's father; same nose and eyes, same noble brow, but a curling ginger beard hid the majority of his features. Both visitors were soaked. Giant puddles had already formed around their feet. The door stood wide, letting in the blasting wind and revealing two drenched nags below on the driveway. Marun looked down at his butler, who sat upon the floor while gaping back and forth nervously.

"Get the horses in the stable," Marun commanded and went back in the library.

Kehfen stared after him. "That's the sorcerer?" he said to Olomo.

"Yes," affirmed the assassin.

Olomo shifted the Vessel slightly and walked toward the library, ignoring the butler, who had risen and was backing off from them. They heard the outer door shut as they looked inside the library door. Behind them, the butler dashed back to the kitchen with his instructions for the stable hands. They paid this no mind. Instead both their gazes landed squarely on the boy's figure and froze there.

"Kehfrey!" his father shouted.

The child pulled his hands from his ears and smiled widely. "Pop! I lost my tooth and swallowed it! I've got a cussed gap the size of a cave!"

Kehfen rushed in and snatched the boy out of the chair. Kehfrey squeaked as the man squeezed him tightly against his sopping chest. "I thought you were dead," his father whispered in abject relief.

"He *was* dead," the sorcerer said.

Kehfen turned with youngest son dangling.

The master had gone to the window and looked out at the rainy scenery. "Who taught your son to read and write?" he demanded.

"What?" Kehfen said.

"Pop! You're squeezing my breath out!" Kehfrey croaked. Hastily Kehfen relaxed his hold on the boy, but he didn't let him go.

"Who taught him to read and write?" the sorcerer repeated, turning to face the thief.

"No one. None of us know how," Kehfen said, his expression tight with suspicion.

"Not even your wife?" the cold-faced man pressed.

"No. She's just a woman."

Someone spoke an impoliteness at the door. Kehfen whirled. A woman stood in the entrance, a very small woman, but also a very beautiful one. She had a straight nose with a slight upward bend at the tip, prettily curved lips and incredibly green eyes. Long, curly black hair hung down her back from one large tail tied together with a ribbon.

"That's Nicky," Kehfrey introduced. "She gave me the stone."

"For once you weren't exaggerating," Kehfen said as he watched the beauty walk in. She halted a few feet inside the room and lifted a sardonic brow at him. Nicky had changed into a clean dress, this one deep red. Her skin was still pale, but she seemed perkier.

"Hi there, Nicky," Kehfrey said. "This is my Pop. Put me down, Pop. I'm not a baby anymore."

"They take after you somewhat, don't they?" the sorcerer commented.

"What?" Slowly, Kehfen lowered his son, his attention now fixed on the sorcerer. The man was surveying him once more, his face impassive.

"Your sons," Marun said. "In particular Kehfrey, although his face seems finer. I assume he acquired the delicacy of his features from his noble-born mother."

Kehfen hardly cared to respond to such inconsequential comments. "What's going on, Kehfrey?" he said, his insides twisting with trepidation.

Kehfrey sighed. Here it goes. "Right, Pop. Sit down."

Kehfen gaped down at him a second and up at the sorcerer once more. The man just eyed him flatly. "Just get on with the explanation," Kehfen snapped, refusing to sit.

"Fine. Gamis showed up half an hour ago. He's in the kitchen, likely wheedling another pie off the cook. Vik got caught a few hours ago. I think someone brought him here and left without him." Kehfrey looked at Marun for confirmation. The sorcerer nodded once. The boy looked back and found his father sinking onto the desk chair, his face white.

"Vik and Gamis are both here?"

Kehfrey nodded.

"Are you expecting any other members of your family, Master Thief?" Marun said sardonically. Kehfen shook his head numbly.

Olomo, who had observed silently from the side of the door until now, stepped forward impatiently. "I have come for the boy," he repeated.

"You sold the boy," Marun snapped. "Do not think I will return him to you."

Kehfen jumped up in outrage. "Sold the boy! You sold my Kehfrey? He wasn't yours to sell!"

Olomo scowled, but his eyes averted in shame nevertheless. "The idea was not mine. I killed the one who sold him."

"You agreed!" Kehfrey shouted. "Bugger off!"

"I was wrong! I have come to right that wrong!"

"And you think I will just give the boy back to you?" the master said sarcastically.

"He's not yours to give!" Kehfen shouted.

Kehfrey saw darkness swell around Marun. He stepped protectively in front of his father. "Leave off him!" he cried.

Marun looked down at him warningly. "Tell your father who you belong to, boy."

"Kehfrey belongs to no one," his father said.

"Kehfrey," Marun demanded.

Kehfrey scowled. Looking his master in the eyes, he gave him what he wanted. Sort of. "I took up service under him, Pop," he said. He heard his father gasp.

"Service!"

"Service!" Marun repeated. He glared at the boy, but then smiled as if he couldn't help the gesture. He glanced toward the woman, who eyed him darkly.

"He has spunk," she remarked flatly.

"Like some others we know," Marun retorted. "Isn't that right, Hanicke?"

"Hanicke? That's a pretty name," Kehfrey said. "Can I call you Nicky anyway?"

She looked at him and barely smiled in response. The tension in the room lightened somewhat as Marun turned away to gaze out the window again. Kehfen knelt in front of his son and held him immobile by the shoulders.

"What do you think you are up to, boy?"

"Have to keep you safe, don't I? What with him looking for whatever Rook stole, none of you are."

"What with Minister Lolte passing information on about your family, but not about the Syndicate, I would say he is correct," Marun added without turning.

"What?" both Kehfrey and Kehfen said.

Marun turned. When he spoke, he spoke to the boy. "I've been working through the Minister of Justice," he told the child. "He's been handing me all sorts of interesting tidbits about your father, assuring me that Master Pehtre of Pehtre Vineyards is wrongfully accused."

Kehfen hissed in anger and looked at Olomo accusingly.

"I knew nothing of this!" the Ysepian protested.

"Why should I believe you?"

"Because he isn't lying," Kehfrey said. Both Olomo and Marun looked at him in surprise.

"Shit!" Kehfen hissed, yet glaring at Olomo. "If you don't, then does Hiswil?"

Marun now stared at the thief, his expression astonished. The boy's father had accepted the child's statement without question. Did the child hear truths?

Olomo forced his gaze up from the boy and onto the father. "I don't know. I don't think he did last night. But he must have gone to Kortin with this report. Perhaps he knows now."

"Why would they want to nail me for this?" Kehfen said.

"Because Kortin is desperate since he can't find bloody Rook," Kehfrey said. He looked at Marun. "Nicky's already seen that Kortin will just betray us if we try to work a deal with him."

Marun's attention snapped toward the woman. "You predict for the boy now?" he said accusingly.

"Leave off her! She almost died looking! You bloody buggering—!"

"Kehfrey!" Nicky said urgently. "Manners!"

The child snapped his mouth shut too late. Marun showed no initial indication he was angry over the outburst, but he wasn't about to let the insult pass. It was time to put the boy in his place. He stepped around a chair and sat in it.

"Come here," he commanded the child.

Kehfrey stomped forward. His father snatched him back. Marun looked at the thief, and Kehfen felt as if he'd been hit in the stomach. His son jerked out from beneath his numb fingers to obediently approach the man he'd admitted, albeit in a highly qualified manner, to being his master.

The boy halted in front of Marun, his expression guarded. The sorcerer crooked a finger at him. Kehfrey perforce stepped closer, exhibiting no fear of a blow, but such was not his master's intent. The sorcerer merely bent forward and whispered in the child's ear. Kehfrey's face blanched, but he listened without moving until Marun lifted his head and stared at the child pointedly. Kehfrey gave him one silent nod and marched back to his father without looking at anyone.

"What did he say to you?" Kehfen asked.

"Never mind," the boy refused.

Kehfen looked at the sorcerer. "Did you threaten my son?"

"No," the man said, eyeing him coldly.

Kehfen gaped at him without understanding, but then it dawned on him. The sorcerer hadn't threatened Kehfrey. He had threatened someone else, someone Kehfrey loved. Kehfen stared at the sorcerer without an expression on his face, but after his features transformed into an enraged snarl. He pulled the knife from his belt and tossed it.

Arrows, spears, even rocks tended to be better projectile weapons than knives. In most cases, knives were unlikely to accomplish a distance kill— until you placed that knife in the hands of a master. Kehfen's attack was almost inhumanely swift, a body-wide movement executed perfectly and with a force far above average. The blade struck where he'd aimed it, right through the heart. The thief straightened, his snarl turning into an avenged smile.

The smile died half born.

Marun looked down at the blade embedded in his flesh, no sign of pain on his face, no expression of emerging dismay. His gaze returned to Kehfrey's father, disdainful, mocking. Slowly he pulled the knife from his chest. It made a sucking sound as it parted from him. When it had come out, he dropped it carelessly to the floor.

Gaping along with everyone else, Kehfrey heard his father's breath pull inward, a long intake of horror. Another gasp echoed from the doorway. Turning, the boy spied Vik standing in the entrance, his dagger in his hand. Even as Kehfrey watched, the weapon slipped from emotionally anaesthetized fingers and clattered onto wood tiles.

"Hi, now! You're not going to faint again, are you?" he called worriedly.

Vik looked over at him stupidly. "I ...," he began. He shut his mouth without ending the sentence. Unhurriedly he turned away and disappeared from view. They heard the front door open.

"Bring him back," Marun snapped. Kehfrey darted out of the library. Kehfen made a move to follow, but the sorcerer froze him with a glare. "Sit," he commanded. Warily the thief seated himself at the desk. "Your youngest son seems to have the gift of a perfect memory," Marun said, ignoring the attempted murder. "In fact, he seems to have more than one gift. Why is that?"

"I don't know," Kehfen mumbled. He glanced at his knife where it lay on the floor to the side of the armchair. There was blood on it, but not much. The sight was numbing. Such a small flecking of red. The sorcerer's life fluid should have spilled over the brocade upholstery and onto the fine woven rug beneath, but the upholstery was spotless and the rug as well.

It struck Kehfen hard then, that his son had indeed taken up service with a sorcerer, and perhaps he had the wisdom of it. He was still alive, his odd little boy. And so were they, the family for which he had done this incredible thing.

"He sees auras," the sorcerer commenced to list. "He perceives truths." He looked at Nicky for confirmation and received a nod. "And he has a perspicacious mind, especially so for a child of his years. How old is he?"

"Seven," Kehfen said.

"That's right. Seven. And at this tender age, he is destined to reach Ishpaäf." Marun glanced at Olomo, his expression withering. Olomo's skin had turned grey beneath his exterior. Marun looked at the bandages over his chest. They were hunter green. Someone had sacrificed expensive cloth for the man. "You are wounded."

"A flesh wound," Olomo dismissed.

"The others?"

"Dead."

"Simre as well?"

"Yes."

"That is regrettable."

Or perhaps convenient. Marun thought this as Kehfrey arrived in the library entrance with Vik. The gamin pulled the youth into the room and guided him to a chair.

Simre lost. An angel gained. Convenient. Very.

The butler appeared in the doorway. "If you please, Master, I shall uncover the glows?"

Marun nodded. In the hush, the servant hastened to do his duty, obedient slave taking no apparent notice of the state of his master's guests. As the black felt came off the glow sticks, the room brightened, but somehow the shadows in the corners seemed darker. Kehfen looked at them and shivered.

Marun turned his cool regard upon Vik, whom Kehfrey had seated in another upholstered chair several feet away. The youth's hair was wet, the shoulders of his suit darkened with damp. His face was pale from shock, and he stared forward without seeing. Kehfrey stepped between, blocking his master's view. Marun fixed his cold eyes on the child's, but the boy refused to back down.

"He stays with me tonight," Kehfrey said. His master's eyes barely narrowed. Kehfrey thought he'd pay for it then, but the sorcerer nodded once and averted his gaze.

As if sensing her awareness, Kehfrey glanced at Nicky. She stared at him oddly. The boy frowned. What was that expression? Amazement? Did he amaze her? He looked away in confusion. He was only sticking up for his family. That's what a person did.

The servant finished his task and bowed. "Supper will be served shortly," he announced. "I shall send a servant with towels." He shut the door as he left.

"I must teach the boy!" Olomo blurted, lurching forward, his urgency almost making him beg. "You must let me have him!"

"I will not," Marun said flatly, "but you will teach him."

Olomo straightened in surprise. "You will permit me to teach him?"

"Yes," he affirmed.

"You wish to reach Ishpaäf?" the assassin said in surprise.

Marun's lips twitched, the barest hint of mockery. "That isn't likely. I've looked in that nuisance box enough to be sick of the sight of it." He stood suddenly, and Olomo started. The sorcerer's sneer grew more evident. "What is it, assassin? Afraid of me? Why? Because you can't kill me?" Olomo swallowed nervously. Marun looked at Kehfrey's father. "And you, thief? Have you finished questioning my right to the boy?"

Kehfen hesitated and then nodded his defeat. "I won't let you hurt him," he gave a last protest.

"Can you stop me?"

Kehfen scowled.

Marun turned away in apparent disinterest. "You will bring the boy's mother here tomorrow," he said, crossing the room toward the window.

"What?"

"Better yet, you will bring her now. And the remaining half-brother." He put a hand on one of the cold panes. The glass had begun to grow misty from the trapped humidity in the room.

"What? Why?"

Marun drew a symbol on the mist, and for a moment the glass beneath appeared darker than it should have. They shivered behind him, wondering what magic he worked so negligently.

"Don't be a fool," Marun said impassively. "Your Kortin doesn't have your best interests at heart, does he? Go get your wife."

Commencing near the symbol, the moisture on the glass fled until it dripped in little rivulets near the window edges. Unimpeded, the sorcerer peered out at the gloomy gardens to the fore of the manor. Kehfen stood and gaped at the man's straight back, and then at Kehfrey.

"Go on, Pop!" the child urged him. "Kortin can't be trusted with her. You don't know what he might pull if he finds out you came here."

"Shit!" he hissed. He bent an irate look upon Olomo.

"I will go with you," the Ysepian offered promptly. He crossed the room and handed the Vessel to the boy. "Do not look within. You are not ready."

"What do I do with it, then?" Kehfrey asked.

"Give it to Nicky," Marun suggested spitefully without turning. "She took good care of it for hundreds of years, after all."

Olomo scowled at the sorcerer, but his ire redirected toward the woman as Kehfrey walked up to her and diffidently handed her the box. She received it with a flat return glare at the assassin.

"Come on!" Kehfen called. He hurried from the library and out of view. Olomo looked at the boy one last time, his eyes limned with fatigue and apprehension, and then followed the child's father out of the house.

Marun turned. "Kehfrey, go and tell Evern to set aside food for your family for later."

The boy nodded, but looked toward Nicky with a questioning expression cast over his alert features.

"The cook," she informed him.

"Right," he said and darted out of the room.

Marun jerked his head at the woman. Obediently she retreated from the library and shut the door behind her. In the entrance hall, she searched the floor for the weapon Vik had dropped, but didn't see it anywhere. Thinking Vik's father must have taken it, she headed for the kitchen after Kehfrey.

Inside the library, Marun walked to Vik and pulled him from the chair. The youth moved without resisting, but kept his pallid face averted. A hand lifted over his slender back, brushing lightly where before there had been heavy possession. Vik's head dipped forward onto a shoulder as a palm cradled his neck, comfort unexpectedly tendered. One single sob burst out of him before he could stop it. He gritted his teeth and swallowed the others.

Marun shifted slightly away and seized one of his hands. Vik's fingers brushed through cloth and met flesh. His focus sharpened. Marun had set the tips inside the rip the knife had created, placed them over his beating heart. Vik attempted to pull away, but the sorcerer's grasp tightened. Dark will and cold insistence sullied the attempt at placation.

"Your brother returned to this life in much the same fashion," the sorcerer proffered.

"He had a rock," Vik whispered.

"Of my making."

"You had no rock."

"Not with me," he murmured.

He pulled Vik's head closer and claimed his lips, once more possession, heavy and certain. Vik shivered again, shivered and damned himself. When Marun thrust their bodies together, he met the need with an obvious response. Vik shook with it. He hated the man. He wanted him. Ah, gods help him, but he wanted him. And the foreboding that had been an icy rock in his guts had become an anchor sinking him further into the chill of this too real nightmare.

The door opened and saved him. "Hi, now! Can't you even give him time to think?"

Marun released him, and Vik moved away from both, ashamed and nearly weeping from it. The sorcerer regarded him and then turned away, his irritation passing onto Kehfrey, the gaze ice cold. But the boy had the fortitude to weather the freeze.

"Supper is ready to be served," he announced evenly, but his eyes were bright with anger, enough to melt an iceberg.

Marun's cold warmed to a thoughtful darkness. Yes. The boy had cleaned up very nicely. Acting thus, he looked a perfectly frigid young gentleman. But his red hair—such a dramatic flame over his white skin. Frigidity rebuffed. "Black doesn't suit you. It makes you too pale."

"If you plan on me being an assassin, I won't be wearing much else, will I?"

"I suppose not," he agreed and strode out of the room.

Kehfrey stared after him and then went over to Vik. "Come on," he said softly.

"I feel like dirt," Vik whispered.

"He does that to everyone."

"You don't understand!"

"Don't I?"

Vik glared down at him through tears. "You're not like me! I'm—!"

"So what if you are? You're still my brother. If that counts for nothing, then I'm not growing up."

Vik laughed, but misery gave weight to the sound. His brief mirth dissolved. "I let him use me."

And it had felt good. In the end, it had all felt good. The heat of flesh, the cold of power, the fear, the need, the uncertainty, the hatred, all of it blurred together into the most intense sexual act he'd ever had.

"Did you have a choice?" Kehfrey asked. Vik blinked at him. "Gods bust it! Vik! I haven't found many choices yet myself. Let me know when you do. In the meantime, stop busting yourself up over it. That's just no good to you." He pulled Vik's hand. "Come on. You need to eat. I need to eat. I lost half my blood. I'm starving."

"Were you really dead?" Vik said, dragged out of the library by his precious, courageous runt of a brother who would most certainly grow up. The sorcerer seemed to admire the brat for some odd reason. Perhaps courage rendered the master of the manor less aggressive. Perhaps he respected such.

"Yes," Kehfrey said. "Dead. Very dead."

"What was it like?"

"Forgot. How do you like that? Must have been the most boring thing that ever happened to me."

This time when Vik laughed, his voice rang with some strength to it. Kehfrey paused in the middle of the hall and Vik's mirth failed. "What's wrong?" he said nervously.

But the answer was as blessedly innocuous as, "Never been to the dining room."

"This way," Nicky called. The boys turned to find her standing beside another door.

"Isn't that the woman who gave you the stone?" Vik asked Kehfrey.

"That's her."

"What's she doing here?"

"She's his slave," his brother informed him with a hushed voice.

"Oh," he said softly. When he looked at her again, he recognised the expression in her eyes. It was compassion. She knew exactly how he felt. "Does he ...?"

"No," she said. "He uses me for other things. And to tempt his marks."

They had reached her by then. Vik gazed past her and saw *him* standing before the head of the table, regarding them coldly. Vik was certain Marun had heard her, but the man didn't seem to care. Vik's attention turned toward the other person in the room. "Gamis!"

"Hello, Vik," Gamis said bleakly from behind a chair, looking very uncomfortable indeed. He was out of place in his dirty handed-down suit of threadbare brown velvet. Vik looked down at Kehfrey, a question expressed on his handsome face, an astounded accusation.

"Don't blame me," Kehfrey said. "He came on his own. He said he was going to bury me."

A surprised laugh burst out of Vik's mouth. Gamis grimaced. Grinning, Kehfrey shoved Vik inward before he could change his mind. "Hi, now, Gamis! If you take more pie than me this time, I'm going to pound you one."

"You and what army?" Gamis said. He opened his mouth to toss another insult, but the scraping noise of a chair froze his thoughts. He turned to see the intimidating master of the house seating himself. Hastily he pulled his own chair out and sat. He huddled in it, looking as if he wanted to disappear.

"Stop slouching," Vik said.

Gamis glared at him and continued slouching, which made Vik grimace in mild disgust. When he pulled his chair out from the table, he performed the task with considerably less noise than his brother and a great deal more grace. The seating of his person was a fluid motion that had less to do with practice than natural refinement. He kept his back straight. He did not look toward their host. Kehfrey, who'd been watching, copied Vik's manners, choosing a chair that placed him between master and brother. Seated, the self-appointed chaperone looked at his master questioningly.

"Hi, now! Why *are* we eating with you? Aren't we supposed to eat with the servants?"

"*You* might later," Marun answered coldly. "So far, the rest of your family aren't servants."

"Right." That was at least good news for Vik. Marun didn't consider him a slave. Kehfrey looked at Nicky. She had seated herself at the further end of the table, just as a lady might with her lord. The boy lifted a ginger brow at her.

"Window dressing," she told him. He frowned suspiciously, uncertain what she meant.

"Hanicke acts as hostess when I need her to," Marun amended on her behalf.

Kehfrey blinked, staring from one to the other doubtfully. The butler interrupted his contemplation, entering with a serving cart and two helpers. They commenced to serve supper.

Gamis, who'd never been one to listen to his mother, ate like the lower class child he was. Kehfrey, wiser than him, watched Vik and copied him move for move. He tried once to get Gamis to smarten up, surreptitiously throwing a pea at him, but Gamis only scowled and continued to eat like a commoner, which looked rather more than piggish in the light of upper class manners. Vik shook his head at Kehfrey's exasperated expression, indicating he should give up, and Marun watched them all. Whatever he thought of their behaviour, he kept it to himself.

They consumed the first courses of their meal without a single attempt at conversation. Everyone seemed satisfied to do so. Kehfrey, for once, didn't feel like livening things up. The air was already charged with too much energy. It was precariously balanced and the slightest wrong move could make it discharge horribly. Kehfrey knew when to shut up. Now was certainly the time.

Chapter Five

Wilf preceded his mother into the manor and paused two yards in to scan the hall, his hand on the knife at his belt, this despite warnings that any such weapon would be of no use. In his opinion, it would at least buy him the time to retreat with his mother if such became necessary.

Left behind in the wind-beset entrance, the butler hurried to round the young man. He bowed, remarking the half buttoned coat, the soiled breeches that matched, the begrimed shoes and stockings. He noted as well that beneath the coat there was nothing but an undershirt badly in need of laundering. The woman was little better attired. The cloth of her dress was worn and faded from too many washings, the hem stained with old dirt and new. She wore a tattered sheet in place of a cape.

However the sorry state of the guests' apparel, the butler gave no indication anything was untoward when he spoke. It was no concern of his with whom his master conducted business, only that he served all with the same polite reticence. "If you would care to come this way?" he suggested. "I shall show you to the dining room. They are still within."

Kehfen crossed the threshold with Canella, who held the baby close. The infant was wrapped within a shawl so old the wool had felted. They halted behind Wilf. Kehfen kept an arm around his wife's waist and a hand on her elbow. She faced the butler, but her gaze darted in every direction. The last to enter, Olomo loomed at their back, a dark and drenched sentinel. A servant bowed to him and shut the door, blocking the sight of the carriage they had hired to transport the woman and child. Kehfen had been adamant that the rain should not touch his newborn daughter, and during their climb of the entrance steps, Olomo had taken the brunt of the storm on his back.

Wilf looked back at his father without speaking. Kehfen urged him on with a quick cant of his head. The young man nodded at the butler, who bowed again and led them up the hall and to a door on the right.

"The remaining members of the family," he announced to the master and stepped aside to let them pass. Marun rose from the table unhurriedly. Vik stood. Kehfrey imitated him, but Gamis remained seated, mimicking Nicky, for which Vik scowled at him momentarily.

"What's that?" Kehfrey said in surprise. "Where's Mum's stomach?"

"She had the baby, stupid," Gamis said.

Kehfrey gaped at his mother. "You had the baby without me!"

Canella, who had been staring fearfully at Marun, looked at Kehfrey and burst into tears. The child hastened around the table to her.

"I'm sorry, Mum! I didn't mean it!" He halted in front of her and stared at the bundle. He looked at his father.

"A sister," the man said, and Kehfrey grinned in brotherly triumph.

"Hanicke," Marun spoke. "Take the woman to a chamber. She should be resting."

Nicky had already risen, expecting just such a request. Her master had sounded polite enough, but he really didn't have the patience for a woman's trifling problems, childbirth being one of them in his mind. "Bring her this way," she said to Kehfen.

She brushed by Wilf just before passing out the door. Such muscles beneath that coat and only a wet shirt to hide them with. He was staring at her. She knew that stare. She stared back, just long enough for him to know he might be welcome.

Kehfen helped his wife follow Nicky into the hall and up the staircase. Kehfrey tagged after his mother. "When did you have the baby?" the boy asked.

"Very early this morning," his father answered. Canella still wept and showed no signs of stopping. Tears burdened the child's eyes from witnessing her misery.

"Kehfrey," Nicky called to him. "Go back to the kitchen. Tell cook to have a meal readied for her. Make sure there's hot soup. She needs fluids."

Kehfrey dashed down the stairs, grateful to be doing anything that might help his mother, but also thankful he had something else to do than blubber like an infant. He'd given up that sort of thing. Mostly. He never cried if he could help it. His brothers always teased him for it. Well, except Vik.

He arrived in the kitchen in seconds. "Mum needs hot soup!" he blurted to Evern. "And something to eat! And fluids!"

"Calm down, boy. I saw the baby. I peeked from the door to the hall. I have hot soup."

Kehfrey gaped at him and then grinned happily. "She had a sister! I mean she had *my* sister."

Cook laughed. "Well, of course. Congratulations."

Kehfrey's grin widened. "I'm a big brother now. Wilf can't call me baby anymore."

Cook smiled placidly and continued putting the tray of food together. Once this was accomplished, he weighed the platter experimentally. "No. Too heavy for you," he said to the child. "You take it," he ordered one of the household staff.

The young man slid off his chair and took the tray, though he did have a sullen look despite his alacrity. Kehfrey followed the servant out into the hall and up the stairs. The man paused at the top of the flight.

"Which one did they put your mum in?" he asked the boy.

"Don't know. Got sent down before I saw her go in."

Guessing that the remaining members of the boy's family would not be housed in rooms along the master's wing, the servant chose the hall opposite from Marun's chamber. A door opened as they tramped along, and Nicky looked out from a chamber and spotted them. She waved the servant forward and relieved him of the tray. He was quicker returning to the kitchen than departing from it, disappearing down the stairs before Nicky had so much as turned back in.

"Go give your mother a kiss, Kehfrey. Then take your father back down," Nicky directed on her way to a bedside table.

As Kehfrey approached his mother, Kehfen stood near the entrance and observed Nicky. He wondered if he should refuse to leave. His wife lay in the bed, covered for warmth, looking far too pale and drained of all strength. He disliked leaving her with this strange tiny woman who had traded a spelled stone for a knife. Why the woman should do such a thing mystified him. Her motivation was suspect. She could have been acting on her master's behalf. Kehfrey could have been the sorcerer's means to get at him and then Kortin. Despite his wealth of guile, the child was only seven, therefore a likely target, susceptible to ....

To what? The boy heard truths. The woman couldn't have lied to him. And the way she looked at Kehfrey didn't seem unkindly.

During his father's musings, Kehfrey had half crept on the bed. He leaned closer and kissed his mother on the cheek. Still despondent, she sobbed loudly and thrust a sheet over her lower face to hide her loss of control. She had the baby clutched at her side. Kehfrey looked at his sister's little face in awe.

"She's so small!" The tiny mouth scrunched up and then moved as if it were sucking. He watched, fascinated.

"Out you go," Nicky ordered. She set the tray down and approached. An amused, benign smile played over her lips.

"Can't I stay?" he pleaded.

"No. I need to see after your mum. She needs a wash. She needs to be checked over."

"For what?"

"Don't worry about it. I know what to do. I've done it hundreds of times."

He gaped at her. "Yourself! A hundred babies?"

She laughed. "No! Midwifing. I've had only twelve." She laughed again as he looked at her flat stomach in disbelief. "Out!" she repeated more firmly.

She gave him a determined shove toward his father. Kehfen still showed signs of rebellion, and she eyed him warningly. The thief decided against protesting. He really didn't want to see the bloody business women must deal with after a birth, and he just didn't feel any ill will from that woman. The boy arrived at his side, and Kehfen guided his son out by a shoulder and shut the door softly.

"She's an elf!" Kehfrey remarked brightly.

"What?" he said, startled.

"A half elf. And she doesn't have red hair." The child marched forward, but his father pulled him back.

"A half elf?" Well. That explained the diminutive, but perfect stature.

"Yes," Kehfrey confirmed. "Marun said so. But she won't tell me how old she is."

"What woman will?" Kehfen said dully. "A half elf. What a rarity."

Kehfrey nodded and started toward the stairwell a second time. "Just a word of warning, Pop," he said, looking behind. "Don't tell Marun your name if he asks. He uses names to enslave people. And don't go wandering, especially not below in the cellars."

"Why not?" his father asked, catching up.

"He's got dead people down there. You won't like it."

Kehfen loosed a disdainful snort. "I've seen dead people before. I've made a few of them."

"I know, but these ones still move, and not because they're crawling with maggots," his son said, stopping to peer solemnly at him. "Don't wander. They'll eat you."

Kehfen stared at him. "You're not telling me a story now, are you?"

"Not this time," the boy said. "Not this time." He continued down the stairs. "Make sure you let Wilf know if I forget. Gamis has already been warned, and Vik's seen them with me."

"Vik saw them? With you?"

"Marun took us down. Don't ask him to take you. You won't like what you see."

Kehfen had a terrible suspicion over what he might see. He considered asking Kehfrey about it, but by then they had reached the dining room. The child entered, bowed politely to Marun as he'd seen the butler do and led his father to a chair. Marun rose, as manners dictated towards guests, but he sat before Kehfen had finished seating himself.

Kehfen had never supped at a table like this. He looked uncertainly at Wilf, who was seated near him. Wilf had large helpings of food on his plate. Across the table, the Ysepian consumed servings of several different dishes, ignoring the cutlery and using his fingers and bread to sop up most everything. Kehfen would have done the same, but there was the matter of the cutlery, and unlike Olomo, he cared what this cold bastard of a man sitting at the head of the table thought of him. He wasn't just some lowborn filth who couldn't learn etiquette. And so he sat stiffly, waiting for a clue. The eldest boy soon gave him one.

"Serve yourself, Pop," Wilf said. "The butler left the dishes for us, since we didn't all come to sit at once."

Kehfen looked at the host warily. Marun eyed him without a motion. Frowning slightly, Kehfen reached for the nearest platter and pulled it over. He picked up the serving spoon and gave himself a healthy heap of whatever the dish was. It smelled heavenly.

"Chicken cooked with Midyin truffles," Vik informed him. He sat across the table next to Olomo, but had nothing left on his plate. He had finished eating and only remained at the table because of politeness. Kehfen looked up, his countenance freezing into cold denunciation. Vik, who'd had a rather tired expression on his face, went hot with shame.

"You broke a solemn oath," his father said flatly.

"I didn't mean to. I came with Lord Rhet to look at the place only. Rhet abandoned me here."

"If you hadn't come with that roach, you wouldn't have ended up here."

Vik's skin paled from red to white. After all that had gone on, after what Kehfrey had been through, the intolerance was too much. He rose and his chair crashed backward. "You son of a bitch! I didn't cause this mess! You did when you led Kehfrey here to his death! Have you seen the mark on his chest, Pop? It goes right out the other side!"

Kehfen glared at him for all of a second, but then averted his eyes, unable to shift the responsibility for their predicament away. He heard Kehfrey stomp away from the door. The child rounded the table, picked up the fallen chair and set it down.

"Right," he said. "No more useless fighting."

"Since when do you give orders?" Gamis hurled at him.

"Since he came here," Marun said.

Gamis gulped and huddled in his chair. Vik sat again, still refusing to look in the master's direction, but Wilf dared to stare openly at the sorcerer, his blue eyes frosty with challenge. Kehfen looked only at Kehfrey as the child took a seat next to Vik. When the boy's hazel eyes met those of his sire, Kehfen reddened and looked down at his plate.

His little boy had died. He'd died, and what had he done after? He had put his life on the line again to save them all. And all he, his father, could do was belittle Vik. Kehfen looked at the child once more.

"I'm sorry," he said softly. Kehfrey gave a pointed jerk of his head toward Vik. Kehfen looked cautiously at the older son. Vik looked back flatly.

"Don't bother," the youth said. He rose in a rush and stalked from the room. This time the chair managed to stay upright, but only because Kehfrey had caught the back with a hand.

"Shit," the boy whispered. He stood, but Marun waved him down. He sat again. His expression was mutinous, however.

"He doesn't need you to coddle him constantly," his master said. "Let him work it out."

"Work what out?" Wilf said. "How to tell you to bugger off?"

Marun focused on the young man. He hadn't missed the unspoken challenge earlier, but had waited for it to take a more definite form, which it just had.

"Tell me?" Wilf said. "This Lord Velmis? He invited me here earlier."

"An acquaintance owing a favour," Marun dismissed curtly. An old lover actually, but Velmis owed him for other favours received. He still owed. Marun lifted his wineglass and swirled the red liquid indolently. "Wilf, bastard son of Lord Ghemet," he recounted icily. "Your natural father was equally accomplished at wooing foolish women from their virtue." He sipped the wine. Wilf glared at him, his lips a white line on his face. "I think it's time you paid your maternal grandfather a visit, don't you?" Marun continued, undeterred by the young man's obvious wrath.

"And what would that accomplish?" Wilf snapped.

"Go and find out," he snapped in turn. "At the very least, he can look up at you from his sickbed and see what a beautiful bastard his daughter gave him as a grandson. He can't do much else."

Scepticism bittered Wilf's angry countenance. "I can't just visit him."

"Yes, you can," Marun countered. "You will go tomorrow. I will give you a letter of introduction."

Kehfrey laughed. His master cast a frosty glower at him.

"And what is so amusing?"

"That is." They all looked at him in disbelief. "Well, it is!" Kehfrey insisted. "Imagine: Wilf knocking on the great door of the castle, the bastard grandson introducing himself with a letter of introduction from the polite evil sorcerer taking over the city. They can't refuse, can they? Wilf will be seated in the great hall with the proper nephews, the proper wives and their proper children, and they'll have to pretend they aren't insulted. Every noble-born bastard from here to Midyi will want to get up on a table and cheer. I'd give my left nut to see the look on Lord Harte's face. Can I go with Wilf?"

"No," the sorcerer denied him. He lifted his wine glass to his lips, but Kehfrey caught the smile he hid behind it.

Wilf gaped at his little brother, at Marun, at Kehfen.

"Well, it just might work," Kehfen said. "The worst that can happen is he'll look you over and send you off again, but he might just decide to see your mother, if you mind the manners she taught you." The thief had already downed his wine in one great gulp. After speaking his piece, he looked around for another bottle.

"I'll get it," Kehfrey offered, guessing what he wanted. He went to the sideboard where several bottles rested in buckets of water. He managed to snag one while stretching up on his toes. He brought it to the table and handed Kehfen the bottle and a dagger.

"Where did you get this?" Kehfen demanded, the dagger an accusing point in his hand.

"Vik dropped it. I only kept it for him."

"You shouldn't be handling this!"

"Why the hells not? I'm not an idiot! There are boys my age with their own."

"You're half the size of most boys your age. You can't take on a boy your age, not the types who own a weapon like this. Best you run."

"I am not half the size! And I'm sick of running! I can handle a weapon as well as any!"

"Kehfrey—!"

"He's about to handle weapons daily," Marun coolly reminded the exasperated father. "Take the dagger back, Kehfrey. The proper tool for opening a bottle is a corkscrew. You will find it near the buckets."

120

While Kehfen stared at the sorcerer worriedly, Kehfrey nimbly lifted the dagger from his fingers. "He's only seven!" the thief protested.

"He only died this morning because you sent him down a chimney to thieve for you. You think teaching your son to burgle houses is any safer than what Olomo plans for him to learn? At least he will learn to fight and defend himself this way. He's right. There's only so much running anyone can do before he must turn to face his enemies."

Kehfrey put the corkscrew in his father's fingers. Kehfen looked at the tool stupidly and then silently worked it into the cork. He had nothing to say to the sorcerer's caustic retort. There was no defence against his folly, but it wasn't as if he'd had a choice. They were a family of thieves with obligations to their guild, gods damn it.

"By the way, Kehfrey? How did you survive the lit fire?" the sorcerer inquired.

"Potion against fire and smoke," the child said.

Marun looked at Kehfen, a brow lifted. "Who makes these potions for you?"

"I don't know. Hiswil gets them from Kortin. Kortin never tells anyone."

"Does this mean you have a rival?" Kehfrey asked Marun.

"It means I have someone to pull in."

Kehfrey didn't bother asking what he meant by that. He knew. Marun intended to gather a coven. "It tasted disgusting," he said instead. "Does it have to?"

Marun shook his head. "The witch can't know much."

"I suppose not," Kehfrey agreed.

Marun actually smiled again. Meanwhile, the boy's father tugged the cork out and served himself a glassful of wine. Without asking, Kehfrey fetched the bottle and presented it to his master, who accepted it and poured without comment.

"What is it that Rook took that you want back?" the boy asked.

"I will not discuss that," Marun said tightly.

Kehfrey frowned at him. Wilf dared to demand what his little brother wanted to know. "How can anyone find it if you don't say what it is?"

"It will be found when you find Rook!" Marun snapped. "The object and the thief will be together."

"You're so certain of that?"

Marun sent Wilf an icy stare. The room grew noticeably colder and the shadows thickened. Somewhere below them, a distant howl erupted from a human throat, only the cry didn't sound very human at all. Wilf jerked in alarm. He stood up from his seat and gaped at the thickening shadows.

"What was that?" he cried.

"A ghoul in the cellar!" Gamis shouted. He screamed and ran out of the room. They heard him thudding up the stairs, crying for his mother.

"Hells!" Kehfen hissed. "That's done it!" He stood hastily. "Excuse me," he said politely and rushed out the door after Gamis before he horrified his poor mother further.

Wilf gawped at Marun in dismay. He looked at Kehfrey quickly. The boy nodded affirmation to his silent question.

"Excuse me," he muttered thickly. He drank the last of his wine in one quick swallow and followed his stepfather out of the room. He would have to take Gamis off his hands. Kehfen would have enough to do calming Canella. As he left the dining area, he noted Vik standing in the middle of the hall and paused in mid-step. Vik regarded him impassively.

"Go back in!" Wilf hissed.

"Why?"

"He's your mark!" the young man whispered. For this, Vik grimaced at him. Wilf couldn't believe his stupidity. "Cussed shitting devils, Vik! Someone has to calm him down! Go in before the ghouls go on a rampage!"

"Bend over and do it yourself!"

"Shit!" Wilf said and stomped up the stairs.

Kehfrey appeared at the door of the dining room. "Do you know where my room is?" he asked. Vik shook his head. "Second on the right, back side of the house. Here." He said this while coming forward. "You dropped this." He held the dagger out to him.

"Keep it," Vik said. He had found it after Marun had parted from him in the bedroom earlier. He remembered thinking he could free his brother from this madness. He knew better now. "It's not much good for anything," he added angrily.

"You might need it later," Kehfrey protested.

"What the hells for?"

"Stabbing would-be admirers," Marun said, coming up behind Kehfrey. "Take it," he commanded.

Vik glared at him, and the shadows thickened once again, but he refused to relent. Ignoring the peril and Kehfrey's outstretched hand, he stalked up the stairs. Marun watched him until the bedroom door shut with a condemnatory thud.

Kehfrey sighed unhappily. "You should have asked him," he said softly.

"I'm not in the habit," his master snapped. "Go to bed!" He turned away and went back into the dining room.

"Can I learn some more letters first?" the boy asked.

Almost ready to burst with displeasure, Marun suddenly calmed. He nodded. "Wait in the library."

Kehfrey smiled and darted down the hall. Marun looked over at Olomo.

"You will start with the boy tomorrow," he commanded the assassin. "Do not plan on having him all day. I shall want him when I am available."

Olomo nodded acquiescence. He could hope for no more. He had lost the boy through his own folly. After Marun passed from view, the assassin

122

rose from the table. "Tomorrow," he whispered. "Tomorrow, the boy begins the path."

He left the dining room. A servant waiting surreptitiously in the hall came forward and bowed. "This way, if you please," the man said. Olomo followed him to his appointed room. He was glad to go. He was tired and needed rest. The boy must have all of his attention tomorrow.

***

"Enough," Marun decreed. "Your head is tipping over the parchment."

Kehfrey snapped upright with a start. There was ink on the tip of his nose. The blemish focused the sorcerer's gaze on the child's skin. Unlike most ginger-haired children, this child had not a freckle on his face. Marun didn't recall seeing any on his body either. But for the small scars the quarrel had created, which might fade over time, the boy seemed flawless.

"Go to bed," Marun said. "Doubtless you haven't slept properly since sometime yesterday. I'm surprised you can do anything, what with that and dying too."

Kehfrey blinked at him, his eyes owlish wide, and put the quill down. He slipped off the chair and walked quietly out of the room. He neglected to bow as he left.

Marun ignored the gaffe. He wasn't displeased with the child. The boy had spent the last hour astounding him, but he had hidden his admiration carefully. He seldom came across anyone worthy of his respect, but this peculiar child managed to pull the emotion from him, along with a bright note of astonishment and pleasure.

Odd how everything seemed darker now that he'd left the library. Marun couldn't attribute the obscurity to his shadows. They'd collapsed within minutes of commencing the boy's lesson. He remembered the strange attraction to light the child had displayed in the cellar, how he'd become a green imp in the dark, how his very emotions had scattered the witch light from his body. Odd. Very odd.

Novices apt to the earthly magics seldom drew the energy to them in such a fashion, out of the very air. It was the most sluggish manner in which to accrue power, unless one had sufficient to create a flow to begin with. Rather, they pulled it up from deep within the earth, generally through their feet and normally with the consent of the Goddess. Only a master already filled with the earth's potency could have done what the boy had done in the cellar, repulse a spell with but a thought.

But Kehfrey wasn't a master. He couldn't possibly be. Even so, that the boy had a gift for magnetising and repulsing power suggested he was strong enough to force a massive flow from the Great Mother. But that he suffered pain whenever spells were cast daunted the sorcerer's enthusiasm. Until he could explain that deficiency, Marun dared not begin educating the boy appropriately.

Pensively Marun looked down at the sheets of parchment the child had abandoned. Kehfrey could write simple sentences already. The letters were perfectly formed. There were a few spelling mistakes, to be sure, but the same error had never occurred twice, except for one particular case.

"The child is brilliant," he said.

He heard noise without, the clatter of hooves, wheels on gravel, a horse whinnying. He went to the window and peered out. A coach had stopped before the manor.

The butler's steps sounded in the hall. Marun heard him halt near the outer door, where he quite properly waited without opening it. The visitor must knock.

Marun turned away from the window. He didn't see the visitor alight from the coach, but he already knew who it would be. He returned to Kehfrey's work and admired it again.

The knock finally came, loud, urgent. He listened to the butler open the door. Once again the servant yelped as someone shoved him aside impatiently. Marun smiled, but the smile was sinister. His visitor rushed past the library door, but skidded to a halt upon spying the master within.

"Marun!" Lord Rhet gasped. He thrust into the library. "Marun! He died! He died horribly! What have you done?"

Marun looked at Rhet. The nobleman was a mess. His hair was uncombed. His kohl had bled around his eyes and dripped down his cheeks. His red and orange suit had the stains of bodily fluids on it, perhaps vomit, perhaps other liquids.

"Marun! You promised to save him!"

"Lolte died," Marun said flatly. "Your uncle's office is hereditary. You are now the Minister of Justice."

Rhet gaped at him. His mouth worked without a noise coming from it. Slowly he sat in an armchair. "Why?" he said. "You promised!"

"Your uncle promised also. Quite obviously he betrayed me. The stone killed him for it."

"Betrayed you? But ...!"

"Your uncle pointed the finger at the wrong person and you helped him," Marun said. Rhet started and his eyes widened with fear. Marun's lips turned down with distaste. "Tonight you will search for all his files concerning Kortin and the Syndicate and send them to me."

"But ...! But I don't want to be Minister!" Rhet cried.

"Sorry to have ruined your days of unending play." He stalked toward the nobleman. Rhet flinched backward into the cushions. A foul odour became perceptible. Rhet stank abominably. "Did you hold him as he died, Rhet?" Marun said, halting near him. "Did his guts spill onto you? Did he wretch his lungs out onto your tunic?"

Rhet gaped at him and shivered. The shadows in the room lengthened, deepened, threatened to surround them. Several of the glow sticks dimmed and then died, the biotic liquid curdled within the glass tubes. Rhet stared at the sorcerer, blank fear in his eyes.

"Tomorrow you will be approached by the Syndicate, Rhet. You will agree to do whatever they tell you, only you will be mendacious. Isn't that right, Rhet?"

"Yes," he whispered.

"Do you know why you will be mendacious?" Marun asked him.

"Because I don't want to die," he whispered.

"At least not like your uncle," Marun amended for him. He walked back to the window. "I killed your uncle because he betrayed me outright. But you? I decided to forgive you this time. Just this once. Don't expect me to do it again." He looked at Rhet from a distance. "If you see the beauty again, be sure to thank him for your life. He's the only reason I decided to spare you. You have good taste."

Rhet nodded silently.

"Leave, Rhet," Marun commanded. The lord rose obediently and headed for the door. "A moment!" the sorcerer snapped.

Rhet froze. He stared at the doorway like a man waiting for the axe.

"Take that chair with you. You've ruined it," Marun spat.

Quaking now, Rhet returned to the armchair. It was a heavy piece of furniture. He attempted to lift it, but found his unworked muscles useless for the task. He was forced to drag it from the room. He sobbed every time the legs screeched on the wooden floor. Marun watched him go in perfect, fascinated silence. After one particularly loud screech of wood on wood, Rhet added a bodily stain of his own to his suit. A puddle of urine formed between his shaking legs. Mortified, Rhet yanked the chair through the door, sliding it through his urine and out of sight. After that, the butler must have taken pity on the man, because there were no further dragging noises.

Marun turned to the window and watched the pair appear on the stairs outside. The butler held one side of the chair, Rhet the other. They carried it to the coach together, splashing through puddles and blinking away rain. The footmen came off their steps and gaped at the piece of furniture in amazement. Marun turned away in disinterest. He walked back to the desk and looked down at the child's handwriting.

Every error corrected but one. He regarded the one mistake, the one mistake repeated tenaciously. He floated his finger across the word and read it softly.

"Kahfrey."

He smiled. He had clearly shown the boy how to spell it, even acceding to Winfellan custom and adding the unnecessary silent consonant to the appellation; but the child had altered the first vowel every time. Every single time.

Marun's finger drifted off the name. He left the desk and walked out of the library, careful to step over the urine, and headed for the stairs. On the second floor, he paused just outside the child's door and stared at it. His expression betrayed momentary irritation. He averted his face, but remained at the door.

What did they look like sleeping together? One angelic, one—

He remembered the child's unconscious face earlier that day. Both angelic, he amended to himself, but the younger of them had a will of steel. He would have to be careful. Steel needed to be fired just so. Then it would fold like a blade of grass.

He walked away from the door and on to his room. He knew how to wait.

***

Pressed up against the child's side, staring at the further wall blindly, Vik shuddered involuntarily. The footsteps in the corridor began again. The sound receded. Even so, he shivered with apprehension. One of Kehfrey's skinny arms wrapped around him, and Vik gasped like a captured bird, his breath almost whistling inward.

"It's all right," the boy whispered. "He promised to leave you be tonight. Go to sleep."

"I thought you were sleeping."

"I was until you turned into a board," the child said sarcastically. Vik shifted away in embarrassment.

"Not that! All of you. You're tense as a primed crossbow."

"I'm sorry," Vik whispered and began to weep.

Kehfrey put an arm around him again. Time for a distraction, he thought; but this day of peril and radical change had rather fixed his brother's predicament in the boy's mind. Sensuality. Coupling. Adult mysteries. Adult miseries.

"What's it like?" he said abruptly.

"What's what like?" Vik managed to utter.

"Fornication?"

Vik laughed in surprise and lost a little more of the tension that had arisen while waiting on the master's decision outside the door. "You're too young, Kehfrey." He wiped his tears away and sniffed.

"I still want to know."

"How can I explain it? It's different for everyone."

"Really? Why?"

"It's like food. Some people like the taste of some things more than others."

"Sex is like pie," Kehfrey uttered then.

Vik laughed again, unable to help himself. "You're a wonder, Kehfrey."

"I was just beginning to notice," the boy retorted. He yawned mightily. "If you quit reminding me, I'll be able to forget again."

"Do you want to?"

"Would you go back to yesterday if you could?"

"Yes," Vik whispered.

"Me too," Kehfrey whispered back. "We were safer."

"No one's safe now. Not with him here."

126

Kehfrey was silent, but he agreed. Marun wanted this city. From there, he would probably just keep on with it, over the years collecting more cities until a hero rose up to stop him. That's what the evil enchanters did in all the stories. It's what they did. Pity the poor heroes. Most of them got banged up but good.

***

The following day, Olomo awakened Kehfrey before the sun rose. Kehfrey's first perception of him came as a cool breeze over his face. He opened his eyes to find the assassin looking at him from the open door. Kehfrey blinked. Olomo left the room without a word.

Kehfrey sighed in resignation, edged out from beneath Vik's arm and slid off the bed. He snatched his clothes from a chair and retreated into the hall with them. He shut the door softly and dressed on the polished wood of the corridor floor while Olomo stood on the steps and watched. When the child had finished, the tall man proceeded down the stairs without a sound. Kehfrey matched his silence and followed.

From the entrance hall, they turned toward the kitchen. Kehfrey hoped they were going to have breakfast, but Olomo altered course before they reached the kitchen corridor and led him toward double doors. Kehfrey shortly found himself standing in a very large bare room.

"What's it for?" he said, thinking such an expansive chamber a waste of space.

"Parties," Olomo answered him. "Dancing. Frivolities."

Kehfrey looked about in wonder. Parties. Frivolities. Dancing. Despite Olomo's deprecating tone, he liked the sound of those words.

"This is where we will begin training," Olomo continued. "And your first task will be to stand and not move." He glowered at Kehfrey pointedly. The child had been whirling slowly as if listening to music in his mind. Kehfrey let his arms drop and faced his trainer.

"For how long?" he said.

"You will not question!" Olomo snapped.

Kehfrey sighed once again and then settled into a comfortable stance. Olomo walked around him and out of sight, where he scrutinized the child meticulously. The boy was balanced, with no signs of disproportion to his shoulders or his limbs. A rarity. His undersized stature was unfortunate, but there were also advantages to this. For an assassin, size wasn't all that necessary and sometimes a detriment.

Olomo stepped to the side of his student. "We begin," he said. "You will do as I do."

He commenced the First Manoeuvre. Kehfrey rounded to the front for a better view, watched Olomo and then attempted to mimic his stylistic motions.

"No!" said the assassin. "You are not a mirror. Use the same arm as I do. The same leg. The same hand."

"Can I stand behind you, then?" the child said.

"I cannot see you behind me," Olomo barked. "I do not have a second teacher to watch your efforts. For this first lesson, you will stand to the side."

The child was difficult. Did he not know the honour he was receiving, learning the ways of Pek when he was no longer of an age to begin? And a complete stranger to the faith! To any faith! Little infidel!

"You will not question my instructions again. What I teach has been passed down in like fashion for centuries."

The child's expression tightened into a mulish glower. "Hi, now! I don't see you looking in that box yet? Who's to say it was done right to begin with?"

Olomo's eyes widened in outrage. He stepped forward to punish the brat, but a lilting feminine laugh echoed through the ballroom and forestalled the motion. He whirled toward the small stage built for musicians. Nicky stood upon it, dressed in boy's clothing. She hadn't been there seconds earlier.

"From the mouths of the innocent, assassin! 'From the mouths of the innocent, the truth can be heard. Listen!'"

"You! Filth! You will not speak the holy words of Amut!"

"Why not? He taught them to me."

Olomo straightened. His expression betrayed disbelief.

"You think I lie? Ask the boy." She looked toward Kehfrey. "Did I lie?"

"No," he said firmly. Olomo turned away from both, but Kehfrey caught a look of confusion cross his face before he stalked away. Nicky jumped down from the stage and walked toward the child. "How'd you get in here?" Kehfrey asked. "I didn't see the doors open. There's nowhere to hide."

"Maybe I was invisible," she tested him.

"Now you *are* lying. Come on! How did you do it?"

"There's an elven path leading out of the house right up there on the stage," she said. "From there, it goes to a house in the city, and from that to another up the hill."

At this, Olomo presented her with a suspicious look. She taunted him with a superior smirk. "This was how you stole the Vessel!" he guessed.

"Of course. I couldn't have gotten past the Pek Tom wards and guards otherwise. I'm not *that* good."

He stepped forward, his expression suddenly calm. "You have given me a gift. Now we know the weakness that led to the loss of the Vessel."

"Now *you* know," she retorted. "Unless you make it back to another faction, no one else will."

"I will return with this knowledge," he assured her flatly.

"What's an elven path?" Kehfrey piped up.

Nicky looked down at the curious child and smiled. He was such a sweet-faced gamin, but with a soul of fire. She knew this was so, because he was a troublesome little mutt of a boy, but she liked mongrels. Every

128

valued breed could be traced to some handsome bastard line that had shown a usefulness that could not be denied. Though the boy wasn't technically a bastard, every noble house would view him as such. His father was as lowborn as they came. Well, too bad for them. The lower classes had won a coup without trying, to have this boy amongst their number. No matter how much influence he gained, Nicky didn't think he was the type to forget his beginnings and ignore his equals.

"It's a path only the elves can see," she said. "Shortcuts from one place to another. They're odd things, the ones in buildings at least. They can exist for as long as the house, then up and disappear when the structure does. The ones outside seem to have existed forever and never disappear."

"That's how the notes appear at Kortin's villa, then," the boy said. "You take them. Did you just take another?"

"The boy is quick," Olomo remarked, to which Nicky nodded wryly.

"What was the note about this time?" Kehfrey asked.

"That is not for you to discuss," his master's voice issued from the door.

They all spun to stare at him. He stood just inside the ballroom, in his habitual drab colours and wearing his usual impenetrable expression. He jerked his head at Nicky and walked away. Nicky hurried after him until they were both out of view. Kehfrey looked up at Olomo. Olomo looked down at him, his brows furrowed with worry.

"He frightens me too," the child whispered.

Olomo glared in outrage, but rather than voicing his discontent, he turned his back on Kehfrey and began the First Manoeuvre a second time, obviously expecting the child to mimic the motions. Grinning hugely, Kehfrey copied him. They were in the ballroom and they were dancing; only Olomo didn't seem to know it.

***

Much later, Olomo saw fit to visit the dining room with Kehfrey, where they seated themselves with the male members of the boy's family for the purpose of breakfast. The sun had risen hours ago. Olomo had only called a halt to training when the butler had announced they were holding up breakfast for the others. The sorcerer was not present, having given permission for the meal to start without him.

Other than needing to build his strength and to expand the stretch of certain muscles, Kehfrey had proven he was destined to be an assassin. He had learned the First Manoeuvre the first time Olomo had performed it completely. He had then learned the Second Manoeuvre and the Third. He had danced them all and, even when his trainer had demanded he quicken the pace, had executed the moves with exceptional skill. The Ysepian was satisfied with the child's progress. He was more than satisfied. He felt serene again and he had not felt that way for months.

"So, then?" Gamis said. He had piled so many servings on his plate, Kehfrey didn't think he'd be able to eat it all, but it sure looked like he was trying. "Are you really training to be an assassin?"

"Yes," Kehfrey answered. He had a pie in front of him. A whole pie just for him. A meat pie. Except for having a brooding raven of a master and a rather cantankerous combat trainer, he was in heaven.

"Can you toss a knife now?" Gamis pressed.

"Haven't had the lesson yet," Kehfrey said around a mouthful.

"You can't toss a knife? What sort of assassin are you going to be? Are you going to kiss your victims and make them cry?"

Kehfrey ignored him and savoured another bite of pie.

"Where's that beauty from last night?" Wilf said.

"You mean Nicky," Vik responded.

"Yeah, her. Where is she?"

"With Marun," Kehfrey mumbled. More pie. More heaven.

"Shit! Does he do both, then?"

"I don't think so," Vik said flatly. This morning he was not his usual impeccable self. He had dark circles beneath his eyes. His apparel was rumpled and his hair had flattened against his head. He needed a bath. He was afraid to take one. When he had awakened alone in the room, he had almost panicked. He'd remained huddled in the bed until Gamis had made noises outside the door, scratching at it for attention. He had let his brother in, for once thankful for his company, annoying or not. Gamis had been his unwitting security since.

"So she's available?" Wilf continued. He still wore only a coat above his undershirt and trousers. The coat gaped wide and his undershirt was unlaced because he was too hot. The room faced east and the sun had already heated it abominably. Despite yesterday's rain, it looked as if they were in for more high temperature and humidity.

"What do you mean by available?" Nicky asked from the door.

Wilf turned, startled. He blushed like an innocent, which elicited a smile from the woman and coarse laughs from both Gamis and Kehfen. Still in boy's clothing, Nicky sauntered in. The trousers were tight. Every male eye but two watched her hips as she moved to take a seat. She smirked at the men while settling. She knew exactly where they'd been looking. The only one who hadn't watched had been Kehfrey. His eyes were almost in that pie.

"Kehfrey, don't swallow it with your eyes," she called. "Waste of good food. Eyes can't taste."

He looked up, grinning around a forkful. She couldn't help but laugh. He was adorable. Devilish, but adorable.

"How did training go?" she asked, ignoring the rest of the staring males.

He swallowed and answered. "Learned to dance three manoeuvres."

"It is not dancing!" Olomo snarled.

"Is too!" he riposted.

130

Olomo was about ready to smack him and then changed his mind. "Is that how you see it?" he said.

The child nodded. "Perfect room to practice in too."

"Just wait till I put you on the roof!" Olomo muttered beneath his breath. His brief moment of serenity had vanished. The impossible child had popped the bubble.

Kehfrey heard and his eyes widened. "Really? Can we go after breakfast? I love roofs! There's never any shit on roofs. Well, except bird shit and sometimes rat droppings. Better than people shit, mind."

Olomo rolled his eyes in exasperation, but Nicky laughed in delight. She, with her elven hearing, had also caught what the assassin had threatened. Olomo ignored her and looked at Kehfrey's father for help.

"Get used to it," Kehfen told him. "Every one of the guild masters either praised him to heaven or pulled their hair out in desperation trying to find something he couldn't do. And no amount of threats keeps him off roofs." Nicky laughed again. Kehfen eyed her in wry amusement. "You think you'd fare any better with him?" he said.

"Oh, I learned yesterday," she assured him. "He thinks quicker than a drugged-out gnome and spits out questions faster than a man with the flu shits."

Everyone in the room roared with mirth except for Kehfrey. He scowled at his pie and killed it off determinedly. Is that what she thought? That he spewed nonsense? Fine! He just wouldn't speak to her, then. He looked at his empty plate furiously. No more pie. Heaven had fallen into his stomach and disappeared. Feeling very unappreciated, he looked out the window at the brightly lit garden.

"Hi!" he cried, losing his bad humour. "There's a door made of glass!" He hadn't seen it last night. The curtains had been drawn. And when he'd come in for breakfast, only the pie had done for his eyes, but now he rushed from his chair to take a closer look at the amazing find. He darted over to the door, found the crystal knob and turned it. Remembering his duty, he looked back at Olomo questioningly.

"Go. But come back when I call," the man said.

Kehfrey grinned and pulled the door open, but then took a moment to goggle at all the prismatic lights coming off a picture etched in the glass.

"Leave it open," Wilf called. "Bloody sweating like a pig in here."

"So take your coat off," Nicky suggested softly. She looked at his chest with a warm gleam in her eyes, and Wilf's lips turned up in an answering smile of anticipation.

Kehfrey, yet standing within the entrance, noticed the silent signals, scowled furiously and stomped out into the garden. Now he *really* wasn't going to talk to her. Ever! Maybe never to Wilf too. Gods busted turd always had to show him up!

"Wait up," Vik called to him. Kehfrey ignored his brother's request and continued thumping away.

"I'm coming too," Gamis said and dashed after Vik.

"That's a good idea. Too hot in here," Nicky said. She grabbed a tart from the table and followed the boys out.

Wilf gaped after her and then stood hastily. "See you, Pop," he said.

Nicky turned at the door. "Oh, no," she denied him. "You have a suit waiting for you upstairs."

"A suit?" he said in confusion.

"That's right. A loan from Marun," she explained. Wilf scowled darkly. "Don't worry," she continued. "I picked it. This one will look good on you. I ordered a bath. Go upstairs. Clean up. You have an appointment to keep." She turned her back on him and strolled out into the open air, biting into the tart as she departed.

"Crud," Wilf hissed.

"The game's not over," Kehfen said, smirking at the youth.

Wilf's usual sparkle returned and he smiled jauntily. With a last look out the window at the next of his conquests, he marched into the hall. Kehfen turned his head to peer outside. Nicky looked back through the glass at Wilf's retreating back. The expression Kehfen caught on her face startled him. Her attention swerved toward him. She surveyed him with almost the same sort of intensity as she'd done Wilf and then smirked and disappeared around a rose bush.

"Well, now," Kehfen said in surprise.

"What?" Olomo said.

"I swear she had the same look on her face as Wilf usually has," he said. "You know? That self-satisfied *I've got you* look."

"She is half elf," Olomo said flatly.

"And what's that got to do with it?"

"Your son is but one of many to her. *She* is centuries old. He is only another toy. It is how their kind think of humans."

"How do you know that?"

"There is a tribe near the Fortress of Pek Tom," Olomo told him. "Their attitude toward us became evident to me when I was younger." He glanced back at the open door. The woman was too distant to hear him. "She had the points of a true elf back then. The legend describes the thief as pure-blooded. That she is not and far from any tribe speaks much of her character. I did not take her for an elf at first for this reason. The half-blooded are not permitted to wander."

"Is she from this tribe in Ysep, you think?"

"No, not her. The tribe near us has darker skin like mine. She is a North Easterner, like you."

Kehfen considered this revelation. If Olomo was correct about elven predilections, Wilf was about to learn he could be a trophy. Kehfen wondered how he'd take it.

***

132

"I've caught a frog!" Kehfrey ran toward Vik with the creature in his hands, but was so excited he tripped in his haste. He stumbled and fell on his front, but he didn't lose the frog. "Look!" he squeaked.

Vik, laughing at his capers, walked up to him and bent down. "That's not a frog."

"Is so!" Kehfrey closed his hands on the creature before it leapt away.

"No. It's a toad," Vik corrected. "Look again. Frogs have bigger hind legs. Their skin is smoother."

"Whatever it is, it pissed on me!" the boy said happily. By now up on his knees, he peeked in at his prize. He squeezed his wet hands around the toad. It had tried to jump out.

"I want to see," Gamis said, coming up to their sides.

"It's a toad," Kehfrey said proudly.

"Let me see," Gamis insisted. Kehfrey opened his fingers warily. Gamis slapped his wrists and the toad shot out.

"Gamis!" Kehfrey hollered.

Gamis hooted and dashed after the creature. "My toad now!" he bellowed nastily.

"No!" Kehfrey darted after him, determined not to let Gamis catch his pet, but the toad had other ideas and leapt to safety beneath a bush.

"Quick! Head it off!" Gamis called.

Kehfrey ran around the shrub and squatted on all fours to peer under it. He saw something slither away. On the other side of the bush, Gamis shrieked in terror.

"Snake!" he screamed. He ran back to the house in a big hurry.

"You can have the toad!" Kehfrey shouted at his retreating back. He dashed around the bush and went after the snake instead. Wasn't this exciting? A garden filled with creatures! He had just followed the snake to another bush when a set of hands dragged him back.

"No, you don't," Nicky said.

"Let go!" he howled.

"Kehfrey! That was an asp!"

The boy ceased struggling and straightened himself. "What's an asp?" he asked.

"A very poisonous snake."

"Really? How do you catch them, then?"

"Kehfrey! You don't!" She pulled him away from the bush to a safer location. City children! They were so stupid when it came to wildlife. She knelt before him. "Kehfrey, promise you won't try catching one." He scowled rebelliously at her. "If you don't promise, I'll tell Marun you're bent on committing suicide," she threatened.

Kehfrey sighed, utterly vexed. "All right. I promise not to try and catch one. Until I know how!" Upon issuing this hastily appended qualifier, he ran off as fast as his skinny legs could carry him.

"Kehfrey!" she shouted after him.

Vik stepped up to her side, looking after his brother worriedly. "Nothing stops him once his mind's made up."

"That's what I'm concerned about," she said.

"If there is a way to go about catching a poisonous snake, you might want to let him learn."

Nicky looked at the youth in astonishment.

"It's better than leaving him go off unprepared," he explained. Her expression turned thoughtful. He looked away. Kehfrey had found a long stick and now poked beneath every bush he came across.

"You're very beautiful," Nicky said.

Vik glanced at her in surprise. "I've been told that. But not usually by a woman."

"Do you talk with any much?"

"No," he admitted.

She surprised him with an unexpected question. "Will you listen to my advice?"

He looked at her warily. "What sort of advice would you give me?"

"The sort that comes from living some nine hundred years," she told him. He regarded her silently and then nodded his head once. "Don't cower from Marun in the bedchamber. If you enjoy him, let yourself go."

"What? Why?" Her words astounded him. This was advice?

"There's no point in guilt, Vik," she said flatly. "There's no point in it at all. It's a completely useless emotion for a slave. Do you understand? Don't regret. Don't feel guilt."

She walked away from him. He stared after her, stunned. In the distance, he heard Olomo shout Kehfrey's name. Kehfrey pulled out from beneath a bush and dashed toward the assassin.

"Got to go, Vik," he cried.

He caught up with Nicky, who was on her way back to the house as well. He raced past her without a word. Nicky halted in her tracks and stared after him. When she began walking again, her pace was slower. Vik stared after both, frowning. It was strange, really. In his own childish way, Kehfrey had said the same thing to him last night.

"Maybe I should stop busting myself up over it," he whispered. After all, he seemed to be the only one who was.

He scowled. None of the others was on Marun's sexual menu. What did they know?

The image of the man filtered through his thoughts. Marun's face, Marun's scarred back. He shivered beneath the hot sun and then turned away from the house and drifted deeper into the garden.

Snakes were safer company.

***

In the manor, the master stood before the window of his workroom and looked down on the garden. Vik was alone. Vik was alone, and he had no time to go to him. Angrily he spurned the view and returned to the table with the single object on it—a wine bottle with an elegant label.

"Pehtre Vineyards," he whispered.

He touched the label lightly and then dropped his hand away. Rook had drunk from this bottle. His spit had lathered the glass mouth, had mixed with the dregs of the wine. Marun bent over the open neck and breathed the scent from it. The residue of the wine had soured inside. He straightened slowly.

Without a name to add to the spit, the bottle hadn't been of much use to him. It had become somewhat more useful last night. He could not enslave Rook with a name passed to him offhandedly. For that, a name had to be acquired with purpose. Still, a name passed along second hand, so to speak, had its uses. With it, Rook could be found. Marun smiled viciously.

He glanced toward the fireplace. The ward to keep out thieves danced as strongly as when he'd spelled it into existence last night. This time he'd set the fiery dervishes marching about the andiron. Satisfied, he picked the bottle up and left the room. The magic upon the door sealed it behind him. He had learned his lesson. His workroom would not be violated again, by window, door, or chimney. Especially by chimney.

He headed down the hall. He had slaves to educate. They would taste the spit of their next victim, the spit on the bottle mouth, the spit in the dregs. They would hear the name of their next meal. Tonight his ghouls would hunt.

***

Wilf was already in the tub when the knock sounded at his door. He looked up and scowled at Gamis. Unfortunately they were sharing the room. Wilf had begun his bath listening to his brother ranting about toads, snakes and that miserable Kehfrey, who'd sicced a venomous asp on him.

"Answer the door," he snapped at the disgruntled boy.

"It's just another servant. Get in here, then!" Gamis shouted toward the entrance.

Wilf's glower strengthened. Gamis! He was common through and through.

The door opened and it wasn't a servant. It was the woman.

Wilf froze with an arm lifted. His other hand had been scrubbing his armpit. She looked at him and smiled in appreciation and then stepped in the room without any evidence of discomfort over his nakedness. Once within, she eyed Gamis pointedly. Gamis looked back blankly and didn't catch on. Sighing, she walked over to him, took his hand and pulled him off the bed.

"Where are we going?" he said stupidly.

"*You* are going out," Nicky told him firmly.

"Me?"

"Yes." She deposited him out in the hall and shut the door on his gaping face. The last he saw of Wilf, his brother was smiling exactly like she had been.

***

A hired coach arrived later in the morning. The butler opened the manor door to find a hesitant cabby standing before it.

"What is it?" the servant demanded.

"I was told to bring some parcels here," the man said.

"From whom?"

"Can't say. Was hired by some fellow in quite a dither. Said to say your master was expecting the parcels. Said it was reading material."

The butler then understood what the parcels contained. "Very well," he said. "Bring them in."

The cabby returned to his coach and hauled the packages out. There were four in total, two of them quite heavy. The butler tipped the man for his effort, ushered him out and directed two underlings to carry the parcels into the library. Marun would be informed once he'd finished with his business in the wine cellar. In the meantime, the butler was anxious to get the master's bedchamber in order. He knew he'd be in for it if the chamber weren't ready before the sorcerer pulled his sweet fresh piece back in there.

"Better the blond whore than one of us," he whispered.

Now that Simre was gone, the master's attention would wander again, unless that beautiful youth managed to keep him distracted, a circumstance for which the butler prayed fervently. He hurried the two younger servants along as soon as they were done in the library. They were of the same mind as him and rushed up to the bedchamber eagerly for once, knowing none of them would be called back into it later, so long as the new trick was handy.

"Let's get a bath prepared for him," one of them whispered as they passed the guest chamber, the only one of the rooms on the master's side of the manor that housed members of the invading family. They looked inside the chamber at the rumpled bedding they had earlier pulled down for airing. Not one of them mistook the speaker's pronoun to mean the master.

"Good idea," the butler said. "Go back down and have cook boil the water."

As eagerly, the fellow retreated down the stairs.

***

Kehfrey turned up in the dining room for the noon meal feeling displeased. Olomo had spent the rest of the morning boring him with

136

circuitous fables and sacred quotations from Holy Amut and some other religious prophet of the Pek who happened to be named Pek, naturally. Olomo had required him to repeat the fables and quotes verbatim. Eventually as the lesson had progressed, he'd dared to ask the assassin why the stories were necessary to his training. Olomo had promptly called him a sacrilegious infidel.

"Your spiritual education must progress in unison with your physical prowess," he had uttered sharply. "You will not reach Ishpaäf as an imbecile."

"If that's true, why don't you just look in the box yourself?" Kehfrey had demanded. "You already know this stuff!"

Olomo had glowered and begun another fable. Kehfrey had listened carelessly at that point and received a backhand for repeating it incorrectly.

"That's it!" he had shouted, picking himself off the floor in a fury. "I bet you looked in the box already and didn't find any Ishpaäf!"

Olomo had sent him tumbling a second time. That time, when Kehfrey had picked himself up, he'd caught a trace of bewilderment mixed with the anger on his trainer's face.

"I guessed right!" he'd bellowed. "You smack me again and I'll shut my trap if I ever figure this Ishpaäf out!"

"How can I teach you if you show no respect for the words of the Holy Teachers?" Olomo had protested.

"You think smacking me on the head will make me change my mind?" he had retorted hotly. "I'm not some stupid little twit! I have opinions! Obviously that's why your cussed holy leader told you I'd figure it out!"

At that point, Olomo had flatly told him to go eat lunch. Kehfrey had stomped away, and Olomo had remained standing in the ballroom, staring down at his feet and scowling fit to catch the floor on fire. Kehfrey hoped the man had his head on straight by the time the training recommenced, but for now, here he was in the dining room too early.

"Crud," he said. There wasn't even a scrap of food anywhere or anyone to talk with.

He left the room and went off to the kitchen. As he expected, the majority of the servants were to be found within. Although the kitchen staff rushed about to get lunch ready, they were working very quietly.

"Why so hushed?" he asked.

"Master's in the cellar," the cook said. He turned back to the fireplace and tasted the soup to which he'd been adding salt

Too curious for his own good, Kehfrey determined to visit Marun and see what he was up to with the ghouls. No one said a word as he left the kitchen by the wrong door. They had surmised already that he was a peculiar child, chosen to be the master's protégé. None of them knew what to do about him really, so they just let him go. If the master didn't like his presence in the cellar, the boy would know soon enough, likely to his detriment.

Kehfrey discovered the cellar door wide open. Down he went, peeking beneath the steps before he got too far in, disliking the idea of something dead grabbing his ankle from below. He heard noises deeper within the dark and squinted ahead. A shadow approached him. He prepared to flee back up into the light, but the shadow turned into his master.

"What are you doing here?" Marun said.

"Seeing what you're doing. Do you feed them? Do the dead need to be fed?"

"Not really," Marun responded. "But they have an urge to eat."

He turned and went back whence he'd come. Kehfrey took that for an invitation and darted after him, keeping close on his heels. Marun didn't bother to create a witch light for the child this time, nor did Kehfrey beg from him the service. He let his eyes adjust to the dimness and peered into the dark warily. The blackness didn't seem as terrible as it usually did. He decided Marun must not be casting those menacing shadows.

The sorcerer halted. Kehfrey bumped into him, but wasn't rebuked. He peeked forward from behind the man's shielding body. The ghouls huddled near the back of the cellar. There were more than two. It was hard to discern the exact number in the gloom, but he thought there might be six. No. Make that four whole and three not-so-complete ghouls.

A foul stench wafted toward him. It wasn't so bad as to make him retch just yet, but he thought he might if one came closer. A few must have been dead for quite some time.

"What are they doing?" he whispered.

"Smelling their next victim's scent," Marun said. His voice echoed back to Kehfrey's ears from both sides of the long, low chamber. The boy knew for certain, then, that there weren't many unnatural shadows. When the sorcerer cast those, echoes were eaten.

"How do they go about doing that? Can they smell so well?"

"It's not so much Rook's scent as his spiritual emanation. I gave them the bottle Rook left here."

"Oh. I take it the negotiations I mentioned are scrapped for the moment?"

Marun laughed in the darkness. The ghouls paused and looked toward him expectantly. "Rook!" he said. "Smell him! Learn his scent! Taste him!"

The abominations huddled over the bottle again, and for a time, Kehfrey watched them pass the glass back and forth. There was no order to their motions. They handed the bottle across the circle randomly. Sometimes the one who had just smelled and tasted the glass took it back again. Sometimes they passed it along the circle one way and then suddenly reversed the direction. Whatever the case, they performed the strange task in gruesome silence.

"How long have they been doing that?" Kehfrey asked after many minutes had passed.

"A few hours," Marun said.

"Why?"

138

"Their brains are dead. They don't think so quickly anymore. I have one victim in mind for them. To keep them focused, they will need to be at the scent of his spiritual residue for the rest of the day."

"It's a wonder they think at all, then."

"I don't know that they do," Marun said flatly. "But something moves them."

"You don't know what?" the boy asked in surprise.

"No," he admitted.

"Then how do you control them?"

"With my will," he said darkly. "With my will."

Kehfrey frowned. Will? Was that all there was to magic? Didn't a witch need spells? He vocalized these thoughts. "Don't you need spells, too?"

"Sometimes," the sorcerer said. "Sometimes not. It depends really. A spell is a means of focusing. A good spell will call power toward you, but if you don't have your own power, your own inner strength, a spell will forever be useless."

Power. Kehfrey looked at the ghouls. There was a power in them, wasn't there? It moved their dead bodies. "What happened to their souls?" he asked.

Marun laughed. "Who cares?"

"They did."

Marun was silent a moment. "Do your parents take you to church, Kehfrey?" he said presently

"No," the boy replied.

"Then why worry about souls?"

"I don't know. It just crossed my mind when you mentioned power."

"I mention power and you think souls?"

"Isn't it the soul that carries the will? Shouldn't the power collect to it?"

Once again, for several seconds Marun stood without responding, and then he knelt at the child's side. "You're right, of course," he told him.

"Am I? Does that surprise you?"

"Why do you ask that?"

"Because you aren't towering over me." Kehfrey could barely see the man, just a glint of light reflecting in his eyes. Marun's hand touched his face. Fingers crossed his lips and slipped past his cheek. They came to rest in the hair at the back of his head, cool on his scalp, but with such a power beneath, a strange energy that wasn't all darkness and chill. Warmth. Human warmth mixed with inhuman potency.

How very odd. If the sorcerer wasn't darkness and chill, from where did he pull the shadows?

"Why aren't you afraid to be down here?" Marun whispered into the silence.

"Because you're here," he said softly.

Marun's hand slowly dropped away. He stood and looked toward the ghouls. "You're quite correct. There is the power of one's own soul, but there is also power that can be gathered."

"From where?"

"From everywhere, but most particularly from the earth. You had better leave now."

"Why?"

"I'm about to bind them with a spell to keep them working at their lesson. You'll just hurt your head listening. I have yet to know why that is so with you."

The boy slipped away. Soon after, the light from the door dimmed, blocked by the child's body. When it had cleared again, the sorcerer began the binding. The ghouls turned their grisly faces toward him, and he pondered over the questions the boy had raised. What in their dead husks listened? It wasn't their souls. Of that, he was certain.

After he finished, he walked away from the hideous creatures, his brows twisted into a heavy frown. He hadn't thought about the soul of another in decades other than to bind one into slavery. This child! This child made him think of soft things. He wondered if that was at all good for him.

Chapter Six

Marun did not find the boy waiting for him above the cellar and his immediate disappointment over this irritated him. He deposited a crate of wine on a counter in the kitchen and snapped at the servants to shut the cellar door. Two rushed out to see after the task before the abominations escaped. Marun smiled darkly. Fools. The ghouls wouldn't leave the cellar of their own determination unless it were night. Somewhat appeased by the fear of his servants, he made his way to the hall.

Domel approached and informed his master of a delivery with his usual professional, subdued voice. "Packages have arrived for you, Master. Reading material, the cabby said. They were placed in the library."

Marun nodded absently. Domel bowed and watched as the sorcerer changed directions and headed toward the library. His master halted just inside the open door. Marun's expression, which had been inattentive, became visibly intense with awareness. Kehfrey was within the library, and so was Vik. They both bent over the desk, but it was Vik who was seated, frowning at a parchment he scratched at with a quill.

"This damned thing doesn't work," he blurted.

"I told you," Kehfrey said. "We have to take the ragged bit off the nib. You just did have to try before I got it ready."

"Fine. Trim it." Vik handed the child the quill while grimacing at the disgusting blotch he'd made on the parchment. "It looks like a smashed fly," he said deprecatingly. He lifted a hand to rub an itch on his cheek.

"Careful," his brother warned. "Now you have a smashed fly on your cheek." Smirking, Kehfrey used the penknife to trim off the splayed tip of the quill.

Vik pulled his fingers away from his face to discover his fingertips were indeed covered with ink. "Blast! Is it any wonder scribes are paid to do this?"

Kehfrey snickered and offered the properly trimmed quill. He had scored the slanted end with several tiny nicks leading progressively to the point. The cuts were designed to make it easier for Vik's novice efforts to result in something legible, but Vik didn't appreciate the difference in the tip. He only noticed the child's fingers were a complete mess and hesitated to take the writing instrument.

"Doesn't he have metal nibs? Why doesn't he have metal nibs? He's rich enough."

"If he does, he's locked them in the drawer. Do you want me to pick it?"

Vik didn't think this was a good idea and shook his head, even yet eyeing the filthy quill with distaste.

"You already got your fingers dirty," his brother pointed out. "Why change your mind now? Metal nibs will likely be just as messy."

"Perhaps you can just teach me to read only."

"You said you wanted to write poetry. You can't just make the words appear on the parchment by themselves," Kehfrey said. "Some poet you will be! You going to pay a scribe to steal your work?"

Irritably Vik grabbed the quill. He dipped it into the inkwell and tried the letter again. This time, it came out a little nicer. "It's bleeding in all directions!" he complained after a moment.

"Too much ink on the quill," Marun said from behind them. Both turned in dismay. He ignored their discomfort and walked toward the parcels. They rested on a large side table near the window. He pulled the smallest of them over and cut the twine with a small knife that had been left for him. He removed the first of many papers from out of the wrapping, sat in an armchair and began reading.

From the second Marun had announced his presence, Vik had stared at him. He sat frozen in the chair now, unable to think. Kehfrey knew it and stepped in front to cut off his view of the man. "Right. Try this letter," he suggested, pointing at one he'd learned yesterday. "It's a vowel."

"A what?" Vik mumbled.

Kehfrey gently shoved his brother's chin in the direction of the desk. "A vowel. For the sounds that open your mouth."

"This one letter?" Vik said in disbelief.

"No! This is just one of them." Kehfrey demonstrated the sound for which this particular letter was responsible. "Almet," he told his brother. "That's the name."

"There are people with that name," Vik said in surprise.

He made his attempt and it was passable. Kehfrey was satisfied with the result and continued the lesson with four other letters. With his brother blocking his view, Vik found it relatively easy to pretend Marun wasn't in the room with them, until the sound of parchment moving against parchment reminded him. Then he inevitably paused to listen.

"This is boring," he muttered at the end of a few minutes. Truthfully, his own apprehension frustrated him. He could barely concentrate.

"You have to get through them to start words," Kehfrey said. "You won't be bored once you can do that." He took the quill and wrote a word with the letters he had taught his brother. He waited to see what Vik made of it.

"Hak!" Vik uttered, blinking incredulously at the strange word.

"Hark," Kehfrey corrected. "Isn't that one of those stupid words I keep hearing you mutter? You know, in those silly poems you repeat?"

Vik scowled. "Remind me never to use that word in one of my own. And they aren't silly poems."

Kehfrey grinned. "Those ones are. You should start a new style. No one talks that way. Except the ones who think you like it."

Sighing, Vik copied the word hark down. His brother had a point. As usual. "If you weren't seven, I'd think you were a genius."

"So what do you think I am instead?" Kehfrey said with a laughing voice.

"A gods busted annoying pest. Give me the next letter."

Obligingly Kehfrey obeyed. Over in the chair, Marun stared at them fixedly. Despite the sound of shuffling paper, he hadn't been reading at all. He couldn't keep his eyes off them. He could only see Kehfrey's back, occasionally a hint of his pale face. Of Vik, his view was limited to the youth's slender figure. The younger brother's carefully chosen position blocked the sight of Vik's head.

An infant's piercing wail drifted down and broke their concentration. Kehfrey looked up and out the door. Vik straightened and did the same. Rewarded for his silent patience, Marun stared at the fine lines of his features.

"I forgot!" Kehfrey cried. "I have a sister!"

Vik turned and caught Marun's stare. His blue eyes went cold with distrust. The baby's cry sounded again. He set the quill in the stand. "That's enough for today," he said to Kehfrey. "Go up and see Mum. She must be feeling better by now."

Kehfrey looked at him uncertainly and then over at Marun. His young face exhibited the same mistrust as his brother. The shadows in the room suddenly darkened. Although the master's expression hadn't changed, his displeasure was evident. Vik stood and shoved Kehfrey toward the door.

"Hurry up! The noon meal will be called soon." He propelled the child out of the library and shut the door on his bewildered face, but afterward stood before the sealed entrance and looked at it fixedly. "Did you read any of those papers?" he said. He heard the sorcerer stand up.

"No," Marun answered. "Do you remember any of the letters he taught you?"

"Only some of them." He sensed Marun step up behind him. He turned slowly.

"You have ink on your cheek," the sorcerer informed him coldly.

Vik nodded. His blue eyes had grown dark, the pupils large. They locked once again with Marun's brown ones. Despite having a colour that should have been warm, Marun's eyes weren't at all. His features were expressionless as he lifted his hand and touched Vik's inked skin. Vik unexpectedly took the last step toward him. He pulled the man's head down and kissed him hard. Marun stiffened and groaned into his mouth. It was he who shook this time, a shiver of need that could no longer be suppressed. He pulled Vik into his arms and crushed him tight.

***

His ear pressed to the library door, Kehfrey listened to them speaking. Presently he heard Marun moan. He straightened when he felt the thump of their bodies against the wood. He shook his head and walked away softly. Vik hadn't protested. In fact, it sounded as if he had started it this time. Considering that his brother had shoved him out of the library, he was fairly certain of this assumption.

Domel had been watching from the entrance that led off to the kitchen. Kehfrey ignored him as he headed up the stairs, but Domel said nothing, only stared after him, frowning. How long would Marun let the boy alone? He'd never seen the master use a child before. Generally he preferred men, occasionally taking one who approached manhood, such as the beautiful brother, but there was something about this boy, something that made the sinister man pause every time he looked at him.

Domel turned away. It didn't matter about the boy. Domel's lot was still the same. He must perform his function. It was time he found out if the noon meal was ready to be served.

***

"She's beautiful, Mum," Kehfrey whispered. He sat at his mother's side, staring with wide eyes at the little face of his sister. Canella smiled and returned to gazing lovingly at the infant suckling on her breast.

Nicky walked past carrying a load of fresh swaddling cloths. She tucked them into a basket that rested near the bed. She had already filled another with rags for Canella. "There now," she said. "That should do until tomorrow. I sent a man to fetch more. And the laundress will show up in the morning and clean the soiled ones."

"You don't have a laundress here?" Canella said.

"He won't keep women about."

"But you're here."

"I have uses other than the usual female kind," Nicky said flatly.

Kehfrey put a finger in the baby's waving hand and marvelled at the difference in size. Canella looked away from Nicky, eager for a distraction. The short conversation had reminded her that she and her family weren't guests, but prisoners. Kehfrey's wondrous expression served her need fine. For the moment.

Her fears edged in despite his company. Her family was in trouble, terrible trouble, and somehow Kehfrey was the reason they weren't all dead or worse. She stared down at his ginger hair and wondered how long their little saviour would continue to keep that sinister man at bay. How long before the sorcerer tired of them all, before he killed them and turned them into the walking dead?

Terror stiffened her body. Her clutch on the baby slowly tightened until she smothered her daughter's small nose against her breast. After a minute, Kehfrey abruptly realized his sister struggled to breathe. Her face had turned blue. He called out in alarm.

"Mum! Let her go!"

Canella started. Realizing what she was doing, she screamed. Kehfrey dragged her stiff arms off the baby and pulled the infant away. Nicky dashed over from where she'd been standing and snatched the baby up. She looked at the infant's blue skin and bent her ear to the small face. Canella's sobbing prevented her from hearing what she needed to perceive. She dashed to the door and out.

"My baby!" Canella cried.

Kehfrey thrust himself upon her and put a hand over her mouth. "Hsst!" he shushed, fixing her eyes with his. "Let her listen. She needs to hear the baby breathe."

Canella stared distraughtly at him. His hazel eyes, so bright in his pale face, refused another sound from her mouth, and she couldn't seem to do anything but obey his will. A few seconds after, they heard the infant wail outside. Kehfrey lowered his hand. His alarming, too perceptive gaze shifted away. Canella gasped because she had been holding her breath and then wept openly.

Nicky appeared at the door and walked back into the chamber. Her face expressionless, she set the baby down on Canella's lap, but the mother shuddered and refused to touch her offspring. The infant wailed and kicked, the small face now a bright, angry red.

"Pick her up, Mum," Kehfrey urged her. "She's still hungry."

"I almost killed her!" she wept.

"No, you didn't," he lied. "She was just pushing a big one out her bum. Look! There it is. It almost got on you. That's why I yelled." Kehfrey pulled his hand off the swaddling cloth and made a disgusted face. "It's green! That's disgusting!"

Nicky laughed. Canella smiled weakly. She looked up with eyes that appealed. Staring down at the tired, worried face, Nicky decided Kehfrey was on the right path.

"Just a big push," she agreed. "Quite a dump in that cloth. Let me see to it for you." She gently plucked the baby up.

"Thank you," Canella said shakily.

"Oh, it's not a problem. Is it, my sweet little dumpy?" Nicky cooed at the squalling baby. She set the infant down on a soft cloth on the washstand and began to wipe her clean.

"Why's it all greeny black?" Kehfrey said. He'd gotten off the bed and edged up closer, but not too close.

"Because. All babies start with greeny black. It'll turn yellow in a few days. You'll see."

"I don't think I want to."

"Typical male response," she said caustically.

"What do you mean by that?"

"Just what I said!"

He glowered at her and then looked at his mother. She watched them despondently. Kehfrey's brows remained furrowed, but they twisted instead with worry. "Where's Pop?" he asked. His mother needed him.

"Gone with Wilf," Nicky answered.

"Where to?"

"To see my father," Canella told him.

Kehfrey returned to the bed and scooted up beside her. "Why did Pop go?"

"Safety," Nicky said. Kehfrey looked inquiringly at her. She didn't look back, but answered as if she'd seen the question on his face. "The Baron's not in the city, but Marun decided travelling alone was too risky, even in the country," she explained, then cooed at the screaming infant.

"So he told Pop to go with Wilf?" Kehfrey said.

"Yes," she answered, speaking loud enough to be heard above his sister's screeches. "They're using his personal coach. If Kortin has any spies placed outside the grounds, they'll just think Marun went off somewhere. Get me another cloth, will you? She's wiggling too much to leave go a second."

He slipped off the bed, grabbed swaddling from the basket and handed it to her. He watched her wrap his livid sister back up. Done, she lowered the squalling baby toward him.

"Here," she said. "Keep her neck supported."

"Oh! Be careful!" Canella cried.

Too late! Kehfrey had the baby. He gaped down at his sister. Nicky was ready to catch her, but he had her firmly enough. In the middle of a desperate screech, the infant suddenly ceased crying. Her little arms stopped waving and with perfect stillness she gazed up at her brother.

"Hi, now! I think she likes me!" He turned toward his mother and grinned mightily.

"Now if you only had a tit full of milk," Nicky said, "we could keep her with you all day."

Kehfrey's proud grin turned into sour grimace. He was coming to think that flower of an ancient woman had too many thorns.

Her fear and shame momentarily forgotten, Canella laughed. "Oh, what a fine mum you'd be!" she joked, but her face was soft with pride over him.

Kehfrey's sourness mellowed somewhat. He looked down at his sister and received a smack in the face for it. He blinked in surprise. "Gods bust it! She takes after you, Mum!"

Both Nicky and Canella laughed. Nicky urged him toward his mother with a gentle push. "Give the baby back, Kehfrey. You're likely missing the noon meal."

Despite the prompt, the boy didn't rush. He walked back to the bed and delicately placed the baby in Canella's arms. He waited until he saw his sister feeding again before he kissed his mother a farewell. She smiled at him, but her lips quivered. She set them firm again on her own, but just to help her along, he decided to give her some encouragement. His sort of encouragement.

"Hi, now! Tomorrow I'll tell you a whopping true story!"

146

"A true story?" she repeated. "That'll be a first. What's it about?"

"Some silly fellow who climbed a mountain and asked the gods to show him how to fly."

"And did they?" she asked, smiling down at his earnest face.

"Tell you tomorrow," he said and dashed out of the room.

Nicky smiled after him and then glanced at Canella. The woman seemed well enough despite the scare. "Someone will bring a tray up for you in a moment, and I will be in later," she promised. "But if you need me beforehand, pull the rope."

Canella nodded. "Thank you."

Nicky smiled again and went out the door. She found Kehfrey standing in the middle of the hall, frowning intensely at his shoes. She shut the door softly before she spoke to him. "So," she said as she approached. "Did he learn to fly?"

He looked at her worriedly. "Don't know yet. Have to finish making it up."

She laughed. "You are a wonder, brat."

"Will she be all right?"

"I think so. With you watching out for her, why wouldn't she be?" She pushed him toward the stairs. "Let's go eat."

"I'm not hungry."

She looked down at him in surprise. How had she missed this? His skin was paler than usual and bluish half-circles had appeared beneath his eyes. He hadn't been like that earlier. She was sure he hadn't. It was as if stepping out the door and away from his mother's anxious presence had sapped the strength from him.

A hand on his forehead, informed her that his skin was hot and clammy. "Oh, dear. You're for bed."

"But I'm not sick."

"Yes, you are. It was bound to catch up with you, child."

"What was?" he said as she pressed him toward the room he had appropriated.

"Everything," she said flatly. "It was a wonder you held up so well."

"I'm still up," he protested.

"Not for long." Into the room she forced him. Despite his objections, she stripped him down and set him in bed. When he edged toward the other side, she crushed his rebellion with a well-chosen threat. "If you don't get well, you'll make the baby sick too."

He sank into the pillow with a white face. "I won't!"

"You will if you take a sickness to her," she warned.

"Do you think I already did?"

"No," she answered firmly. "Rest. You will feel better if you rest. Do you understand?" He nodded solemnly. "I'll be back with some soup," she said. He nodded again. "And some pie," she offered, eyeing him closely.

He didn't rise to the temptation. Truly alarmed then, she left the room and went to find help. After she had gone, feeling more tired than he could ever remember being, Kehfrey shut his eyes and drifted away.

***

"It's poison," he heard a man's deep voice state.

"What? The staff wouldn't dare!"

That was Nicky. He knew that was Nicky.

"No. They didn't do this."

Marun. Kehfrey lifted heavy eyelids. The sorcerer sat on the bed next to him. "What poison?" Kehfrey whispered.

"Likely the fire and smoke potion you drank early yesterday morning," Marun informed him.

"But that was so long ago!" Nicky blurted. "And he had the rock!"

She stood at the side of the bed. Kehfrey could barely see her. His eyes refused to focus. And he was cold. He was so very cold.

"The poison hadn't worked through his system," Marun said. "Some poisons take time. The rock wouldn't have cured it because a cure wasn't needed yet."

"How can you be certain it's poison?" she said.

"Look at his tongue," he answered. He slipped his finger into Kehfrey's mouth and held it open. It was the second time he'd done so, but the child had slept during the first examination. Nicky bent and saw that the boy's tongue had taken on a deep purple hue.

"This poison comes of a herb contaminated with disease," Marun said. "You see the effects a day later after the germs have thrived in the gut."

"Is it deadly?" she asked, and Kehfrey discerned fear in her voice. How wonderful. She really did like him. If he weren't so very tired, he'd smile, but smiling seemed such an effort, breathing too. This was a rather less shocking way to die, he supposed. Not a bad poison at all.

"Not this time," Marun said. Gently he lifted the child up.

Kehfrey had no strength left in him to raise his head and the sorcerer put a hand beneath his neck for support. "I was fine just an hour ago," he whispered.

"That's how this poison works," Marun said.

Kehfrey squinted at him. Was that a green glow over the man? Where'd all the black go? Marun's head came down and blocked out his vision. He felt lips on his own. They were wonderfully warm. He felt strange then. He was floating. He was floating in green. Before his wonder developed into further questions, he drifted away a second time.

Marun lifted his lips from Kehfrey's. A flush of rose had returned to the boy's pale skin. Marun pressed the child's soft lips open with a thumb and peered into his mouth, to observe that the tongue was no longer purple.

"I didn't know you could do that," Nicky said quietly

148

He ignored her. He didn't care what she thought of his act of healing. He set Kehfrey down, but remained seated to his side, gazing down at him thoughtfully.

"I don't understand," the woman said. "Why would Kortin poison the boy? It makes no sense."

"I think it was coincidental," he responded.

"How can you say that? How can poison be coincidental?"

"As you seemed to have noticed, it doesn't make sense that Kortin would go out of his way to poison a child. I suspect that whomever he purchased the potion from mishandled a batch."

Nicky looked down at Kehfrey worriedly. "I saw this," she whispered.

Marun focused on her. "Why didn't you tell me?"

"I didn't see the sickness. Only you holding the child in your arms. I thought ...." Her words faded off.

"You thought I intended to use the boy!" he accused.

She stepped away from him. His eyes were hot with anger. She shivered. His eyes weren't cold! Marun's eyes weren't cold!

"Get out!" he spat.

She darted from the room, shut the door and stood shaking before it. That had been close. Too close. He had come a knife's edge away from punishing her. Still shaking, she slipped away from the door. Marun's punishments could be extraordinarily cruel. She had reason to know. She looked back at the door as she crept down the stairs.

Marun was in love with that boy. She didn't think her master knew it. Not yet.

***

Baron Harte observed the young man fixedly. Wilf regarded him in turn, his expression impassive. He laid the fork he'd been holding down, exactly so, and picked up the glass of wine. It was old glass, hand cut and rimmed in gold. He sipped from it and set it down. His motions were precise, his manners impeccable. Around the long table, every face was turned toward him, staring or gaping, some angry, some just curious. Most of the attending family weren't eating, some because they refused to partake of the meal while he sat at the table, others because they were too fascinated by the drama unfolding before their eyes. Wilf ignored them, but for his grandfather. Him he stared down without a sign of discomfort.

What was Baron Harte to him, after all? Worse had pinned him with a glare—cutthroats, murderous whores, the infamous Kortin, boss of the thieving ring. Baron Harte? He was nobody really. He only thought he was somebody because he'd been born with a title.

Another cut of the knife, another delicious mouthful, another swallow. His skin prickled more from the chill draught blowing through the large hall of the old castle than the cold stares of the noble family who sat the table with him. Long banners hung from the upper walks and were so old as to have lost most of their colour, but they were pride and they were tradition and would not be traded in for new rags to cover the ancient grey walls.

Wilf was the new. He was the unwanted. Even so, he would have enjoyed taking another look about the immense vestibule that served as both entryway and place of court, but the narrow stares of the men kept him from gawping at history not permitted to a bastard-born son of the blood. He would not look twice, refused to give them any opportunity to mock him. He was not a lowbred boy who'd never been in a castle, who must gawk at the faded signs of tradition and family honour. Odd how clumsy the older castles were. It wasn't any wonder the old man was ill.

"I see that she taught you some manners at least," Harte said suddenly.

Wilf smiled, a bare hint of curve at the corners of his mouth. "Manners can be useful," he replied lightly.

He picked up the knife and sliced a bite-sized morsel from the breast of chicken on his plate. The plate was the finest of old china and bore the family coat of arms, a buck leaping over a silver river. The dish had a crack, and tiny lines threaded throughout the glaze. Wilf had supped on finer, but of course the dishes had been new. The widows of merchants made much better marks; at least they were still rich.

"Manners! Yes! Manners! Useful for worming your way into the right circles," the nobleman seated near the further end said.

Wilf regarded the man calmly. Unlike the older generation of Winfellan upper class, this fellow wore a powdered wig over his head and painted his face with whitening makeup. He would be a cousin of his mother's, likely the one who stood to inherit from the austere Baron.

"Have you another use for manners?" Wilf retorted.

"Unlike you, I have manners because I was born into polite company."

He was a large fellow, boasting wide shoulders that he held very straight. He seemed roughly Canella's age. Wilf thought he saw a vague resemblance to his mother. Perhaps the eyebrows. Yes. The brows had a similar arch. The Baron had that arch too.

"Well, I'm sure your uncle appreciates you for them," Wilf replied.

The man stood with a menacing glower. "You will leave this place!"

"You did not invite me to sit," Wilf pointed out frigidly. The nobleman put a hand on the ornamental dagger at his waist. Remaining outwardly calm, Wilf tensed for a fight.

"Sit down, Rhendel!" Baron Harte snapped. Rhendel opened his mouth to protest. "Sit!" Harte roared. He coughed afterward, the noise hoarse and arriving from deep in his chest. The spasm shuddered through his body. Bloody mucous had splattered his handkerchief when he pulled it away from his mouth.

"You have consumption, milord," Wilf said flatly.

"Not so," Harte wheezed. "The priests say it is a result of over-imbibing the Amek weed. The smoke has blackened my lungs. A recent ailment has worsened the condition."

"Can they not cure you?"

Wilf had heard that his maternal grandfather suffered an addiction to the Amek drug, but he was surprised Harte admitted to the vice so easily. It was said the Baron smoked to forget the deaths of his sons. Wilf chanced a look at Rhendel and wondered how much responsibility for those losses lay at the door of his powdered cousin. If Rhendel were to be judged by the murderous sentiment in his eyes, Wilf guessed he held the weight of several dead men on his head. But what did this matter? Ghosts weighed next to nothing.

"They say I am called," Harte answered Wilf's polite inquiry.

"I see. Then you are fortunate." Fortunate enough to have been left alive to name his brother's son his heir, the sorry old goat.

"So they say," Harte said, to all appearances unimpressed. "Does she take you to church?"

"No."

"Why not?" That question had issued from a woman. She was handsome and stately and sat to Rhendel's left. Wilf had earlier decided she must be the nobleman's wife.

"The church had little useful advice for my mother," he answered.

"Of course not," Rhendel said derisively. "A whore has no need to strengthen her virtue."

"Her virtue, Lord Rhendel, belonged to her father," Wilf uttered coldly. "And he failed to protect it."

"You blame my uncle for it! She opened her legs on her own!"

"On her own? How did she manage to get *on her own*? A woman's virtue belongs to the man who owns her," he re-stated, glaring at his self-righteous cousin.

"You only say that to avoid the truth, you bastard of a whore."

Wilf laughed at him. "The truth? You wouldn't know it if you tripped over it." He looked contemptuously at the young women lined up next to Rhendel's wife. "Are you willing to follow your uncle's example? Send for a midwife and check them all. Let's see if you choose to throw them out after."

The elder pair of the four blanched. The younger two were just too immature to have known temptation. Wilf smiled mockingly at the eldest set.

Rhendel roared, knocked his chair over and went after the insolent upstart. Two of his sons leapt up as well. They were on Wilf's side of the table, but he moved more quickly. He freed himself from his chair and backed away while they still lurched from their seats. The women screamed. The Baron shouted and then coughed uncontrollably. Rhendel ignored his uncle's incoherent protests and charged, his fighting blade raised to knife his victim's chest. It was a damned clumsy attack, and Wilf was somewhat surprised to see it. He'd have thought a nobleman would be better trained. All the same, he thanked the gods it was bad manners to come to the table wearing a sword. Rhendel was doubtless educated in the proper use of a lord's weapon.

Wilf sidestepped the inept rush and caught the man's arm. With a practiced twist, he sent his cousin flying. Rhendel landed with a heavy thud on the stone floor. He groaned and rolled to his front. The last of his sons joined the first two, and the three moved in unison toward their unwanted guest. Wilf pulled free his dagger. If he must leave, he preferred to do so intact and still breathing.

"Back off! I'm more proficient with this weapon than you! Not one of you pampered asses has ever had to fight in Demon Alley!"

The young men paused. He had named the most disreputable street in all of Wistal, purportedly the place where any sort of cutthroat or professional criminal could be hired, also the second best location to look for a dumped body when the docks had already been ruled out.

"You're bloody on my turf without a sword!" he sneered at Rhendel. Still trying to get his feet underneath himself, the elder cousin cursed Wilf. Wilf laughed. He'd thumped the perfumed buffoon a good one. "Interesting luncheon, Grandfather," he said sarcastically. "It seems my cousins are no less prone to blood sport than my usual company. My compliments to the cook. I think I shall be going now."

"Wait!" the old man wheezed. He coughed again, but managed to restrain his inflammation enough for speech. "I will speak with you in my chamber."

"What?" Rhendel protested. "You can't do that!" He had lifted himself at last and was ready to continue the battle.

"Shut up, Rhendel!" Harte hissed. He shook his fist at his nephew. A crumpled sheet of parchment flashed. Rhendel blanched at the reminder and backed off, which was just as well. Harte choked on his own fluids again.

Harte's manservant pressed a fresh handkerchief over the old man's mouth. Harte's shoulders heaved helplessly before he was able to continue, but Wilf's noble adversaries hesitated long enough for Harte to recover from the fit. Presently the old man lifted his head and indicated to the manservant that he wished to rise. With the aid of the servant, Harte faced off with his bastard grandson, a determined, proud expression cast over his tired features.

"Go up to my chamber with me. I will speak with you alone."

Wilf's gaze flashed from him to his cousins and back again, distrust plain in his eyes. The old man lifted his hand and opened it. The crumpled letter of introduction lay upon his palm.

"I can't very well ignore this, can I?" Harte said hoarsely.

Wilf inclined his head in a sardonic agreement. "No more than I could ignore the command to visit you."

"You were commanded?"

"It wasn't my idea," he admitted.

Harte's frown turned quizzical. "So you wouldn't have come?"

"I never intended to."

"You can't believe that whoreson!" Rhendel interjected.

"Shut up!" Harte snapped. He turned away. "Come," he called to his grandson. "I need to speak with you without the constant distractions."

Wilf perforce followed, marching warily between Rhendel's sons, but the letter had been enough to make them think and they kept their weapons lowered. Even so, Wilf didn't sheathe his dagger until he had followed Harte half way up the steps winding along the wall of the great hall, and he looked behind regularly until they had walked into the Baron's chamber at the head of the stairwell. The manservant assisted Harte onto his ancient four-poster, covered him with a throw, and took up station before the door. Wilf eyed the fellow cagily.

"Ignore him. He's loyal to me," the old man said.

Wilf considered his grandfather. This was likely how he'd end up when he aged. All in all, it wasn't too bad. Harte's back was still relatively straight. He hadn't grown fat. He was shrivelled, true, covered in age spots, but he looked dignified for all that.

Harte settled comfortably into his bed and regarded Wilf without speaking for a minute. He didn't ask the youth to sit. "I was straight and strong like you once," he eventually said, mimicking his grandson's thoughts in a backward fashion.

"I was considering how I might end up," Wilf admitted.

"Does it frighten you?"

"No. Not getting there does."

Harte barely smiled. "You sound as if you've had cause to worry."

"I have."

"Chased by a jealous husband perhaps?"

"No, actually. Jealous husbands haven't been much trouble."

"Your step-father's cohorts?" the old man pressed.

"Sometimes. Mostly it was just working for the Syndicate when I was younger. I got stuck in a chimney. Took me hours to free myself from the flue. I've had trouble with small places since."

Harte found it interesting the boy didn't think gang fights all that worrisome. "They send children down the chimneys?" he said, not commenting on Wilf's obvious self-assurance concerning his fighting prowess. "So that's how they do it."

Wilf smiled darkly. "I was too clumsy, so they sent me off to do my own thing."

"Whoring." The derision of Harte's tone was nearly as solid as a gob of spit.

"Yes, whoring," Wilf affirmed coolly. "I'm very good at it. I take after my natural father, you see. Just about any woman I want to bed gets into bed with me. I get money from the older marks. I just use the younger ones. They generally have nothing to give me but the virtue their fathers and husbands are so careless with."

Harte stared at him. The boy's expression was flat. He didn't boast. He wasn't proud. He just stated fact. "Your mother taught you to blame me for what she did," Harte rejoined.

"No, my stepfather did. Considering that he never lost her virtue in all the time he's had her, I have to believe him."

"You cannot tell me she didn't whore for the Syndicate!"

"I can!" Wilf spat. "Kehfen never betrayed her. She's only lost her purity once, and because *you* didn't see after her properly. Don't think I am blind, old man. My mother is no better than any other woman. A well-delivered line, a careful pose, power, money; any of these can turn a woman. *Any* woman. I just know what it takes to prevent it."

The old man averted his face. His eyes blinked rapidly several times. Wilf stared in amazement. Did the unforgiving old creature weep?

The Baron astounded him with his next question. "How is she? Is she well?"

"She just gave birth to my first sister," Wilf said, staring at a suddenly eager face. "Blond again."

"Blond again? There are more?"

"I have three brothers. One blond, one red-haired like Kehfen, the other with sandy brown hair. Is that what you want, old man? News of my mother? You should just have her visit."

Harte scowled and waved the crumpled letter again. "What have you to do with *him*?"

Marun hadn't sealed the letter of introduction, but this hadn't mattered. Wilf couldn't read, but he knew enough to realize the sorcerer had signed the paper with just an initial. Apparently an initial was all Marun needed to get doors opened, that and the fear his initial engendered.

"What have *you* to do with him?" Wilf countered. "How do you know him? How is it that a letter of introduction from him got me in your door?"

"He came to me recently. With an offer."

"In return for a favour, I suppose?"

The old man nodded.

"Did you refuse?"

"You don't refuse a man like that," Harte said tightly. "I told him I would think about it."

"What did he offer you?"

"My life," Harte admitted. He thumped the bed sternly. "Now you; how do you know him?"

"He has my family under his wing at the moment," Wilf said.

"Under his wing? Why? Of what interest is a family of thieves and whores to him?"

"I couldn't begin to guess," Wilf said. The old man glowered at him, and Wilf relented. "He does seem to think my little brother might have a use as an apprentice."

"An apprentice! One of your brothers?"

"Yes. Is that so surprising?"

"That darkness doesn't come from my side of the family," Harte said, turning his eyes away.

Wilf took offence at the scathing dismissal of his brother's worth. "You don't even deserve to know Kehfrey exists, old man."

"Kehfrey, is it?" Harte whispered. "Did you know you were named after her eldest brother?"

"Yes."

"My Wilf died when your mother was twelve. She adored him. What are your other siblings named?"

"Gamis and Vik. They haven't named the girl yet." He didn't say why, but Kehfen had told him it was because they were afraid to do so. They knew what Marun did with a name.

"Common names," Harte said flatly.

Wilf would not stand at attention and be further insulted. "I grow tired of this interview, *Grandfather*. If you are quite done, I shall leave. And even if you are not quite done." He headed for the door, set to move the servant physically if he must.

"Wait! I know why he sent you!"

"Do you? Why?" Wilf rounded on the Baron. Rather than answer, Harte looked him up and down slowly. His expression was almost hungry. "Answer me, old man!" Wilf snapped.

"You are my bribe," Harte said. "He knew. He knew I'd be tempted by you."

"Did he? What tempts you? Memories? Or do you think he will give you your youth back?"

"No! He gives me a Harte back!" the Baron roared. He coughed weakly after. Wilf stared at him, incredulous. "Tell me," Harte said after a minute. "Did she marry your step-father before you were born?"

"Yes," Wilf answered truthfully.

"Hells!" Harte hissed. "Where is he?"

"Why do you want to know?"

"Because he owns you, boy. He owns you legally. I can't very well adopt you and call you my successor unless he abandons all claims to you."

This statement elicited not a word from Wilf. He gaped at the old man as if one of the cousins had just crept up behind and knifed him in the heart. In his stunned mind, a knife in the heart was still more likely than Baron Harte wishing to claim a bastard grandson as his successor.

"Have you lost your wits? Did you understand what I just said?" Harte demanded urgently.

"Yes. I just find it hard to believe." And hard to speak and sound so composed. Harte had just offered him legitimacy. Legitimacy and the lifelong enmity of Rhendel. Rhendel's enmity seemed more real by far. Rhendel's enmity was a certainty.

"Believe it," Harte said. "I am sick to death of that useless wheedling lot downstairs. They think I can't hear them going on about wanting me to drop off and die sooner. My lungs have gone! Not my ears!" He coughed again. "Now! Where is he? Your step-father."

"Waiting in the coach for me," Wilf said numbly.

"Quick, man," Harte called to his manservant. "Fetch him! Get him up the servants' stairs. Don't let anyone know who he is. Then go send someone after the magistrate. Bring him now! Get witnesses! Lords Mehtle and Kess will do. Do what it takes. Bribe everyone!"

The servant nodded and rushed out. Wilf looked at the door that had just thudded to, and snapped his mouth shut almost as loudly. "You aren't serious!" he said to Harte. "Just like that? You expect to instate me as your successor just like that? Your nephew will gut me in my sleep!"

"That's why I'm going to evict him tonight," the old man said. He laughed wickedly. "I've grown tired of listening to that pompous ass. I've seen his two eldest girls go off behind his back. Yet there he sits in his powdered wig and goes on about what a good father he is. His fine sons! His fine girls! As if he were better than me because all of his boys are still alive." He snorted. "I should have called your mother back long ago."

"Then why didn't you?"

"I was ashamed. I was too proud. I was afraid Rhendel would kill her. I was afraid of how you had turned out, afraid of what Rhendel would say and do to you." He laughed again. "But you held up fine. You have a tongue on you. You have wits. And you have *that man* backing you. Rhendel will pause before making an attempt on you now."

Wilf just looked at him in awe. The old man really meant it. He wanted to make *him*, the bastard grandson, his successor. In all his life, Wilf had never considered it possible. He had dreamt of it, certainly, but he had known how very unlikely it was.

It was still very unlikely. "Doesn't matter what you say while you're still alive. Once you're dead, the House of Lords won't ratify it."

"We'll let your patron deal with the House of Lords, shall we?" Harte answered. "She taught you the manners to go with your blood. She was wise, my girl. She knew you might need them."

"Yes, she's wise. She learned the hard way what counts for what."

The old man flushed beneath Wilf's heated gaze. "I can't change what's gone on. I can only change now."

Wilf gave him a curt nod and turned toward the window. Below in the courtyard, the manservant rushed up to the coach. Kehfen leaned his head out to listen. His hat was off and his ginger hair a bright flame in the sunlight. Strange how it sometimes sparked a truer red than red hair should, but only where the sharpest of curls bent the filaments and only

156

when the light was this bright. Funny little man, but a truer father than one could ask for.

"Tell me about your life, Grandfather?" Wilf said as he looked down at the enigma that was Kehfen, who revealed nothing of his past, of his parents, of siblings, of home, but who had never failed to be there when Wilf had needed him. "What is it like to be a lord?"

"Ha! You'll find out soon, won't you? Let me keep my voice, boy. It pains me enough to speak, and I'll like as not use my throat enough to make me mute when your mother's keeper arrives."

And so Wilf had no choice but to wait in the stiff silence and suffer the famished stare of a wasted and bitter old man who saw a Harte in a bastard.

Sometime later, a noise at the door focused both their eyes on the oak panels. The manservant re-entered followed by Kehfen. Rhendel's voice could be heard, demanding the identity of the stranger being conducted into the lord's chamber, but the manservant pressed Kehfen forward without responding. Kehfen stepped inward warily. The manservant left and shut the door again.

When Kehfen spotted Wilf, his relief was evident. He relaxed and let loose the air from his lungs, the exhalation audible in the quiet. "Thought I was going up to a trap," he said sharply.

"Then why'd you come?" the old man demanded.

Kehfen eyed Baron Harte distrustfully. He'd seen the lord before, but only from afar. "Had to make sure Wilf was all right, didn't I? He's family."

Pleased by this answer, Wilf crossed his arms and presented the old man with an arrogant sneer. Kehfen, inches shorter and with no resemblance to Wilf physically, still managed to seem similar if only by the way he carried himself. He crossed his arms as well and glowered at the Baron.

Harte looked from one to the other. "Yes, you're family," he said. "Pair of arrogant thieves. Now then, Wilf's stepfather, are you prepared to disown the boy?"

Kehfen lifted a brow at this remark. "And why should I do that?"

"Because he can't be the next Baron Harte without the name Harte, can he?"

Kehfen peered thoughtfully at the sick man. "I suppose that stands to reason," he said at last.

Harte smiled and nodded his certainty. "Quick, then. Lock the door before Rhendel tries to interfere. He's got to be down there shitting his breeches by now."

Kehfen's smile was wicked as he locked the door. The old man crowed again and paid for it with racking coughs. Watching his tortured gasps, Wilf took pity and brought him another handkerchief, his own—or rather Marun's, but he didn't say so. Harte nodded a thank-you and huddled back into his pillow.

"Do you think Marun might let me have that stone of healing after all?" he wheezed. "Just to let me live long enough to see Rhendel doesn't get me declared an idiot?"

"Could Rhendel do that?" Wilf said uneasily.

"He could try," Harte whispered. "He will try."

Kehfen approached the bed, a worried furrow between his brows. "Is it worth being a baron? I mean for Wilf? He's not going to have it easy, is he?"

"No one's going to have it easy anymore. Marun is here again," Harte said darkly.

"What do you mean *again*?" Wilf asked.

"He was born here, in Winfel. Did you not know? He's as Winfellan as you or I."

Kehfen found a seat nearby. He grabbed it and set it closer. Sitting, he leaned in toward the nobleman. "You have a story to tell us, Baron. If you're up to it, we'd be happy to listen."

Harte looked from him to Wilf. The youth leant against a bedpost, his attitude expectant. Harte remembered someone like him once, in his aged mind someone very similar. He thought he saw a resemblance to his younger self, the jaw perhaps, the set of the eyes. He wasn't sure exactly. The nose might be it. The nose was broad like his. But then, so were a lot of Winfellan noses, including the nose of the man who had fathered Wilf. Ghemet, that deceitful son of a bitch.

"I was your age when Marun was whipped," Harte said, keeping his voice low for the sake of his raw throat. "Only his name wasn't Marun then. It was his name of birth they called him when they lashed him to the poles. Tehlm Sevet he was." He looked away from Wilf and into the past. "Tehlm Sevet was Prince Cehtre's lover, the one for whom the prince jumped off the tower."

"Crud!" Wilf hissed. "That was him? That's impossible! He's younger than you!"

"Think, boy!" Harte snapped. "He's a sorcerer. He was already half my age now when this happened; only no one knew it then. They only knew it afterward, when King Sihmuen forced the details from out of his son."

"How could anyone have captured him to whip him?" Wilf said.

"He was surprised in his lover's bed. He was still apprenticed to the sorcerer before him, back then. You understand? He wears his master's name now."

"So exactly how did they capture him?" Kehfen asked.

"As I said. They took him by surprise, straight from the bed he shared with Cehtre. They gagged him immediately, which saved all their miserable lives. The king had him whipped in front of his son and sold into slavery. I remember what he said. I was there with my father. King Sihmuen said, 'Sell him to the Mehto as a ship's whore. He'll get what he wants daily, then.' "

"And then Prince Cehtre threw himself out of the tower," Wilf ended.

158

"Not until after his father had all the information out of him," the old man said. "And then the first Marun came and punished us for the loss of his apprentice. The king was killed within days. The older Marun appeared magically, popping into the palace anywhere at will, taking lives as he saw fit. The rest of us were saved only because the Carmet monks set wards to trap him. They cornered him and blasted him to ashes."

"What was our Marun doing in Wistal back then?" the thief said.

"No one knows," Harte answered. "Some think he came across Cehtre while the prince was in Labelen Province hunting. He may have followed him here."

"Gods' balls," Wilf whispered. He looked at Kehfen. "Why didn't he come back before now?"

Kehfen shook his head in mystification. They both looked at Baron Harte.

"I don't know that either," Harte said, "but I've made a guess. I've heard that his kind has a weakness where water is concerned. He may not have been able to return because of it. He was on a ship destined to circumnavigate the continent. Think of it! Trapped in a small compartment in the forward hold, men relieving their bowels in a cabin just ahead, coming to him in the darkness, using him while he smelled the never-ending stench, powerless to stop them. Think what he must have endured and done to get back here."

Harte looked at his grandson and then at the man who had raised the boy. Both their faces had whitened with consternation. Harte didn't need their anxiety clarified. Wilf had already told him. Marun had their family under his wing. That was cause for concern. That was cause for outright dread.

***

As Nicky walked into the dining room, she noted that Olomo waited for the boy. Idling near the window, he barely acknowledged her presence, a mere shift of his attention that immediately drifted away again. But Vik, who stood near his chair, looked over at her and stepped forward, his brows furrowed into a question.

"What did you want him for?" he said. He was still upset over the interruption.

If she weren't so shaken by her recent brush with her master's wrath, she would have found his irritation amusing. As it was, she just wanted to keep the youth calm. It wouldn't do to have him barging upstairs and annoying the sorcerer further. "He needed to take care of something urgent," she said.

Vik eyed her cautiously. What sort of something urgent? She had shouted some sort of foreign jabber from beyond the library door and driven Marun from him. But what would make the man pull away like that, in the middle of what they had both wanted so badly?

"What language were you using before?" he said, circling around the question he really wanted to ask.

"Elven," she said. She moved away from him and over to the table. She nodded to the butler. "He's not coming down. Send something upstairs for him. You may serve the rest of us."

Domel nodded politely and began to set the serving dishes on the table. "To which room shall I have a man carry the tray? The workroom, or the bedchamber?" he said.

Nicky frowned. This was about to get dramatic again. "Kehfrey's room," she answered flatly.

"What?" Vik said. "What's he doing in Kehfrey's room?" He started toward the dining room entrance. Nicky managed to get there before him.

"Don't go up there. He's watching over Kehfrey. The child is ill."

Vik, his face turning white, only tried to dart around her. She shoved him back harshly.

"Get out of my way, woman!" he barked. Next time he would hurt her if he must.

"I said stay here. He won't want you up there."

Olomo approached from the other side of the table. "I would know what has occurred with the boy. He was fine just an hour ago."

"Yes! He was!" Vik said. "Get out of the way!"

"He was poisoned," she said, stunning them silent.

"Poisoned!" Domel uttered in horror. He almost dropped a dish from his benumbed fingers. "But ...! None of us would!"

"He knows that," she reassured the man. "He says the fire and smoke potion was misbrewed. A contaminated ingredient."

"But the child drank that over a day ago," Olomo said.

"It's slow acting poison. He's fine now. Marun healed him. Please, both of you, just go sit. He doesn't want you up there."

"But he's my brother," Vik asserted. He attempted to push her aside.

Olomo placed his large hand on the youth's shoulder and hauled him back. "You will do as she says," he commanded. Vik slapped his hand away. "Think, boy," Olomo said. "The child must not be disturbed. You and the sorcerer have ... *issues* to resolve. Wait until later."

Vik glared at him and Nicky. She knew perfectly well the *issues* had been in the process of being resolved when she'd interrupted them. Nicky glowered back and then lifted a sardonic brow, waiting for him to remember what reason she'd had to disrupt the resolution. Vik scowled and turned away. He stalked over to the table and sat down angrily. Unhurriedly Olomo followed his example. Nicky, eyeing Vik suspiciously, sat as well.

The noon meal commenced in resentful, worried silence. The atmosphere only livened up momentarily when Gamis rushed in late, at which point he was brought up to date on where all the absent members of his family were. Then the concerned hush settled over them once more.

He couldn't leave. It was a terrible nightmare. He couldn't get out of it.

The old man moved again, pulling the naked child closer, his grip firm, merciless.

"Please, Grandfather! I don't like it!" the little boy wailed. "It hurts!"

The old man smiled in a kindly manner and then struck the child across the face. It wasn't a soft blow. When he lifted the sobbing boy onto his lap, the child bled from a broken lip.

Hovering in an upper corner of the stone chamber, Kehfrey watched. Horrified, he rotated and tried to slip out of the crack again. Somehow he just couldn't squeeze through.

This is impossible! I'm not here! I can squeeze through a not-here crack, can't I?

The child whimpered, and Kehfrey's attention reverted to the old man. Now he thrust the little boy up and down upon his lap. Kehfrey whirled once more. He didn't want to see that! He didn't want to be here! He had to get out of this nightmare!

He tried the crack in the stone again. Once more he was unable to force himself through the gap. And beneath him, the ghoul with the gaping wound in his throat swiped at his invisible presence. It gobbled wordlessly and spat up yellow drool on its chin.

"Get away from that corner!" the old man snapped at it.

The ghoul shifted away, but continued to look upward with its sunken eyes. The child wept louder. The old man continued moving the little boy up and down. After another few thrusts, gnarled hands parted from bruised hips and lifted toward the head of the sobbing child. The old man gave an ecstatic, mad shout and snapped the small neck. The crying ceased instantly.

A hand that had murdered reached now for a smooth grey stone on a small table nearby. Fingers curled over the oblong shape. The old man shuddered in rapture. The pleasure seemed to torture him. His face twisted with agony as he spent himself in the cadaver.

Horrified and unable to turn away, Kehfrey watched darkness waft up from the floor and over the old man's legs. The dark curled around his hips, crept over the dead child like thousands of viscous black slugs and sank into the limp body. The corpse twitched. A skinny arm moved. The old man groaned and thrust the body against him one last time, the stone still in his hand, the grey surface touching the child's waist. The boy's eyes moved. The blank gaze drifted upward. Despite the broken angle of the neck, the pupils rose until they fixed on Kehfrey's position.

And then Kehfrey was in.

He screamed. The sound came out as a faint wordless protest.

"There now," the old man croaked. "Be a good boy." He shoved the child off his lap.

Kehfrey felt himself sprawl on the ground. He couldn't move his head. Why couldn't he move his head?

It wasn't his head! He was in the body! He was in the body!

He screamed a second time. Once more it came out as a barely discernable grunt.

Everything was wrong! It didn't feel right! The heart was dead! The blood was still! It was dead! The child was dead!

"There now," the old man said again, this time more calmly. "You've been such a good boy."

Somehow, desperately, Kehfrey forced the body to move. He rolled it, but the head remained turned at the wrong angle. He lifted a hand and pulled it over by the hair. The old man came into view. His eyes were cold, his face impassive. He rubbed the stone against his spent flesh. As Kehfrey observed, the man's penis slowly grew tumescent again. Kehfrey fixed the child's dead gaze on the stone.

The stone was the reason. It was why he was here, why he was trapped. Something in the stone had drawn him into this nightmare.

"Come here, my good boy," the old man whispered. "Come to me."

Kehfrey refused to let the cadaver move.

The man frowned. He shouted. "Come here!"

Although the limbs jerked with the need to obey, once more Kehfrey stilled the life-emptied body.

The old man scowled petulantly. "Did I ruin you?"

He lifted off the chair and towered over the child he'd murdered. The boy's dead limbs jerked in a spastic reaction to its master's movement. Kehfrey grimly forced the body still. The man crouched. He brought the stone closer and touched the dead chest with it. Kehfrey snatched the rock and rolled away.

He heard the man roar. He felt the stone's power. He recognised a presence, a confused, angry presence, and then he saw the path out, back to a place, a manor, a room, a man. He grasped the link and slipped away.

***

Marun started as the child bolted upright in the bed. Kehfrey stared blankly forward and then screamed in pure horror. The sorcerer knocked the small serving table over while rising. His tray of food crashed to the floor. He darted toward the boy.

"Kehfrey!" he called. He grabbed stiff shoulders. Kehfrey gasped and pulled away from him.

"You! How can you be here? You're not here! You're not here at all!"

Marun straightened and stared at him in astonishment. The sounds of thudding steps preceded the opening of the door. It slammed wide and revealed Vik, Olomo just behind him.

"Kehfrey!" Vik rushed into the room, snatched his brother into his arms, and pulled him off the bed and away from Marun. "What did you do to him?" he said accusingly.

"I did nothing. He woke from a nightmare."

Vik glared at Marun distrustfully while Kehfrey shivered uncontrollably in his arms. Vik had never seen his brother like this. Never. "Kehfrey?" he called softly. "Kehfrey what happened?"

"Had to get out! Had to get out!" the child repeated dazedly.

"Out of where?" Marun demanded.

"Leave him alone!" Vik shouted.

The master stepped forward, his comportment rigid with menace. "Put the child back in bed."

Vik hesitated. Shadows rose: whirling, ominous darkness that curled visibly around the man who had summoned them.

"Put the child back!" the sorcerer said through his teeth. Terrified, Vik stumbled toward the bed and set Kehfrey on it. "Now let him go."

Shaking with fright, the elder brother endeavoured to part from the younger, but discovered himself unable to move away. Kehfrey had snarled his fingers in Vik's suit. Both small hands were white with the pressure he bore on them. "He won't release me." Vik looked up to see the shadows thicken over Marun. "It's true!" he protested fearfully. "He won't release me!"

The sorcerer stepped forward and grasped the child's wrists. The shadows sank into Kehfrey's arms. His little hands snapped open. So did his mouth. He screamed, but not a sound came out of his throat.

"Kehfrey!" Vik called.

"Get out!" Marun directed. "Both of you!"

Vik dared to hesitate again. A hostile glare, a silent promise of murder sent him flying from the room. Throwing his faith upon the words of his holy leader, Olomo stepped out after Vik and shut the door.

"Kehfrey!" Vik whispered his distress.

"He will not be harmed," Olomo said with a fanatic's conviction. "He is destined." With utmost calm, he treaded away from the stunned brother.

Nicky rushed past Vik, and he abruptly realized his mother called from her room. She sounded frightened. He pursued Nicky in that direction, but she pulled up when she perceived him.

"No!" she refused with a hushed voice. "You'll only frighten her more. Go back to Gamis. He's still cowering below."

She opened the door, slipped in and shut him out. He stopped in the middle of the hall and stared at the entry blankly. He turned again. There was no one with him. He was alone in the hall, alone with his fear for Kehfrey.

***

"Kehfrey!" the sorcerer called. The boy stared at the hands on his wrists, frozen with a scream on his face. Marun released him and slowly backed away. "Kehfrey," he called again, this time more softly.

The child blinked. His head turned. When he looked at Marun, the hazel of his irises was so bright the colour seemed luminous.

"Don't touch me," he whispered. He shivered then, one violent convulsion. He looked down at his naked body and snatched a blanket over his middle. "Don't touch me," he whispered again.

"Tell me where you were," Marun said.

"I don't know."

"Tell me!" he insisted.

"I don't know! I couldn't see a way out! I was trapped!"

"Then how did you get back?"

"I grabbed the stone from his hand. I saw a way and fled." Kehfrey scrambled backward as the sorcerer stepped forward. The man's features had tensed with excitement.

"Where? Where were you?"

"I don't know!" the child shouted. "You! You were there! Why don't you know?"

"My own spells blind my sight!" Marun snarled. "They bind me against the man who has the stone."

"How can you do this? How can you move? How can you seem to be here when you're not?"

"Your body was breathing while you were gone, Kehfrey. It works the same way. There's a link whether you see the path the link makes or not."

The boy stared. He swallowed, but nothing went down his throat. His mouth was so dry.

"Tell me how you grabbed the stone?" Marun said.

"He killed his grandson," the boy whispered. "He used him. He broke his neck."

"You went into the grandson," Marun guessed. He'd gone into a dead child! Gods above! What was this boy? What was he to dare such a thing?

The boy shivered. He stared at Marun with intense distrust. "He killed his grandson," he repeated. "He made a ghoul out of him. Just like you can!"

And the sorcerer's amazement intensified. To occupy a ghoul was to displace an evil that not even he fully comprehended, and yet this child had done it, this small shivering child who demanded justification for the horrible journey he had undergone. Marun stared at him, immobile from astonishment.

How could he explain it? How could he possibly comprehend this child's power? It was unlike his, so very unlike. It was freedom and fire, a smouldering blaze lurking in a tiny body, a blaze that leapt the ether and to places he could not, dared not.

"Why does he have your power?" the incredible child demanded.

164

"I spelled the stone," he explained, crouching to get at eye level. "I took a risk placing my essence in it. My body is protected from death, but the stone is a weakness."

"What did you do exactly? What sort of spell did you put on the stone?"

"I made it desirable. I made it addictive. I made it so any who touch it cannot bear to destroy it, but it gives them some of my power."

"He did what you want to do!" Kehfrey accused. "He used him! He killed him! He pumped his seed into his corpse!" The accusation rose in a panicked crescendo, and the last word spat out with foamy saliva. The child shuddered and almost vomited, as if his own spit had horrified him. He pressed the sheet to his white face and stared with huge, wounded eyes at the sorcerer.

"I would not do that to you," Marun whispered into the distraught silence that followed. "The stone only reflects my thoughts. It magnifies them in the wrong hands. It warps them. The man you saw was out of control."

"Will you be? Will you be when you get it back?"

"No! I swear to you I won't."

The boy stared at him, his expression doubtful.

"Kehfrey! I'm not lying! You know I'm not!" Marun pleaded.

"It wasn't a lie yesterday," Kehfrey whispered, and Marun blanched. "Why did he kill his grandson? Did you think it? Did you think it about me?"

"Kehfrey!"

"Answer me!" the boy screamed.

"Yes! The day I met you! I have since decided otherwise, as you well know." Marun's countenance darkened with anger. "What I think and do are not always the same, just as it is with you. Do you do everything you think? Everything you imagine?"

"*He* is *doing it* for you!" Kehfrey accused.

Marun scowled. He couldn't justify his feelings. Feelings were never rational and the ones he felt for this boy were the quintessence of irrational. No child had ever made him feel this way, and he wished to all Creation his madness would just go away. But knowing now what he did about this child, he was uncertain it would. There was something inexpressibly compelling about Kehfrey, and the sorcerer was convinced the boy would only grow more so as he matured. Power attracted power, and this child was filled with it.

He refocused the argument on the object of his hunt. "Who was he? Was it Rook?"

"I don't know. I've never seen him before," the child said hoarsely. "It can't have been Rook. It was his grandson he murdered."

Marun considered the child. Presently he stepped around the bed and went to the washstand. He poured a cup of fresh water and brought it to him. Kehfrey watched him mistrustfully. Marun hated the sight of that sentiment on the boy. A day ago he hadn't deserved it. His dismay fought free in an outburst of anger.

"Take the cup!" he snapped. He watched the child lift his shaking hands toward the vessel. His little fingers fumbled over the bottom. When the tips inadvertently connected to flesh, the boy gasped and pulled his hands away. "I will not hurt you!" Marun said, once again hiding his mortification with impatience.

"I remember what you threatened last night," Kehfrey said.

"I threatened someone else."

"I saw the legs missing from that ghoul. I saw all the ghouls."

"My enemies," he reminded flatly.

"Not the servant!" the boy croaked.

Marun sighed his defeat. The servant he couldn't justify. That murder had been an object lesson to the others, who at the time had thought to collude with the monks of Carmet. But the boy would only see this retribution as excessive cruelty, and he would perhaps be right. The servants were slaves. A simple command would have brought them to order, but he had been angry and sent one to his doom. Regardless that the boy was more sagacious than his age warranted, Kehfrey still had the uncomplicated morality of a child, and the sorcerer apprehended that he could say nothing to justify the servant's presence amongst the ghouls.

And so he threw away any attempt to validate his act of cruelty. Wordlessly he knelt with one knee on the bed, intending only to help the child assuage his thirst, but Kehfrey cried out and tried to draw away. Once again the sorcerer's impatience undermined his kindness. He grabbed the boy by the back of the neck and pulled him closer. The child was too weak to fight off his grip. Marun set the cup to his lips.

"Drink!" he snapped.

Shivering uncontrollably, the child opened his mouth and let the water flow in. His eyes shut momentarily in abject relief, but then the lids fluttered open again, and he glared just as fearfully as before. Marun pulled the cup away and released him.

"You are a stubborn child," he muttered as he set the vessel aside. He returned to the bed and sat on it, but he didn't look at the boy. He pondered almost furiously his predicament. Why he felt so strongly, he had no idea. He only knew he must secure Kehfrey's confidence. Whatever he said, however truthful, wasn't good enough. Not now. Feelings changed and the truth of a moment could become the lie of tomorrow. The boy knew this. Something more was required to recapture his trust.

Not far away, on a small dresser, Vik's dagger lay athwart a leather harness. Marun's eyes narrowed. He rose and went toward it.

"What are you doing?" the boy exclaimed.

Marun smiled darkly. The child was too quick. He'd spotted the direction of his master's interest and come to the wrong conclusion. "I am about to win your trust back," he said flatly.

"How? By turning me into a ghoul? That's pretty effective!"

He heard the boy's body thud to the floor. Marun sighed again, this time cynically. He lifted the dagger and sliced his palm with it. He dropped the knife on the dresser, and turned with his hand fisted tight around the wound, crumpling the laceration, preventing it from shutting properly. As he'd guessed, Kehfrey was on the floor, half risen, both hands on the bed for support. On shivering legs, the boy watched uncertainly.

"My name is Tehlm Sevet. I swear to you by all that I am, I will not kill you," Marun said as he walked.

Kehfrey gaped at him. Then his mouth snapped shut. Immediately he opened it again. A demand popped out. "And my family?"

Marun sighed a third time. "And your family," he agreed. The child's lips opened once again. "Do not ask more!" the sorcerer snarled. Gods help him. He couldn't give him more. He could only give him certainty of a future.

Kehfrey scowled and swallowed his attempt. Marun knelt to the side of him. He brought his fist up and opened his hand. Blood welled on the palm. He set the edge of his hand against the child's mouth. Kehfrey glared into his eyes fixedly. He did not blink.

"Open your lips," Marun whispered. Slowly the child obeyed. The blood dripped inside and onto his tongue. Marun bent forward and set his lips on the boy's. Power lifted. Green swelled over them.

Kehfrey's eyes shut. He felt his heart beating erratically. Then he felt another heart, a slower, bigger heart.

Marun's!

Something ... something was beyond that. It thrummed in time with Marun's heart. Something deep and mysterious. Something ... *familiar*!

He pulled away with a gasp. Marun stared in mystification, fresh blood smeared upon his lips. Kehfrey hastily wiped at the stain he was certain must be on his own, but only managed to spread the blood further. Marun grabbed his head and compelled him to be still. By this time the preternatural green had vanished beneath the sorcerer's skin.

"What did you sense?" he demanded.

"Your heart! Let go!"

"And?"

"Something ...! Something old!" The child struggled. "I don't want to know!" he shouted. He tugged his head futilely.

Marun relented and let him go. "You stubborn child," he named him a second time. He picked Kehfrey up and set him back on the bed. "Cover yourself. Go back to sleep."

"No! You need to let Vik in. He's out there crying."

Scowling, Marun hauled a blanket over him. "I will take care of Vik. You sleep. I need you tonight."

"Tonight? What are we doing?"

"Following the hunters," he uttered. He turned away.

"Wait!" Kehfrey cried.

"What now?" he said impatiently.

"The blood! Get it off! He'll just go mad seeing it."

"Shit!" he hissed. The boy was right. He grabbed a towel at the washstand, wet it and wiped the blood away. The wound in his palm had already sealed, not because of the soulstone spell, but because of the green of healing, a green he had not summoned.

Odd. So very odd. It had erupted out of him as if the child had called it, and the Mother Goddess had risen higher beneath the crust of the world, only the boy had pulled back before she'd fully manifested. Frowning, Marun approached the child and cleaned the blood from his lips and cheek. Kehfrey permitted him the familiarity. He lay on the pillow, all the protest gone out of him, at least physically.

"Why did you kiss me?"

Marun's attention sharpened on Kehfrey's eyes. From their placid expression, he surmised the boy understood the act had not been about desire, at least to start. "To share the blood," he answered.

"Why?"

"To bind the oath. The life fluid is a potent element."

"Why the green?"

"I don't know. It rose of its own accord." Drawn out by this child, this strange, compelling child. And the interest of the Goddess had been piqued. But now she rested further down again, brooding. For some reason, Marun was disinclined to send even the faintest of questions down to her. Sometimes she would answer him no matter where he stood on the world, but this time he had a presentiment a question would bring more damage than answers. The boy had rejected her approach, and this boy was nothing if not a bundle of canny instinct and power. Marun had to respect that. Questioning the Goddess would have to wait for a more appropriate moment.

"I don't want to sleep," the boy whispered.

"Why not?"

"I might go back!"

"I'll send Nicky to you."

The young face immediately relaxed. This angered Marun, but he quelled the emotion. At the dresser, he wiped the dagger blade and tossed the towel aside. He glanced at the tumbled table, the spilled food, and turned away. Let the woman clean the mess.

His face an impassive mask, he strode from the room, but his mind was a turmoil of conflicting emotions, some of them so violent he could barely breathe. His chest was tight and his muscles tense. When he departed from the chamber, he saw before him the balm to soothe both his body and soul. There were no words in him to pacify the object of his desire. He grabbed his salvation and crushed it to his chest.

***

Tears tracked Vik's face. His lids were swollen and his eyes reddened. He started when Marun opened the door of the room. He had a brief glimpse of Kehfrey shifting restlessly in the bed, and then the door shut.

"Kehfrey!" he whispered.

He moved forward, his eyes only on the door. Before he had another thought, Marun clutched him and kissed him with a violence that bruised his lips. For the next few seconds, he could only listen to his thundering heart and feel the cold power burning beneath his lover's skin. He thought he tasted blood.

He shivered uncontrollably by the time the sorcerer released him, fear and desire so thoroughly entwined as to make him dizzy. Muted by his confusion, Vik watched Marun pull one of his chains out from beneath his tunic. Vik remembered the weight of them on his back, that first time alone in the master's bedchamber, how light they had been, yet how heavy with cold power. Now he saw one used.

"Hanicke!" the sorcerer hissed. His fingers gripped one particular charm. Vik started again as the door to Canella's room banged open. Nicky stepped out into the hall, her expression almost panicked. "Go see after the boy. He's afraid to sleep," the master snapped.

She nodded hastily. She glanced back into the room at Kehfrey's worried mother, smiled faintly, shut the door and fled. She didn't look at Marun as she rushed by him and into Kehfrey's chamber. Vik had a fleeting impression of Kehfrey yawning mightily. The door shut on the vision. This provoked him enough that he found his voice again.

"Let me see him!"

"No!" Marun snarled. He dragged him away from the door and toward his own.

"Marun!" Vik protested.

"*Shut up!*"

"I heard him! The things he shouted! What the hells is happening to him? What have you done?"

"Shut up!" the man snarled more heatedly.

He thrust Vik up against a wall and the youth grunted from the breath rushing out of his lungs. The sorcerer's lips sealed his again. He gasped for air when he was freed.

Marun hauled his door open and threw Vik inward. He needed Vik. He needed him now.

He needed him because of Kehfrey.

Chapter Seven

"I did what you said!" Rhet blurted. "I agreed with everything they asked!"

He knew he'd come at a bad time. The sorcerer paced back and forth, hardly calm at all and improperly dressed. His tunic was absent, his linen undershirt rumpled and half hanging out of his breeches, which hadn't quite been done up right, and his stockings drooped. As well, his hair was awry, his forehead wet with perspiration, and he moved jerkily like an animal in a cage, an animal that hadn't been fed for days. Rhet, standing in the centre of the library, shook uncontrollably to see him thus. He hadn't taken a seat. He didn't dare.

Marun paused in front of the library window and glared out. "Were you followed here?"

"No! I came in disguise. I took a hired coach."

"Yes! I can see that!" He turned to face off with the nobleman. Rhet was dressed in contemptible gaudy women's garb, a hood thrown over his head concealing much of his face. He looked like a low-priced slut hiding from her pimp. "What did the ringleaders demand of you?"

"That I continue feeding lies to you about the Syndicate."

"And nothing else?"

"No. I don't think they trust me."

"Why do you say that?"

"Because they know I ...."

"They know what?" Marun said impatiently.

"They know I am like you," Rhet whispered. Marun laughed at that. He roared with laughter. Rhet shook all the harder.

"Like me!" the sorcerer spat. He laughed again. "You imbecile! You aren't like me!" He stalked toward Lord Rhet and punched him hard in the face. Rhet fell to the floor. "Contemptible idiot!" his attacker hissed. "You should have come as usual. Now they likely know you are in collusion with me."

"I'm sorry! I'm sorry!" Rhet cried. He tasted blood in his mouth. Red dripped onto the wooden tiles. Where the blood landed, darkness swelled up out of the floor. More lurched into life around the sorcerer's feet. "Please, no!" the nobleman begged.

The library door opened. The sorcerer's head snapped toward the intruder. It was Vik.

"Lord Rhet," the youth greeted sourly. "So I have you to thank for this latest interruption."

Marun, who'd been about to shout at him to leave, shut his mouth instead.

"I'm sorry!" Rhet said. He knew the boy had just saved his life.

Vik shut the door and walked in toward him. "You cheap slut. Can't you even get something decent on? What poor taste."

"I'm sorry!" Rhet repeated, kohl-decorated eyes begging for protection.

Vik answered the silent plea with withering disdain. His expression contemptuous, he looked at Marun. "Are you planning to kill him?"

"I was considering it." The sorcerer was patently calmer than before and Rhet's hopes soared.

"Gods! Don't put his ugly ghoul in the cellar," Vik uttered in abhorrence. "He'd look like a skinny hag next to the men."

"Please, no!" Rhet cried again, abruptly realizing Vik was no shield at all.

"What do you suggest, then?" Marun said. His voice was completely composed now.

"He's dressed for the part. He's already on his knees."

Marun smiled darkly. "Such cruelty, Vik. What other secrets do you hide from your family?" he inquired over their victim's whimpers.

Vik stepped toward him. "It's none of their business," he said and dragged his lover's head down.

At their feet, Rhet shivered and waited for them to use him. If he was good, they might decide not to kill him. He had to be good.

***

When Kehfen and Wilf exited the coach, they paused on the white gravel to gaze at a hired vehicle that waited further along the curve of the driveway. "Let's find out who he brought?" Wilf suggested, looking curiously at the bored cabby.

Kehfen nodded agreement, but just as they were halfway over, the door to the manor opened. A dishevelled man stumbled out into the sunlight. He was ridiculously thin and ugly, dressed in garish women's garb, the skirt torn, the bodice drooping and revealing a hairy chest. The cloak sagged off one shoulder, leaving the other bare. In utter silence, Wilf and Kehfen watched the stranger totter down the steps. Noting their presence, the man froze in alarm.

"Nice black eye you got there," Kehfen commented.

"Fine fat lip too," Wilf added. "You come here regularly?"

The man laughed. The noise was high and wild. He spun away from them, his eyes crazed, and staggered toward the hired coach, into which he dragged himself. The vehicle set off. Kehfen and Wilf turned toward the house in trepidation. Up there, Vik stood in the doorway, as composed as a young lord and likely more handsome than any currently living in Wistal.

Handsome be damned! Kehfen had no use for such and glared accusingly at his pervert of a son. Vik hesitated and then walked down the steps. "Did you do that?" his father demanded.

"Some of it," he admitted.

172

"You little bastard! Why?"

"What's your problem? As if you've never smartened one of your associates up."

This logic forced Kehfen to take a mental step backwards. Momentarily. Curiosity forced him to question again. "So what did the fellow need smartening about?"

Vik shrugged. "Don't know. I fucked him over because Marun would have killed him otherwise," came the simple if coarse answer. "Buggering him seemed the nicer thing to do."

Kehfen goggled at him, blatantly astonished, but Wilf chortled. "You soft-hearted fairy!" he insulted and gave Vik an approving slug on the arm. Vik danced away, smiling slightly and rubbing his abused limb.

Mystified, Kehfen looked from one to the other. Vik had saved that man's life? By buggering him? Was that preferable?

He spotted Marun within the entrance, and the possibility that it might be settled home. He remembered what the sorcerer did with the dead.

Sinister fucker. He was perfectly collected, even dressed only in breeches and an undershirt. If torture sex didn't get him flustered, Kehfen was certain he didn't want to know what did.

"Hey! You won't believe what happened!" Wilf said to Vik, not noticing the sorcerer above.

"What? The old bastard decided to adopt you?"

Wilf gawped in surprise and then scowled. "Shit! Was it that obvious? *I* didn't expect it." He heard the noise of footsteps and looked aside. The sorcerer approached them. Wilf stiffened with distrust.

"Did he ask for help with his illness?" the sorcerer said.

"Yes," Kehfen replied. Wilf seemed more inclined to run than answer. Though calm enough, the sorcerer had a disturbing ambience. The moment he had walked out the door, the daylight just hadn't seemed as bright. "He thinks his nephew will challenge the adoption and have him declared incompetent by his peers," Kehfen added. He glanced at the undershirt again. There was a bloodstain on the hem.

Marun nodded as if unsurprised. "Is the adoption legal yet?"

"Oh, he got it done right and proper, with a magistrate and noble-born witnesses. How did you know he'd do it?"

"Opinions change with age. They change with reminders of what once was." Marun looked at Wilf pointedly.

Wilf's gaze shot up, away from the red stain he'd only just noticed. "He did think I looked a bit like him when he was younger," he admitted.

"Did he? Perhaps you do a bit. You take after your mother most. And she? She doesn't much take after Harte at all. I remember Harte well from his younger days. He was standing just ten feet before me when I was whipped." He walked back up the stairs and into the house.

"What?" Vik said. "Whipped here! In Winfel? You were whipped here?" He started after Marun, his curiosity bursting out of control, but

Kehfen hauled him back. For some reason, his too handsome son couldn't seem to feel the cold terror creeping along in that man's wake.

"It was him," Kehfen whispered. "Prince Cehtre's lover."

Vik stalled. Having occurred just under fifty years ago, the story was so horrific it had become almost mythical, but the lace marks on Marun's back made the legend compellingly real. Murders had happened. Bodies had disappeared and returned mangled. Cehtre had thrown himself from a tower.

"Does he have the marks?" Wilf asked. "The whip marks on his back?"

"Yes," Vik said, almost inaudible.

His father shook him roughly. "Don't you fall in love with him," he hissed. "Don't you do that. The man's an adder. He can't be trusted."

Vik could only stare at him. But surprise evaporated and bitter scorn replaced it. "What do you care?"

"You idiot!" Kehfen cried. He hauled his son in and squeezed him hard. "Don't you dare get hurt! You hear me?"

The choked words didn't match the angry look beforehand. Shocked, Vik gaped over his father's shoulder at Wilf, whose brow furrowed with the same worry as Kehfen's. Vik's truculence vanished. His arms rose around his father's back in forgiveness. Kehfen shook him a second time and let go. Stepping away, he scowled and wiped his eyes clear.

"Brats! You're all annoying brats!" he muttered, embarrassed to have wept like a child, if only for half a minute.

Wilf smiled weakly. Vik, who was now the one weeping and unable to stop, turned away. Kehfen smacked him on the back of the head.

"Ow! What did you do that for?" Vik said, glaring at the father.

"Stopped you crying, didn't it?"

Vik smiled unwillingly. Kehfen hadn't kidded like that since he'd learned of his son's sexual preference. "If I'm a brat, it came from you!" Vik joked back, but it was also a test.

"Yes, well, can't plead innocent all the time, can I?" Kehfen said ruefully.

Vik sighed noiselessly. His father had passed the test.

Kehfen stepped toward the house. "Everything all right with the rest of them?"

Vik glanced at the house. Wonderful. He just had to be the bearer of bad tidings. "Fine now."

"And what do you mean by that?"

"Do *not* panic, Pop. Everything *is* fine now."

"So tell me what it was when it wasn't!" Kehfen said. Gods bust it! What had bloody happened this time? Vik proceeded to inform him as they walked into the manor. "Gods bust it!" he cried afterward. "My Kehfrey was poisoned!"

"Shit!" Wilf said. "There's going to be more dead boys for certain. Are we going to warn them?"

A denial assailed them. "Not yet."

They halted in the hallway before the stairs and turned to see Marun standing in the library entrance.

"Why not?" Wilf said.

"First of all, the Syndicate doesn't deserve my consideration," he answered as he approached. "Second, Kortin probably wants you all dead. Lastly, I have a job for us tonight and I don't want him tipped off."

"What job?" Kehfen asked.

"I'm going after Rook," the man said flatly.

"Going after him? How? No one can find him."

"I can. Now, I can. You will come," he informed Kehfen; then looked at Wilf and added, "but not you. You will remain here to guard the household."

"Bloody balls! That's all I ever get to do!" the young man complained.

"That's because you're good at it," Kehfen said, slapping him on the shoulder. "Mum will be glad of your company."

"So will Gamis. He's been freaking over ghouls and snakes since he got here," Vik said. "I wonder where he's taken himself?"

"You have plenty of time to find out," Marun said. "You are remaining behind as well."

Vik stared reproachfully at him, but his lover's expression brooked no argument. Lips thinning with resentment, Vik averted his face and stalked away, a silent promise of reprisal in his piqued carriage. Marun sighed infinitesimally and looked toward the boy's father.

"Don't look at me. He got that from his mother," Kehfen said and actually saw a smile slip past the man's defences.

"I think perhaps Kehfrey takes after you. He spits out retorts as fast."

"That he does," Kehfen admitted. "I suppose I must thank you now for saving him." But Marun merely eyed him flatly and turned away.

"Doesn't look like he cares much for gratitude," Wilf commented after the sorcerer had disappeared into the library again.

"No, I suppose not. Gratitude counts less than favours owed." Kehfen headed up the stairs. "I'm looking in on Kehfrey and then your Mum."

"Right. I'll see Mum first," Wilf said and followed him up the stairs. "Mum's going to be thrilled!"

***

Within the room, the light was dim. The drapes had been shut. At the door, Kehfen studied the pair of figures in the bed. Both slept, the boy cradled against Nicky's bosom. Lucky child. Too bad he was too young to properly enjoy the cushion. Smiling, Kehfen shut the door. His Kehfrey was fine, just needed his rest. Kehfen planned to see him later, before he and the sorcerer went after Rook that night.

He stepped onward to the guest room where his wife waited. He found her blubbering on Wilf's shoulder, the discomfited young man patting her back. It was such a feeble attempt to make her stop that Kehfen laughed.

"Pop!" Wilf protested. "She's crying!"

"That's not crying. She's so happy she can't let it out right."

Wilf gaped, but then heard his mother laugh against his shoulder.
"Oh, Mum! You've just snotted up Marun's loaned suit for nothing."

Kehfen and Canella both laughed. "Snot will come out," she retorted.
She sniffed and turned her head away proudly, reminding them both of
her higher birth. Kehfen bent and kissed his lady wife.

"How's the new brat?"

"Oh! She's fine!"

The sharpness of her tone didn't fit with the reassurance. He looked
askance at her. What had gone on here? He knew that way of his wife's.
She was worried over something, but seeing the haggard droop of her skin
beneath the eyes, he decided to save the questions for a private moment.
The last few days had been hard on her. Hells! They'd been hard on
everyone. He let her be and squatted to view the basket in which their
infant daughter rested. He smiled. She was a sweet little bundle.

"Our first daughter. I was getting sick of boys."

"Well now you can get your fill of her," Canella said dryly. "Just you
don't wake her up."

"Oh, come on. I haven't seen her all day."

"Hsst! You get over here."

Kehfen straightened with a smile and returned to his wife. He bent
and kissed her again. "Your father said he'd like you to visit once you're
able," he mentioned. She almost began crying again, but he made a
pretend dodge toward the baby. That stopped her cold. She hissed at him
to come back, but smiled at his devilish expression.

"You always know what to do, don't you?" she said.

"Fast on my feet. Yes, that's me." It wasn't an idle boast. He had to be
quick, physically and mentally. His life depended on his rapid evaluations
just about daily.

"He says I'm going to have to train with a sword," Wilf told his
mother, pleased with the prospect.

"Of course you will. Knives are for common folk," she said
complacently.

Kehfen pulled Wilf off the bed and pre-empted the place next to
Canella. "Hi, now, woman. You complaining about your common
husband?"

"I am not," she denied. "My husband isn't the least common. He's a
prince in disguise."

"Is he, now?" Kehfen said with a teasing smile. "Well! Aren't you
lucky."

Wilf laughed. "I'm leaving. You two look like you need some privacy."

"Ah, hells! I'm not getting much farther than that for months," Kehfen
told him. Canella smacked him hard on the arm and he laughed.

"No, really," Wilf said with a smile. "I'll just see if Vik has located Gamis yet. Knowing Gamis, he's eating or trying to cheat the staff of their wages, *if* they get any, that is."

"That's Gamis, all right," Kehfen said. "Must have a tapeworm packed in that greedy gut of his." Wilf grinned and shut the door. Kehfen's answering smile dropped away. "Tell me what happened, then," he ordered his wife.

This time when she burst into tears, he knew it was for real. The confession came out with little prompting. Afterward he folded his penitent wife in his arms and shut his eyes, hiding his sadness, his anxiety, his thankfulness that Kehfrey had been there to save his little sister. That boy seemed always to be where he was needed most, but what he might have to pay in the future for their continued protection filled Kehfen's mind with trepidation.

***

Above an unused alley that separated two warehouses, Olomo crept down the roof of the westernmost. He slid from the ridge, aiming for a place from which to drop down. Ahead lay the port the warehouses served. There, the masts of ships made a forest of spires and twisted hemp vines. The wind, fortunately for the proud captains, currently blew seaward, but Olomo only smelled the stench of human waste lifting off the ground with every gust. The violent rains of yesterday hadn't been severe enough to wash the worst of the squalor off the streets. Even high above the alleys, the stench was enough to wrinkle his nose. He ignored the reek as best he could and continued on with caution. His mission was an important one. There was a boy to train. There were articles needed for this crucial task.

Spying a likely bit of gutter, he slipped down the remaining distance of roof. The gutter proved as sturdy as he had hoped. He hung by his fingers and dropped to the wood planks of the massive wharf built over the rocks of the harbour. He paused to check the alley for observers and then walked down the narrow passage toward the open end, which was just barely visible beyond the heaped garbage lazy dockworkers had shoved into the convenient receptacle. At the end, he peered cautiously outward, looking for anyone from the thieving guild. Members of the smuggling guild were no doubt present, but they didn't concern Olomo. The guilds weren't particularly loyal to each other. If any smugglers saw him, they'd pass the information along to Kortin's gang, but in their own good time, time enough for him to disappear again.

Many smaller perpendicular piers jutted out from the main wharf into the bay. Most had more than one ship lashed to the mooring posts, cargo vessels primarily. There was a large ship moored to the nearest dock, a different one than yesterday. All along the raised thoroughfare, people wandered. Sailors and dockworkers moved about, some with loads, some with business to see to, some looking for hire. They cursed. They greeted.

They stomped past without a word. The cacophony of merchants hawking wares and whores hawking flesh mixed with the general din. Everything was as it should be and with not a sign of a thieving guild representative.

A man with Olomo's skin colouration walked by. It was a Get tribesman, of no interest to the assassin, just a hired kraken killer from southern Ysep. Olomo paused to watch him stride onward, only doing so to admire the great harpoon he proudly carried. Once he'd passed, Olomo stepped out into the open.

He was watched of course, but this was unavoidable. He continued on in a relaxed manner until he arrived at the correct warehouse. The guard nodded a greeting, took his bribe and let him pass. Olomo hurried into the darkness beyond the gaping doors. Near the centre of the structure, he climbed crates to the rafters and hefted himself up onto the closest beam. He followed it until he saw them, Simre and his followers laid out end to end upon a wide rafter on the further side of the warehouse. In the centre of the line of corpses, the bundle lay undisturbed. The trap had not been sprung.

Olomo smiled briefly. The guard had assured him that he was familiar with the death traps of Pek assassins. A few of his mates had crossed Simre, and he'd been the only one left living to learn the lesson. Frankly the guard had been happy to be of service. His mates had been avenged. It didn't matter to him that another Pek assassin had done the job.

Olomo approached the bundle. He stepped over it and took position in the only safe location. Crouched above a body, he threw a small stone he'd taken from the sorcerer's long driveway. The trap within the bundle went off. Two flat wooden sticks flung the flaps of canvas aside. Dozens of wood slivers flew up from out of the primed weapon. The slivers whizzed past him, some hissing by only inches from his body, each of them tipped with deadly poison. There was no cure. Death occurred within minutes.

Silence returned. Not one projectile had pierced him. With the chill of excitement fading in his limbs, he checked for misfired darts, but found none in the contraption. He pressed the wooden sticks down, forced the springs to remain in place with a leather strap and stored the device in an airtight case. Without the slivers in the holes, the poison inside was exposed to air, which rendered it useless. Packed properly, the trap was reusable. He tucked it within the bundle and after tying the collection shut, he hauled the package up and made his way back down the beam, stepping carefully past the bodies of the Pek Tol followers. He returned to the guard at the warehouse door.

"What about them, then?" the guard said, referring to the bodies.

Olomo gave him what remained of his money. He no longer needed it. He had everything he required now. "Get rid of them," he told the man. "It matters not how. They are but shells to be cast aside."

"Right," the guard answered flatly, unimpressed. "Anything important I should know? Traps?"

"There are slivers of wood scattered around the warehouse. Do not go in for three hours. By then, the poison will have degraded."

"You sure about that?"

"I am sure. The poison loses potency exposed to air." Olomo stalked away. He returned to the alley and disappeared within it. He scaled the wall and fled back up the roof. He must leave the city at once. He must return to his charge, the boy.

He smiled in expectation. The weapons he had taken from Simre and his men were secure. Tomorrow the boy would learn to dance with knives.

***

Kehfrey turned in his sleep. Something soft and fragrant tickled his nose. He sneezed. The arm that had been wrapped loosely around him clutched him tight. He almost screamed, but stopped himself just in time. He recognised the scent of the one who held him.

"Nicky." He shoved a lock of hair off his nose. "You smell."

"You brat! I almost peed in the bed! You scared the wits out of me!"

"You made me sneeze. Why do you put on so much perfume? Do you stink without it?"

"I do not stink!" she objected. "Perfume smells good. It makes me feel ...."

"Feel what?"

"Never mind." She shifted away to look him over. "Do you feel better?"

"Yes."

"Would you like some pie?"

He grinned. "Yes," he said again.

She smiled at him wryly, but there was relief in the gesture. "Tell me what happened," she said.

His smile disappeared, and he shook his head.

"Fine, then, but at least tell me if he hurt you. I can see after that."

"He didn't hurt me."

"You're sure?" she said, watching narrowly.

"I'm sure. I would know."

"Sometimes children lie about it."

"Some children know what to lie about and what not," he retorted.

"You are a very odd child. If your father had the right colour eyes, I'd think you were a half elf."

"What does that have to do with it?" He shifted away from her.

"Elven children tend to be precocious like you."

"Well, I'm all human," he said angrily. "And what do you mean by precocious exactly?"

"That your perspective on things is more adult than usual," she said. She smiled at his hurt. "I didn't mean to offend." She grabbed him and gave him a kiss on the cheek by way of apology, but ruined the gesture when she deliberately shoved some of her long hair up his nose.

"Gaah!" he cried. He laughed and scurried away. In his haste, he fell off the bed.

Nicky tossed herself across the mattress and peered down at him anxiously. "Are you all right?"

"You just did that to see me naked again," he accused.

Her serious expression disappeared. "There's nothing that interesting to look at yet."

"Well, it's still bigger than the whanger Astabe painted the other day." He grabbed the pot beneath the bed and made use of it, turning about for privacy. He heard Nicky giggle.

"A whanger! That's a good one. Trust you to invent another name for it."

He grinned. Once finished, he shoved the pot back under and searched out his clothing. Nicky sat up and watched him haul his breeches on. He plunked down on the floor and groped about for a stocking, having inadvertently seated himself on one. He found it eventually.

"You don't seem too worried about being naked today," she remarked.

"What's the point? You saw it yesterday. You slept with it today and yesterday. Not much more to discover, is there?"

"Kehfrey?" she said, serious again. "Are you sure there isn't any elf in your bloodline?"

"Crud, woman!" he shouted. He almost threw a shoe at her. "I'm not an elf!"

"All right!" she said, lifting her arms in defence. "I just had to ask. You aren't like any human child I've ever met, including my own."

"You had human children?" he exclaimed, lowering the shoe.

"I'm half human, Kehfrey," she said wryly. "They can't all come out half elf when you couple with a human father."

"What if you couple with an elf father?"

"Then you get whole blooded ones," she said flatly. "Sometimes."

He noted her stiff expression and realized there was a sad story behind it, somewhere in her long history. Someday he hoped he'd get it out of her. "I can't find my other shoe," he muttered, looking around in pretended bewilderment.

"It's on your foot."

"Oh! Right." He smirked and received a cynical smile in response. He tugged the second shoe on and then looked up at her solemnly. "Can I see your ears?" he asked. He'd seen them yesterday evening, but wanted to verify that his memory hadn't failed him.

"What for?" she said.

He just looked at her expectantly and waited. Relenting, she pulled her hair aside for him. They were nice round ears, perfectly human in appearance, just like last night.

"Half elves always have human ears. It's how the full-blooded ones tell us apart."

"But you look completely human," he pointed out.

180

"The eyes, Kehfrey."

"Those green eyes are elvish? Humans have green eyes."

"It's greener than human green."

"There's no other eye colour?"

"There is a tribe with a lot of blue-eyed members, but it's a rare trait in general."

"No brown eyes? No hazel?"

"No."

"Well! See? Counts me out completely, doesn't it?"

She smiled at his logic. He was right, of course. She'd never heard of a hazel-eyed elf, even a half-blooded one. He finished with his shoe and stood. She observed pensively as he pulled on his tunic. When his head popped out, he grinned with the irrepressible enthusiasm of youth. His ginger hair was askew, one side flattened, the other straight up over his head.

"Where's that pie, then?" he said.

Without answering, she pulled him over and pressed the high side down. The wave sprung back up. Recalcitrant curls, they were just like their owner, obstinate, and so she let them be and walked toward the door.

"Let's see what cook has cooling on the counter," she suggested. "He won't mind if you have a little something to tide you over."

"Does an entire pie count as a little something?" he wanted to know.

"Today it does," she said firmly. He grinned, and she couldn't help smiling back. He was adorable. Devilish definitely, but adorable.

"Nicky?"

Ah. Questions. Here they came. No doubt a slew of them. "Yes?"

"You said elven children were precocious, right?"

The impish cast to his countenance had fled and now he was all gravity. Nicky eyed this development with growing distrust. Whatever the questions concerned, she doubted they would be easy to answer. "Right," she admitted guardedly.

"So when do they start fornicating?" he up and asked.

She blinked. Then blinked again. "Fornicating? Children?"

"You said they were precocious."

"I didn't mean that!"

"But when do they get interested in it, then?" he insisted.

"If they ask about it, then they're interested," she said.

He blinked at her and blinked again, and a pink flush crept over his cheeks. "Um ... how old is that, roughly speaking?"

"Around ten or so, but no one takes them seriously."

"Why?"

"Because they're children!" She shoved him at the door. "Of all things, Kehfrey! Why must you ask about fornicating? You can't compare humans to elves. Elves have an entirely different culture."

"I'm interested!" he snapped. "So there! Ignore me! Nothing to take seriously, is it? I'm only gods busted seven!"

He stomped out ahead of her, and she followed him to the stairs, shaking her head in mystification. He was a very odd child.

***

The papers were in no particular order. Rhet had dumped them one on top of the other before packing them off. Marun sorted them himself as he read. Eventually the piles alone told him a story: receipts written out to the late Lord Lolte, receipts for wine purchases from Pehtre Vineyards in particular; delivery orders to various houses in the city, of which some of the addresses Marun recognised; deeds to establishments throughout Wistal and beyond. The story was very clear indeed.

Lolte had been in charge of the whoring ring of the Syndicate. This fact alone set many mysteries in the light, the largest of them how the Syndicate had formed and managed to survive as a powerful, structured entity for so long. Lolte had seen to it. The Minister of Justice, he had been the perfect leader, the perfect organiser of a crime ring.

Lolte had been lying to him all along.

Marun scowled at the papers. Lolte had lied. The alliances he had arranged through the Minister, the so-called favours he'd asked handled: any number of them may never have happened. Months of careful manoeuvring had only seemed to take place. Because of Lolte, he was back at the beginning again.

"Damn him!" he hissed. He would gladly have killed the Lord Minister of Justice all over again knowing this, killed him more viciously. "Damn him!"

The rage that filled him grew beyond his tolerance. He clutched the table and threw it over. The papers scattered and drifted everywhere. The noise of the crashing furniture resounded throughout the room. Shortly after, Domel came through the library door and stared inward fearfully.

"Get the master thief!" Marun snarled.

As the butler rushed out again, the master of the manor stalked away from the devastation and toward the writing desk. Kehfrey's work still lay on it, Vik's as well. The sorcerer calmed slightly, reminded that not all was the same as a few months earlier.

While he stood there pondering Vik's hesitant scrawl and Kehfrey's sure one, a noise sounded at the door. He turned to find the gamin there, looking in at the overturned table and the scattered papers. Just beyond him, the woman hovered nervously, her inhumanly bright eyes showing fear. Her master was fit to kill someone just now and she knew it.

"Hi, now!" the boy piped up. "Are all those scraps for me to work on?"

Marun laughed despite his anger, but he turned the laugh into a scowl. The child was still far too pale. He looked sleepy and his hair was an absolute mess. He should go right back to bed. "What are you doing out of bed?"

"Hungry," the child told him. "About to wheedle a pie off Evern." He stepped in a pace. "Want me to get some for you?"

"No!" He turned away angrily. Abruptly he changed his mind. "Yes!" he said. "Get me some."

Gods! He was hungry. He only just realized it. He hadn't eaten all day. He hadn't had breakfast, and he'd dumped his noon meal on the floor of Kehfrey's room.

"Back in a minute," the boy said. He dashed out the door. The woman hastened after him.

Marun sat at the desk and picked up the paper Vik had written on earlier. "Hak," he read incorrectly. He smiled. The smile faded. "What the hells has happened?" he whispered. He answered himself immediately. "I have taken in a family of thieves, jesters, whores, poets and geniuses."

Was that better than having Lolte?

But he'd never had Lolte. He scowled again.

The thief entered the library just then. There wasn't a sound, but Marun sensed his presence. A moment of silence ensued as the man observed the state of the room, and Marun waited to learn his reaction.

"Well, now," Kehfen said, announcing his entrance. "Kehfrey's going to like all that."

Once again Marun smiled, but he kept his head turned away. Family of arrogant jesters. "I know about Kortin and the Minister of Justice," he said. "I need to know who the other ringleaders are." The smile was gone by the time he turned.

"So you figured Lolte, did you? Is that what the papers are about?" Kehfen stepped inward and approached him.

Marun regarded him darkly. The man was Kehfrey grown up, only not so delicate of feature. Even so, Kehfen was a very handsome man. He had a way of moving that suggested he meant business. Marun almost smiled again, remembering what business he'd received yesterday evening. The bloodied knife had disappeared from the floor, likely retrieved by the butler. Kehfen didn't look in that direction. He showed no sign of discomfort, but Marun knew he feared. Kehfen hid it well. He'd doubtless had a lifetime of practice.

"You know who Kortin is. He's in charge of the thieving ring," Kehfen said. "Then there's his half-brother, Drayhven. You would know him as Lord Avehlt."

"Gods!" Marun hissed. The Minister of the bloody Port! "What's he in charge of?"

"The protection and gambling racket. Also contraband and smuggling. He's got a stranglehold on every market in the city and beyond. He's not a good man to owe a debt to."

"Are there any more?"

"Just the pickpocket and beggars' ring. The leader isn't much to worry over. His name is Chimet, a common fellow with no noble-blooded family connections. He pretty much does what the others tell him to do. No one else wants his end of the Syndicate. Too little gain, too much risk." Kehfen stopped beside the desk and looked down at the sorcerer impassively.

Marun considered him just as dispassionately. "Lolte is dead," he said, watching the man carefully for his reaction.

"Is he? The Syndicate can't hold up for long without Lolte. I heard his successor is a bit of a useless twit."

"I have his nephew under control," Marun said flatly.

"Do you?"

"He was the man who fled the manor when you arrived."

Kehfen laughed before he could catch himself. Marun barely smiled. At that moment, Kehfrey popped back into the library, holding a tray in his hands.

"I've got two pies!" he blurted happily, staggering inward under the load. "And stout!" He set down the heavy tray before Marun. "The stout's too warm. The heat wave, you know."

"The staff should keep some in the cellar," Marun muttered absently.

Kehfrey grinned at him wisely and whisked a pie away along with a fork. He saw a crease form in Marun's cheek. The sorcerer had almost smiled at his own forgetfulness.

Just as Kehfrey set his plate down on a small table, Kehfen grabbed the boy's mug of stout off the tray. "Hey!" Kehfrey protested.

"No, you don't," his father denied him. "I'm not having you whirling about like a drunken fool and telling us stories again about how the world is round like a peach and spinning off in the void faster than a bloody bird." He tossed a gulp of stout down and scowled at its warmness. In the process of drinking the stout as well, which he generally didn't care for, Marun suddenly coughed and spat the brown liquid everywhere. Father and son looked at him in surprise.

"The world is round!" the sorcerer gasped hoarsely.

"It is so!" Kehfrey cried angrily. "I saw it clear as your spit!"

Suddenly the master laughed outright. He actually howled with mirth. Kehfen looked at his son and eyed him as if to say *I told you so*; even the sorcerer thought he was foolish. But Kehfen quickly lost the amused expression when Marun stood and went to a shelf nearby. The master brought a heavy book down and thudded it onto the end table next to the chair Kehfrey sat in. He pressed it open at the right page and whirled it about. There, sitting prettily above a carefully printed paragraph of writing, was an illustration of the world depicting the outlines of their continent. It was round.

Kehfrey grinned hugely.

"The world *is* round!" Marun repeated, his meaning quite clear this time.

184

Kehfen gawped at the page in awe. "But how does anyone know?" he said. "You can't just get drunk and wake up with a story!"

"Apparently your son can," Marun said firmly. Not only that, he could be deathly tired, pop out of his body and get momentarily trapped in a dead one possessed by dark magic. Marun's lips began to curl again with mirth. He turned away, grinning wider than he'd done in decades.

A family of thieves, jesters, whores, poets, geniuses, *and mystics*. That *was* better than having Lolte.

***

Supper commenced, and Kehfrey managed to find room for more despite recently devouring an entire pie. Gamis, on the other hand, had been in the sugar bin stealing crystals whenever Cook hadn't been looking. He left the table in a hurry and they heard him vomiting out in the hall. Domel sighed heavily and retreated from the dining room to see that his staff cleaned this latest mess. Since that family had descended on them, there seemed to be mess after mess to right.

"The pig!" Wilf said in disgust. "Cook almost cut both his hands off the last time he saw him in the cussed sugar."

Vik smiled. "He won't go in it tomorrow. I told him Evern was going to put an adder in the bin, just for him."

At the head of the table, Marun sat through all this without a word, but Kehfrey saw the dimple in his cheek creasing again. The sorcerer lifted a goblet of wine to hide the emotion. He seemed to appreciate their banter, but didn't want his enjoyment noticed. He had a reputation at stake, a dire one that he refused to ruin with constant laughter, family of jesters or not. Even so, his latest and youngest servant thought it was good for the man to remember he was still human, or at least human enough to laugh.

His master's gaze darted toward him, and Kehfrey lowered his quickly. Well, however much it was good for the man to laugh, Marun didn't want it remarked, and that was that.

"I say we make him stuff his guts with sugar until he can't stand the sight of it," Wilf put forth. His eyes wandered toward the other end of the table. Nicky sat there, a vision of false purity in a white dress. He thought about the very wicked bath they'd shared earlier and wondered if she'd like a go at another. Unfortunately she was acting extremely sedate and circumspect at the moment. Wilf thought it likely Marun's cold presence was the reason.

Kehfen spoke and drew Wilf's attention back to the centre of the table. "Won't work. Short memory," the thief said. Gamis wasn't his brightest. There was no getting around that.

"I saw the pastry boy on our old street make a snake out of dough and paint it with colours," Kehfrey said. "We could put one like it in the bin and make Gamis shit his drawers."

Vik laughed in delight. "Could you paint it up just like an adder?"

"Remember the asp this morning? I could do that. It was just grey and black. The soot in the hearth will do fine for paint."

"I don't think cook will want soot in the sugar bin," Marun remarked dryly.

"Right," the child said in disappointment.

"He could, however, make you a food-based paint that will do the job," the sorcerer continued blandly. The boy grinned at him. It was quite an evil little smirk, Marun noted.

To the other side of the table, Olomo released a noise of disgust. "You have no time for such nonsense. You will begin training again tomorrow morning."

"He will be resting tomorrow morning," Marun denied him. "Tonight he will be out helping me track Rook down. You will come along."

"Kehfrey can't come," Kehfen objected. "It's too dangerous. He's been through enough."

"He will come. He has skills that might be useful tonight."

"Skills? What skills? He's just a little boy! He can't come!"

"He will come!" Marun snapped. Kehfen started to protest again, but the master's threatening chill changed his mind. Kehfen shut his mouth and glowered. Marun stared the thief down until he averted his head in submission.

"That's it!" Vik barked, making his attempt the second his father's defeat had been concluded. "If Kehfrey goes, I go!"

"You will not," the master contradicted.

Vik opened his lips to dissent. Marun's expression darkened and the intense disquiet in the room deepened. Obstinately Vik inhaled for a rebuttal. A pea landed in his mouth.

"Gak!" he said and spat.

Kehfrey snickered. "Point!"

"Little devil!" Vik blurted.

Kehfrey picked up another pea and waited for his shot. Vik snapped his mouth shut. Why did he care about that brat? Why did anyone? He cast a resentful look at Marun, but the master gazed upon the gamin, his expression amused. The tension in the air had vanished. Vik looked down at his plate and grimaced. Damned brat.

The gathering went back to eating, except for Kehfrey and his master. The child smirked at Marun and began piling his peas on top of his carrots. Marun wondered what the boy was imagining.

Having calmly watched all that occurred, Olomo set his dinner knife down and spoke to the child. "Are you able to throw anything else accurately other than food?" he said dryly.

"Darts," the child answered, still intent on his plate of food.

"Just darts?"

"There's darts at one of the safe houses. Won a silver off someone the other day."

"Indeed. Did you hit what you aimed at?"

"Yes. Why?"

"Just wondering."

"Do you want to play darts with me?" the child asked, taking his attention off the fortress of pea-besieged carrots.

"No. Later we will toss knives perhaps."

"Knives! Fine by me!" the boy said excitedly. "No one ever lets me touch them usually. Want to go at it now? I'm done."

Olomo stared at the enthusiastic little face guardedly. "You haven't been taught yet."

"No bother. Give me a few practice shots." The boy rose hurriedly. Remembering his manners, he sat back down and looked to Marun for permission.

The conversation had piqued the master's interest. Marun stood. The carrot and pea pile would obviously not be eaten, and he wondered what the boy could do with a knife in any case. "This should be interesting. Let's go."

Olomo inclined his head in agreement and rose. "I shall return shortly with the weapons," he said stiffly.

"Where will this contest take place?" Marun asked.

"Not a contest. A lesson," Olomo amended firmly. "There is an hour of light left. If there is a tree that you do not care for overly much, we can sacrifice it." Marun nodded his consent, and Olomo left the dining room.

Kehfen eyed Kehfrey intently. "Well, boy? What's your bet?" he challenged

"No bets this time," the child refused.

"You took a silver off Scoss just two days ago. Why not your Pop?"

"I know how to play darts."

"You were all up for a game with Olomo."

"There wasn't going to be any betting. Just fun."

"What's that? Fun without betting?"

"We don't even know what I can do yet," the child protested.

"Fine. Let's bet on whether you'll hit the target the first time," Kehfen suggested. "I've got five silver says you can't."

"I get a practice shot first."

"That's not the first time, then," Kehfen retaliated.

"Fine. First shot. I got a silver."

"I'll take it. Five to one. Quite a gain if you make it. Let's let Wilf hold it."

"No, Wilf's betting, too," Wilf said. "I bet he makes the shot. Ten silvers."

Kehfen grinned at him wisely. "No five to one odds for you, boy. We go even."

"I've got fourteen hanging about somewhere," Vik said.

"For or against?" his father demanded.

"For." Vik scowled at Kehfrey. "You better not miss, brat."

"If it's bigger than your mouth, no problem," the child taunted. Vik rose from his chair and charged at him. Kehfrey squealed and ran out the door.

"Don't break his arms! He needs them!" Wilf shouted. He raced after the two, but suddenly skidded to a halt and rushed back in. "Here!" he said to Nicky. He handed her his pouch and hurried back out again.

"Looks like you're holding," Kehfen said. Grinning, he counted out enough silver to cover the bets and handed it over to her. He strolled out after the boys.

Nicky looked at Marun. He returned her regard, his expression impassive. "For or against?" she asked. "Which would you bet?"

"I don't bet," he said flatly. He turned away and walked out of the room.

"No, I suppose you don't," she whispered. Marun made sure of everything by owning, threatening or killing it. "They don't know him," she said tightly. "They don't know him at all."

***

Olomo used a piece of soft limestone gravel from the driveway to draw a circle in the middle of the trunk. He made the target fairly low, this so the child would have a good chance at it. As he drew, he listened to Kehfen mock the boy. At the same time, the two eldest brothers encouraged him. Gamis had shown up to enjoy the entertainment. He was still feeling queasy and sat on the grass out of the way. He hadn't placed a bet. He'd lost all his silvers in the safe house.

The Ysepian was not pleased by this turn of events. This was a sacred duty. It was not an entertainment. He scowled at the tree and then set his face into a calm mask. The bet didn't matter, only the child's education.

Once the target was prepared, the assassin returned. He had left the bundle on the ground. Marun stood next to it, observing with his usual unsmiling expression. Ignoring the sorcerer, the assassin knelt beside the canvas and unrolled it. Awed silence settled the moment he unveiled his cache.

He had them all, every weapon and trap Simre's team had owned: the swords, the daggers, the throwing knives, the throwing stars, the poisons, the devices, the garrottes, the cases, the sheaths. Everything. It was an impressive arsenal and he knew it, but he made no indication he felt so. Ignoring the longer daggers meant for close combat, he lifted a set of short knives. Olomo already had his own strapped on the limbs of his body. These were for the child.

"These are throwing knives," he said. "Do you see that they are shorter than daggers, the tangs small and covered only with enough leather to ensure a good, quick grasp? They have been weighted perfectly for throwing."

The boy had come to crouch at the other side of the bundle. "I see it, but what are the round thingies?" he asked, ignoring the short-bladed weapons.

"Throwing stars. They are for later." The child had no patience. Olomo lifted the canvas and wrapped the remaining weapons, hiding them from the boy's curious eyes. "You must never go into this without my permission. There are poisons within that have no cure. Do you understand?"

"Yes," the boy answered.

"You will promise!" Olomo demanded.

"I promise," he said solemnly.

Satisfied, Olomo rose. He carried the knives across the lawn and set himself ten feet before the target. One after the other, he sank the blades into the tree. Despite that the target had been adjusted for Kehfrey's height, the weapons formed a neat circle in the centre.

"Did you watch me?" Olomo said. He ignored the impressed silence of the spectators.

"Yes," the boy responded.

"Go and get them."

Kehfrey jogged over to the tree and tugged at the first one. He had a time of it. Olomo's overhand throws had seemed indolent when he'd tossed the blades, but they'd hit with a surprising amount of force. The blades had sunk in rather deep for Kehfrey's strength. The jeering commenced.

"Hi, now, boy!" Kehfen called. "Get your feet on that tree for leverage and pull! If you're lucky, you'll only bust your head and not your butt when you land."

Gamis snickered. "Nothing useful in his head."

Olomo moved forward and helped the child pull the knives out.

"I'm never going to get any in that deep," Kehfrey hissed at his teacher.

"It only matters that you get the point in the tree, not how deeply. Your strength will increase with time."

"Right." Kehfrey took the knives, all five, careful not to nick himself on an edge, and set off after Olomo. Back at the line, he set four down at his feet and hefted one experimentally. His family watched in dead silence. Marun shifted slightly forward to where he could observe the child's intent face.

"It's not like darts," the boy said.

"No," Olomo agreed. "The blade must arc toward its target. It must strike exactly so."

"Well, here it goes," Kehfrey said and tossed the first at the tree. He mangled the throw badly. The weapon struck the target flat sided and fell off. Kehfrey groaned and thumped onto his back, the image of mortification. He had missed!

Kehfen laughed in victory.

"Fuck!" Wilf shouted.

"Wait a moment!" Vik snapped. "He hit the target!"

"Not so," Kehfen said. "It fell off."

"But not before it hit the target," Vik insisted.

"That's right," Wilf put in eagerly. "He did hit the target. You didn't say anything about him getting it stuck inside."

"Go piss off, you pair of cheaters! The target never got stuck, so the strike doesn't count."

"Aww! Leave off!" Kehfrey cried from on the ground. "Pop's right. I missed."

"Little rat!" Wilf said. He stomped up to the supine child. "I lost ten silver on you!"

"And I lost fourteen!" Vik shouted.

"I'll pay it back!"

"How!"

"I'll make every other shot! I'll bet the pot for it!"

"You've got no money to bet with," Kehfen said, stomping up to his youngest son. "You lost, boy. And so did the rest of you."

Wilf and Vik scowled at each other. Their accusing eyes fell on the boy once more, who remained flat on his back while staring up mutinously.

"I'll back him," Marun interposed coldly.

Kehfen looked at the man in surprise. "You will?"

"That's what I said," he confirmed.

"I bet twenty silver extra that I can get them formed in a square!" the boy shouted.

Marun's head snapped down toward him. A smile broke his immediate scowl, forced out by the child's impenitent character. Kehfrey grinned at him like a wild fool. "Brat!" the sorcerer named him. "Get up and make your play." He looked at Kehfen. "Are you taking that bet?"

"Hells, yes!" Kehfen said. "Get up and do it, fool boy! I have just the thing in mind to buy with all my gains."

Kehfrey sprang up, still grinning. "That's it, then!" He picked up the knives, one after the other, and shot them into the tree without pause. Each arc was perfect, not a wobble or overspin on any blade. When he was done, he had made a square formed by their points.

His father gaped at the tree. He walked over to it and stared. He turned about. He roared into the silence. "You little trickster! You fouled the first shot on purpose! You've practiced before! You conned me!"

"Of course I practiced before. I had Vik's dagger all last night. These knives are easier to toss." Gleefully he started his victory dance, bottom waggling an insult.

"Shit!" Vik said. "But you were sleeping! Weren't you?"

"You sleep like an axed cow," the child cried. He looked at Marun. "Sorry about the dresser. I only ruined the back side."

Marun laughed. "What were you going to do if I hadn't backed you, you little thief?"

"I have two gold and five silver in my other pocket. I stole it off Hiswil the other night

"How can you have money?" Nicky said. "I threw out your clothes. There was nothing in them."

"I hid my stash before my bath yesterday."

"Gods bust it!" Kehfen cried in further outrage. "You stole from Hiswil! You don't steal off your own!"

"I was practicing! I was going to give it back!" The child jumped up and down in protest. "I just died before I got around to it. Doesn't matter now anyway, does it?"

His father stared at him. Kehfrey stared back, the victory dance forgotten. Kehfrey waited to see if he was in for it. By the way his father's lips worked to repress a smile, Kehfen was about to decide not, but he wasn't going to let Kehfrey get away with all of his ill-gotten gains. He thrust his palm out.

"Hand it over," he snapped. Grumbling, Kehfrey stomped over and passed the stolen coins to him. "Where's the silver?"

"I get my share of the gains!" the boy objected. Kehfen curled his fingers shut, barely stopping a smile from forming.

"Where's my winnings?" the child demanded.

The smile escaped his father's lips after all. He shoved the two gold coins back in his son's fingers. "Go see Nicky for the purse, brat!" He cuffed him on the head lightly. "You owe me change for the gold pieces."

Grinning, Kehfrey walked toward Nicky.

"Hi, now!" Kehfen called.

"What now?" his boy answered, stalling halfway.

"When'd you lift the coins off Hiswil exactly?"

"When he helped me off the horse. I pretended I was afraid and grabbed the loose coin in his pocket while I was hanging on."

"Brat," Kehfen muttered. He looked at Wilf and Vik. They were both grinning at him. "Were you in on this scam?"

Vik stopped gloating. "No! I swear! I had no idea he practiced last night."

"You really must sleep like an axed cow," Wilf teased.

"I was exhausted. I don't sleep like that at all normally."

"Nicky says she only snores when she's exhausted," the child piped up.

"Hsst!" Nicky hissed. "Leave off that or I'll toss your winnings in the pond."

"You can't run in that dress," Kehfrey retorted. For answer, Nicky hefted her skirt up and was off, shapely legs flashing beneath the white dress. Kehfrey laughed and chased after her.

"Hi, now!" Wilf cried. "She's got what you owe me!" He raced off behind her, passing his little brother quickly. Kehfrey stopped running. He stared at the bushes they'd disappeared behind. He could hear Wilf thudding away still.

Vik stepped up beside him. "What about your winnings? And what you owe me?"

"Wilf will get it," Kehfrey responded flatly. He was probably going to get something else as well. Kehfrey didn't want to be around to see that. He went back to Marun.

"Here." He proffered the gold to his master. In response to this, Marun lifted an inquiring brow. "For the broken back of the dresser," the boy said. "I shouldn't have done it, but I just couldn't resist."

Marun accepted the coins without comment, but his cheek twitched again. He turned his head toward Olomo. The tall man was glowering at Kehfrey, had been since he'd discovered the child had scammed the lot of them. "He seems to be well along with knives," Marun said pointedly, pricking Olomo's pride further.

"That he does," Olomo agreed and then turned on the boy. "I asked you if you knew how to throw anything other than food!"

"I gave you an answer," Kehfrey said.

"You will not lie to me again!"

"But I didn't lie. I just didn't answer completely."

"I asked you if you could throw more than darts."

"Well, I kind of avoided that answer, didn't I?" the child admitted. "But I didn't lie."

Olomo scowled. The child was incurable. He was a rebellious little infidel, through and through, and yet he must be taught. "What am I to do with you? You are disrespectful."

"Can you show me how to throw those stars, then?" the boy asked.

"You goad me!" Olomo shouted.

"What? No! I really want to know. I'm sorry I misled you. I promise not to do it again. Please?"

Scowling, Olomo considered the begging child. After a moment, he crouched down and unwrapped the packet of weapons. He rose with three throwing stars in his fingers and shot them into the tree all at once without turning his head.

"You will begin with one," he snapped. Grinning, the boy dashed away to fetch the stars.

"Are they poisoned?" Marun questioned hurriedly.

"Not these ones," Olomo informed him gruffly.

The sorcerer nodded and settled into a relaxed stance again, but Olomo was not pleased to have seen the flicker of fear in his eyes. A covert chat with the servants had indicated the master tended toward adults, but the slaves had also admitted he occasionally bedded younger flesh, though never before anyone as immature as Kehfrey. Olomo didn't want the boy to become a first in that category and determined to remove him from the master's path whenever possible.

And how difficult would this prove when the man stood there as the boy jogged back and looked upon him with such a cool and possessive gaze? Olomo had seen such regard before, upon the faces of men who had purchased fine horses for their stables, or perhaps a prized piece for a rare collection. The assassin supposed this calculating scrutiny was better than the untoward attention of a man with perverse lusts.

"Can you show me again while standing up and facing the target?" the child asked, not even glancing at the man who owned him.

There were many shadows of the future and the majority did not always come to pass. There was no point in worrying over the sorcerer's feelings for this boy, so long as those feelings remained cool and remote. Wordlessly Olomo took a star from the child's hand and demonstrated the casting of it.

Kehfrey ran off to fetch the star and returned a second time. He set himself in the correct throwing position and tried a shot. The star thudded into the tree, but well aside from the circle. The child's eyes narrowed and he sent another off. This one spun where he'd aimed it, between the daggers he'd cast earlier. Dead centre. Olomo cursed something in his own language. The boy whirled about and scowled at him.

"I am not an elf!" he shouted. He dropped the last star and ran off into the growing dark.

"Kehfrey!" Kehfen called after him, but the child vanished under some bushes. "Blast!" He turned on Olomo. "What the hells did you say to him?"

"He called him a misbegotten elf," Marun said icily.

Olomo glowered between the two men, no hint of penitence to his stolid features.

"I find it hard to believe he learned that much Ysepian in this short a time," the sorcerer said.

"I taught him none of it. The child has the gift of tongues," Olomo said tightly.

Marun stared at him, his face a blank mask. His eyes turned toward the boy's father, but Kehfen was gaping at Olomo in surprise.

"What do you mean *gift of tongues*?" Kehfen said.

"He hears a language and understands it instantly," Olomo told him. "I have been teaching him the Pek fables and holy words in Ysepian all morning. He repeats it all back in a perfect Winfellan translation."

"What?" Kehfen cried. "I don't believe you!"

"It doesn't matter what you believe. The child has the gift. He understood Amek just as easily." Scowling, Olomo retrieved all the weapons and bundled them away. Ignoring both stunned men, he stalked off toward the manor.

Marun continued to stare at Kehfen. "What?" the thief said nervously.

"When was the child born?" the sorcerer questioned.

"Seven years ago. I told you yesterday."

"The date, man!"

"What's that got to do with it? I know he's an odd child, but he's not a monster."

"I didn't say he was," Marun replied, calming himself, "but he is unusually gifted. Can you explain it?"

Kehfen shook his head. "He's always been peculiar, from the moment he was born. He looked me in the eyes, and I almost thought he knew who I was. It was the strangest impression. The first light was shining through the window, right onto his little face. His eyes, they almost seemed to glow. He didn't cry, not during his birth, not when I held him then. Just looked me dead on like he could really see me. Babies don't do that."

"The date of birth, Kehfen!" Marun insisted. "I need it!"

"What will you do with it?"

"Make his star chart."

"You think you'll find answers in the stars?"

"It's possible. *If I have the date!* Now give it to me!" the sorcerer commanded, his patience at an end.

"Well, there's the thing. I don't actually know it," Kehfen admitted.

"What?" Marun hissed.

"Well, it was early winter. That's certain."

Marun cursed a string of the foulest oaths he'd ever learned, many of them in foreign tongues. He thought he heard a muffled childish chortle somewhere in the gloom and desisted. "Does your wife know?" he asked the thief.

"Why would anyone want to put his fist up a god's ass?" a small voice whispered across the darkening lawn.

"She might, yes," Kehfen said, his eyes darting nervously toward the bushes and back to the sorcerer.

"Why would any god let him in the first place?" added the small voice, this time from another location and further off. "But it was a good curse all the same. I suppose I'll keep it. That one outdid the best of Nicky's."

The sorcerer's eyes narrowed. He'd uttered that imprecation in the Midyin language, yet the child had understood it clearly, and it appeared Kehfrey had also been subjected to Nicky's considerable array of invectives, many of which were not of Winfellan origin. The irredeemable brat most definitely had the gift of tongues.

Marun turned toward the manor, intending to see the boy's noble mother about his date of birth, but the thief father, guessing what the master was about, didn't like that at all.

"Hi! Wait up! You'll scare the wits out of her! Let me ask!" He darted after the ominous man.

Marun stopped walking. "Go, then. And get the hour of birth as well."

Kehfen nodded and jogged away.

Behind and standing together, Vik and Gamis stared nervously at Marun's turned back. They watched the shadow of his body grow darker than all the other shadows in the garden. Gamis whimpered softly. Vik held him by the shoulder and led him toward the manor. Gamis broke free once he reached the limestone gravel of the driveway and raced toward the house as fast as his legs could carry him. Vik halted and let him go. He sighed softly. Gamis was not the bravest of them, but he was conceivably the wisest. They should perhaps all think of running.

He heard footsteps and turned. Marun approached purposefully.

"Find your little brother," he commanded. "He's hidden himself somewhere in this murk."

"Hi, Kehfrey!" Vik shouted. "I found another toad!"

"Liar!" the little voice hailed from somewhere in the shrubbery and not too far away either.

Vik looked at Marun pointedly. The sorcerer's scowl altered into an unwilling smile. "Now to get him out of the bushes," Vik said. "That's another matter altogether."

Marun's smile actually deepened. "Kehfrey! Come here!" he snapped. He watched Vik's face as the child appeared at his side a few seconds later. The youth's eyes narrowed. Was it jealousy? He was extremely attached to his younger brother. Could he resent his lover's control over the boy?

Vik looked away from Marun and down at Kehfrey. Something wriggled in the child's hand. "What have you got now?"

"Don't know," the boy said. "Found it under a bush. Looks like a worm, but it has a head and tiny legs."

Marun squinted down. "It's a salamander," he said. Suddenly the gamin was no more than a simple child. Marun was mildly astonished by the transformation.

"What does it eat?" Kehfrey begged to know, just a little boy with a potential pet.

"Very small bugs and worms," the sorcerer informed him. He crouched down. "You must put it back, Kehfrey. Then you must go upstairs and rest. We leave at midnight, and you have just admitted that you spent part of last night breaking the back of a dresser. Go rest some more."

Kehfrey scowled, but jogged away to deposit the salamander. Marun lifted up and waited for him to finish. Presently the child returned. He shot a glance at his master, wondering if he might be able to change his mind, but the implacable expression was a definite no. The boy sighed and made off to the manor without a word. Marun started after him. Vik arrested his retreat with a question.

"Did you love him?"

"Love who?" the sorcerer said, a note of irritation in his tone.

"Prince Cehtre?" Vik said, regarding the sorcerer fixedly.

Marun did not turn to face him. "No," he said after a moment. He began walking again.

"Then he jumped out of the tower for nothing!"

The sorcerer whipped about. He approached Vik, his face grim and his eyes blazing. "He jumped out of the tower because his father ripped every last ounce of self-respect from him."

"You did love him," Vik mocked.

Marun struck him across the face. Vik's head snapped back, but he righted it immediately, neither remorse nor fear in him, only a deep and burning anger. He tasted blood and realized his lip bled. He didn't feel the

195

cut. He laughed softly and lifted his eyes to the sorcerer. He knew exactly what he felt then.

Marun's heated expression altered. Vik stepped into the arms that opened to grasp him, but the kiss he gave his lover was as defiant as the resentment in his heart.

Chapter Eight

Kehfen waited on the steps, stood there a long time, searching the dark for a hint of human shape, uncertain and wondering where the sorcerer had gone. Eventually Marun turned up, strolling across the darkened lawn, one arm over the shoulder of Kehfen's firstborn son. Vik had his arm around the sorcerer's waist.

With the sight of them together, the thief's trepidation transmuted into a smouldering sense of insult, but he said nothing, merely watched them approach, a mute on the topmost step. The recently acquired grass stains on his son's blue suit gave him the answer to the sorcerer's unexpected absence. Kehfen's lips compressed to a rigid line, but other than that, he showed no sign of his disapproval. When they had crunched the gravel to the bottom step, he descended the flight to meet them.

"Did you get the information?" Marun said. His arm remained over Vik's slender shoulders. It was a challenge, an insult, a declaration.

"You aren't going to like it," Kehfen said flatly, his eyes flitting away from the mocking possession he read in the sorcerer's gaze.

The sorcerer frowned. "She didn't know?"

"It's not as if we had calendars! We can't read them anyway!" Did his son have a bruised lip?

Damn them both. He did.

"Then what did she tell you?" Marun said impatiently.

"She remembers that the Ahams brothers were all hung the day before. It'll be in the city records." Kehfen's eyes fixed on Vik's. Vik's skin flushed pink. The youth's gaze flicked aside.

"And the hour of birth?" Marun said.

The thief's attention reverted to the sorcerer. "Dawn. Some time around it."

"Did you see the light? Was it the light before the sun actually rises? Or the light after?"

"Like I said, I lifted Kehfrey up before the window when I first held him. The dawn light was on his face. It was just minutes after he was born."

"Yes, but when he was born? Where was the sun?"

"There was only a glow in the sky when he was born. The sun hadn't risen yet, not until I held him up to the light."

Marun looked away, his face pensive. He had hours of calculations ahead of him. Days of calculations! He would have to make a chart for virtually every hour, perhaps every minute of that morning. "Was there a midwife?" he said, looking at the father again.

"Yes, but that'll be no help to you. She couldn't read or write either."

"She wouldn't necessarily remember one of hundreds of births that year," Vik pointed out. "Just face it. No one keeps track of the days except those who are church going and have clerics to tell them."

The boy was correct. There was nothing to go on but the date of a hanging and the vague memory of the hour. Marun loosed Vik's shoulders and walked up the stairs without him.

"Where are you going?" Vik asked.

"I have things to see to," he said. He continued on without turning back.

Vik scowled. He heard his father sigh heavily and glanced over. "What now?"

"I told you not to fall in love with that man."

Vik cursed and stalked up the stairs. Kehfen let him go. There was nothing he could do about it now. It wasn't as if he had a choice in the matter. His family was well and truly trapped, as the sorcerer's mocking arm over his son's shoulder had declared.

A small sound carried on the night air. A pair of dim figures approached from beneath the trees. Their shapes solidified into Wilf and the woman. They had managed to ruin her white dress. She had green grass stains all over it. She didn't seem to mind. She laughed at Kehfen when she spotted him.

"What are you doing alone out here?"

"Worrying," he responded truthfully.

Wilf, who had been following her so that he might watch her fine backside, caught up quickly. "Worrying about what?" he said.

Kehfen noted that Wilf had his tunic on inside out. "Everything."

"That's a lot to worry about," the woman said. "Too late to bother now. Everything will just keep happening. Come inside. I'm heading for the pantry."

"And what's in the pantry?"

"Brandy," she said with a smirk. "The answer to all useless worrying."

Kehfen followed her up. That was a fine backside. Very fine. She was a delectable little piece, to be sure. "Brandy sounds like a good idea," he said casually.

He wondered when she'd get tired of Wilf. He wondered if Wilf would get tired of her. He doubted Wilf would. The boy never got tired of them until he thought he had them completely. Then, unless they were high paying marks, he dropped them flat. But Kehfen knew Wilf would never really have Nicky. She was just toying with him for her own amusement.

Did that mean he had another son to warn off? Wouldn't do to have Wilf fall in love with her. Wouldn't do at all.

"Gods, but she's a piece," Wilf whispered and shoved by him.

Kehfen's anxiety evaporated. He *was* worrying too much. The boy was bound to get burnt eventually. Nicky at least looked as if she wouldn't singe him too badly. What had she to be angry over? She was a slave. She took her pleasure where she could. Wilf could never have her completely. It was a simple fact.

Tossing any remaining concern for Wilf aside, Kehfen followed Nicky through the hall and on toward the kitchen. "Brandy sounds like a very good idea to me," he repeated firmly.

My, but that was a very fine bottom.

***

Some time during the day, the bottle had been dropped. The shards lay on the flagstones and the ghouls crouched around broken glass, passing only the neck along—silently, intently, mindlessly. Satisfied with their readiness, Marun turned his back on the abominations and headed back up the stairs. His slaves were prepared. In just a few hours, he would call the dead to hunt.

He barred the cellar door behind him. As he walked by the pantry, he heard laughter and paused. A man's voice, then a woman's—it was Hanicke and someone else. A third voice sounded from within. Kehfen. She was with Kehfen and Wilf. She was dipping in the cooking brandy again.

No longer interested, Marun stepped onward through the kitchen and on to the main hall. He froze when he saw Vik in the library, brooding before the window. More quietly, the sorcerer ascended the stairs. He was disinclined toward having another row with his lover. It seemed that he and Vik were either hating each other or fucking, and never anything in between. He preferred the fucking and had to admit the hate made this pastime more intoxicating, but he could do without the argumentation beforehand.

When he arrived at the child's room, he saw that Kehfrey had for once obeyed him and was where he should be, sleeping in bed. Marun entered the chamber and seated himself in the chair from which he had watched before. He sat, he stared, and he wondered about the boy. The child was a mystery. There were too many gifts, too many powerful gifts. Why all in one child? Was there a destiny in hand for him? Was it only this idiotic Ishpaäf?

Was Ishpaäf actually worth seeking?

He grimaced. Of all the religions of the world, the Pek factions were the only ones that worshipped no gods. Instead it was this blasted Ishpaäf, the unattainable, cryptic aspiration. Well, at least unattainable for him.

He sighed noiselessly. He would solve the mystery of the child eventually. He must be patient. There was time for it.

The boy unexpectedly shifted toward him. "I thought you wanted me to sleep," he said crossly. "If you're going to just stare at me, I might as well get up and do something."

"I thought you *were* sleeping." Marun didn't feel apologetic. He wanted to speak with the boy.

"I was. I heard you come in."

"You sleep lightly."

"Sometimes. Do you?"

"Yes," he admitted.

"Pop says I have a twitchy mind. Can't stay asleep because of it."

"He may be correct." A twitchy mind? It was as good an explanation as any.

"Why did you come in?"

"I was wondering why you had so many gifts," he said.

"What gifts?"

Marun smiled in the darkness. "You don't know?"

"Do you mean the knife thing? I practiced."

"The *knife thing* is a virtual impossibility for the average seven year old."

"Oh."

For a moment, they were both silent.

"Do you mean the Ishpaäf thing, then?" the child proffered next.

"That's part of it."

"What else is there?"

"The way you think far ahead, seeing the consequences like an adult."

"Didn't you mention that yesterday?"

"You know I did." He got off the chair. "Are you still dressed?"

"Yes," came the response. "Didn't want to waste time dressing again later."

"Come, then." The sorcerer walked away. Linen rustled. Small feet thumped to the floor. "You don't need your shoes," Marun said and disappeared around the bend of the door.

Kehfrey hurried from his room. The sorcerer led him down the wing, past the master bedchamber and on toward the workroom. Marun stopped before the spelled door and stared at the polished panels. Kehfrey remembered this door. This was where Marun had kept the Vessel. This was where Nicky had been locked in to suffer the terrible, stifling heat as punishment for saving his life. He would never forget her pale, tormented face. Never. But as Marun willed the ward away from the handle, Kehfrey kept his anger hidden.

Presently the black of the ward shifted. The sorcerer set his hand on the latch and opened the door. He urged Kehfrey inward, keeping an arm up to guard him. "It wouldn't kill you," he responded to the child's cautious glance, "but it would render you useless for the night. If there is any possibility that you might lead me to my soulstone, I would have you with the hunting party."

"So why'd we come back here?"

Kehfrey stepped forward. The heat that assailed him after he passed under the lintel almost made him flinch. Some of the warmth was from the recent sunlight—the awful heat wave had continued unabated despite yesterday's storm—but as well, the ward in the fireplace had kept the temperature up and driven off the moisture in the air. With the window shut, the work chamber was a furnace. Kehfrey was surprised nothing had caught fire beyond the hearth.

"Why do you still have a fire ward up?" he asked

"To keep thieves out," his master replied.

"Oh .... Are you planning to put the wards in all the fire places?"

"No. I have something I wish to read to you," Marun said without a sign of emotion. He uncovered a glow stick standing on the table. He didn't seem the least bothered by the heat, but Kehfrey supposed the cold black he hid beneath his skin took care of it for him.

Marun moved to the further side of the room where the small shelf of books stood against the wall adjacent the hearth. He removed one volume, selecting it without hesitation, and set it on the table. Kehfrey peered at the book curiously. The leather cover was embossed with three strange symbols. Gold gilded the indentations.

"What's that, then? You didn't show me letters like those yesterday."

"These are glyphs," his master replied. "Each symbol has a meaning."

"Really? What do they say?"

Marun read them in the exact language they were written. "Mahall's Words," he said in modern dwarvish.

"Who's Mahall?" the boy questioned. He spoke in Winfellan as usual.

"He's a dwarven god."

"A god! A dwarf? Are they real?" And would one let a man put a fist up his ass? Kehfrey seriously doubted it. Be the last thing that fool mortal would do. Probably only had to lift a single insulting finger into the air and that was the end. Mayhap a mortal only had to think the thought and thereafter die. Could a god read one's mind?

"Yes, they are real," Marun answered. "Why shouldn't they be? Elves are real."

"Have you seen a god?"

"Yes. Once. A dragon."

"A dragon god? Not a dwarf god?"

"No, not a dwarf god."

There was no way anyone could put a fist up a dragon's ass without getting lost in the dragon. One little squat, and farewell mortal; until he got shitted out later, of course.

"Oh. Then how do you know if a dwarf god is real?" Kehfrey said with a serious, ever so guileless expression.

Marun laughed. "I've seen dwarves. Will you settle for that?"

"Fair enough, I suppose," the boy answered half-heartedly.

Marun smiled at his reservation. He relented and gave the boy some tidbits of information just to please him. "Dwarves aren't as folktales would have them. Not as short, not as squat, and not nearly as ugly. Most pass for human. The true name of their race is the Ryn."

"If they aren't so different from us, why do folktales have them otherwise?"

Marun sighed. He shouldn't have bothered. It would be one question after the other and never to the matter at hand. "It's only because they're shorter than most humans and never get taller, no matter how well fed."

"Oh. Will you tell me about the dragon later?"

Apparently the child could tell he was becoming irritated. Well, good.

"Of course." He retrieved the book and sat in the only armchair the room boasted. He opened the tome to a particular page. Just before he began reading again, the child interrupted him.

"Why were there three symbols, but you only said two words?"

"The smaller symbol is for ownership. It's the one in the centre. It shows that the words belonged to Mahall, that he spoke them. Do you see that the two are attached by a small scroll?"

"Oh," Kehfrey said, apparently understanding.

Marun smiled again. The boy was quick. The sorcerer took a breath and read a passage, once more in the language the words were written. "*They shall not rise but for those who know their wants,*" he uttered.

"What are we talking about here?" Kehfrey said, again in Winfellan.

"Dragons," Marun responded in the modern dwarf tongue.

"Dragons!" the boy cried in Winfellan, delighted. Marun seemed bent on telling about them after all. "So this dwarvish book is about dragons?"

"Not entirely. It's a compendium of Rynnish legends concerning the god Mahall."

"Oh."

Marun repeated the line he'd read. "Now you say it," he instructed.

"They shall not rise but for those who know their wants," Kehfrey said in Winfellan.

"Say it the way I did," Marun demanded, still in dwarven.

"I just did."

"No, you didn't," his master refuted. Kehfrey eyed him askance and muttered something barely audible. "What was that?'" the sorcerer snapped, now in their native tongue.

"You're doing like Olomo."

"And what exactly do you mean?"

"He was like that yesterday. And this morning! Acting like he was saying something different than he was saying."

"He was. Only you have it wrong. He was saying something different from what you thought you were hearing." The boy gaped at him. Marun eyed him intently. The child really had no idea.

"Come here," he directed, his tone gentle. Kehfrey approached obediently. Marun turned the book about and pointed at a symbol. "Listen carefully," he said and uttered the word dragon. "What did you hear?"

"Dragon."

Once more the child had responded in Winfellan. Marun sighed and bolstered his patience with a calm reminder that the boy was only seven and really quite innocent and ignorant, odd little thief though he was.

"Once again, Kehfrey," he said. "This time look at my mouth. Don't assume you know anything. Listen to the exact sounds I am making."

The boy frowned. His expression was confused. When he looked down at the strange symbols on the page, he did so with a worried glint to the hazel of his eyes. Marun hauled his head back up by the chin. Carefully, slowly, he pronounced dragon again. There was an instant wherein the child looked at him blankly, but then his eyes just grew wider and wider. Marun's smile matched the motion, growing wider and wider as well. The child had finally understood.

"Gods bust it!" Kehfrey whispered.

Marun nodded. "You hear it now?" He released the boy's captured chin. Kehfrey nodded, mute with awe. "Good." Marun turned the page. "Listen to this."

He spun the book back to rights and read off a line that had escaped him for ages. He looked at Kehfrey eagerly, only to find the boy gazing at him blankly again.

"Kehfrey, I want you to translate this time," he directed firmly.

"What?" The child blinked in surprise. "I was listening to all those rough sounds coming out of your mouth. How are you doing that?"

"Never mind that now! Just translate!" Gods! Had he ruined the boy's gift? He repeated again. This time when he looked up, the child was frowning. "Did you understand?"

"That's all wrong. You make no sense at all."

Marun shut his eyes in disappointment. He had ruined it. He should never have forced the child to comprehend his gift.

"Say it again, but more slowly," Kehfrey asked.

Marun raised his eyelids. He repeated a third time, this time without looking down. He was certain he was not going to have a translation. The child glowered throughout.

"It's not the same language as the first one, is it?" the boy said.

Marun blinked. Was that it? Could that be why? "It's a dead language," he disclosed.

"Dead! How can a language be dead?"

"No one speaks it anymore," he answered simply.

"Then what's it doing in a book?"

Marun rotated the book again and permitted the child to scrutinize the glyphs properly. "This line is a transcription from the face of a rock in the Jahama Mountains. This is all that remains of Mahall's original written word, scored upon the granite with his nail some two million years ago."

"Two million years!" Kehfrey repeated with due reverence. Though he'd never heard the word *million* before, he acquired the clear sense it was a massive figure. "He must be dead by now. No one can live that long."

"Mahall is a god, Kehfrey," Marun reminded patiently. "The gods have existed in their immortal state approximately two hundred and fifty million years. However, about one hundred and fifty thousand years ago, the dwarf gods all disappeared. Every remaining portion of their written works is precious now."

Kehfrey squinted thoughtfully. "Two hundred and fifty million years? Is that like the beginning of time?"

"For our world, not even close. There are gnomish texts claiming the existence of the world at five and a half billion years."

Kehfrey frowned, his expression rather aggravated of a sudden, partially because the word billion—which he sensed was certainly more massive than a million—just about gave him a headache, but also because he couldn't conceive of going on and on forever like an immortal god. "How can the gods possibly exist that long without becoming utterly bored?"

Marun tried to repress a smile, but couldn't quite. "Of all the comments to make of immortality, you make this?"

"What else is there to bother a god if not boredom? Death doesn't seem to be the spectacular problem it is for us. Seems to me they might wish they could die after too long experiencing the same things over and over."

"Damn it, but you are too wise, boy. But just to let you know, I've read that a god ofttimes falls into a sort of waking sleep in which he mentally drifts as the aeons pass. Apparently they've been known to do so synchronously until events occur that attract their notice and bring them back to our sphere. And I can tell you now; they've been stirring for the past thousand and more years. A great deal of attention is focused here on this area of the world. You have been born into interesting times, for the gods at least."

"Really?" Kehfrey said. "Odd creatures, aren't they? I wonder if they keep their eyes open when they sleep so they can see if something interesting happens. Must be what is meant by a waking sleep." And this was possibly the only time anyone might have a chance at sticking a fist up the ass of one and also surviving the insult.

As if dismissing the topic, Kehfrey tapped the book. "What's a transcription exactly? That wasn't very clear to me."

"Basically something copied. This transcription is very valuable. It's perhaps the last remaining example of the wisdom Mahall passed on to his mortal progeny. Since the disappearance of the dwarven gods, most of their written records were destroyed."

"Doesn't seem so valuable at the moment," Kehfrey said. "It's garbled."

What a disappointment. Marun repressed his irritation. He couldn't blame the boy. He'd thought he was close, but he'd wrecked his opportunity by forcing the child to comprehend his talent. Some mystics were better left innocent of their powers, and apparently Kehfrey was one of them. The failure was his master's fault. Even so, when Marun looked down at that head of flame hair, he couldn't suppress a sigh of discontent.

Kehfrey heard him, but pretended not to. He was interested in the symbols on the page and he bent closer to inspect them. These were large glyphs again, different from the others, but this stood to reason since they all meant different things. "Why isn't there a translation into the other language?" he asked.

"This book was written by gnomes studying dwarf tribes," came the answer. "The dwarfs have a tendency to be closed-mouthed about many things, and so too the gnomes, unfortunately. If the gnomes knew what this passage meant, they didn't see fit to translate the text, only to record it for posterity."

"If this is so, how can you even read it?"

"My master read it to me once. He knew what it meant."

Kehfrey eyed him narrowly. "He read it and then didn't tell you what it meant?"

Marun turned a little pink around his neckline. "If you must know, I was a lot younger then and he didn't trust me to control myself." The smirk playing at the corners of the child's lips was just too much. "I think it's time you went back to bed," Marun added sharply.

"Not just yet," said Kehfrey. He pointed at the first glyph. "Say this one again." He received no response and looked at his master. Marun yet glowered at him for having been amused at his expense. "Oh, come on! I'll really try to understand it this time."

Marun obliged, but only because he was curious what the boy made of all of it. Kehfrey scowled the moment he finished.

"It's dead all right," he accused. "You killed it."

"What do you mean *I* killed it?"

"Try it again, only don't gut it with that big thundering kkkkk thing you do."

Marun stared in surprise. Kehfrey looked back, watching with an expectant gleam in his eyes. Slowly Marun repeated the word, only he made the consonants flow more softly.

"Almost," Kehfrey whispered.

A hint of something shivered through the boy's gaze, something odd, something unnatural. It receded and then returned stronger. Marun observed the change in silence.

And then the boy said it.

The hairs rose all over Marun's body. Kehfrey had said it. The word had flowed out of his mouth without a stammer. His pale face had become an unnatural, serene mask, his eyes strange with the intensity of whatever mysterious force pressed outward from inside him. Something burned beneath the hazel, and the sorcerer could only think it was the smouldering blaze that could leap the ether, but just now, it had been harnessed to fire a dead language into a conflagration of knowledge.

Softly Marun uttered the next of the glyphs, altering his manner of speaking in accordance with Kehfrey's previous instruction. The child corrected him. Marun said the next, following the rule just demonstrated. This time the boy nodded. Marun read to the end of the line with only one further correction. He stared at Kehfrey in anticipation. With his eyes half shut, almost as if he dreamt, the child spoke.

"They who would call the flightless wyrm must lure the beast with a generous serving of the great mother's waste."

Marun continued to stare in awe. The child had spoken entirely in modern dwarf. He'd translated an ancient, disused language, and done it using one of which he'd only heard a few words.

"How are you doing that?" Marun blurted.

"What?" Kehfrey said. He blinked and looked at Marun in confusion. "Doing what?"

"You just spoke modern dwarf! You translated an ancient text! A dead language!"

He watched in astonishment as the child's eyes rolled up into his head. Kehfrey abruptly fell over. Marun shoved the book off his lap and crouched at the boy's side. The child had fainted. The whites of his eyes still showed. Marun felt for a pulse in his neck. It was there, but it beat erratically.

"Kehfrey?" he called. The boy's skin had become very pasty again. It was clammy. "Too hot!" Marun hissed. He carried him out into the hall, willing the door of the workroom shut behind. It thudded loudly. The child jerked in his arms.

"What?" he cried again.

"Be still. You fainted from overheating," Marun said. He carried him back to the open door of his bedroom. There, he discovered Vik inside the dark chamber, frowning worriedly.

"Kehfrey!" The youth looked at the sorcerer. "What have you done?"

Again it was hatred and accusation. "I taught him ancient dwarf!" Marun snarled. "Go downstairs. Tell them I want a bath of unheated water up here now."

"How can ancient dwarf do that to him?" Vik demanded.

"You should hear it," Kehfrey muttered weakly. "It just about makes you strangle on your own tongue."

"Get the bath!" Marun snapped. Vik hesitated, prepared to argue further, but changed his mind abruptly. He fled the chamber, hurried on by his lover's darkening glare. "Gods!" Marun hissed. "How can he do that? One moment he trusts me, the next moment he thinks I'm abusing you!"

"He doesn't know what you promised," Kehfrey said.

"You didn't tell him?" Marun set the boy on the bed and began to strip the clothes from him. The child shook his head in response to the question. He didn't display the least indication he felt distrust or distaste over the ministrations performed on his body, which soothed the sorcerer's hurt somewhat. "Why not?" Marun asked.

"If I told them, they wouldn't be afraid, and then they'd make you go barmy."

Once again the child's surprising wisdom forced laughter out of him. "I may go barmy anyway," he said. He finished his task and went to the

206

window to shove it further open. The night air hadn't cooled yet. Staring out, he thought perhaps he might have to wait until tomorrow to go after Rook.

Unless he used the green of healing .... Should he?

Damn it. The goddess's reaction earlier when he made the blood oath with Kehfrey, the brooding that still continued: he hesitated to raise the green. He'd called on the gentler powers too often these past days. She must have noticed. She might question him if it happened again. He didn't want to speak to her of the boy, not yet, not when he still hadn't recovered his soulstone. There would be no end to her mockery if she learned of his stupidity.

"Hells." There was nothing harder than hiding things from the goddess, whose skin was the crust of the world.

"What if I kept a wet towel wrapped over my head?" the boy suggested.

Marun looked at him sharply. "Do you read minds now?"

"No," the boy responded. "It's just sense. You might not take me if I don't cool off. I was only trying to come up with something to avoid that."

"I was thinking of waiting until tomorrow night."

"Oh. Well. That won't do. You'll snap everyone's heads off by breakfast time."

Again Marun laughed. He heard noise coming up from the entry hall. Shortly after, Vik entered followed by Domel, who bore a bright glow stick. A line of servants trailed them. A pair set the copper tub on the floor, and the remaining commenced to dump buckets of water within it. Marun didn't wait for them to finish. He set Kehfrey in the tub before the second bucket had been tilted.

"Keep filling it," he commanded.

"Aie! It's freezing!" the child protested.

Marun felt the water. It was tepid. "It's not. You're overheated. Just relax. You'll feel better in a moment." He straightened and directed Domel to fetch salt. The butler had just uncovered a glow stick standing on the dresser. He bowed and left the room.

"Overheated!" Vik repeated. "Why didn't you say?"

"I seem to recall an immediate accusation rather than a concerned inquiry," Marun said with a scathing glance.

Vik reddened in the dim light. "I'm sorry," he said softly.

Marun wasn't ready to forgive him. "Feed him a spoonful of salt when it arrives. Give him water to drink, lots of it. I will be back to check on him later." He stalked out the door and headed back to the workroom, where he fetched the book off the floor and opened it to the page.

"*They who would call the flightless wyrm must lure the beast with a generous serving of the great mother's waste.*"

It all made sense now!

"They eat earth magic," he said. He pulled the chains out from beneath his dull tunic and touched the golden charm with the dragon

207

symbol on it. He could do it now. He could summon an earth dragon. It was so incredibly simple. He was elated, but the triumphant smile playing over his lips faded.

Kehfrey! What had he seen behind that boy's eyes? The sorcerer had a deep foreboding the answer to that mystery would be just as difficult to expose as this one had been. And he had taken years on this one. A lifetime by normal human standards.

He thumped the book onto the table and left the workroom. He was in time to see Domel arriving at the child's chamber.

"Domel!"

The butler started in alarm. Salt spilled everywhere. Marun ignored the servant's jumpy manner. He ignored as well the two boys who stared as he came into view.

"Go to Lord Rhet. Tell him I want the date of a hanging. Three brothers. The Ahams brothers."

Domel nodded, deposited the remaining salt on a table just within the bedchamber and hurried down the stairs. Marun looked in at Kehfrey, found him alert and curious, and shut the door without a word. He followed Domel down, but diverted toward the library. He had an astrolabe tucked in a cabinet there. He would see if there had been any obvious and unusual alignments or eclipses seven years ago.

"In the early winter," he added to himself.

At the very least, he might get some hint of an answer this evening before he set the ghouls after Rook. He found the astrolabe in the case and carried it to the desk. In his haste to find an answer, he shoved all of Kehfrey and Vik's work off the table. The parchments scattered all about, but he'd already forgotten them before they landed.

***

"What the hells was that all about?" Vik demanded.

"Don't know," Kehfrey said tiredly. Yes, he did, but he didn't care. He sank into the water until only his hair capped the surface.

Vik hauled him back out by both armpits. "Don't do that!"

"I was holding my breath!"

"Don't do it anyway! Gods, Kehfrey! I swear I'll be the next to faint if anything else happens."

"You had your turn yesterday."

Vik shoved Kehfrey's head back under the water. The boy came up spluttering.

"Hey!" he burbled, spitting water. "Knock it off! You just told me not to!"

"I changed my mind."

Kehfrey splashed water over him. Vik took a giant swing and smacked the surface hard. Water slammed into his brother's face. Kehfrey answered in kind. Soon there was as much water out of the tub as in. At the end of

208

the war, which was considered to be a draw, Vik fell back on the floor, soaking wet and feeling immensely better.

"Much cooler like this," he remarked.

"You wear too much," Kehfrey said. "Nicky and I prefer being naked."

"What?" Vik laughed in disbelief. "She does not."

"Does too!"

"Maybe she does, but not with you."

"Yes, she does!"

"Oh, knock it off, Kehfrey. You're too young and that's that."

"Gods busted Wilf!"

Vik heard the resentful curse and at last understood. So. That was it. "You know Wilf. He'll get tired quickly." He lifted up on an elbow to better see his brother, who had before been only a crop of ginger poking up from a copper bastion. Kehfrey was scowling in the middle of the tub, completely unappeased. "You're too young, Kehfrey," Vik said again. "Someone else will come along by the time you're ready."

"She's a half elf! She'll still be here!"

"So hurry up and grow." He grinned at the grimace the boy bestowed upon him. "Kehfrey! Come on! You can't expect a woman to wait on a seven-year-old boy."

"I suppose not," the child admitted unhappily. "Not much use to her, am I? Can't keep a stiff much longer than to have a pee."

Vik shook his head in exasperation. "You're unnatural, Kehfrey." Kehfrey looked at him wisely. Vik flushed. "I know what I am. That's not the problem we're discussing."

"*Is* it a problem?" the boy questioned, all curiosity again.

It was Vik's turn to scowl. "Generally, yes," he admitted.

"Then why do you?"

"I don't know. I wish I did."

"Why? Would you change it, if you did?"

"Yes."

Kehfrey considered that. "What if you can't?" he said eventually.

"That's the way it is now, Kehfrey."

"Oh. Well. Don't worry about it, then."

Vik shook his head in exasperation a second time. "That's not so easy. Look at you about Nicky. Have you stopped worrying?"

"Oh. Right."

The brothers glowered at each other. Kehfrey abruptly sent a huge splash of water at Vik. Vik lunged for the tub. Grinning hugely, both boys cleared their troubled minds while drenching their surroundings. They vaguely realized Domel would be really pissed when he returned, but that didn't stop them. Domel wasn't going to do much about it. He knew who Marun favoured. It wasn't him.

* * *

In the bedroom down the other wing, Canella nursed her little girl. She lay on her side in the plush bed, the baby pulling on a breast, surrounded by comforts she hadn't enjoyed since she was fifteen. A rich carpet, sumptuous furnishings, a feather bolster and satin sheets—it was like a return to heaven, but she knew it would all go away again. Once the sorcerer tired of Vik's company, she'd lose this small glimpse of paradise. For the first time in her life, she wished her beautiful son would please a man so well his benefactor would think to keep him longer, perhaps even be so impressed as to make a companion's contract. Canella couldn't set her hopes on her father. Her father might change his mind about Wilf, and if not that, her cousin Rhendel might declare Harte incompetent and Wilf would be just a bastard again.

A heavy sigh eased from her lungs. The baby suckled on, oblivious to all but the warmth and comfort of mother. Lucky child. Everything was so simple when you were an infant. Canella heaved another unhappy breath.

Vaguely she thought she heard the noise of boys laughing, and her mind rose from the deep abyss of melancholy. Happy sounds drifted in through her open window. She smiled. So much had happened, so many terrible and frightening things. The ingenuous laughter made it all seem less sinister. But then she heard the branch creak again, and her pleasant humour flittered away. She looked at the bough warily. A tree loomed just outside her window, a huge elm gnarled with age. She didn't like it. It was always creaking.

"I hate that tree," she told the infant. Perhaps she should have the window shut? But it was just a tree. Undecided, she stared at the branch waving in the light wind. Laughter flowed inward again and the smile revisited her face.

"Do you hear that?" she asked her daughter. "Those are your brothers, Vik and Kehfrey." Their happiness was such a good sound. Her little Kehfrey was feeling better. And Vik! She wished she could see him laughing. He'd been solemn for so long.

"Trust my Kehfrey to make him laugh." She stared out the window, dismissing the desire to shut it. She listened to the distant noise of her sons' cheerful shouting and drifted contentedly to sleep.

***

Marun called them together several hours later. By then the air had cooled sufficiently he was certain Kehfrey would not overheat again. Having sent servants to summon the others, he visited the child's room himself. He halted when the area rug squished beneath his feet. He looked down in surprise. The tub was still in the room. It seemed empty. Another squishy step forward and he guessed where all the water had gone.

He waited for his eyes to adjust to the gloom. After a moment, he distinguished both brothers on the bed. The covers had been thrown down, refused because of the heat. They lay naked side by side. The faint light from the hall glowed on their pale skin.

The green kiss .... After Kehfrey's nightmare, he'd intended only to give an oath and win the child's trust, but the green had risen out of his flesh and revealed his protestations as lies. "Power rises to power," he said faintly, and his had risen for this child, this enigma who seemed a lens upon which all gifts collected.

He'd lied to himself earlier. He had many good reasons to hesitate curing Kehfrey's heat exhaustion with the green kiss. The one reason he hadn't faced was this: he wanted to kiss him. Gods help him, but he'd fallen in love with an immature boy.

He didn't like these feelings. Mortification. Anxiety. He was a sinful man, but some sins he didn't want to live with.

"Hi! Don't slip on the floor," Kehfrey whispered suddenly. Marun's gaze snapped toward the child's face. The boy's bright eyes peeked out from beneath the mop of wild hair.

"Get dressed!" his master whispered harshly and turned away. He discovered the assassin in the hall upon his emergence, and this cooled the fire in his groin as effectively as an icy bath. Olomo was fully prepared, his weapons in place, his black suit repaired, and his demeanour bleeding the usual Ysepian disgust for any sexuality other than the prescribed one.

"I will see the boy down," Olomo informed him, in his dark eyes disapproval unwisely proffered. The sorcerer did not, just then, wish to spare the time to correct the impudence. He nodded curtly and descended the stairs. The thud of the door shutting was a thinly veiled repudiation; it came from an assassin who knew better than to be noisy.

Below, Kehfen stood with Wilf and Nicky. Nicky had dressed in boy's clothing again. Marun frowned, remembering the three had been dipping into the brandy earlier. They had best not be drunk.

"I want you to set a watch," he ordered Wilf. "Get the servants to stand it with you."

"Are you expecting trouble?" Kehfen asked.

"No, but caution is advisable just now." He looked at Hanicke pointedly.

"I see nothing," she offered hastily.

"And as you are always so fond of saying, you can't see everything," he said witheringly. He looked back at Wilf. "My workroom is completely warded. Do not approach the door. Though the wood seems plain enough, there is magic on it. It needs none of your attention. It is your family you protect. Do it diligently or not. It is up to you."

Wilf nodded solemnly, and his father gave him an approving slap on the shoulder.

After another minute, Olomo appeared at the top of the stairs with Kehfrey before him. The child, still somewhat pale, seemed alert enough. He had crowned his head with a white turban of wet cloth. Some of the moisture had dripped down onto his tunic. He looked silly and he knew it.

Grinning, he darted forward, jumped on the banister and slid down with a childish whoop, slipping off before he met the knob at the end. He thudded down before them and bowed, making a wide flourish with both arms. The towel tumbled off his head and plopped on the marble floor.

"Don't want to meet that knob with my jewels," he joked. He grabbed the towel and rewound it over his head

"Brat!" his father hailed him. "I bet you've been looking to do that since you first saw the banister."

"Well, it's not much good for anything else. You'd have to be pissed drunk to fall off those stairs. Look at the width of them!" Truly the breadth of the grand staircase was much wider than the rickety and narrow flights he was accustomed to scurrying up and down.

"What's with the wet turban?" Wilf said.

"Head got a little hot earlier. Just a precaution."

This statement prompted Kehfrey's father to frown misgivingly and open his mouth to argue that the boy remain behind, but Marun abruptly walked away. The thief glowered after him. "Where's he off to?"

"Going for the ghouls," Kehfrey told him. "I think you should all wait outside now."

"What for?" Wilf said.

"Because they stink. It's going to get worse in the heat. You'll tough it better outside."

Olomo descended the last step and stood behind the boy, not looking the least concerned about the proposition of meeting malodorous walking dead, but Kehfen and Wilf glanced at each other, wondering just how bad the stench could be if the boy had toughed it in the closed space of the cellar earlier. Olomo clapped his hand on the child's shoulder and pushed him forward. Shrugging, Kehfen followed after them, but Nicky stayed put. Because she did, Wilf did as well.

"Why can't you see everything?" he asked her.

"Decisions get made and changed constantly," she said frankly. "That makes the future alter. Tonight I see nothing at all. A lot of decisions are being made and changed tonight. Here and elsewhere." She frowned at him curiously. "How do you plan on going about this watch of yours? The servants will do as you say, but they aren't fighters. They're just as likely to run screaming as tell you where the trouble is."

"I have a few tricks to help us. Got an axe anywhere?"

She grinned. "What are you planning to do? Scare any would-be intruders off with it?"

"No. Cut wood." He laughed at her surprised expression. "Come on, then. Do you?"

"In the back, outside the kitchen."

"Let's go, then." Smiling, Wilf set off. She followed, a bemused expression on her face. Out in the yard, the bemusement changed to appreciation when he stripped off his upper clothing and set to work.

My, but he had a fine set of shoulders and back, didn't he? Very fine indeed. And didn't she just adore strong young babies like him.

***

Marun didn't conduct the ghouls through the main hall of the house. He summoned them out of the cellar and brought them directly into the open by another door. He was accustomed to ignoring the stench of decomposition, but he didn't appreciate it. The choice of door was practical. Domel's staff would have less cleaning to do, and the putrid reek would not spread as far through the manor.

While skirting the kitchen gardens, he discovered Wilf chopping a log of wood into wedges, Nicky watching him. Wilf stopped in surprise when he spotted the sorcerer, but Marun passed without a word. The ghouls followed him into the lantern light. In all their gruesomeness, they lurched past Wilf and the woman. A stifled gasp escaped Wilf, and he commenced to retch. Vomit erupted from his throat before he even bent. Marun smiled grimly and continued on. The little boy had more fortitude than the rest of his family put together. Odd child. So very odd.

At the front of the house, Olomo, Kehfen and Kehfrey waited on the gravel driveway next to three horses. Stable hands struggled with the horses meant for Olomo and Kehfen. Having sensed the approach of the walking dead, they whinnied and threatened to bolt. Marun halted the ghouls beneath a tree and continued forward alone. Taking the reins of his well-behaved gelding, he noted that Olomo had placed protective hands on the child's shoulders. His face impassive, Marun mounted, but once astride ordered the assassin to pass him the boy.

"He will ride with me," Olomo refused.

"He will not," the sorcerer countered.

The Ysepian's expression tightened into another rebuff, and this ended the patience of the boy's master, who gathered the darkness from out of the night shadows and drew them toward him. Kehfrey perceived the threat before the others and interrupted the confrontation. He shrugged out of Olomo's grasp and put a trusting hand up toward his master. Marun pulled him up and in front. Olomo glowered at both and then jerked his mount's reins from the servant. Kehfen took control of his horse as well, his expression tight.

"Stay here a moment," Marun ordered the two men and set his mount off toward the dark figures waiting beneath the tree.

"If you blast him, I'll never get to play with those other weapons," Kehfrey hissed.

"If I blast him, I'll be certain to let him live just so you can," he hissed back. He smiled over the boy's head. The child was irrepressible.

The ghouls watched with dull eyes as they approached. The gelding sidled somewhat, but Marun settled the beast quickly. Unlike the other horses, this mount was accustomed to the strange creatures with which his owner consorted.

"Go," Marun commanded the ghouls. "Find Rook. Take me to him."

They staggered toward him, and he backed the horse away. When it appeared that they weren't going to turn toward the gate, he cursed in irritation and guided the horse aside, to then angle around the ghouls and watch from behind.

"Seems they're heading in a straight line. Like you said, they don't think so quickly anymore," Kehfrey said.

Marun could only agree. He'd forgotten how stupid ghouls could be. Unless they had specific instructions, or some sort of inset training to fall back on from their former lives, they tended to be an erratic lot. But what else had he to use here? There were virtually no monsters worth summoning in this area of Winfel, and malevolent ghosts would be impractical, like as not leech the life out of everyone they approached.

"What if they meet the pond? They could fall in," the child said.

"That's why I need to follow them," Marun said flatly. "Get out of the way, man!" he shouted at Kehfrey's father.

The servants had already fled, but the thief gaped at the ghouls, horror-struck. Fortunately he was already astride. As the undead approached, his mount cantered away with a frightened whinny, but Kehfen continued to stare at the ghouls, no longer aware he was mounted or that his horse retreated with him.

That was Mur in the lead. That was Mur with dead eyes and a gaping mouth, his skin a ghastly, bloodless white. And that thing in the back? That bloated, legless carcass had been Ofmen.

Kehfen turned sideways on his horse and vomited until all he could do was spit bile. Someone grabbed the reins from his numb fingers and pulled his mount around.

"You will hold on," Olomo directed brusquely. The assassin sent both horses after Marun.

Kehfen snatched the pommel and clung to it. Blinking tears, the thief realized they were headed toward the small lake they'd skirted that first fateful night when they had come to break into the manor. The sorcerer's horse thumped hooves just to the rear of the abominations. Kehfrey's high voice drifted back to the father.

"This is going to take forever. See the two without legs. They slow the rest down."

The two crippled ghouls dropped to the ground, completely lifeless again. "Any other advice or criticism?" Marun demanded.

"Can I take this towel off? It's falling in my eyes."

Marun laughed, pulled the towel off his small head and cast the cloth away. He dragged his fingers through the boy's wet forelocks. "I'm surprised you complain about the towel. This mess gets in your eyes more."

"It didn't before the bath."

Marun gave the hair a tug. "You will let Nicky trim it for you," he decreed.

Kehfrey yelped and grabbed at his head. "Ow! Leave off! I can trim it myself!"

"Can you? I doubt it will look any good." He released the boy's hellish locks. "Nicky will do it," he said firmly. He kicked the mount forward; the ghouls needed to be headed off. "Around the lake!" he roared, setting himself in their path.

The five remaining walkers paused. The dead thief, Mur, was in the lead. After a small, tense moment, he turned right. The others followed. Marun looked past them toward Olomo and Kehfen. The assassin led Kehfen's horse. Beneath the light of the moon, Marun clearly made out Kehfen's sickened expression as he passed the two abandoned corpses tumbled on the grass. Marun supposed it didn't help that one of them had dropped in a strangely twisted position, the stumps of its legs crossed beneath in a seated arrangement, its head turned and staring upward blindly. The cadaver's expression, a pensive and questioning air, falsely mimicked life. Kehfen averted his face and his cheeks bulged spasmodically.

"Pop's not taking it well," Kehfrey muttered.

"He'll be fine. The horror wears off eventually." Marun turned his mount about. The ghouls were halfway around the small lake. After a further minute, they continued on without rounding it further. "Mur's not going toward the city at all. He's taking them up into the hills."

"That's the direction of Kortin's villa," Kehfen said breathily when Olomo escorted him up.

"Is it? Well. This should be interesting." A fell light in his eyes, Marun kicked his mount after the hunters.

***

Though Nicky assured him all the windows had warding glyphs marked on the frames, Wilf didn't care to leave the matter to faith. Rightfully so. Wards were absolutely useless on an open window. Thus every room that wasn't in use, or whose occupant was currently absent, had a thorough check and its windows were shut. Under Wilf's direction, a servant followed him into each chamber with a bucket of broken glass and shattered pottery. The servant spread shards inside the unlit hearths, positioning some in piled logs where groping hands or unprotected legs might touch them. A number of empty wine bottles had been sacrificed for this, and also one cracked plate.

Finally there were the doors. Already impressed with Wilf's fireplace traps, Nicky watched as he set a wedge before each door along the lower and upper halls. Carefully, using a bit of dough when necessary, he balanced an overturned bottle so the mouth rested flat on the wedge and at an angle against each door. He made cook waste several cups of flour for the dough.

"We use clay usually, but Marun seems to be such a rich bastard, why bother looking for mud at this hour?" Wilf joked. "Someone pulls open the door, he's going to tip the bottle over. That will let us know he's in the house and where he is too."

"Simple, but practical," she said.

By the time they arrived at the servant's stairwell leading up to the attic quarters, Wilf hadn't a single empty bottle left. He settled for posting a guard in the hall of the attic. For the remainder of the house, and since the main rooms were secured against intrusion, Wilf instructed servants to stand watch at key positions in each hall, after which he went to check on Vik, Gamis and his mother. Gamis was awake and staring worriedly out the window of the room he shared with Wilf.

"Get your butt off to Mum's room," Wilf said.

"I saw the ghouls," Gamis cried. "I saw them. Kehfrey was sitting with that Marun. He was smiling like a demon."

"Kehfrey always smiles like a demon," Nicky said.

"Not him! The sorcerer!"

Nicky glowered. She was disturbed over how much that odd red-haired brat made her master smile. The affability between them did not bode well at all. Marun never failed to possess entirely anything that pleased or delighted him. With regard to his slaves, he used them without compunction. So far the child had managed to innocently amuse his master, but there would come a time—

"Get off with you!" Wilf repeated to Gamis.

Nicky blinked, momentarily wrested out of a vision, torn from an adolescent boy determined to overcome his slavery to a master who would drag him through the blackest territory of the spirit. Ah, gods! Why had she saved that poor child? He would have been happier dead.

"Why can't I stay here?" Gamis whined.

Nicky frowned in mystification. Such hair. The colour had gone from ginger to crimson. What had he done? Dye it? Why do that? And how had he managed the metallic sheen? Must be oil. Had to be oil. No human had hair like that.

"Not tonight. You keep Mum company," Wilf said.

But there was a stink of magic to the transformation. Yes. Not dye. The Shadow Master's attention had drawn lines of power over the boy. He had changed because of it. Even now, he changed. If the humanity weren't torn from him spiritually, it would be burned from his body. Tehlm Sevet would see to that. He wouldn't make a ghoul of this child of destiny, but he'd make of him a tool of destruction, whatever way he could.

"I don't want to sleep in her bed. It'll smell. Remember what it smelled like with Kehfrey?"

"I remember what it smelled like with you," Wilf snapped. "Get going."

216

"You just want the room so you can ball her," his brother griped, pointing rudely at Nicky.

Nicky forced out an unashamed grin as Wilf chased his brother from the room. Gamis was quick getting into Canella's chamber. Wilf looked in at his mother. She slept despite Gamis's outcry. The baby was awake, however, quietly waving her little arms up and down.

"Hsst!" Wilf whispered. "Leave our sister be. If she wants attention, she'll let Mum know herself."

"I'm not touching her," Gamis hissed in disgust. "She stinks."

Wilf paused in the process of shutting the door, noting the wide open window and the large branch waving outside it. He stared at it suspiciously. He didn't like that branch. Better to have the door open. If there were trouble, he'd hear it.

"I'm leaving the door open," he whispered to Gamis.

"Good. It'll let the air in. Bloody hot in here," the boy grumbled. "And stinky!"

Shaking his head in exasperation, Wilf left the room. In Kehfrey's chamber, Vik slept soundly. The window was wide, but there wasn't a branch to be seen outside. Still, Wilf didn't like it. Once again, he decided to leave the door open, though Vik stretched naked over the bed. For propriety, Wilf stepped in to cover him, but when his foot squished on the rug, he paused. A second tentative step met with the same moist sound. An empty tub sat on the floor, hinting from where all the moisture had originated.

"Gods busted Kehfrey," Wilf muttered.

"Hi, now! What are you doing?" Vik said, sitting up.

"Coming to cover you. I was leaving the door open because of the window so I could hear if there was trouble."

"They've gone already?" Vik said in surprise.

"Kehfrey was right. You sleep like an axed cow."

"Oh, get off!" Vik slid out of the bed, went to the window and shut it with a bang.

"What the hells did you both do in here?" Wilf said.

"There was a storm in the room," Vik responded testily. He flopped back on the bed, sprawling over it carelessly. "Shut the gods busted door!"

"You'll boil."

"I'll boil naked! In privacy!"

"You're on watch later," Wilf warned him.

"Fine! By then I shall have finished cooking."

Grinning, Wilf shut the door. Vik. He never woke up pleasant.

The elder brother recoiled as he turned. Nicky had been watching from behind him, and her regard was keen with interest. "He's very beautiful," she confessed her admiration.

Wilf frowned, realizing Vik, damn him, had seen her and made no effort whatsoever to hide his exposure. "He's not your type."

"He is, but unfortunately I'm not his type." With a wise smile, she wound her arms around his neck and pressed a mocking kiss on his handsome, scowling face, though she only managed to reach his chin. "What's the matter, Wilf? I'm not allowed to look? I bet you look all the time. I bet you know exactly what to look for, rich or poor."

The bitch! Wilf pulled free and stalked toward his room. He heard her follow him.

"Are you planning to leave your door open, then?" she asked.

"Yes!" he snapped.

"Good. It'll let a breeze in."

He turned to give her a set down. Not a word left his mouth. She'd already stripped the tunic off her torso. She walked past, dragging the garment behind, the smooth skin of her back just too much of an invitation to resist. A motion in the hallway attracted his attention. The servant he'd set to guard this floor stared at him. The man had moved several feet closer. Slowly, Wilf backed until he was inside his room. By the time he turned, Nicky stood naked in front of the bed.

"He'll come and watch," Wilf said hotly.

"So?" She bent over the bed and crept on it. His eyes on her beautiful curved bottom, Wilf didn't worry about the servant further.

***

"They did just have to go up a cliff," Kehfrey said deprecatingly.

"I let them get too far ahead," Marun berated himself. One of his hunters, the one missing an arm and part of a face, had broken its back falling off the sheer face. It was useless now. Fortunately he'd arrived in time to call the rest back down. They stood with their dead faces pointed toward him, waiting with gruesome, blank-eyed patience.

"Better drop that one," the boy said. Fascinated, Kehfrey watched the false life vanish from the twisted body.

Marun turned toward Kehfen. The thief directed his mount on his own now. "This path? Does it head toward Kortin's villa eventually?" the sorcerer asked.

"I'm not sure. These little tracks are for farmers and grape pickers. I've only gone up using the main road."

"We'll have the ghouls follow it up anyway. Once we get past this cliff, we will see which way they head."

"Why bother with them?" Kehfen said with evident disgust. "If you think Rook is being hid by Kortin, let's just go without them."

"Do *you* want to be the one to break into Kortin's villa?" Marun asked.

Kehfen scowled and shook his head. Better to let the dead go first. They were at least already dead.

"They'll scare Kortin's heavies off, Pop," his little boy said brightly. "Come on. It's not that bad. They're already dead."

Just what he'd been thinking. His boy was correct. Still, he didn't like it. Ofmen had been left behind at the lake, but Mur was still with them. Looking at his animated corpse, Kehfen shuddered in revulsion. He caught a sinister smile forming on Marun's face and turned away from the man's knowing stare. The sorcerer ordered the four remaining ghouls up the small path.

"Why didn't you just use Nicky's elven path before now?" Kehfrey asked him.

"Humans can't walk elven paths."

"Why not?"

"The paths are odd. Human eyes can't seem to see them properly. There is a tendency to forget one's purpose and get lost while in them."

"Oh," the boy said in disappointment. He'd been hoping to go with Nicky into one.

"You should have sent the woman to assassinate Kortin," Olomo said contemptuously.

"She's not an assassin," Marun retorted. "At best she is a middling good thief because of these paths, also a useful messenger. Other than that, only her seeress powers interest me."

"And her skills as a hostess," Kehfen reminded with a cynical voice.

Marun looked back at him. Kehfen's expression suggested the man was thinking of something other than hostess duties. "Yes, there is that," Marun said dryly. He smiled faintly as he turned away. No doubt Nicky would give Kehfen a turn when she tired of Wilf. It looked as if Kehfen hoped she would.

They followed the ghouls for a further half hour, passing field after field of night-blackened grape vines, the smell of death and sweet rotting fruit in their nostrils. The violent storm of yesterday had sundered cluster from vine, breaking the skins and spilling the aroma of grape into the air. But the reek of the ghouls added a foulness to every scent they breathed.

The path crested the top of the cliff, coming out on a low-rising plateau where the night breeze blew the heavy smell of decaying corpse and decomposing fruit away from them. Another trail crossed theirs. The undead ignored it and turned into a plot of carefully staked vines. They thrust the vegetation aside, snapping the curling foliage and pressing through.

"I know where we are," Olomo said. "If we take this path here, it'll turn about and head straight for the back of Kortin's villa. We are no more than minutes away."

Marun called the ghouls back and set them on the indicated path. He was pleased with the turn of events. The ghouls had not led them into the city. That alone saved him trouble. The hunting party hadn't met a soul during the countryside foray. He wouldn't have to deal with angered city officials on the morrow, and it wasn't likely there would be open reprisals against him by the nobility. An attack by the undead upon one paltry wine producer would raise an outcry within the ruling council of Wistal, certainly, but it wouldn't unify the members against him, especially not without proof he was responsible.

Publicly Kortin was a respected landowner with no connection to his half-brother, the Minister of the Port. Lord Avehlt would have to act on his own to avenge this assault. If he dared. Marun suspected he wouldn't. Without Kortin, without Lolte, Avehlt would have to work through greedy underlings, many of them wanting to grab power while they could and possibly not willing to work under the minister as a minor figure. After tonight, the Syndicate might be broken beyond repair, unless Avehlt was wise and collaborated.

Even so, once Kortin was taken care of, a key position in the criminal ring would be vacant. Marun had considered his options since yesterday and come up with an ideal solution. Kehfen knew how things worked. He had shown, when he'd come to fetch Kehfrey, he could be sufficiently vicious to hold the title of head thief. He loved his children enough to cooperate for their sakes. Kehfen would be a perfect replacement for Kortin.

Marun heard the thief whisper to Olomo. "Do you think Hiswil will be with him?"

"It is possible," Olomo answered.

"That son of a bitch."

"He may not have known," Olomo pointed out.

"Doesn't matter. I have to kill the bastard now. Kehfrey took his cussed money."

"Crud, Pop! I said I was going to give it back," the child hissed.

"Quiet! All of you!" Marun snarled. This family! Why did he put up with them?

The child squirming between his legs was answer enough, but he did wish he'd stop doing that. It was becoming too distracting.

"Stop the horse!" Kehfrey whispered.

"Why?"

"I drank a gallon of water before leaving. I can't hold it anymore."

Marun shut his eyes in exasperation. He pulled the horse to a halt and helped the boy slip down. Dancing on his feet, Kehfrey hauled his tunic up and lowered his breeches. He didn't take the time to run to the side of the path. He didn't have time to spare.

"You should have said earlier," Marun remarked dryly.

"I didn't need to go earlier."

"You are a nuisance, Kehfrey."

Kehfrey glanced up worriedly, but his master looked down at him with an amused expression on his face.

"Are you almost done?" Kehfen snapped. "We're losing sight of them."

"We can catch up quickly enough," Marun said with equanimity. The ghouls weren't rushing. Ghouls hardly ever rushed unless you made them want to .... Or if they were close to prey.

Kehfrey had stopped dancing and was now sighing in utter relief. "I swear I got a bull-sized bladder full of piss in there," he grumbled. "Look! It's still coming out."

"Kehfrey!" his father snarled.

"Well, it is."

"We can hear it!"

"Right. I'll try to make it quieter."

"Kehfrey! Just finish!"

"Are you in a rush now, Pop?"

"I'm going to kill that brat."

"Not before I do," Marun interjected, and that basically meant never. "Force it out and get up here."

Grinning, Kehfrey hauled his breeches back in order and grabbed Marun's hand. Marun sighed in annoyance. The boy's hand was damp.

"Sorry," Kehfrey said sheepishly. Shaking his head, Marun settled the gamin in front and kicked the horse forward. The boy belatedly wiped his palm on his tunic front. Marun wiped his there as well. All the moisture might as well go on the same cloth.

They caught up to the ghouls in time to see them approaching a shut gate. Marun sent the barrier flying open with words of power. Kehfrey reacted with a squeal and clapped his hands over his ears, while the ghouls trundled through the opening without pausing.

"What's wrong with him?" Kehfen said anxiously, kicking his mount in line with the sorcerer's.

"He suffers from a strange reaction to magical chants," Marun told him.

"He does? Why?"

"I don't know yet."

Still with his hands over his ears, Kehfrey stared forward fixedly. Kehfen reached over and pulled one arm away. "Kehfrey?"

"What?"

"Are you all right?"

"Yes."

"Why did you keep your hands over your ears, then?" Marun asked.

"I was trying to follow the echoes," the child answered.

"Echoes?" Kehfen said in confusion.

"Did you manage to do so?" Marun questioned.

"No. They faded away. I wonder why?"

"Echoes generally do," the sorcerer responded. Echoes. The boy had said yesterday the words rang in his head. This phenomenon must be the same thing.

Ahead of them, the ghouls turned a corner in the path, disappearing around a rose-covered trellis. Terrified screams ripped the still night.

"Here we are, then," Kehfen remarked.

As one, they quickened the paces of their mounts. They charged around the corner to the sight of a man fleeing while also desperately hauling up his trousers. A woman, still screeching high and shrill, lay curled beneath a bush. Her bodice was unlaced and her legs visible beneath hiked skirts. The ghouls had already passed her. They moved quicker now. Their prey was near, but the woman, who wasn't their intended victim, continued to shriek. Irritated, Marun sent her consciousness flying with an assault of shadows. The screaming cut off abruptly.

"Saw her a few weeks ago," he muttered tetchily. "Bloody annoying woman. Screamed constantly."

"She's one of them you kidnapped, then?" the child said.

"Yes."

"What did you do to her?"

"You don't want to know."

"They say all of them wake up with nightmares," the child continued.

"They would," his master responded flatly. Yes, they would.

"Yes, well, how did you kidnap them?"

"Lolte provided thugs who did the work."

"And they caught the useless ones who knew nothing, of course," Kehfrey surmised.

"Another reason I gave Lolte a very ugly death," Marun said. Kehfrey glanced at him with a frown. Marun put a hand on the child's crown and forced him to look forward. "Don't ask," he said.

The fleeing man had reached the villa. Shouts filtered back to the riders. They crested a small hill and there it lay, sprawling downward on a gentle slope, a well-built villa that climbed the hill like stairs, one story high in every section. Marun pulled his horse up. His companions followed his example. The ghouls were not twenty feet from a back door. Men had come out to see what the fleeing cohort bellowed about. They spied the abominations rushing toward them and ran back in. One of them was short, bald and sported a large, well-formed moustache.

"Well, there goes Hiswil," Kehfen said as the door slammed shut.

Marun's ghastly hunters thumped against the heavy wood. They wailed and screeched, the anger in their cries not the least human.

"Block your ears, Kehfrey," Marun commanded. The moment the boy had his arms up, he spoke the words to send the door crashing inward.

Chapter Nine

Despite having his hands over his ears, the words of the spell rang violently inside Kehfrey's head. He hunched in agony as the echoes boomed louder and louder, this time not fading at all. The horse pranced in excitement, and Marun's arms tightened around him reflexively. Kehfrey barely felt the grip; the echoes threatened to overwhelm him.

The instant the beast settled, the sorcerer's cold hands rose to cradle Kehfrey's aching head. Green blossomed beneath Kehfrey's eyelids, a beautiful wash of soothing light, and the horrible pounding diminished. The sound of a beating heart replaced the echoes; just his own heart, he thought, until he recognised as well the rhythmic thundering of Marun's. So strange to know a sound so intimate and yet without pressing an ear to the chest. But it was there, a beat slower than his own. He heard it or perhaps felt it: Marun's heart. And deep beneath, somewhere mysterious, a pulse of pure power kept time with the sorcerer. Such a seductive noise. Potent murmurs of intelligible meaning. Exhortations to plummet further down. He thought, as he edged toward the source, he could hear those horrible echoes again. Just before he tipped over the peculiar precipice, Marun snatched him from the brink. The sorcerer's presence wrapped around Kehfrey's spirit and yanked hard.

"Kehfrey!" Marun snapped.

The child jerked in his arms. His little body straightened. "I know where the echoes went," he whispered hoarsely.

"I know. I felt you there this time. Stay with me. You aren't ready for that."

"What was it?"

"The source of power. I can keep your head from aching, but you must stay close. We dismount now."

The sorcerer descended from the saddle. The air felt cool on Kehfrey's hot back. He shut his eyes, welcoming the freshness of the night air ... and drifted again. The power still called. So alluring. So dark and deep. He thought something sparkled in the pit of shadows, something brilliant and sharp. Like teeth.

"Kehfrey!"

He looked down at Marun.

"Stay out of it!" the sorcerer snapped.

"Why is it calling me?"

"Because it can. Because you hear it. Refuse to listen! It must never be given all it wants."

"Why not?"

"We have no time for this now." Marun lifted Kehfrey off the horse and set him down, but kept a hand on a small shoulder to be certain of the boy's balance. "Your father and Olomo have already gone in. Let's go." He pulled the boy through the shattered doorway.

Kehfrey noticed the damage for the first time. Marun's spell had not only opened the door, it had blown the entire frame inward. An unconscious man lay beneath the splintered wood. The victim shifted and groaned as they swept past. Blood, lots of it, seeped beneath his body.

Further within the villa, screams filtered through to them. A lamenting woman burst out of a door and ran toward them. Marun pressed himself to the side of the hall, squashing Kehfrey to the rear. She fled by without stopping.

"Hi, now! I can't breathe!" Kehfrey protested.

"She would have run you down," Marun said testily.

"Well, at least I might have seen something nice as she passed over," the child retorted smartly.

Marun scowled. "You are an unnatural child, Kehfrey." He towed the boy down the hall toward the screams and shouts.

"Vik just said the same thing earlier," Kehfrey told him.

"Vik is very observant."

Another woman ran toward them, this one with a child in her arms and two trailing behind. Marun shoved the boy aside a second time. Silently they watched the group flee past. They were about to step into the centre again when a short man crashed through an open door and hit the wall just ahead of them. He sank to the floor, burbling red-flecked spit out of his mouth. A large gash in the throat poured his lifeblood out.

"There goes Hiswil," Kehfrey pronounced.

Holding a bloody knife, his father stepped out of the doorway. "Will you look at that? His gods busted moustache is still perfect."

So it was. Perfect. Not a hair out of line. Must have glued it in place. "Did you really have to kill him?" Kehfrey cried angrily. "I hate like shit owing money!"

"Yes. Look at his hand."

Kehfrey peered down again. Hiswil had a knife in his grip and red on the blade. Kehfrey looked up hurriedly. Blood leaked down his father's forearm.

"Don't worry about it," Kehfen said. "Only a scratch." His gaze shifted to Marun. "The ghouls have gone down the cellar. Most everyone else ran out the loading doors. Olomo's gone the other way to check the front of the house."

"Lead me to the hunters," Marun commanded. The thief guided him toward the cellar. They passed another dead man. He lay on his stomach. His head was canted to the side, and his eyes were wide open in a surprised stare. Kehfrey recognised Lerny.

"Why did you kill him? He was harmless."

"Was he?" his father snapped, continuing onward. "There's a crossbow under him."

224

A second more careful look, and Kehfrey spotted the wing of a crossbow peeking out from beneath the old man's chest. He couldn't see what had killed him, though. "What did him?" he called to his father, but both he and the sorcerer had disappeared around a corner.

"Kehfrey!" Marun shouted impatiently.

Sighing dismally, the boy jogged forward. Death and more death, and he was certain to commit his share of murders, what with learning to be an assassin. He didn't really like the idea and decided there and then he wouldn't do shit in the way of murder if Marun asked him to. Magic could do anything a man might, so what did a sorcerer need with an assassin anyhow?

Kehfen and the sorcerer were descending a dark stairwell. Kehfrey darted after them. Marun grabbed the boy's collar. He held it the rest of the way down, disinclined to losing track of the child again.

The cellar was enormous. It had been cut out of the rock over which the villa had been built. Barrels of wine lay on top of each other, row upon row. A large pair of loading doors stood open, letting in the moonlight. Kehfen stopped within the shadows at the end of an aisle and peered at the entrance suspiciously. Marun halted just behind him. He peeked out over the shorter man's head.

"There could be enemies in the shadows here or out there waiting for us to pass," Kehfen hissed. "The light from that door will make us perfect targets from either direction."

Marun pulled Kehfrey in between them and placed his palms over the boy's ears. A chant commenced. Kehfrey's little hands clutched his father's back, digging in as if he were in agony or extremely terrified; Kehfen wasn't sure which. He pulled the boys tight fingers off, knelt, set his dagger on the ground and added his own palms over Marun's.

Blackness swelled inside the cavernous cellar, unnatural and heavier than a simple lack of light. Somewhere further along, the ghouls screeched and howled, greeting the deepening obscurity with pleasure. Kehfen glared into the murk, but could see absolutely nothing. As the incantation progressed, several frightened screams filtered through the black and then more. There was movement, panicked stumbling. Something large crashed to the ground. Beneath the racket of a barrel rolling away, choking noises sounded, but no longer the voice of the dark practitioner who had summoned the murderous power into the cellar.

"What's happening?" Kehfen whispered.

"Do you really want to know?" Marun asked.

"No. Never mind."

Between them, little Kehfrey was more a stiff effigy than a boy. Kehfen blinked. He thought a faint aura of green glowed beneath his fingers, just where the sorcerer's hands rested.

The shadows began to break apart. Moonlight shot through the open doors. Kehfen snatched up his dagger and stood. Just ahead, a dead man lay on the stone floor. His face was distorted. A grotesquely swollen tongue stuck out of his mouth. Further along, the legs of another body stretched out from an aisle. One more casualty of dark magic sprawled near the loading doors, the tongue also protruding.

"Let's go," Marun urged and pulled Kehfrey past his father.

Kehfen dashed after them, skin prickling. Whatever Marun had called into the cavern, the sorcerer seemed certain it had done its task and departed. Even so, the thief was unwilling to permit the master of the shadows to stray too far ahead, just in case *something* had been left behind.

They headed into the darkness past the large entrance. The ghouls were creating a wordless racket, hoarse voices raised in protest. Shifting to the side, Kehfen just barely made them out. They scratched and banged at a small door in the cellar's stone wall.

"Where does that lead?" Marun shouted above the din.

"The older cellars in the foundation where it's coolest," Kehfen answered, "where Kortin does some business that needs to be kept quiet."

"What business, exactly?"

"Torture and punishment mostly, and the occasional body he doesn't want to rot too quickly before it can be disposed of." Kehfen grimaced at the yowling ghouls. "Can't you shut them up?"

Marun willed his hunters to desist. A welcome silence ensued, but for the footsteps of the living as they approached the door. Then the wailing and protesting began again. Marun scowled and ceased walking. He lifted a hand. A green light burst into life on his palm. Beneath the eerie glow, it became clear his ghouls were not responsible for the outcry.

"It's them!" Kehfrey cried.

"Who?"

"The two I saw when I was trapped here!"

Marun felt the boy turn. Before the child could dash away, he tugged him back by his tunic. "You mentioned one ghoul only."

"What's going on here?" the boy's father demanded.

Marun ignored him. He listened suspiciously to the noise from beyond the door. There were definitely two sources. Some of the bawling had the high pitch a child's vocal cords might create, but some were lower in tonality, evidently created within the throat of a dead man.

The clamour discontinued suddenly. A scratching noise sounded at the door. Then the wood shuddered under an impact. The sorcerer pulled Kehfrey back, stepping on Kehfen as he did so. They almost tumbled down.

"Move!" Marun hissed.

"What's going on here?" Kehfen repeated.

"There are ghouls behind that door."

"So?"

"So? They aren't under my control!" They listened to another impact on the door.

"Right," said Kehfen. "Time to leave." He began to back off.

226

"Take the child. I need to get in there." Marun shoved Kehfrey at his father, who caught him quickly.

"What the hells for?" the thief demanded. "You'll let them loose on us!"

Marun turned back to snarl his displeasure. The door burst open. The first ghoul fell on the broken door. It lifted its head and stared forward, sunken eyes vibrant with unnatural intent. The slashed throat gaped bloodlessly.

"Rook!" Kehfen spat.

The abomination's mouth widened in an unholy and ravenous grin. It began to rise. Behind him, a naked child stepped out, its little head dangling sideways. The small body was pale except for where the blood had sunk down the legs. There, the limbs had swollen purple with congealed fluid. Slowly the child ghoul turned its body until the head hanging from its useless neck pointed toward them.

Marun had lunged aside when the door crashed outward. Now he crouched on a knee, one hand raised, the other palm resting on the packed dirt of the cellar. He whispered beneath his breath, drawing power from the earth. The glowing ball in his palm grew larger and brighter. Gradually it began to swirl with orange. The corpse of Rook uttered a loud choking cry that lifted out from both his slashed throat and his hanging mouth. He stumbled forward. The smaller cadaver lurched alongside, tittering in a grotesque mimicry of childlike happiness. Both ghouls passed Marun without looking at him. The sorcerer stared in shock, momentarily frozen with astonishment.

Clutching his boy in horror, Kehfen backed away. Rook's ghoul charged forward. Kehfen bellowed and jerked Kehfrey aside. He expected to feel the bite of the stinking corpse, but the event didn't happen. Dead Rook wheeled and grabbed Kehfrey.

"No!" Kehfen shouted.

His protest was echoed from beyond the abominations. Marun darted forward. As the sorcerer rushed to the child's aid, Kehfrey twist into a ball in the ghouls grasp. His little feet came forward to shove the foul mouth back. Marun's grasping hand helped the attack, pulling the head back by the hair, away from Kehfrey. The snapping of Rook's neck sounded loudly in the air. The sorcerer's other hand, still filled with an eerie glow, flashed into the undead face. Fire erupted over Rook's head.

Once-living reflexes saved the child. The ghoul released the boy to smack at its burning head. Kehfrey dropped to the ground, thudding onto his back. The breath whistled out of him. A little body fell upon him and slammed the rest of the air out. The small ghoul, most likely no more than four when he'd died, smiled at Kehfrey hungrily, his head flopping with every movement. Kehfrey stared at him breathlessly, his mouth wide in panic. Cold little fingers clutched his neck and dug in.

Marun hurled Rook's burning body away. "Get it off!" he shouted at Kehfen.

He didn't wait for an answer. He landed at Kehfrey's side and pulled at the icy fingers on the boy's neck. They resisted. He broke a digit and another. Kehfrey's father thudded down at the other side and prized a hand loose. Kehfrey choked and wheezed a breath in, eyes starting from his head. Suddenly he scrabbled out from beneath the struggling child corpse. A flaming body landed where he'd been, sending both Marun and Kehfen backward in alarm. The child ghoul, trapped beneath Rook, clawed at Kehfrey's legs, catching one before the boy could free himself entirely.

Kehfen's arm was aflame. He shouted and rolled, desperate to put the fire out. Marun worsened the thief's predicament when he added to the infernal heat. Uttering enraged words of power, the sorcerer sundered the gloom with a conflagration. The magic engulfed the torsos of both ghouls. Kehfen yelped, rolled further off and yanked free of his smouldering jacket. He tossed it aside and looked back toward his son.

The sorcerer rose, stepped on the arm of the dead child, and lifted Kehfrey. The hand continued to grasp, tearing a strip of the boy's breeches away.

"Fucking bastard spelled them to endure!" the sorcerer spat. He crunched the small arm again and at last the child ghoul released Kehfrey. Just in time. Rook's ghoul swiped an arm in Marun's direction. The sorcerer skipped backward and nearly fell. He came up against a stack of barrels and steadied himself against it, clutching Kehfrey tenaciously.

Dizzy from anoxia and the horrible banging in his head, Kehfrey felt as if he were floating in the air. A too-bright fire worsened the tears flooding his eyes. The blaze lurched up and toward him. Something dark stumbled past and met the staggering light. Both tumbled down. Another shadow rushed past and thudded onto the first. Kehfrey blinked, wondering what he was seeing.

Marun edged away. He'd summoned his ghouls. They pressed Rook's corpse down as it burned. The child ghoul, scorched but no longer aflame, crawled toward Kehfrey. The sorcerer sent two ghouls after it and ordered them on the pyre created of Rook's flaming body. Marun cradled Kehfrey's ears between his arm and chest and commenced the spell that would take the unnatural life out of all of the abominations.

Kehfrey shrieked in pain. His head pounded as if his heart had crashed inside it. His heart, Marun's heart ... and the thing. The thing in the depths, it searched for him, thrumming now, the hugest heart of all. He felt himself falling toward the pit, the great dark cavern where all the echoes went. So familiar. So very familiar. What was it?

"Kehfrey!"

His body shook.

"Kehfrey!"

Again his body rattled. He opened his eyes. It was awful. The stench!

"Gaah!" he cried. He turned his head and vomited.

"Get him out of here!" Marun snapped.

Someone lifted Kehfrey even as he retched. With his head hanging down and vomit erupting out of his mouth, he was borne away. He gasped in agony and almost choked on another heave.

"Kehfrey!" his father cried. "Don't choke on it, boy! Let it out before you breathe!"

Very good advice. Only it wasn't working out so easily, was it? He heaved again. He felt as if his stomach were ready to disgorge from his mouth. His father set him down on his knees. Kehfrey gasped and choked on acid. Quite unhelpfully Kehfen smacked him on the back. It took even longer to get his breath back.

"What has happened here?"

That was Olomo. Fine time to show up. A master assassin and he misses all the murder and mayhem. Kehfrey wheezed air inward and tried to listen to what his father said.

"There were more ghouls in the cellar. One was Rook," Kehfen related, his voice echoing horror over the encounter.

"Rook is a ghoul?" Olomo questioned.

"Was," Marun called from further off. Kehfrey heard his booted feet crunching gravel. "All of them are destroyed now."

"Is that what this foul smoke is about?" Olomo said. A noxious cloud billowed through the loading doors. The light of flames danced on the many racks of barrels.

"There was no other way to destroy them," Marun answered harshly. Kehfrey felt himself rise in the air again. "We must leave. It isn't here."

"Gods bust it!" Kehfen said. "Tell us what it is that you seek!"

"No!" Marun shouted.

Held in the sorcerer's arms again, weak and dizzy, Kehfrey looked back at his father's scowling face. The boy lifted a hand to shush him. Kehfen paused, but the assassin stalked after the sorcerer and forced the matter.

"If this thing is not here, then where is it?" Olomo said.

"With Kortin!" Marun screamed, rounding on Olomo. "Find Kortin and we find my—!" He swallowed the end of the answer and averted his gaze.

"Your what?" Kehfen bellowed, ignoring his son's distraught expression. "We find your what?"

"His soul, Pop," Kehfrey said. "Now shut up about it."

Kehfen stalled in mid-step. Had he heard right?

Marun squeezed Kehfrey, angered by the revelation.

"We get to Kortin and you touch nothing on him," the boy wheezed out. "The rock is spelled. It'll undo your mind."

"A rock! We seek a rock?" Olomo cried. "There are rocks everywhere!"

Snarling, Marun answered. "We seek a rock on Kortin's person! The location is specific!"

"What does it look like, then?" Kehfen said, facing off with the man.

"It is a smooth, oblong, river-polished piece of granite," the sorcerer spat. He headed in the direction he thought the horses might be. "You shouldn't have said," he hissed, easing up on the child's chest.

"No choice now," Kehfrey whispered. "We have to get it back tonight. He knew you were coming."

Damn it! The boy was right. Where the hells was Kortin?

***

Canella turned with the baby and settled on her other side. She exposed a breast and helped the small lips catch on. She winced as they did. Babies never failed to get it wrong the first week. She had blisters on the ends of her nipples that hurt abominably. With that and her milk coming in, she was in agony. She worked a finger in the corner of the child's mouth and broke the suction. The baby bashed her in protest.

Aie! That hurt! Her poor swollen breast!

"Try again," she said softly. "No. Open wider."

She teased the distended nipple against the infant's lips. The mouth opened wider and she pressed the little head forward quickly. She sighed in relief. The baby had latched on properly. A few seconds later, she hissed in anguish. Her milk came down, rushing into her ducts like a river flowing in spring thaw. At the same time, her uterus contracted painfully. As her front soaked with milk that spurted copiously from her free breast, between her legs the blood of birthing flowed out of her body.

"Gods! Having babies is such a mess!"

Of course the baby just had to grunt and do her business right then. Canella looked at Gamis snoring softly next to them. She considered waking him. He wouldn't help with the baby, but he could get Nicky. Nicky knew what it was like. She wouldn't mind coming to help.

"Gamis," she called. She gave him a shove. "Gamis! Wake up!"

"What?" he said stupidly.

"Go get Nicky. I need some help."

"Oh, Mum!" he protested. He rolled onto his side.

"Get up!" She poked him in the back.

"Mum!" He sat up and glowered at her. His eyes darted away and widened in surprise. Canella watched blankly as his mouth opened in fright. Then Gamis screamed.

***

"Where would Kortin go?" Marun demanded as they approached their mounts.

"Could be in any number of safe houses," Kehfen responded. "This could take all night. Days actually. Kortin won't be easy to find, and he'll have his gang ready to fight us off."

Marun cursed in some strange language, for which Kehfrey laughed. "That's a good one," the child said. Marun angled his head down and glowered at him. "Well, it was. I'm collecting them, you know."

Marun shook his head in exasperation. Incorrigible child. Almost killed *again* and he still couldn't be subdued. He set the boy on his mount and lifted up behind him. "Give me the likeliest place he'd go," he ordered Kehfen, settling his champing horse.

"We can try the waterfront," Olomo suggested.

"No," Kehfrey said firmly.

"What would you know?" Kehfen said. "You've never even met Kortin. You don't know how he thinks."

Kehfrey canted his head up and looked at Marun. Marun, who had been glaring at Kehfen and Olomo, seemed to freeze. The two men watched his face become cold and expressionless. The change filled them with dread.

"Where does the road in front lead to?" the sorcerer said, his tone flat.

"Out to Portway road," Kehfen answered, frowning. Marun jerked his reins and hauled the mount's head about. He sent it thundering toward the front of the villa. "Hi, now!" Kehfen shouted. "Where are you off to?"

Kehfrey answered. "The manor!"

"Ah, gods!" Kehfen cried. He mounted his horse and galloped after them. He caught up quickly, because a human barrier of neighbouring vine growers and field workers had come up the private road, led there by anxious members of Kortin's household. They blocked the gate between hedges. Marun pulled up his horse to face off with them.

"You!" someone shouted. "Who are you?"

"Innocent visitors," Marun said. "Be careful. There are monstrous creatures back there. You should run."

"Look!" someone shouted. "The villa is on fire!"

"By the gods! What is that?" another person screamed.

Marun glanced back. A figure in flames stumbled down the road toward them. "Gods!" he hissed. Rook's ghoul resisted destruction even yet. That damned Kortin had spelled the abomination to endure attacks a typical ghoul could not: snapped spines, fire and counter spells included. "Run!" he shouted at the people blocking their path. "The demons are coming!"

The mob screamed and shouted. A full-blown flight ensued, into which Marun kicked his horse forward. He barely avoided trampling a man bearing a pointed farming tool in his hands. Behind, he heard Kehfen cursing. After a few dozen yards, the horses surpassed the last of the fleeing citizens.

"Slow down!" Marun heard Kehfen shout.

"No time!" he shouted back.

Kehfen managed to get his mount up next to them. "How do you know Kortin is at the manor?" he hollered.

"Kortin has the stone. He wants what I want."

"Gods!" Kehfen cried. His family! Vik! "Will he hurt Vik?" he shouted.

"Not if we get back in time."

The thief cursed heatedly. Marun knew he did it to prevent fear from overwhelming him.

"It's not Vik he wants," Kehfrey said, but not loud enough for his father to hear. "The ghouls were set for me."

"I know!" he hissed. "I know." But if Kortin did manage to get in and didn't find the child, Vik *would* be hurt. Kortin would look for Vik in Kehfrey's absence, just as he would.

***

Canella twisted to look back. A high-pitched scream ripped from her throat. A man watched them from just outside the window. A rope fell away, back toward the tree branch it was hooked onto as the intruder pulled himself in. While Canella lay frozen in the bed, clutching her baby in horror, the man straightened and smiled at her. His left hand reached inside his jacket front. An oblong lump bulged from an inside pocket.

That face? Didn't she know that face?

Gamis was not so bewildered as his mother. He thudded onto the floor and dashed toward the door, still shouting wordlessly. A strange darkness swept into the room, and the door slammed shut just before he reached it. He banged into the wood and fell to the floor, where he moaned piteously.

"There, boy," the intruder said, his tone gentle. "Be a good boy. Come over to see me."

Gamis rolled to his fours. His nose bled. He looked at the intruder and cringed away. He'd seen enough angry and damaged men in the safe houses to recognise the insane gleam in the old man's eyes.

"Kortin?" Canella said. His attention returned to her, smile unwavering. She almost smiled back before she remembered why she was there in the manor. Cold terror filled her mind. This man was no longer an ally of her husband's.

"Hello? Aren't you Kehfen's noble-born slut?"

Something thudded against the door. Gamis yelped and scuttled out of the way. Wilf shouted from outside.

"Mum! Gamis!" The door thudded again. "Mum!"

"Shall I open it for him?" Kortin said, still with the most pleasant of voices. He crossed to Canella, and she cowered in the bed. She wept silently now, the tears almost blinding her. Not heeding a frightened whimper, he probed the sheets that covered her. She'd hauled them over the baby's head. He pulled the linen down. "Isn't that impressive?" He scrutinized the newborn sucking obliviously on a swollen breast. "The milk has come in, hasn't it? They're as big as melons. Does it hurt?"

"Yes," she whispered. He reeked like something dead. She almost retched. He bent closer, and she did retch. Her vomit scattered across the pillow and onto her daughter's small head.

Kortin pulled away and laughed. He turned toward the sobbing boy on the floor. "Where is the child?" he said, his tone soft, appealing. Gamis moaned and scurried under a table. "Come now, boy? Where is he? Your little brother?"

"He went with the sorcerer! Leave me alone!"

Kortin scowled. "With him? He went with him? That little whore!"

The false amiability vanished. Kortin bent over the bed and pulled the baby off her mother's breast. Canella gasped as the suction broke in the most painful manner. He held her child up by an arm, and the infant shrieked in pain.

"My baby! Please! Give her back!"

Kortin turned to the door. It slammed open, but not from Wilf's assault. A mysterious force had moved it. Just about to crash into the panels again, Wilf pulled up sharply. He spotted Kortin and shouted.

"You! You bastard! Let her go!"

"It's a girl, is it?" Kortin remarked. He swung the infant carelessly. "How useless."

His face impassive, he watched the young man approach. Wilf wore only his breeches. Barefoot, shirtless, with just a knife to defend his family, he crouched in a fighting position. Beyond him, a small woman paused within the door. She was dressed in nothing but a man's tunic, obviously his. It hung almost to her knees. Kortin glanced at her and then averted his gaze, scorning the sight of her. Wilf was more interesting to look upon. Fine looking young man. Very fine indeed.

"Put the baby down, old man," Wilf said. "Gently!"

The intruder laughed as if the demand were a joke. His left hand retreated from his jacket front. At first wary that a weapon might appear, Wilf stared in surprise. Kortin had nothing but a rock within his fist. Was the man mad? Where was his weapon?

"Wilf!" Nicky shouted. "Back off!"

"What? It's just a rock!" he called without turning. Rocks were easily dodged, especially when there was only one.

But tossing the stone wasn't Kortin's intention. Darkness welled up around Wilf's feet. Its cold sank into his bones, sapped his strength, numbed his body all over. The knife fell from his hand. Blood pounding in his head, he thumped to his knees, only vaguely hearing his mother's alarmed cry. A boot kicked his head, and he spun away to lay sprawled on the floor, senseless.

"Where is the boy?" Kortin shouted above the infant's wailing. He lifted the baby. He would dash its brains out now!

"Stop!" a new voice assailed him.

He paused with his tiny victim high over his head. There, within the doorway stood a youth of surpassing beauty. Dressed only in breeches, he was unarmed but for a bottle he'd broken on the floor. Vik had fled his room unable to find his dagger and had created this crude weapon in its stead. His foot bled from a gash. He'd stepped on a shard in his haste.

"A beauty," Kortin said. "A rare beauty."

"Please! Put the baby down," the adolescent begged.

"Come to me. I'll put her down," Kortin bargained.

"No, you won't. Put her down first."

"I'll bash her head in now! Come here!"

Vik set the broken bottle down and walked forward. He could not pry his gaze from Kortin's eyes, which were bloodshot and wild with madness. The stench hanging over the thief settled into his nostrils. He gasped and tried not to retch in revulsion.

Kortin lowered the infant with each step Vik took. "Yes! That's it! Come to me!" he whispered eagerly.

Vik arrived within reach. Kortin dropped the baby and snatched him by the upper arm. The baby plummeted and screamed on the hardwood floor. Kortin ignored everything but Vik. He jerked the youth closer, forcing Vik to inadvertently kick his sister's little body. Vik cried a wordless protest. Kortin wrenched him closer and dragged him out of the room. Vik had a brief glimpse of Nicky's white face. He heard his mother screaming, Gamis weeping, and then he began to struggle.

"No, you don't!" Kortin shouted.

He hit the boy on the head with the stone. Vik slumped against him, and Kortin laughed. He caught one arm again and dragged the youth along the corridor. As he approached the stairwell, he spotted servants, all of them motionless and staring at him warily. He laughed at them. They weren't going to interfere. He was master here now.

He stomped to the further hall, dragging the boy through shards of broken glass. He heard a hiss and then a strangled cry of pain, and the boy's arm stiffened in his tight hand. There would be blood, Kortin realized. Yes, there would be blood.

He stopped before the one door, the special door. Here, the master's workroom. Here, the seat of power. With the stone against his chest, the interloper glared at the wood. The ward over it shimmered into visibility, black and oily and reluctant. Under the force of Kortin's will, the ward buckled and scattered. The door slammed inward violently. The hinges at the top broke. When the power settled, the door hung off the frame crookedly. Kortin laughed again and dragged the youth in.

***

"Wilf!"

Someone pinched the skin on his chest.

"Wilf!"

He opened his eyes. His jaw ached abominably. Nicky knelt beside him, her expression anxious. He remembered the intruder. He tasted blood in his mouth.

"Nicky! The baby!" His voice came out slurred. His tongue felt swollen in his mouth.

"She's safe with her mother. Gamis took them out of the house."

"Out of the house?" he repeated.

"Yes. We must go. Get up!"

"Go? We have to get Kortin."

"Do you remember nothing? He has the stone!"

Urged on by her pulling hands, Wilf rose to his feet. "What is it with this stone?"

"It's what Marun wanted back. Kortin has it. It means he's had it all along." She tugged at his arm, but he refused to move.

"And that means what exactly?" He spotted his knife. It had fallen only a few feet away. That insane old man hadn't taken it.

"It means he's been leeching power from Marun for weeks," Nicky said. "It means he killed Rook to get it long ago. It means we're all in danger. The man's been driven mad by the stone."

Wilf jerked upright, his knife in hand. "What? He killed his own son. That's crazy!"

"Gods! Wilf! That's what I'm trying to tell you!" She yanked him about and shoved hard. "Come on!"

"Is everyone else out?" he asked. She didn't answer right off. "Nicky!"

"Yes!" she said. Her tone was more panicky than impatient.

He glanced at her. She was staring down the hall. Wilf followed her gaze. A faint, wavering light cast an angular pattern on the corridor floor and wall. It issued from the open door of the chamber she'd named Marun's workroom. He stared at the illumination as they continued toward the stairwell. She began the descent when they reached it, but he stepped onward.

"Wilf! Wilf, don't!"

She grabbed his arm to pull him back. He shoved her off. There were sounds coming from that room. Someone sobbed. Someone moaned. His hackles rising in trepidation, he strode forward.

"Wilf!" Nicky cried one last time. She stopped and would not approach further. Fearfully she waited to see what would happen.

Wilf stepped softly toward the open entrance. He wiped blood from his eyes and blinked. The doorframe had been damaged. The wood was splintered along the top and side. He came within view of the chamber and there he froze in horror. For a moment, he could do nothing but stare. He found his voice belatedly. "Get off him!" he shouted.

Kortin looked toward him and smiled. With a hand on his victim's back, he pressed Vik against the heavy table. With the other, he rubbed the stone along the youth's spinal column. A trail of darkness bled from the granite, swelling with each violent thrust of Kortin's hips. The old man moaned in pleasure, and Vik hissed in pain, shivering violently as if he were wrapped in ice. Vik stared into his brother's eyes; then his eyelids shut and agony twisted his features.

"Get off him!" Wilf shouted again. The shadows in the corners of the corridor billowed to the ceiling. Wilf yelped in alarm and backed a pace.

He hesitated on the verge of running back to Nicky, gaze shooting from the end of the corridor to the room and the violence happening within. The stairs leading up to the servants' quarters seemed more a gaping black maw with jagged sideways teeth than a stairwell.

"Where is the boy?" Kortin demanded. He pushed into Vik again. "Where is that slut?" He lifted the rock from Vik's back. Blood smeared the underside.

"I don't know!" Wilf said. Who was he talking about?

"You know!" Kortin insisted. Vik struggled beneath him. The old man turned his weathered angular face toward the youth and struck his back with the stone. Vik grunted and jerked against the table. A whimper escaped him.

"No!" Wilf cried. "Don't hurt him!"

"Get me the boy!" Kortin screamed. "Get him now!"

"Tell me who you mean? I'll get him."

"The child! The child with flame hair! Bring him to me or this whore dies!"

Kehfrey! He wanted Kehfrey? Wilf backed off from the door. Why did he want Kehfrey?

"I'll get him," he lied. "Don't hurt Vik. If you do, the boy will never come."

"I can wait," Kortin said, almost whispering. "I know how to wait."

Repulsed, Wilf gaped at his face. The eyes had half shut in ecstasy, but the lips twisted as if Kortin were in pain. Wilf stared once more into Vik's horrified eyes and then fled from the sight. Nicky stood in the centre of the hall, just a few yards away from the main stairs.

"You! You lied! Vik is here!" Wilf sobbed.

"I had to get you out! There's nothing we can do for him!"

"We can stall for time," Wilf barely breathed. He grabbed her small shoulders and shook her hard. "You stay here and listen. Do you hear me? If anything happens, if he wants anything, you come tell me."

She nodded. Wilf stared down at her white face and then rushed down the stairs and out the open front door. They all waited beneath trees bordering the driveway—the servants, his mother, Gamis, the baby.

"Is she alive?" Wilf cried, ignoring his mother's sob of relief at the sight of him.

"Yes," Gamis said. "Mum's feeding her. We think her arm is broken."

Wilf looked down at his mother. She sat with her back to a tree. Her front was exposed. The baby suckled fitfully on one swollen breast. Wilf noted a bruise on her crown. The bastard had dropped her on her tiny head. He knew then the infant might die later in any case. He didn't say so.

"The man took Vik," Gamis said. "He said he'd bash the baby's head in if he didn't go with him."

Wilf shut his eyes in horror. Oh, Vik! What was he to do? What was he to do?

236

Thundering hooves brought him whirling about in fright. Three horses charged into the drive. "You!" Wilf shouted at the first of the riders. "You! He's got Vik! He's hurting him!"

Marun swept off his horse, leaving Kehfrey up on it. "When did this happen?"

"Not more than ten minutes ago," a servant told him. He stepped forward from beneath the tree. "The intruder came in through the woman's window and hurt the infant. That boy, Vik, exchanged himself for her."

"No!" Kehfen exclaimed.

Wilf looked beyond Marun. Kehfen had rushed closer to listen. Now he charged past Marun toward Canella.

"Canella!"

"He hurt the baby, Kehfen!" Canella wept. "Her little head is all swollen. She's so quiet now! Her arm doesn't move right!

"Oh, no! Oh, no!" Kehfen whispered.

"Help her, Marun!" Kehfrey shouted from atop the horse. "You can help her!"

Marun snarled silently. He looked toward the house and hesitated.

"Vik is still alive!" Kehfrey said. "The baby won't be soon!"

Unable to ignore the boy's logic or the likely consequence of utter hatred for ignoring the plea, Marun strode toward the woman and crouched down. Green swelled in his palms before he touched the infant, before he even knelt. There was dead silence as those around gathered in to watch. Grimly the sorcerer sank healing energy into the baby.

***

Nicky had moved closer to the workroom entrance, close enough to hear Kortin's abusive comments and Vik's helpless cries, but far enough to run from the blackness lurking at the end of the corridor. A clatter sounded to her rear. She wheeled around, panicked and searching for unnatural shadows. She saw none.

Someone was charging up the steps of the main staircase, but the footsteps didn't sound right. They were too light. The creator of the noise rose into view, and her eyes started in her head.

"No! Kehfrey! Go back down!"

The child ignored her and continued forward. He looked like hell. Vomit covered his side. A leg of his breeches was torn and hanging off. Something black and greasy soiled his face, and he smelled like rotted flesh. She attempted to grab him. He dodged aside.

"Kehfrey!" she shouted.

"Kehfrey!" the intruder roared. "Come to me!"

Nicky grabbed at him again. He darted away and pointed a warning finger at her. He backed off as he spoke. "No, you don't," he said coldly. "This isn't up to you."

"He'll kill you! He wants you! He wants you because Marun does!"

"I know that," the boy hissed. "Shut up."

By then, he had reached the open door. Nicky dashed toward him, but the boy stepped in through the entrance. A wall of darkness rose and barred the woman's path.

"Kehfrey!" she screamed.

***

The distant cry shivered through the dark. Marun jerked away from Canella's daughter and the glow on his hands died. He recognised the faint voice, the name it had called. He scanned the area in growing alarm. There was no child sitting on his mount. The boy wasn't among the gathered crowd.

"No!" he whispered. He lurched up and ran toward the house. "No!" he shouted. "Kehfrey!"

Another mouth repeated his call, a man's voice. Kehfen's. The sounds of other runners beat the air behind him. He flew up the stairs, taking them three at a time. He thumped into the far wall and careened off it, directing his body toward the eerie firelight illuminating the end of the hall. Nicky stood before the workroom door, half dressed in a large tunic, her face white with terror. A dark cloud of shadow was forcing her back from the entrance.

"Kehfrey!" she screamed again.

Marun dashed up toward her and shoved her aside. He was there, in the room. Kehfrey was there. "Kehfrey!" Marun cried. "Come back!"

But the boy didn't turn. He walked forward slowly, resolutely.

The boy's father thundered up next to Marun. He shouted the child's name and tried to press forward, but the darkness whirled about his limbs and sent him tumbling. He collapsed to the side, groaning in agony. The boy ignored the commotion.

"I won't do it," he said. "Not unless you let him up."

"You come here," Kortin hissed. "Come here, or I thump his brains out before you!" The man lifted the rock.

"Stupid bastard! You do that and there's no reason for me to cooperate, is there? You think catching me with threats will make me sweeter?"

The expression on Kortin's sun-weathered face froze. He stared at the boy, his hand still high. Shortly after, he lowered his arm without force and laughed. Beneath him, Vik whispered at Kehfrey to run. Neither abuser nor next victim paid heed to him.

"You are an incorrigible child," Kortin said.

Kehfrey nodded his guilt. "I know you like it," he said. "You don't need, Vik. You can have me. Let Vik go. You know I hate it when you use him."

"Yes. You do, don't you?" Kortin looked straight into the eyes of the sorcerer. "Yes, boy. Come to me," he urged.

"No!" Marun shouted. He stepped forward into the unnatural shadows. They bent sluggishly, rebelliously, but still twisted away, true to the relentless will of their proper master. Kortin bellowed angrily. Clutching the rock tight, fingers white around the grey, he said a word. The floor in front of Marun caught fire. The sorcerer staggered back, vaguely aware of Olomo jumping back with him.

"Let him go!" Marun roared. He didn't wait for an answer. He summoned darkness to him, the shadows and the freezing cold of his hatred.

"Mine! He's mine now!" the old man shouted. He looked down at Kehfrey, his face contorted insanely. The boy had paused. His features were distorted with pain.

"What is it, boy?" the man called. "What hurts you?"

"Get off Vik! I want you to touch me! Not him!"

"No!" Vik wept, but Kehfrey stepped forward the remaining distance and tugged at the hem of Kortin's undershirt like a little boy demanding attention. His words were not so innocent.

"Get off him and touch me instead! Put yourself in me!"

Kortin smiled down in triumph. He pulled his hips away from Vik and lowered the stone toward Kehfrey, who watched with an expression that seemed a mix of frustration and yearning. His eyes were unusually bright. Kortin stared into the hazel glow as if mesmerized.

"Yes! Touch me!" Kehfrey hissed. "Touch me with it!"

He lifted his small hands toward the man's distended penis, and Kortin loosed an excited, choking noise deep in his throat. Vik rolled weakly off the table, protesting to Kehfrey, begging him to run. Cold stone touched the child's smooth cheek. On his flushed skin, the boy felt the sorcerer; yet behind him, he also heard the man cursing futilely, the dark cold of his wrath growing with the passing seconds. Beneath that, woven into the pattern of Tehlm Sevet's spirit, there lurked the miasma of an ancient power hidden within a cavern deep below, a cavern formed of crystal teeth.

Kehfrey sensed the anger of that power, and even as the fear and bloodlust of his master brushed his soul, his skin prickled with longing for the blackness beneath, this familiar and all-consuming hunger to dominate and to own. He wanted it, and he hated it, and he didn't know what the blackness was, only that he must not let it find him. This standoff had to end. Quickly.

A sinister mix of emotions reflected from the stone and toward Marun's body, and then returned and hit the warmth of Kehfrey's cheek. It made his teeth ache, his guts twist with nausea, and it tightened the cold determination in his mind. And Kortin felt the Shadow Master's fury, too. The lust, the hunger, the fear. He felt it all and he wanted it all. Kehfrey looked at the old thief's tortured, twisted face and knew Kortin couldn't live without the stone now. He couldn't live. The boy gave him a smile, his best smile, his sweetest, the one his mother loved.

Kortin sighed and caressed him with the stone, rubbing vomit and the greasy soot of corpses. With his other hand, he curled fingers in wild copper hair. There was gentleness in the gesture, but also the sure grasp of possession. Kehfrey eased closer, the welcome on his face almost sad, the hazel of his eyes more luminous than before, as if tears threatened.

"Yes," Kortin whispered, transfixed by the child's poignant, angelic face. "Touch me! Touch me!"

"No!" the sorcerer screamed.

"Yes," Kehfrey said gently and reached for the wet member that jerked with eagerness.

A hairsbreadth from the man's genitals, the boy's fingers paused. The smile left his face and his expression became strangely distant. Kortin frowned down at him and watched in mystification as the child's small hand pressed on his right wrist. Then, somehow, the boy clutched a dagger in his fist. As Kortin stared in bemusement, the child thrust the point into his groin.

Kortin's fingers twisted violently in the boy's ginger hair. Kehfrey ignored the pain and gutted his victim, almost as an afterthought taking off the appendage that had insulted his brother. The old man's face twisted with shock and utter agony. The stone dropped from his hand and thudded to the floor. He bent forward, screaming, both hands groping at his eviscerated flesh. Without a sign of emotion, the child finished the murder and cut his throat open.

Standing over the doused, smoking floor, Marun stared inward blankly. Kortin's shadows, his own, they broke and scattered into nothing. The assassin moved past his stunned figure and approached the boy. Tall and proud, Olomo stood next to the child, bent his head slightly and watched Kehfrey's first victim die choking on blood. Kortin lifted a pleading hand toward the impassive child. The last of his air bubbled through his open neck, and he went limp.

Olomo turned his head and subjected Marun to a cold glare of disdain. "The boy is destined!" he said fervently. "He belongs to you only because he decides it is so. Never forget it!" He walked stiffly past the silent sorcerer and out into the hall.

Her arms wrapped around her shaking frame, Nicky walked in until she stood with her master. Marun scarcely noticed her presence. "Kehfrey," he whispered.

Kehfrey refused to look at him. He dropped the bloodied dagger and darted around the table. He threw himself on his brother and sobbed. The misery he had repressed poured out of him almost violently. He clutched at Vik's head, pressed his face into flaxen hair and moaned wordlessly against his brother's neck .

Marun stepped up to their sides and crouched. Vik was bloody, cut along his legs and on his foot. He had swelling bruises on his back and

240

buttocks, a lump on his head. Wanting to ease his pain, the sorcerer reached toward him.

"No!" Kehfrey shouted, lifting his head. "Did you finish saving my sister?" Marun stared at him. He hesitated. "Go back down!" the boy shouted. "I had it under control! Go fix my sister!"

Marun straightened and stared down at the uncanny child, too amazed by far to be angered. After a second, he walked over to the fallen stone, snatched it up and left the room. He passed the child's gawping father and older brother. They didn't look at him, only stared in at Kehfrey as if they couldn't seem to recognise him. Marun continued down the hall, feeling a chill that had little to do with dark shadows and cold power.

Inside the room, Vik sobbed and put his arms around Kehfrey. With his face pressed against his brother's small stomach, he wept abjectly. "I'm sorry," he gulped. "I'm sorry!"

"It wasn't your fault," his brother said. "It was mine. I let him like me."

Vik wasn't sure what he meant. "Kehfrey! I want out of this room!"

Kehfrey brushed the tears from his cheeks and pulled gently away. "I'll help you," he whispered. "I'll get you cleaned up."

Vik nodded and turned until he could get on his knees. Nicky stepped forward and pulled his breeches up as he lifted himself. At last upright, wobbling between both woman and child, Vik looked toward the door and saw Kehfen staring inward, Wilf next to him. His father's eyes were filled with tears. He remained motionless at the door, but Wilf moved forward a step.

"Don't touch me!" Vik cried.

Wilf gaped in shock. "I wouldn't hurt you!" he said, his tone wounded.

"No! I know. Just don't touch me now," Vik said. His voice lowered to an exhausted whisper. He didn't want anyone to touch him, no one but Nicky and Kehfrey. He limped toward the door, held up between them, wincing with every move.

"Wilf," Nicky said. "Go downstairs. Call the servants back into the house. Tell them I want the bath filled again, this time with warm water. Tell them they had better move it."

Wilf left hastily, grateful to leave the horror that was the aftermath of one brother's rape and the other's first murder. Vik perceived this revulsion and shut his eyes, willing himself not to cry. Oh! A bath! He wanted a bath so badly. A sob escaped his throat despite his resolve. He felt hands on him then, other hands, and cried out in fear. His eyes opened to the sight of his father.

"Let me carry you," Kehfen offered, compassion plain on his features.

Grief welled up and spilled out of control. Vik fell against his father. When Kehfen lifted him, he turned his head into his father's shoulders and sobbed brokenly. Without another word, Kehfen carried Vik to Kehfrey's room and laid him on the bed, where he cradled his son's head and wept silently above his racking shoulders. Nicky left the room to see about bandages, but Kehfrey stood in the doorway and watched, the tears of his remorse drying on his face. Kehfen looked over at him. The child gazed back steadily, his features filled with sorrow.

There! Kehfen saw it clearly. That was the look of a man who knew what killing was. Kehfrey had lost his childhood.

But as he witnessed that haggard stare, Kehfen could not help wondering if the loss had really occurred this night. The boy who had murdered Kortin, he'd been something other than a child, something unnatural. Kehfen understood then. He'd never really had a third son at all, but some strange being who only seemed like one. From the moment he'd first held him, the child had looked at him just like that, like an old man, wise and distant, and infinitely lonely and sad.

Kehfen blinked and looked away. He suddenly couldn't bear the sight of his little boy, because it made him feel guilty. He had no idea why.

***

Domel arrived at the manor only minutes after the infant girl was finally healed. He sat his horse and peered owlishly at the frightened faces of his staff gathered beneath a tree. His gaze sidled to the dishevelled woman and disturbed infant. The woman's face was swollen from crying. She made no effort to hide the nakedness of her upper torso, seemed too in shock to do so. The boy, Gamis, his face as puffy, stood before the sorcerer, stuttering an account of Kortin's invasion of the house. Discovering why they had all come to be out there, the butler dismounted and hurried over to his silent underlings.

"You! You! You!" He pointed. "Pick this woman up and get her back inside now. Fetch a clean tunic for her to wear. Change the linens of the bed. We will deal with getting her properly clothed tomorrow." He grabbed one man and pulled him closer. "Where is the kitchen staff?"

"Boiling water for a bath."

"Tell them to boil more. Enough for several baths."

Even from his position, he could smell a noxious stench wafting from the master, who looked like he'd dragged himself through a hell. Marun was covered in foul-looking greasy soot, and his face beneath the grime was grim and white.

"Make sure you get his clothes when he's undressed tonight," Domel continued to instruct in a hushed voice. "They will need to be burned. And burn the clothes of anyone who went with him." The butler pushed the younger man toward the house. "The rest of you get these horses in the stable. Wake the damned stable hand up. He slept through it, I suppose. Then get back in and start putting the house back in order."

The other three had already gone up the steps with the woman and her baby. The master released Gamis, and the boy rushed up the stairs after his mother. Marun turned toward Domel.

"Did you get the date?" he asked. His face neutral, Domel gave him the information. Marun nodded absently. He turned toward the house, but then changed his mind and walked back to his servant. "Go back to Rhet," he said. "Tell him he is to go to Lord Avehlt with an invitation. They are both invited to supper tomorrow."

"Yes, Master," Domel said. Well. Now he had to get that nag back. He kept his irritation to himself and, with long strides, hurried to the stable.

***

Upstairs, the door to Kehfrey's room was shut. Voices sounded beyond the burnished wood, hushed and considerate. Marun continued toward the workroom, for a moment pausing at the entrance to examine the broken frame. The damage irritated him, but a different slight fuelled a harsher anger: a pair of brothers shunning him from behind a shut door. Marun thrust his unreasonable resentment down and stepped into his workroom. Inside, the body lay just as it had been, abandoned by everyone, its murderer, the murderer's family, that damned assassin who'd disappeared like assassins always did after a killing. They'd left the messy details to the master of the manor.

"Kortin," Marun uttered angrily. His grip on the stone tightened. Bitterness clawed at the walls of his self-reserve. He stepped over the corpse and toward the hearth. The shadows earlier had doused the marching dervishes. He set the stone on the andiron and murmured the spell. The dervishes reformed, and the stone levitated until it floated within the ring of flames. Coldly, he considered the result.

He should have done this before. He'd been such a fool, leaving the stone on the mantel, never realizing thieves would send small children down the chimney to do their breaking in for them. This chimney of all chimneys.

He rose, still staring at the magical fire. This chimney. This room. If Rook hadn't disobeyed Kortin, Kehfrey would never have come to the manor. Despite the danger he'd been in, the sorcerer could not regret that part of what had happened. If fate existed, he'd been stupid just so the boy would be with him now.

Destined. Yes, the child was destined. He was destined to be with him. Olomo was nothing but a blind fanatic.

Marun walked toward the corpse, hissing the necessary words of power to raise the dead into a semblance of life. With the ease of long practice, darkness swelled up and around the body.

"Get up," he told it after. Kortin rolled in his congealing blood, and his gaze lifted toward Marun. The glint in the glossy eyes bespoke a ravenous need. "Are you hungry?" his master said. Marun kicked forward a worm of flesh that lay shrivelled on the ruined carpet. "Eat that."

The sorcerer watched intently. Kortin's dead face turned down. Weathered hands reached. The smile on Marun's face grew more sinister with each second as Kortin's ghoul lifted his own genitalia off the floor and brought it toward his mouth. If horror were a balm for bitterness, then this ghastly entertainment was a shadow master's best solace.

***

The sun just hinting the new day, Kehfrey stood before his window and stared out. Far above on a distant rise, the glow of flames also lit the dying night. Kortin's villa yet burned, perhaps his fields as well. It had been so close to them all this time: the goal, the rock, Marun's soul. Had they known, they could have retrieved it sooner, perhaps without the accompanying personal disaster.

He heard the door open and, turning, discovered the reason for that disaster standing in the entrance, clean and dressed in a fresh suit. Kehfrey moved forward before the man entered. Vik wasn't ready to be in the same room with Marun. Kehfrey wasn't ready either, but he didn't have a choice. He hastened to set the man outside before his brother awakened from a troubled sleep.

"Out!" he whispered.

He pushed the sorcerer back with a small hand. Marun moved backward obediently. A little surprised by this, Kehfrey peered at him misgivingly, but no sign of resentment or anger visited the sorcerer's face over the abrupt expulsion. This led the child to suspect his master's blacker emotions had gone beneath his skin, where they habitually brooded in a bath of old power and dark longings. Not all those longings were Marun's. Having touched his soul, Kehfrey understood this now, but he had to wonder if the man comprehended this truth as well. Did Tehlm Sevet know how much the ancient power of crystal teeth and cold desire had twisted within his soul? Did he?

Marun shut the door softly. He looked down at the suspicious boy and scanned his small figure narrowly. Kehfrey had washed. He stood in nothing but a large borrowed tunic that almost enveloped him. He seemed nothing more than a sleepy innocent child, but Marun knew he was not. He was anything but.

He knelt to be at eye level with him. "Will you let me heal Vik?"

He asked. He did not demand.

"I don't know," Kehfrey hedged. "He couldn't bear Pop to stay with him after a while. Nicky and I helped him wash."

Marun remembered wanting to wash once, desperately wanting. Years had gone by before he had properly done so. Years.

"If you went in and asked him?" he suggested. He watched the boy consider it. "Please, Kehfrey. His insides may have been torn. He'll be in agony for days. Infection could set in and kill him later."

"I'll go ask," the boy relented. He opened the door, slipped inside and shut it again. Marun rose and waited, wishing Vik wouldn't be proud for once.

244

His wish was granted. Kehfrey opened the door and nodded. Marun followed him in. Vik watched tiredly, his eyes bruised with fatigue, his face pallid. Kehfrey climbed up on the bed next to him and held his hand comfortingly.

"Kehfrey said you saved my sister," Vik said.

"You saved your sister," Marun told him. "Just you."

Vik averted his head, shutting his eyes on the sight of the man. He could see it, the pity. He didn't want it.

The bed sagged under Marun's weight. A voice breathed into Vik's ear. "I remember," it said. "I remember what it was like."

The warmth of human presence retreated from his skin. Vik turned to stare at Marun. He recalled scars crisscrossing the sorcerer's back. He remembered why they had been put there and what had been done afterward. "I hurt inside," he whispered.

"I know," Marun answered. He bent forward and set his lips on Vik's.

Riveted, Kehfrey observed the glow spread around them, warm and green and comforting, touching even the hand that grasped his brother's. He shivered, wondering how a mouth of crystal teeth could create something so unutterably enthralling as this breathtaking light that flushed their skin. He felt only a fraction of the power Marun levied out to his brother and wished secretly, guiltily, it was him having the supernal kiss of healing. But that wouldn't do. That wouldn't do at all.

Vik's hand tightened on his, but after a moment, his clasp grew limp. Kehfrey kept his fingers laced with his brother's all the same and waited until Marun lifted his head away. When the sorcerer looked up, he saw nothing of the longing in Kehfrey's heart, only the fascination his master's demonstration of power had engendered.

"He'll sleep the rest of the day," Marun said. He tucked the blankets around Vik better and glanced at the boy again.

"I don't understand," the child said.

Ah! Here it came. More questions. The child couldn't seem to bottle them up, even under the direst of circumstances. "What don't you understand?" Marun asked patiently.

"Why do you need to say spells some of the time and not at others?" Kehfrey said, his voice lowered for Vik's sake.

"How to put it?" Marun murmured.

"Try food. Food imagery works well for me."

The sorcerer smiled, and it was beautiful, just mirth and astonishment, none of that dark cynicism mixed in. Not this time.

"All right," he said. "Magic is like a jelly that is poured into a mould. A magician is the container that initially holds the magic. Spells are his moulds. A practitioner collects the power inside himself over the years and uses it as he sees fit. If he uses it often enough for the same thing, he eventually doesn't need a spell. The mould forms automatically. It has become a part of his nature."

"Nicky said you got caught and hurt once," Kehfrey mentioned.

Marun gazed at him pensively before he answered. "Did she?" he said carefully.

"I was wondering about your back," the boy confessed. "I asked her while Vik was sleeping, when I took my own bath. Why did you stay caught when you didn't need to worry about being gagged? You could have thrown shadows. You can do that without a spell."

"Not as well then as now," Marun said, "but I also had a concussion back then. The guards who surprised us struck me on the head before the shadows were properly formed. After that, I could barely think. I just watched. While I was trapped on the Mehto ship, I had nothing to do but remember what I had watched. A witch loses power over water. Don't ask me why. It's just the way it is, and now is not the time to discuss it." He tugged at the blankets Kehfrey sat upon. "Let's get you covered. You should rest."

But Kehfrey didn't need to ask why, and he had no intention of resting yet. "Water isn't the territory of the cavern of crystal teeth," he said. "Earth is."

Marun's mouth relaxed into a small gape of surprise. "I constantly forget how astute you are," he said after a second, "but you never fail to remind me. That is one theory. Weaker, inexperienced witches fail to thrive over water. They rely too much on a continuous link to ley lines. They lose that link over water."

Kehfrey thought Marun's strong connection to the source of power might also have been a problem, but he didn't say it. That thing in the depths of the earth, it didn't lend power without penalties. His gut said as much, and his mother had told him to always trust his guts. "You were like that. Inexperienced," he said instead.

"Yes," Marun admitted.

"So you learned more and then came back to avenge yourself, only this time you put your soul in a rock for safe keeping," Kehfrey said flatly. "Now no one can give you a concussion."

"Basically. Most importantly, no one can kill me," the sorcerer added firmly.

"Unless they harm the stone," the boy amended. "Did you protect it this time?"

"Yes."

"Is it worth it?"

"What do you mean exactly?"

"Revenge?"

Marun couldn't mistake the challenge in that question. "You tell me?" he said icily. "You murdered your brother's abuser earlier this morning."

The boy looked at him quietly before answering. His next words flayed Marun to the quick, worse than the whip had ever done. "It wasn't Kortin's lust that brought him here," he said softly. "It wasn't his needs. It wasn't his revenge driving him. It was yours, yours that hurt Vik, yours for which I had to kill. I might become the most formidable assassin this world has

246

ever seen, Tehlm Sevet, but I shall never kill at your behest. You have my word on it."

Marun rose from the bed without another word and left the room. He shut the door quietly, but Kehfrey knew, by the whiteness of the fingers on the latch, that Marun refrained from exhibiting the rage roiling within. Kehfrey slipped his hands out of Vik's loose fingers, went back to the window and peered at the distant rise. The morning sun hid the glow of the flames, but the smoke of the fire was clearly visible. It loomed high above them.

"Kortin's family has no home," he whispered.

But his family did, here with a sorcerer who might be the most evil man to have ever existed. The child looked at the door, wondering if he should lock it. The sorcerer, despite his barely contained darkness, didn't concern him just now. It was another thing. He was certain Kortin's ghoul hid in the cellar. The black life in that corpse was far more disconcerting than another visit from Marun. His master's barely-checked lust was only physical, but the ghoul's ....

Something fell motivated the walking dead. Something told them to eat. That something was a thing blacker than the sorcerer's shadows, blacker than the ancient power that was his source. The power beneath the earth's crust, it lived; but the power in the ghouls was a gaping hole wanting all life to cease.

"It's tainted," he whispered, head slowly turning toward the window. "Marun's power is tainted. There's something further down, beneath the cave of crystal teeth, beneath the ancient thing that feeds him."

He frowned. An odd glow reflected on the window, a set of white dots the size of silvers. He put his fingers on the pane and the glow settled on his flesh, large and luminous, like a pair of eyes.

"What ...!"

He blinked. When he raised his eyelids, the light had disappeared. With it, his feeling of presentiment vanished, but a sense of disorientation had replaced it.

What had he been thinking of? Oh, yes. Shadows beneath shadows. Unsettled, not wanting to see a glow again, he shied away from the subject and backed from the window.

"My imagination has been tainted. That's it. As if my eyes would glow. Stupid!"

He scooted up onto the bed next to Vik and endeavoured to kick consciousness out. He failed most miserably and was grateful, an hour later, when Nicky slipped into the room, lay on the bed with him and cradled him in her arms.

"How did you know?" he whispered.

"I'm a seeress," she reminded.

"Are you certain seeing isn't catchy?"

"Positive."

"Oh. Good." He twitched and threw off wakefulness at last.

Nicky smiled. "Sweet child of destiny," she murmured. "You have no idea how bright you shine."

She kissed his forehead, wishing, wishing so very fervently that somehow he'd shine on despite their master's darkness. His distant future, when she tried to look, was incomprehensible. She only discerned a brightness, but as if through murky glass. She thought the obstruction was her master's black emanations clouding the lens of her power, because the few clear images she caught were full of pain and fit only to dim the child's brightness further.

Chapter Ten

Olomo stood in the centre of the ballroom, staring thoughtfully at a distant window. One of the double doors opened. The assassin turned, expecting the boy. It wasn't, and Olomo scowled with displeasure. The boy's unwanted master had entered the room.

Marun stopped six feet in and looked at the assassin flatly. Outfitted in black as usual, Olomo was a dark, uncompromising shadow in the large empty room.

"What is it you want?" Olomo said. His eyes squinted into a suspicious stare. Anything out of the ordinary the sorcerer did, the assassin viewed with mistrust, and today the sorcerer had dressed for an outing, adding riding boots to his usual muted attire. He'd traded in the frock coat for a sturdy summer jacket that had yet to be buttoned.

"I want to know what you think of this confounded boy," Marun answered.

"Have your star charts done nothing for you?"

Marun heaved an impatient breath. Olomo didn't believe in the efficacy of astrological forecasting. He'd said as much a week ago, when he'd come into the library to demand more time with the child. Irritated by his arrogance, Marun had refused the request. Olomo had looked over at Kehfrey, who'd been sitting at the desk learning gnomish script, and snarled that the sorcerer was turning the child into a useless scribe. Now, a week later, Marun stood before the contemptuous assassin, begging for help. It galled him no end.

The charts had forecast nothing untoward about the boy. He would lead an interesting life in interesting times. Bloody useless drivel! Any fool in a disaster would have an interesting time until he died of it.

Marun stalked toward the tall assassin and scowled. "Tell me what you think, Olomo. You have your own ideas about the boy. You've hinted as much."

"Ah! Now you choose to ask me? Have you cried defeat, O Sinister One?"

"Do not goad me! You only live because the boy wants to learn from you. Now start talking."

"The concept will be beyond you," Olomo sneered. The room darkened with shadows, but Olomo ignored them. Marun could threaten all he liked, but he was desperate to keep the boy content and part of that contentment was having an Ysepian assassin teach the child the ways of Pek.

"Olomo," Marun uttered softly and coldly, "I will not ask again. One doesn't need to cause permanent damage to make another suffer."

Olomo rethought his position. "I believe the child to be a reincarnation of Holy Amut," he said. There, sorcerer! Make what you would of that!

"Holy Amut?" Marun cried, his voice lifting in disbelief. "Why do you think that?"

"Amut himself said children often see the simplest path. Amut must have come back to teach us the simplest path to Ishpaäf. This boy is Amut."

Marun snorted in contempt. "Amut! He set himself on fire."

It was too close to Kehfrey's initial outburst upon learning the hallowed story. Olomo's hostility fanned all the hotter. "He endured his immolation without pain! He was in Ishpaäf! No pain harms one who has reached it!"

"He died!" the sorcerer said derisively.

"And came back in his own time!"

"Hundreds of years later. Why take so long?"

"We have perfected the Pek ways in that time. We are ready."

"Nicky foresaw that *none* of you were," Marun pointed out with a mocking sneer.

"Not without the boy. I am *with* the boy. I *will* reach Ishpaäf. He is Amut!"

They glowered at each other, a pair of bulls ready to butt heads. At that moment, the calf in question came in from the ballroom's back entrance, ready for his next lesson. He stopped just inside the door and eyed the men wisely. "Here, now?" he said. "Are you two at it again? Fine! When you're done, you can come and find me." He darted back out before either had a chance to deny him.

"Gods!" Olomo said irritably.

"Oh, he's leading you to Ishpaäf, all right," Marun said with a victorious folding of his arms. "Is he still hiding from you because you said he couldn't conceal himself from a blind and crippled rat?"

Olomo made a ferocious face and chased after his student. The brat! He would hide all day now, while Marun watched and laughed.

Indeed, even as Olomo hurried out, he heard the sorcerer laughing. Olomo deeply regretted scolding the boy for thumping about in his usual rambunctious manner. "Kehfrey!" he roared. "I do not want you to hide at this time!"

Again Marun's laugh sullied his ears. Damn that man! Damn that boy! Amut! He had come back as a devil. "I know you test me," Olomo whispered. "I will be calm. I will prevail." He strode down the back hall, listening carefully, looking for signs, and went around the corner.

To the rear, Kehfrey slipped out from behind the door, crept back into the ballroom and lifted a finger to his lips. Marun smiled. The boy was an unconscionable brat and he loved him for it. He knelt and waved him closer. Kehfrey stepped up quietly. "I want you to come with me today," Marun told the child

"Where to?"

"An old place. I find answers there sometimes."

"What do you need me for?"

"The answers concern you."

The child groaned at him. "Come on! Why do you have to keep trying to figure out why I do this, that, and the other thing?"

"Things! Other things! I must know! I have to know!"

"But why?"

"Because I hate not knowing."

Kehfrey laughed. "You! You call me stubborn. You're more stubborn than me."

Marun smiled, but this time it was a grim gesture. "And I never give up," he added.

"Nor do I," Olomo barked from the doorway. He had backtracked, guessing the child had attempted to trick him. "You will not go without me."

"Fine." Marun rose to a stand. "Get ready. We leave in fifteen minutes." He marched away to the main hall.

"Hi, now! Did you hear us speaking?" Kehfrey said.

"Yes," Olomo admitted.

"Well! I guess I *can't* hide from a blind, crippled rat, after all."

Olomo roared wordlessly. The child squealed and ran in the other direction, but the tall assassin caught him. He held the boy high and glared outrage at him. "You devil! You infidel! You unholy fiend!"

Kehfrey squealed again, but it was just childish laughter. There was no fear in his comportment whatsoever, even when Olomo shook him in further indignation.

"Have you no fear? I am Olomo, First Line of Pek Tom! I have taken thirty-three lives by the old ways! Twelve more when I was but a boy and tested! Twenty-one in battles of no consequence! I could snap your neck in an instant!"

"That would be bloody useful," the boy retorted, hanging limply from between Olomo's long arms. "Come on, now. You can't take a joke? You think thirty-three kills and umpteen other murders have helped you? You have no damned sense of humour. Come to think of it, neither did that Amek fellow, Pek. Is it any wonder Amut Ishpishied off somewhere else."

Olomo froze for an instant and then gently set the boy down. "Pek assassins have no use for humour," he said.

"You laughed at me two weeks ago," the boy pointed out. "Remember? Nicky said I asked questions faster than a man with the flu shits."

"I remember. I also remember you didn't like it."

"Well, no. But I saw you laugh. You *can* laugh. Come on! Next time, I won't hide. You can. Let's see how good you are."

"You want me to hide?" Olomo said flatly.

"Why the hells not? It's good practice." Kehfrey did not mention fun. That wouldn't do at all.

"Yes, it is good practice," Olomo agreed thoughtfully. "In its place."

"Then you'll hide next?"

"I will do better than that."

"What do you mean?" the boy said, turning his head sideways as he looked up at the giant of a man. His little face was lit with suspicion and hope.

Olomo knew the boy couldn't resist a challenge. "I will hide, but I will also leave traps. If you miss them, they will mark you. I will know how observant you are."

"Mark me? How?"

"Paint."

Kehfrey laughed. "Fine, but marks on my fingers don't count." He lifted his hands high. Both sets of fingers were blotched with colour. "My fingers are always inked."

"Fair enough. For now," Olomo agreed.

"Now that you're finished settling that," Marun interposed sarcastically from the doorway, "you can both get ready."

Surprised, the boy and the assassin turned to stare at him. The sorcerer marched away a second time. Kehfrey thought he heard him cursing. "Must have come back to be sure you weren't killing me," he remarked to Olomo.

"That man is too protective of you," his teacher responded, tone disapproving. "He coddles you. Every bruise, scratch and cut healed without a trace. Where is the learning in that?"

"You don't like him protecting me? Oh, come on. I keep on with the training despite cuts, bruises and scratches until you call a halt. A little bit of healing isn't so bad." And was often the only pleasant thing he experienced after a day's hard work, wherein he was knocked in the head, butted in the chest, and wrenched about in general. He really didn't want to lose the magical touch of healing green, especially now that Olomo had managed to convince the Shadow Master he mustn't bestow the gift with his lips. What was the danger in a light brush of the fingers?

"It is not a little bit of healing," Olomo refuted. "He steps in whenever he notices you have taken the least harm. There is no learning without pain."

"You can't honestly say I'm not learning or that I've not suffered pain."

"No. No, I suppose not, but I don't like his reason for interfering." Olomo pushed Kehfrey forward by the shoulder. "Beware, boy. He is not to be trusted. You know what he wants from you."

Yes, Kehfrey supposed he did, but right now, with his family so firmly entwined with the machinations of the Shadow Master, he had no choice but to act like he did trust him.

***

"What are you doing here?" Marun snapped.

He stood on the lowest step outside the manor, awaiting Olomo and Kehfrey, neither of whom had come out yet. Over fifteen minutes had passed since the incident within the ballroom, and their tardiness had only added to his irritation. This surprise visit augmented his annoyance further. The pimp Someren had just shown up in a hired coach—painted, perfumed and smiling prettily.

"Oh, Marun! Don't be evil about my little visit." Someren pouted and drifted forward, mincing in an over-decorated yellow silk dress. Gold embroidery twisted in all directions across the cloth, swirling in intricate patterns. Gold powder dusted the pimp's cheeks and eyelids. His hair had been dusted as well. Today Someren was a golden statue. Too bad he talked and moved.

"*What* are you doing here?" Marun repeated, but with a more frigid tone.

"Oh! It's that useless Rhet! He takes no advice. You just did have to let him think he was in charge," Someren complained. "How can I run the business with that twit? He has no clue what men want in women." After he said this, he turned his face away and made a dramatic moue with his mouth.

Marun stared. Interesting choice of complaint. "I will see Rhet about it," he promised flatly. "Now leave."

"Marun!" Someren wheedled. He sauntered up to the sorcerer and passed a hand around his waist, pressing in toward him suggestively. "Oh, please! You can't just send me away. I've come all this way just to see you."

Must he always speak as if he were exclaiming? "I have no time to deal with your problems with Rhet and the whorehouses. Go now!"

Someren's cultivated facade of feminine wiles cracked, and he scowled at Marun like any man. "At the very least you could loan me Vik," he said, his voice deepened to his natural tonality. "He can help me with the business. Rhet is useless! I've got rude bitches trying to call the shots in the women-run establishments."

Asking for Vik was the poorest choice of suggestion. Motivated by a hot flash of jealousy, Marun put a hand on Someren's gilded face and shoved him away hard. The pimp spun about, almost lost his balance, righted himself and turned back. His winsome smile returned, brought on by anticipation.

"Go away!" Marun snarled, but Someren moved forward instead.

"Do you really want me to? Let me stay, Marun. I would do anything for you." His voice once again issued from his throat feminized. He slid a hand over Marun's thigh and crotch. "I'd let you do more than Vik would."

"You disgusting pain lover," Marun said coldly.

"Yes, we both know what we like," Someren whispered sardonically.

Displeased, Marun retreated a step, but the pimp stepped up with him, rubbing at him persistently. Marun felt his body relenting even though his mind was not ready. He'd been abstinent since the night of

Kortin's death. Gods! That painted slut in front of him was beginning to look good.

"You! Why are you here?" an angry voice intruded.

Marun started and looked behind. Vik was on the top step, just outside the door, his beautiful face rigid with anger. He wore a new suit of simple cut, the fabric a medium blue. The plainly dressed youth looked much better than Someren, far better. He was magnificent.

"Vik!" Someren cried low in surprise. With his next words, his tone shifted into an affectionate wheedle. "Vik, my love! Convince this nasty man to give me a loan of you. I need help. Rhet is being a dreadful bore about everything."

Vik glared at the overdressed tart and, when this did not convince Someren to back off from Marun, stomped down the stairs without a word. Just as he reached their sides, his hand shot out and grabbed Someren by his falsely curled, gold-powdered hair.

"Oh! Oh! Vik! Not my hair!" Someren screeched.

Vik ignored the protest. He dragged the man down the steps and toward the hired carriage. Someren danced madly to keep his balance, and Vik continued hauling, his face an uncompromising hostile mask. He lugged the overly prettified rival along until he had the pimp forced back inside the vehicle. Someren scowled, opened his mouth to protest over the rough treatment and received a vicious punch on the side of the head for his temerity. He grunted and sagged sideways. Vik retreated from the coach and looked at the cabby.

"Take him back now!" he snarled, whipped about and stalked away. The bullwhip cracked and the coach rolled off. Across the white gravel, Vik marched. Marun stared at him from two stairs up, lips smiling in appreciation and perhaps something more. Was that desire? After avoiding him for two weeks! Did he actually think he would get it that easily now? The bastard! "Oh? Did you enjoy that? Why do I see two horses standing out here?" Vik called.

Marun didn't answer right off. His smile faded.

"Where are you going?" Vik insisted.

"For a ride," Marun said.

"With whom?" Vik asked, almost at the steps and watching the sorcerer's expressionless face intently.

"Olomo."

Vik halted directly in front and fixed Marun with a scathing glare. "Olomo," he repeated. "And Kehfrey! Don't pretend otherwise. You bastard! You were going to leave me alone here."

"I thought you were too unwell to ride."

"Lying bastard!" Vik hissed. He hadn't been unwell for over a week. Marun had locked himself in the library since that night, fiddling with papers and charts and declining to see him, all on the pretext of being too busy. Vik knew the truth. Kehfrey had always been permitted entry. Why? Because the man was obsessed with Kehfrey.

254

Vik refused to be abandoned in the sorcerer's lonely household or to let Marun abscond with Kehfrey. But for he and his little brother, none of the family were present in the manor. Wilf had gone to his grandfather. Kehfen had taken Canella, Gamis and the baby to a new home in the city. There was only him left to watch out for Kehfrey.

"I'm coming," Vik said firmly.

"Vik," Marun began.

"I'm coming!" Vik roared.

Marun scowled. Damn this family. He was mad to have taken them on. Irritated all over again, he grabbed Vik by the neck and tugged him up roughly. "I've left you alone for two weeks, but not tonight!"

He punished him with a harsh kiss. Rather than responding with defiance, Vik melted against him. An immediate groan of pent need escaped Marun's throat. He'd left it go too long, left Vik to recover from his ordeal until there would be no chance of nervous withdrawal, but Vik had only taken his well-meaning reticence for rejection. Clearly the rape had been forgotten enough that intimacy could recommence. And recommence it would.

"Hey!" Kehfrey's high voice exclaimed. "I think we might be staying after all. Let's go hide!"

Marun pulled upright hastily. "No!" he bellowed.

He turned, outraged beyond words, only to see the child was in no hurry to dash off. Kehfrey grinned down with a mischievous cast to his angelic face. Truly, there was little of the angelic about him. He was wide-awake and ready for trouble, or ready to make it.

"The brat!" Marun hissed through his teeth.

Olomo, staring down with a faintly disgusted expression, shoved the boy forward. Kehfrey skipped down toward them. "Where's Vik's horse?" he said. "You can't carry him on your lap. He's too big."

Marun shut his eyes. He wanted to throttle the boy. He almost felt his slender neck in his hands. He wanted it so bad. He wanted—!

"Marun!" Vik hissed, jerking his neck out of tightening fingers. "I'm coming with you."

"Fine. I'll have another mount readied." A glare was enough to send the servant holding the reins dashing off to the stables for a third horse.

"When are you going to let me ride my own horse?" Kehfrey asked.

"Never! Not until I know you won't cause trouble on top of it."

"Trouble?" The child peered up from his master's side now, his expression carefully offended. "What could I possibly do on top of a horse?"

"I don't want to even think of it," Marun said flatly. Ignoring Vik's white-lipped glower, he grabbed the boy, descended the stairs, and set him on his mount. Olomo cursed something in Ysepian, but his voice was too low for the words to be understood.

"Let Kehfrey ride with Olomo," Vik said, following after the sorcerer.

"Shut up," Marun directed. Vik's mouth opened to continue arguing. Marun snatched the front of his tunic and hauled him in closer. "Shut up!" he said more severely.

"Vik," Kehfrey said hastily. "Back off. He's not doing what you think."

"Yes, he is! He would take any excuse to touch you! I've seen him watching you! I know what it was about with Kortin two weeks ago!"

"If you don't like it, leave!" Marun dared him, eyes fairly blazing from his head.

Vik's face whitened further. He jerked out of the sorcerer's grasp and retreated back to the steps. He paused at the lowest and refused to look at Marun again. After this, they waited in silence for the third mount. Eventually it clattered into the driveway, the servant jogging along in front. Vik grabbed the reins from the servant and mounted. His fancy buckle shoes weren't appropriate for riding, but he didn't care. He stilled the champing horse and looked down at Marun, his answer to the earlier dare evident. He would not leave, not without his brother. He wouldn't abandon Kehfrey to the Shadow Master.

Marun looked away from him toward Olomo, who had descended to claim a mount. The Ysepian's expression was fairly much in agreement with Vik's. Scowling, Marun lifted himself into the saddle. He pulled the boy in closer and jabbed his heels into the horse's flanks. They set off at a thundering gallop. The rushing pace did nothing to alleviate his anger. He hadn't endured anyone's censure for decades. He hadn't needed to. He had a fine method for handling disapproval. He got rid of those who disapproved. This approach had worked fine until now.

"Are you happy I made you that vow, boy?" Marun snarled down at his head.

"Yes," the child said. He was leaning to the side and staring at the ground hurtling past. Did the horse have all its hooves off the ground just then?

"Are you afraid I'll do what they think?"

"No."

"Isn't that odd. You're usually the first to figure things out."

"I've thought it out," the boy objected.

"And what did you decide?"

"That I haven't much to worry about until I'm about Vik's age."

Marun grimaced and crushed him closer. The boy's breath hissed out. "Your brother is right! I want you!"

"But you won't!" the child squeaked. Four hooves in the air. Definitely.

"And why not?"

"Because you don't want me to act like a whore."

The sorcerer pulled his mount up so quickly it almost ran aground. The other horses charged past, unable to stop in time. Marun looked down at the boy. Kehfrey turned his face up toward him, the expression on it solemn.

A front. A perfect wall of false indifference. And with the indifference, words to repress. "I'm not like you and Vik. You know I'd only pretend. You know I'd hate it. You know you'd hate that I was pretending."

Marun shut his eyes on the child's wise face. Kehfrey suppressed all hint of compassion and continued with a boyish dismissal meant to gouge the remaining hope from his master's heart.

"You know, I think the horse had all four hooves off the ground just then. Kick it onward, will you? I want to check again."

Marun opened his eyes. Both Olomo and Vik had their mounts blocking the road ahead. "I think we should let the horses go at a more sedate pace now," the sorcerer said. His voice was unemotional.

"Aw!" Kehfrey said grumpily. "Come on! Someone piss him off again."

"Kehfrey!" Vik snapped. "Shut up!" The child let out a string of curses so vile that both Olomo and his brother's expression grew long in shock. "Kehfrey!" Vik exclaimed.

"Nicky's lot," Kehfrey said calmly. "Want to hear the elven ones? I'll translate."

"No!" they both responded.

He looked at Marun.

"I've heard them already," the sorcerer said flatly.

Kehfrey grimaced and turned away, apparently disgruntled. After a second, Marun kicked his horse into motion. Their two companions turned their mounts and set themselves to either side. They watched Marun from the corners of their eyes. He seemed completely in control of himself. A few minutes later, they relaxed.

Kehfrey knew better. Marun as yet crushed him tight. The fingers of his hand were misleadingly flat against Kehfrey's abdomen, but the tips dug in. Kehfrey had wounded his master, but he couldn't do otherwise. For his sanity's sake, he dared not do otherwise. However cruel the sorcerer might be, Kehfrey knew Marun wouldn't force an immature child, and now that the green kisses had ended, so had Kehfrey's worst temptation. He was back in control. He had time still, time to free his family.

The problem was, the sorcerer had given his family whatever they wanted most. Kehfen, outwardly posing as a shipping merchant, was now leader of the thieving ring. Along with a socially acceptable husband, Canella had a fine house in the city. She was living like a noblewoman again. She had servants. She had highborn friends calling on her daily. Her firstborn, Wilf, was with his grandfather, mixing in circles he'd never had access to before the legal adoption. And Vik?

Vik.

Kehfrey's spirit plummeted like a rock in a lake, sinking into gloom and despair. Vik was trapped more than all the rest of them. He didn't have what he wanted, not completely. Vik loved Marun, but believed he was kept only because the boy the sorcerer really wanted wasn't ready to receive. Vik was suffering. Kehfrey's guilt over this was acute. Marun hadn't touched Vik since the night Kortin had abused him, but Kehfrey had heard the promise on the steps.

Tonight Vik would whore on his behalf. He would whore because he would not abandon his little brother to the Shadow Master. He would stand between them for as long as he could. Of all his family, Kehfrey wanted to free Vik the most. He just couldn't see a way to go about it. If he disappeared, Marun would make them all suffer, vow or no. But if he stayed, only Vik would endure torment, albeit a torment that wasn't physical. And the rest of his family? They would gain power as Marun rose within the ruling circle of Wistal. The more power they had, the less likely it became they would want to leave. He was caught no matter how he looked at it.

"I know what you think," the sorcerer whispered.

"So. Now you read minds," the boy replied.

"I make educated guesses," Marun said. "You've gone too quiet."

"And?"

"You are deciding what you can and cannot do."

Very good guess, the boy thought. "I can't breathe!" he retorted tightly.

Marun's arms relaxed over his chest. "I won't let you go," he promised. "Not ever."

Kehfrey didn't answer. Marun's head lowered to permit lips to press upon the boy's recently cut hair. The sorcerer ignored the sudden icy glares of their chaperones, and pulled Kehfrey up until he could speak softly into a small ear.

"I never give up," he repeated. "Never!"

Kehfrey's spine tingled as he was settled back on the sorcerer's lap. He scowled at the road ahead. Well, he wouldn't give up either, would he, then? No, he wouldn't! Gods busted Marun! He had maybe six, seven years to figure this mess out. He had time to prepare. He would find a way.

***

They passed through the city gates a half hour later. The summer heat had alleviated during the last week and the streets were crowded. Heavy rain had cleared much of the waste from the cobbles and flushed out the sewers. For once, Wistal wasn't completely rank with human stench, but Kehfrey, who'd never been gone from the city before his ill-fated first robbery attempt, wrinkled his nose in disgust. Rained out gutters or no, Wistal still stank.

"What is that smell?" he cried.

"That?" Marun said. "That is how you smelled when I first met you."

"I did not!"

Marun squeezed him slightly. "Yes, you did," he insisted. They could have caught the boy by his smell alone. It had been almost solid.

Kehfrey refused to answer, obviously deciding to disbelieve him, though he did look at the city folk more intently, particularly the lower class denizens lined up for work along the section of the boulevard called the employment wall. Most of those men were a sorry mess of ragged clothes and unwashed necklines. If their hands were clean, likely it was because they'd done washing jobs in the factories the day before. Amused, the sorcerer smiled over the boy's head, just the faintest of twitches at the corners of his lips, hardly a smile that anyone would recognise as one, but for two brothers who understood him better than most.

Emboldened by that small gesture, Vik at last spoke to his lover. "Where are we going?" he said. A familiar laugh occurred right then, and Vik turned to search over the heads of the pedestrians.

Marun looked toward him and caught the youth staring at a crowd of flashily-dressed young men. As he watched, one of them lifted a hand in greeting toward Vik. "Who is that?"

"An acquaintance." Vik averted his head without returning the greeting.

The distant youth glowered in disappointment. His eyes met Marun's. The young man quickly avoided his gaze. Marun faced forward again, thinking of Rhet's punishment weeks ago, thinking how it would feel to watch Vik do the same to that hopeful slut who even now stared covertly at him.

"You haven't answered my question," Vik reminded.

"We're passing through Wistal to a place on the further side."

"Where exactly?"

"The ruins on Held Mount."

"That place? Why? It's haunted."

"Is it?" Kehfrey said. "Ghouls?"

"I hope not!" Vik answered. He'd come out of their room the night Lord Avehlt arrived with Lord Rhet. He'd wandered to the head of the stairs at exactly the wrong time, the moment when Marun called Kortin up from the cellar to show Avehlt and his men what would happen to them if they didn't cooperate. The ghoul had crossed the stairwell below as Vik stood on the topmost step. Vik had hobbled back into his room and stayed within for three more days, until Kehfrey had sworn he'd made the sorcerer rid the house of the dead thief. Vik didn't want to see another ghoul again. Ever!

He glanced at Kehfrey. From his brother's expression, the boy regretted mentioning ghouls. Kehfrey had followed him out of the room that night, but he hadn't fled back in. No, he'd gone down to the library and watched Avehlt cower away from his mutilated, dead half-brother. Kehfrey refused to speak of all the things he had witnessed afterward, no matter how much he was pressed. Vik supposed he was glad of that.

Ever alert to the subtle signals the brothers passed between each other, Marun noticed the fear flash through Vik's eyes. Kehfrey must have seen it too; he averted his face and heaved a silent sigh. The boy had disturbed his precious older brother's equilibrium and berated himself. "The temple is not haunted," Marun said.

"Temple?" three voices answered.

"This ruin was a temple?" Olomo continued. "Of what divinity?"

"The followers worshipped the earth."

"And you seek answers about the boy there? Why?"

"Because the earth can answer. You know nothing. Be quiet."

Olomo would not be quiet. "Kehfrey must not be polluted with earthly magics. He is meant to reach Ishpaäf, not have his essence corrupted by the old worship."

"I said be quiet!" Marun hissed. "If you speak again, I will send you off that horse and leave you lying in the street for all to pick over."

Olomo grimly shut his mouth. He looked at the boy. Kehfrey glanced at him and away, a muted indication to desist. Olomo sucked in an angry breath and endeavoured to calm himself in the ways taught by his masters.

"Why would the earth answer?" Kehfrey asked Marun, wishing to distract him from Olomo. The sorcerer opened his mouth to reply, when a peremptory voice interrupted.

"Vik! Vik! Where have you been?"

The four of them turned their heads in surprise, but Vik also pulled his mount up. Assassin and sorcerer matched the motion. Kehfrey smiled from within his master's arms and named the arrogant man striding toward them.

"Oh. It's the *Great* Astabe."

Marun scowled. Yes. Astabe. Vik's lover before him. He knew that much from what Rhet had hinted. The artist strode forward with an offended scowl on his proud aquiline face. He pushed between bystanders without excusing his rudeness. He was obviously someone to be reckoned with, or so *he* thought.

"Vik! You left me in the middle of a project!" Astabe said. He looked at the youth resentfully. "I was forced to use someone else to finish."

"What? You couldn't remember his ass enough to finish it from memory?" Kehfrey said. "Now there's as plain an insult to your beauty as you get, Vik."

Astabe started and focused on the other horse. With a myopic squint of his eyelids, he located and recognised the boy before he identified Marun. He didn't bother to look up after that. His eyes fixed on the boy with the intensity of a predator with a prey animal in sight.

"You! The devil."

Marun smiled above the boy's head. So. Kehfrey had introduced himself at some time. As much as this initially amused him, his smile quickly frosted over, because Astabe stared at the boy in just the wrong way.

"Vik? Who is this boy? I know you know him," Astabe questioned. He stepped closer to examine the child. "If you get him to pose for me, I'll forgive you." Vik was strangely silent in response, but Astabe didn't care.

260

His hand lifted to touch the child's leg. Kehfrey kicked the appendage away.

"Hands off, Astabe! I'll gut you beforehand!"

Astabe's gaze darted upward in outrage. He fixed on the boy's flat stare, and then his attention seemed to be drawn further up, tugged higher against his volition. His eyes met thunderous brown, and he blinked in sudden fear. "Marun!" he whispered. His skin turned white.

"Have you finished the project?" the sorcerer demanded.

"No! Not yet. Just a few more touches. Another devil. The boy, for example, would be perfect. A juxtaposition of purity and evil."

"Unless you have him committed to memory, forget it!" Marun kicked his mount onward, knocking into Astabe. Astabe jumped out of the way and apologized as if he'd committed the blunder. "Get it done, Astabe," Marun issued coldly.

Vik gaped down at the white-faced artist and then hurried to catch up with his lover, nudging his mount forward with anxious kicks of his heels.

"That bastard!" Marun hissed. "I'll kill him!"

"Why?" Kehfrey asked.

Vik called to Marun before Kehfrey had an answer. "You knew each other!" he cried. Marun rebuffed him with a cold look, but Vik would not be deterred. "How do you know him?" he demanded.

"I commissioned Hell's Gate from him. The lazy bastard is taking forever to finish it."

"*You* commissioned it?"

"Did you commission the one with the tiny whanger, too?" Kehfrey said.

"What?" Uncertain what the boy meant, Marun looked at Vik. Oddly Vik was blushing.

"The one with the reclining naked man with the tiny whanger," the boy detailed.

"Let me guess. A whanger is a penis?"

"Right. Well?"

"No."

"Oh. Well. I wonder who did?" the boy said with a perplexed frown.

"Somebody with a fear of big whangers, I suspect," Marun murmured dryly. Vik had turned his head completely away from them. "Would you happen to know who, Vik?"

"No," Vik said quietly.

That very quietness caught his brother's attention. "It was you! You modelled it! He got nothing right!"

"I told you! Big whan—! It offends some people!" Vik scowled at his little brother, looked up and saw his lover eyeing him coldly. "What? I modelled for your commissioned work as well."

"And Astabe carefully hid you from me and then made an unflattering portrait of you, no doubt intending to use it to put me off. I'm going to kill that sleazy bastard!"

"Gods! You didn't even know me! Why kill him now?"

"I saw the angel! I asked him about it! He said he'd painted it from his imagination!" Marun commenced to squeeze Kehfrey, so angry he didn't notice what he was doing. "All this time, coming to me, begging for funds for more paint, more models, more everything! All this time he's been buggering you and painting a portrait with a small whanger!"

Vik set loose an indignant hiss. Kehfrey squealed. "Hi, now! My ribs!"

Hastily Marun relaxed his grip, but he continued to glare at Vik.

"I tell you what," Kehfrey said. "You tell Astabe to go piss off, and I'll finish both works. Or fix them. Whichever! Just quit arguing."

"You! Finish the artist's work?" Marun exclaimed. "This isn't a dough snake to frighten Gamis with." Although that snake had been very good actually. It could have fooled him.

"I can do it!" Kehfrey shouted. "Astabe is an idiot! He can't paint! He dabs his brush like a butcher cutting tripe with a cleaver! He paints like he glued his brush to a wobbly, useless penis too small to pick up with tweezers!"

Marun almost laughed for more than one reason. The child was hopeless. And wise. The entire matter had become amusing. "I want him to finish, Kehfrey," he refused. "Thank you for the offer all the same."

"Oh, that's just fine!" the boy said in irritation. "You can at least get Vik's small whanger number and let me fix that."

"Kehfrey!" Vik protested.

"Fair enough," Marun agreed. That would serve Vik and Astabe right. Let Kehfrey turn the portrait into a caricature. It could hang in the entrance hall, just where the big whanger would catch the most light.

"Oh, Kehfrey!" Vik said. He would never live this down. All his friends would laugh behind his back. If that cold bastard Marun let anyone near him again.

Kehfrey scowled. "You think I can't!"

Vik didn't reply at first. He knew Kehfrey was good with a piece of chalk or charcoal, but he was only seven years old. Vik's anger burst out. "Come on, Kehfrey! I've seen you make houses and stuff! But this is different!"

"Stuff! Just because the rain washed the best ones away before you visited, they're all stuff?"

"Rain?" Marun asked.

"Only had the sides of buildings to work on," the boy told him.

Marun grinned. "Now you'll have a nice piece of canvas," he said, shooting a nasty look at Vik. "And if I like it, I'll get you to do more portraits of your brother."

"Like hells you will!" Vik glared repressively at Marun, but his lover only smiled, promising he would dare. "Gods bust it!" Vik said.

"Hi, Vik! Don't be so pissed. See? He's jealous. He does love you."

Vik's mouth shut on a second curse. He stared at Marun. Marun stared back. The man abruptly averted his face.

262

The damned brat! This family! Why this family? They would drive him mad!

Vik watched the sorcerer's frozen expression and slowly smiled. He looked down to find Kehfrey grinning at him. Vik's smile warmed further, and his blue eyes brightened with delight.

Well, that's better, the boy thought. Vik wasn't going to feel like a substitute anymore. At least for a while.

***

The temple was indeed a ruin. The giant slabs of granite that crowned the worn hill had tumbled some time in the very distant past. Vegetation coated the rocks; so much so, the stones were nearly buried. Kehfrey climbed one massive block and jumped up and down experimentally.

"What are you doing?" Marun demanded. He had walked in past the granite and stood in the centre of the broken circle.

"Checking for echoes," the boy answered tersely.

"Echoes?" Was he talking about the echoes in his head again?

"If it echoes, there's a cave under it. If there's a cave under it, there could be treasure."

Oh. Those sorts of echoes. "Thief," the sorcerer uttered quietly.

Kehfrey didn't hear him or pretended that he didn't. He clambered off the fallen slab and took off for a second one. Marun followed his progress, turning slowly to keep track of him. They were alone on Held Mount. He had ordered the assassin and the boy's brother to remain below with the horses. The chaperones had kicked up a fuss, but he had squelched the rebellion. Eventually.

The aggravation of that altercation still pricked Marun. Vik had been adamant, refusing to back off until the sorcerer had given him a black eye. But this had prompted Kehfrey to jump him, and then Olomo had pulled a knife before remembering knives were useless. With shadows pressing in all around them, Olomo had opted for pulling Vik away from the sorcerer, and Marun had carried enraged Kehfrey part of the way up the mount, just to keep him from running off in revenge for Vik's injury. So here they both were, standing within the ruins of an ancient temple, participants in a wary truce.

Kehfrey gave up on the second slab and dashed over to a third, this one half supported by another. Thumping on that one was useless. Of course he just had to go beneath instead. He disappeared into the cavern, and Marun stared at the dark hole, wondering if he'd have to chase after the child, but Kehfrey poked his head back out quickly.

Insisting that he must continue to wear black, Olomo had made of Kehfrey a small dark child with only white skin and flaming hair to set him off from shadows. Just now, he looked like a floating head. The rest of him crept out, ruining the illusion. He carried something in his hand, something that wriggled and weaved angrily.

"Kehfrey!" Marun barked. He had an asp in his hands! The sorcerer rushed forward in alarm.

"I had to catch it! It was going to bite me!" the boy said in defence.

"Did it bite you?"

"No. I got it by the neck when it darted at me."

Losing the initial panic, Marun peered closely at the writhing snake. Kehfrey did have it behind the neck and quite securely. It was a thick serpent, with a vicious, ridged head. The mouth gaped open, revealing fangs dripping toxin. Kehfrey held the asp further away, and Marun stared in bemusement. The boy had caught a venomous snake during its biting lunge. Exactly how fast did that make him?

"Don't tell Nicky!" the child begged.

"What?"

"I promised not to catch any. I didn't have a choice this time. I swear!"

"You caught one before?"

"No, but I wanted to," he admitted. "Nicky made me promise not to. You won't tell her, will you? She'll tear my head off. She doesn't like me playing with snakes."

The child seemed very concerned, and it was Nicky who had generated the emotion. Marun was beginning to loathe that woman. "Throw the snake back under the rock!" he snapped.

Obediently Kehfrey returned to the crossed slabs. He unwound the sinuous body from his forearm and tossed it in the opening quickly. He darted back to Marun, skipping backwards the first few steps to be certain the serpent didn't come after him. Once assured that it would not, Marun knelt in the centre of the circle and pulled at the dry grass, digging in and ripping out chunks along with their roots.

"What are you looking for?" Kehfrey asked.

"A slab."

"Another one? How big?"

"This one is smaller." Marun thrust his fingers into the soil and he felt it. Someone had uncovered it perhaps a year ago, making the task of ripping loose turf a little easier. He pulled a hunk and found the slab. There was a groove in it, which told him he was near the edge. Kehfrey bent and touched the groove. He pulled his hand back immediately.

"What did you sense?" Marun asked. Kehfrey shook his head. He looked ready to fly off. Marun grabbed his arm and pulled him closer. The boy resisted. "I won't hurt you," Marun said.

"There's something bad here!" Kehfrey exclaimed. He didn't bother accusing Marun of lying. He was worried about the other thing more, the thing hiding below the slab. Here, in this circle, the cave of crystal teeth was closer. Strange as this seemed, Kehfrey knew it was so.

"It isn't bad. It isn't good. It's just there," Marun said firmly.

"Why is it the source of power?"

"I don't know. It just is."

"What is that mark on the rock? Is it writing?"

264

This, Marun didn't answer. He couldn't tell Kehfrey, not now. The truth would only frighten the boy. "Kneel," he directed, but again Kehfrey resisted. Marun hissed in frustration and pulled the child down forcefully.

"I don't want to touch it!" Kehfrey protested.

"You will!"

He set the boy in front of himself, grabbed a small hand and shoved it down until it splayed flat over the exposed sacrificial stone. The child's thumb settled into the blood groove. Kehfrey tried to pull away, but the sorcerer pressed him too firmly against the cold granite. Crouched above, Marun began the words of summoning.

Kehfrey cried out in pain. He put his free hand to an ear and ducked the other into Marun's chest, but heard the sorcerer's voice all the same. Each uttered word resonated in the child's head, the next compounding on the previous. He screamed in an attempt to drown the echoes, but his desperation amounted to nothing. The words reverberated louder and louder. Through a mist of tears, he watched shadows creep between the stones toward them, while beneath their bodies an aura of green swelled until it enveloped his splayed hand. The touch of this glow was intrusive and exquisite. The pain receded, but he was still panicked and gulped huge lungfuls of air. Presently he grew dizzy and fell into the echoes.

Marun felt the child go limp. Even so, he held the small body aloft, permitting nothing but the hand to touch the stone. The chant was almost over. They were almost there, their souls, in a dim, vast cavern where crystal teeth threatened from above and all sides, a place even luminous gods seldom broached. But he would. To solve the conundrum of this child, he'd dare question the Goddess at last.

He commenced the final verse, and the emerald glow rose and swallowed them both. He groaned the last of the summoning. It seemed his every muscle had become unendurably rigid, and he quivered with the tension. He ached so much he could have screamed, but the great entity of their world approached. There, where an opening served as the throat leading down, her presence darkened the entrance. He must not scream, and he must show no weakness.

Speak!

The forceful demand almost rendered him senseless. He resisted. He pulled his mind into a freezing, relentless purpose and dove to where the boy had drifted. Kehfrey's spiritual self floated impassively at the top of the cavernous mouth of crystal. Marun gathered him in and held fast.

I would know about the child, he told the entity.

The child? she whispered. He sensed surprise and then desperation. *Give him to me!*

Marun's mind almost recoiled out of the cavern. Physically her thundering bellow shook the earth beneath his knees. He tensed once more and drove his will at her.

No! Tell me what he is!

I want him back!

Back? She wanted him back?

"Tell me who he is?" he shouted with his body. Mentally he pulled away from the deeper place, dragging Kehfrey up with him. There was something very wrong here, something perilous for the child.

I take him back! she whispered. A bodiless force tugged the child's essence down.

No! The sorcerer fled upward. The entity defied him, and the child's spirit gained weight. Marun snatched Kehfrey's fingers from the stone slab. The psychic burden vanished, and they both sprang free. Thwarted, the entity coiled angrily beneath them.

He was mine! He will be mine again! she threatened.

Tell me who he is!

Rebirth means nothing without me! The ground shuddered. *All come back through me! I will not let him go again! When he comes to me next, I will keep him forever!*

Tell me who he is? Marun shouted one last time.

He is the torn one, she whispered. *He is the broken one.*

"Is he Amut reborn?"

The ground shook with mocking laughter. *Serenity! Let him teach it. He cannot keep it forever. He will be driven mad with loneliness. Then he will return.*

Why does the magic harm him? He felt her refuse. She withdrew. "Tell me why?" he screamed. "Tell me why?"

He is not ready to remember! The power of her spite shook him. *Force him at your peril!*

She left, but not without a sacrifice and punishment. He shuddered and shuddered again. Falling to the side, still gripping Kehfrey tightly, he groaned in agony as he spent himself against the child's back. At the same moment, the entity locked his mind down, pinning his will and driving him back from the solution to the boy. He knew then, knew absolutely, he could well stumble across the truth and never recognise it, because the perilous dark mistress of the earth would not have him do so. For daring to rebuff her, she had crippled his mind.

When she at last receded and the glow of her power had collapsed, Kehfrey lay in his arms without moving, and Marun gasped with his face in red hair, unable to do more than hold the boy until the intense, agonizing spasms lessened.

"It was female," said the child. His voice was calm, terribly calm.

"Kehfrey?" Marun whispered hoarsely.

"You're grunting over me because you communed with a monstrous female thing!" Now the voice was not calm.

"Kehfrey, you're safe now."

"You bastard!" the boy hissed. "You almost tossed me into a big toothy cave with a big, not good, not evil, possessive mother thing!"

"What?"

"You heard me! Buggering roach! Buggering roach's pulled out runny shit! The only female you can couple with is that?"

Marun thought he felt the ground tremble. A trace of cold amusement perhaps? "Kehfrey, I had to summon her to learn about you."

"And what did you learn! That we all come from there and all go back! That's what! Thank you very much! I am so relieved. I am comforted. I have a nice place to look forward to at the end of my bloody buggered up days!" The boy struggled then.

His limbs no longer gripped with seizures, Marun pulled him back in. "You! She said you don't want to remember. What? What is it that you can't bear to know?"

"Gods bust it! I don't know! I do know I'm going to tear out your tongue if you ever do that again!" Kehfrey squirmed around and kneed Marun in the crotch.

Soul harboured elsewhere; it didn't matter. In that place, a blow still hurt abominably. Marun loosed the boy and gasped in shock. Kehfrey rolled away, lifted himself and dashed down the hill.

"Kehfrey!" Marun croaked. Again, the ground quaked. Somewhere deep in the earth, the goddess laughed at him. She roared with laughter. "Oh!" he gasped. He should be angry. He should send a shadow down to swallow the child, but he couldn't. He loved Kehfrey.

The entity laughed all the harder. Marun rolled away from the slab so he wouldn't hear her anymore, but he still felt the earth shake beneath.

***

The journey back into Wistal was tranquil. Outwardly.

Kehfrey sat in front of Vik. He had clambered onto the saddle himself, refusing to look in Marun's direction. Silently Vik had mounted behind him. He mimicked his brother and kept his head turned away from the cold man.

Minutes earlier, Vik and Olomo had met the boy halfway up the worn and ancient peak. The trembling earth had alarmed them, overbalancing their fear of Marun's wrath. Kehfrey had refused to answer questions, continuing downward mutely, his face bearing the angriest glower Vik had ever witnessed upon it, the expression nearly as frightening as one of Marun's cold stares. Something had been odd with Kehfrey's eyes. The hazel had almost glowed. But now his eyes seemed normal, if angry.

Only Olomo dared to observe the sorcerer openly. That one's face was haggard, his clothing rumpled and dirt-stained. A telltale blot sullied the front of Marun's breeches. Olomo had spotted the stain when the sorcerer mounted for the ride back. Standing, his jacket had hidden the wet mark. Up there on the mountain, something had shaken the earth and shaken the man. From the expression on his cold face, the sorcerer hadn't found true pleasure in it. Whatever he had done with Kehfrey, he hadn't spent his seed inside the boy.

Olomo glanced at Kehfrey again. The boy's face was yet a rigid mask of anger. On a grown man, his expression would have been alarming. On the child, the dark look was strangely disturbing. Olomo wanted to speak to him, but he could not before the sorcerer. That man, he consumed as much time gazing at the two brothers as the pitted road, more perhaps. The need in him was obvious. It drove him. He could not stop staring. He wanted both, but Olomo knew he would only dare to take Vik. Vik he needed. The boy he loved. From the boy, he wanted love. The assassin was certain the sorcerer would fail to achieve that desire. Young as he was, the boy loved Nicky.

"This is a very tangled household," he whispered in Ysepian. The boy's gaze flashed over and away again. The child had heard and understood. Olomo refrained from speaking further.

Eventually they passed through the gates of the city and journeyed on through the markets clogged with merchants and shoppers, where they ignored the cries of hawkers calling their wares and the beggars pleading for compassion. Marun led them away from the heavy traffic and into less cluttered avenues, until they crossed into the rich quarter where beggars were not permitted, where the townhouses were built of higher quality cut stone or brick, and where city sweepers cleaned the streets daily. Here the strollers paused to look at them, suspiciously or curiously, but all with the arrogance of higher social standing. Marun disregarded the stares and continued until he found the building he wanted, a red brick house with window casements of wood painted white. He looked at it silently and then turned toward the boy.

"Go up there," he said. "This is your mother's home. You may visit with her tonight." Kehfrey stared at him. Vik looked as well. Vik's injured eye was turning from red to purple.

"Vik too?" the boy asked.

"No," Marun denied flatly. Kehfrey remained frozen in place.

"Go," Vik directed his brother. He gave him a shove.

The boy cursed and pulled a leg over the horse's neck. He slipped down with a thud and stomped up the steps. Marun watched him without reproach. By way of knocking, the boy kicked the door rudely. It opened after a few minutes. The butler looked down at the gamin with a disdainful expression.

"What do you want?" he demanded coldly. He'd never seen the drably garbed waif before.

"Come to visit Mum. Move your butt," Kehfrey snarled. He shoved past the man and thumped into the building.

The butler looked down in astonishment and then out at the men below. He blinked at the strange group—the tall dark man with the hair of rope, the beautiful youth with the black eye, and the cold man who glared with a warning in his eyes. The butler blinked again and hastily shut the door. The strange child could be dealt with after they had gone.

Marun turned his head away and set his mount in motion. Vik and Olomo followed after him. "Olomo?" the sorcerer said.

"Yes?"

"You may go with the boy." He heard the man guide his horse about.

Vik edged his mount up next to Marun's. "What are you doing?" he asked.

"Show me where you lived," Marun said.

"Why?"

"Because I want to see it! Are you going to argue over everything I ask?"

"Probably," Vik admitted. "You never explain anything." Marun looked at him. His eyes were hot with need. Vik understood then. "Why did you wait so long?"

"I was busy."

"Liar," Vik retorted.

"I didn't want to force you," he said then.

Vik stared at him in disbelief. "You forced me the first time," he pointed out.

"But you wanted me," Marun retorted.

Vik didn't deny it. "You thought what happened may have changed my mind?" The sorcerer didn't answer, only averted his face. "I haven't changed my mind," Vik said.

Marun looked at him again. "Show me where you lived," he asked once more.

Vik turned his horse down an alley and lead him there.

ʌ ʌ ʌ

"Oh, Mum!" Kehfrey protested. "Enough!"

"Kehfrey! My beautiful boy! You will not wear black constantly!" Canella pulled the tailor over to the shop window and spread a bolt of cloth out in the light. "What about this one? Will it go with his skin and hair?"

It was a very strange blue. There seemed to be some green in it, but it wasn't the type of green Kehfrey wanted anywhere near his body. Better to make it into a curtain or something. Something that would stay far away from him.

"Teal, Mistress Ihmel. Yes, it would suit him. Not many can wear this blue successfully."

"Good. Make up a suit of this as well."

"Of course, Mistress."

"Mum!" Kehfrey complained. "It's curtain material!"

"It is not curtain material. It's a lightweight velvet," she informed him.

"The very best, young master," the tailor added, smiling politely.

Canella glided over to the stand on which her youngest son sulked. He looked peaked. She pulled off a silk glove and touched his forehead, but

269

found his skin cool enough. "Are you hungry? I have the most amazing cook," she said.

"Are we going back now?" Kehfrey asked.

She nodded. Kehfrey sighed in relief and yanked away the different swaths of cloth draped over his body. Some of them smelled musty, as if they'd just been pulled from storage after months waiting for a client willing to be badly dressed in gaudy colours. And didn't his mum just have to arrive with him in tow. The only bolt he'd liked was the dark brown tweed, and she'd rejected it.

Dismissing his disgruntlement as childish nonsense, Canella turned toward the door. Olomo stood before it, glowering at her. She glowered back. Dratted foreigner! Why did Marun have to send him with the boy? She swept toward him, daring him to stand in her way. He moved aside. With a superior smile, she breezed through the door the tailor hastened to open for her.

She was all lace and bright silks. She was a flower hanging downward. She was a bell made of rich cloth. She was an annoying, arrogant snob. At last having managed to get to the door, and without a trailing tail of cloth, Kehfrey looked at Olomo and shook his head in frustration. His mother had more airs now than someone who'd eaten lentils for an entire evening. Olomo looked down in commiseration and followed his student out of the shop.

"Get used to it, boy," he said in Ysepian. "She has found her place again. This is how you would have been if she had found it sooner."

For this unwelcome observation, Kehfrey wrinkled his nose at him. "I would not have. Any arrogance I have is due to innate merit."

This loosed a smile from the assassin, but with his typical stubbornness, Olomo forced the curl of his lips into an expressionless line again. "If you were not so conscientious a student, I'd call you cocky and break your fool neck."

"Made you smile," Kehfrey retorted.

"What are you speaking of?" Canella demanded. She had paused with her hand on the frame of the coach door. Her other was still on the footman's palm, and he waited with unassuming patience to hand her into the vehicle.

"He said you have good choice of colour," Kehfrey lied. Olomo snorted behind him.

"Did he?" Canella muttered. Her eyes narrowed on the man. She doubted it. She averted her head, which she held high and proud, and stepped up into the coach. Kehfrey ignored the footman and climbed in on his own. Olomo's weight made the structure tip until he'd seated himself across from them. Canella glared at him. He glared back. Kehfrey decided he needed to distract them again.

"Want to hear a new song, Mum?"

"Mother! Call me Mother."

"Want to hear a new song, *Mother?*" he repeated snidely.

270

"Yes. I love listening to you sing. I should keep you tomorrow. Then you can see the church and listen to the monks of Carmet chanting."

Kehfrey looked askance at her. "Church?"

"Yes," she said firmly. Her expression was very righteous.

"You never went to church before."

"I did too. I couldn't attend here. I was gone from the city, after all."

"Is that the story? Where did you go, then?"

"Lordun."

"Goat droppings! Too close! Someone who's been to Omera will figure you out quick."

She scowled. "It's too late to change our story now. I have to stick with it."

"Then find someone who's been to the city and have him describe everything in detail. The way people talk, the establishments that cook the best food, where people of your station go for a stroll. Everything! Then say you visited seldom because you lived in the countryside. That will account for no one ever seeing you. You'll get caught for sure otherwise and feel like a fool. And make sure the person you hire doesn't talk after."

"Best to kill him," Olomo said flatly.

Kehfrey glanced impatiently at him. "Best to bribe him, then threaten him till he's scared silly," he amended firmly. "You can have Olomo glower at him." Olomo glowered at the boy. Kehfrey, who wasn't impressed anymore, smiled sweetly back.

Canella sagged back into the seat and bit her fingernails. She remembered herself and pulled her hand away quickly. She had to stop doing that. Her hands were a mess. They were as rough as a peasant's. She pulled her glove back on. "I can have your father look into it for me. I'm sure he can find someone."

"When will he be home?"

"Tomorrow. The next day," she said absently.

Kehfrey did a fair imitation of his peevish mother, pouting in a slump on his side of the vehicle. His father had gone on a trip with Lord Avehlt. Apparently Kehfen and Avehlt had hit it off quite well. They were in on a pirating venture just now. They had decided that some unlucky Omeran with a shipload of Anasinian wine needed his burden relieved. Kehfen, since he was posing as a merchant, needed stock to sell for the legitimate side of his business.

"I want you to stay with me tomorrow," Canella said firmly.

Kehfrey didn't answer. It wasn't up to him.

His mother frowned in irritation, realising the same. She hated Marun. She hated him for what had happened to her little girl and her Kehfrey and Vik. But she needed him. He had given her back everything. Wilf! Her Wilf looked like a young lord, just as he should. She owed Marun her allegiance. She still hated him. Tomorrow she would pretend she didn't and beg him to let Kehfrey stay longer.

"You will like church. The singing is so wonderful!" She paused, thinking about the prospect of Kehfrey singing in the church choir, but at last noted his glum face. Sighing, she lifted his chin with her gloved and perfumed fingers. "Sing me the song, then," she said to mollify him.

His eyes brightened with that wild light that betokened mischief, while Canella's narrowed with suspicion. Kehfrey sang. He had a beautiful voice, clear and of perfect tonality, worthy of the church choir, but she snapped his mouth shut after the first line and peered out the coach window, hoping no one she knew had spotted them. "Kehfrey," she said tightly, seething inside.

He grinned at her. "You don't like it? Pop will."

"Oh! To be sure!" she hissed. "Who taught you that nasty song?"

"Nicky."

"That slut!" First Wilf. Then Kehfen. Although she wasn't sure about Kehfen. She only suspected. Wilf suspected nothing, the blind young fool.

"Don't call her that!" Kehfrey said.

"She is!"

"She does no less than Wilf or Vik. Call them sluts."

"They're men!"

"And so they can't be sluts? Don't you find the rules a bit unfair?"

She frowned. He was the only one of her sons who'd ever noticed, but this didn't make up for the humiliation to which he'd almost subjected her. "Of course I do. But I can't change them."

"Well, she has!" Kehfrey tossed at her. "She doesn't care if you call her a slut."

"Then why should you?" He glared out the window. Oh, Kehfrey! She stared down at him in wonder. Not her little boy too? "You're too young to understand!" she snapped. It was a command really.

"Yes, Mum," he said obediently.

She glanced at Olomo. He wasn't glowering at her for once. Instead he looked sympathetic. Oh, Kehfrey! Not with Nicky! That slut!

Kehfrey caught the exchange of meaningful looks, but he didn't let on. It didn't matter really what his mother thought of Nicky. Her opinion couldn't do squat to the woman or to him. No, his mother was no longer a power to be concerned with in his life. He was unwilling slave of the sorcerer Tehlm Sevet, and his master knew exactly whom to hurt to make him do anything he wanted. But by the gods, he'd free Nicky before he'd let the cold man use her to make him bend!

Grimly, the boy looked out the coach window and considered all he must learn to subvert his master's control over him. Such a thorny path to traverse, his future, but traverse it he would.

.

***

The Soulstone Chronicles continue in *Bound in Stone: Volume Two.*

www.ingramcontent.com/pod-product-compliance
Lightning Source LLC
Chambersburg PA
CBHW061552170626

46811CB00001B/172